What would you do, if you knew for certain,
that Satan wanted to murder your entire family?

THE
BATTLE

A HEAVENLY REALMS CHRISTIAN SUSPENSE NOVEL – BOOK 2

Rick Stockwell

Fervent Publishing

ISBN 978-1-7326484-3-2 - eBook

ISBN 978-1-7326484-4-9 - Paperback

Soli Deo Gloria!

I dedicate this book to my children—John and Abby—and their spouses, Ally and David.

However, as it is written:
"No eye has seen,
no ear has heard,
no mind has conceived
what God has prepared for those who love him"

1 Corinthians 2:9

Author's Note

The Battle is the second installment in the *Heavenly Realms* series. I strongly recommend reading Book 1, *The Wall,* before this novel, as many events from the earlier book are referred to, and it's assumed you have some familiarity with the characters.

The Battle is an imaginary journey into the heavenly realms. I've done my best to follow the letter and spirit of the Bible when writing this book but have also used Scripture-filled, extrabiblical sources such as Randy Alcorn's *Heaven* and John Burke's *Heaven Revealed,* along with my educated imagination and other sources, to enhance the reader's experience and fill in gaps where the Scriptures are silent. This can be dangerous, as I don't want to misrepresent anyone dwelling in the heavenly realms, especially God. I don't believe it's possible to visually illustrate scriptural truths through story in a way that is exciting and gripping without using my imagination to guide the characters through the unseen world awaiting all of us.

Extensive informal endnotes are provided at the end of this book, which indicate where quotes, ideas, or concepts came from.

You can have one hundred percent confidence in the accuracy of the Bible but cannot assign that same level of confidence to the way the heavenly realms and its inhabitants are portrayed in this book. *Sola Scriptura!*

Chapter 1

Critical Mission

SATAN SAT ATOP a throne with six opaque marble steps leading up to it and a blood-red carpet runner stretching up the middle. Massive red marble-covered colonnades ran along the sides of the dark cavernous chamber, leading to a throne area at the rear illuminated by perhaps forty burning torches. His throne was covered with ivory, overlaid with fine gold, and its backrest was rounded at the top. Seated golden lion statues resided beside each armrest, and identical statues sat on the outer edges of each of the six steps.

Agliarept and Satan's other senior commanders were milling around before his throne.

"Silence!"

The hundreds of side conversations immediately stopped. No one dared invoke the wrath of their master.

"I've brought you here today for a vital purpose. As you know, our comrade Ra was recently imprisoned in hell per order of the Nazarene. What you may not know is that before his incarceration, he was engaged in battle with a mortal in our realm. Such a battle has never occurred before. Ra grabbed hold of the mortal's leg as he was fleeing and was pulled into a new time-travel device. Then, our enemy, Mekoddishkem, subdued him. There must be something special about this man, and I demand to know what it is. He may be the key to unlocking the ancient prophecy of our doom. I've learned the man's name is Jackson Trotman. I had him killed yesterday. He is now with the Nazarene.

"It may be that the Nazarene had a crucial purpose for this Jackson Trotman. But since he's dead, it means I've thwarted his purpose for now. But if his descendants become followers of the Nazarene, I fear the worst may happen—the resurrection of the enemy army. You all know the ancient prophecy—if we don't stop the people of God, we'll be thrown into the lake of fire and remain there, suffering in agony, for all eternity. This is my world, and I will crush anyone who tries to take it from me. I will not allow these pitiful mortal weaklings to usurp my rightful place on the throne. We must move quickly and kill every one of Jackson's descendants immediately. Agliarept!"

The demon Lord Agliarept fell before Satan's throne, trembling. "Yes, master."

"I am placing you in charge of this mission."

"Yes, master. I will not fail you."

"Very well, I will hold you to your promise. You may go."

Agliarept turned to the rest of the assembly. "I will severely punish anyone who does not carry out my orders to the letter." Agliarept turned back around and faced Satan with a smile.

Satan smiled back. "Oh, and what punishment do you have in mind for anyone who does not follow your orders to the letter?"

"They will be hung on a meat hook from the ceiling in my chamber."

"Hmm." Satan paused, then shouted, "I'll show you what severe punishment is!" Satan reached over and touched the head of the lion on his right and then the head of the lion on his left, and they came to life. The other commanders backed away from Agliarept.

Satan pointed at Agliarept. The lions leapt off the throne and mauled him. He screamed in agony as the jaw of one of the lions latched onto his right thigh and ripped a clump of flesh from it, while the other lion ripped his left arm right out of its socket.

"Enough," said Satan.

The lions returned to their assigned posts beside Satan's throne and turned back into solid gold.

Agliarept lay in a heap on the floor, groaning from his wounds.

Satan took the scepter from his lap and slammed its base against the stone surface supporting his throne. Then, he pointed to Agliarept. "This is what will happen to any of you who fail to carry out this urgent mission. I will hold *you* personally responsible, not your lieutenants. You must not fail me! Do you understand?"

The crowd of commanders responded in unison. "Yes, master."

After they had left, Satan stepped down from his throne and stood above Agliarept, who was still moaning on the floor beneath him. "Have you learned your lesson?"

Agliarept scowled. "I have, master."

"We shall see." Satan reached down and touched Agliarept, and his servant's body returned to its original form.

Agliarept exhaled.

Satan sneered menacingly. "I will do far worse to you if you fail me."

"Yes, master."

C H A P T E R 2
N O T H I N G I M P U R E

JACKSON SHUDDERED AS he watched his murderer being grabbed by two demons and whisked off to hell. The man would be in horrible agony there, at least for a thousand years, then he'd be thrown alive into the lake of fire where he would writhe in burning sulfur for all eternity. "Mekoddishkem?"

"Yes, Jackson."

"I actually feel bad for him."

The angel huffed. "He just shot and killed you, and yet, you feel bad for him? That is admirable, Jackson. Remarkable... Your Savior would be very pleased that you gave your life for Monica Baker, your sister-in-law, knowing she would have gone straight to hell if you had not."

"Good. I want Jesus to be pleased with me." Jackson put his hand over his mouth. "Am I really dead now?"

Mekoddishkem nodded. "In an earthly sense, yes."

Tears streamed down Jackson's face. "Why now? I mean, I just got married to McKenzie yesterday."

"It was your time. Don't you remember me saying you had five months?"

Jackson drooped forward. "I didn't realize that meant me. I

4

thought you were giving my wife five months to become a Christian. I had no idea you meant I was going to die in five months. Are you sure I can't go back?"

"I am sure. It is written, 'All the days ordained for me were written in your book before one of them came to be.'"

Jackson wiped the tears from his face and straightened up.

The angel placed a hand on his shoulder. "Do not worry, Jackson. God will wipe away every tear."

They walked away from The Wall along a fifty-yard slate gangplank toward a door. Jackson looked back briefly. He'd probably never see The Wall again. It never got old seeing the translucent white structure supporting trillions of gold-encircled portals, each three feet in diameter, suspended in the heavenly realms. Stars and galaxies sparkled in the distance behind it.

Mekoddishkem turned the golden handle on the door at the end of the landing. Lightning-bright light burst through, enveloping both of them.

The light was so bright it blinded Jackson. He heard the door shut. What was going on in front of or around him? He reached out, trembling, fumbling in the air, trying to grab hold of Mekoddishkem's robe. Was Jesus sitting directly in front of him? Or far away? People were mingling nearby, whispering, but their voices were indecipherable.

Mekoddishkem eventually placed a forearm under his protégé's left arm. Jackson grabbed it with both hands.

"Do not be afraid."

Jackson's fear abated, but he continued struggling with all his might to see. His eyes felt as if they'd just been dilated at an eye doctor's appointment. Slowly, gradually, his eyes began to adjust. A huge round structure came into view. It looked like a gigantic pure white ball about forty feet high and thirty feet wide that acted as a gate. The gate glistened with light. He must be imagining things, but then again, the Bible said the gates to heaven are made of pearl. As his eyes adjusted further, he stepped back because a colossal angel stood menacingly in front of the entrance, wielding a massive blade.

Behind the gate was a great high wall, extending as far as he could see to the left and the right. At the base of the wall were twelve foundations, each apparently made of different minerals. Light emanated from the stones.

Outside the gate, a multitude of people were standing, all dressed in white linen robes. He immediately recognized his mother's parents. He ran toward them, then abruptly stopped and reared back as he got closer. They were so young.

His grandmother hugged him and kissed him on the cheek. "Welcome to heaven, Jackson!"

He was speechless. Another woman approached. She looked vaguely familiar. "I'm your other grandmother, Jackson, your father's mother. I died when you were only four." He embraced her, then looked around for her husband, who had outlived her. Pappi wasn't here.

One of his Sunday school teachers from when he was a little boy approached. They shook hands vigorously, then hugged each other.

A tiny toddler ran up to him, saying, "Daddy, Daddy!"

Jackson was dumbfounded. Who was this little girl? Of course. Mekoddishkem had told him about her. She was the fruit of his one-night stand with Cassandra Alvarez, who had taken a morning-after pill the next day. Jackson scooped her up in his arms and held her close, kissing her all over her face. Suddenly, it dawned on him. He didn't know her name.

"Jackson, Jackson!" A girl of around seven ran up to him and clasped her arms around his waist.

He looked down at the face beaming up at him. It was his sister, Susan, who had been killed in a car crash more than twenty years earlier. He fell to his knees, put down his daughter, and wrapped both his arms around Susan in a bear hug. Tears of joy dribbled down his face. It didn't matter what the people around him might be thinking.

After collecting himself, Jackson grabbed all his family members in a group hug. Mekoddishkem was standing nearby, waiting patiently.

Jackson glanced at the angel. "Can we meet Jesus now?"

"Yes."

A knot clenched in Jackson's gut. He was going to meet the God of the universe, the holy and righteous Savior of the world. *How will Jesus react when I approach him? Will he be angry or pleased? What will he say?* Jackson cautiously meandered toward the gate with Mekoddishkem. Another angel came out through the gate, then began searching through an enormous book resting on a golden lectern. *This was the most important moment of his existence. Would he be allowed into heaven or not?* The angel opened it, perused it for what seemed like an eternity, then nodded at the angel guarding the gate.

The angel lowered his blade, returned it to its scabbard, bowed, and allowed them to pass. How odd that an angel that powerful would bow to them. *Mekoddishkem must carry a lot of influence here.*

Jackson walked up to the gate entrance. Intense joy infused him instantly. Everything around him was pure white, from the floor to the arched ceiling. He reached over and touched the right side of the entryway—it was as smooth as one of his mother's pearls.

Then he entered a tunnel that extended through the wall. His sight became exponentially keener. The sides of the tunnel were made of sparkly multicolored stones that he'd never seen before. "How thick is this wall, Mekoddishkem? It seems to go on forever!"

"One hundred and forty-four cubits."

At some point, he'd learned a cubit was the length of a man's forearm, but he couldn't translate that into something understandable. "What's that in feet?"

"Two hundred and sixteen."

"And how high is the wall?"

"One hundred and forty-four cubits."

Twelve times twelve in each direction—perfect symmetry.

As Jackson continued walking through the tunnel, his clothes turned filthy. A tingling sensation ran throughout his body. His skin and hair twitched as if he were walking through a massive microwave. Looking behind, he saw his old clothes had been burned off. They flamed up and quickly dissipated into nothing. Mekoddishkem handed him a sparkling white linen robe with a red sash and bright white sandals to wear.

Jackson gaped at Mekoddishkem. "What just happened to me?"

"Come with me. There is one more thing we need to do."

They departed the tunnel through a side entrance. His guardian angel transported him to the edge of a clear, bluish-white river. Jackson looked upstream to his right. At the end of the river was an incredibly bright light, like that produced by a thousand arc welders, overwhelmingly blinding for normal eyes, but somehow, he could see it without any ill effects. His gaze dropped down to the water. Light proceeded from every molecule in it.

Mekoddishkem signaled for Jackson to move forward. "Walk to the middle of the river, then come back to me."

He tilted his head while studying the angel. *Why walk into a river?* Then he remembered Naaman being told by the prophet Elisha to cleanse himself seven times in the Jordan River to be healed of his leprosy. *Perhaps this is a cleansing.*

His feet twitched as the water reached his ankles. The tingling continued as he trudged forward up to his knees, then to his neck. His whole body was now prickling as if being scraped with a wire brush. He looked back at Mekoddishkem. What was going on?

The angel motioned him forward with his right hand. "Go all the way in, Jackson, above your head."

He held his breath, then dipped beneath the water, walking along the river bottom. Strangely, there was no moisture in the water. It felt completely dry. Jackson continued to the deepest part of the river, stepping gingerly on the golden gravel beneath him. Light exploded from each stone. Something told him to take a breath. Incredibly he was able to breathe, even though underwater. *"How?"*

The tingling and brushing became more intense, progressing to a burning sensation. Then suddenly, everything stopped.

Bright light from above infused the water surrounding him, like sunlight streaming through rain clouds after a summer storm. He basked in the dancing beams.

Jackson lifted both hands in front of his face. As he did, his robe slipped backward over his elbows. His hands and arms were now sparkly white, exploding with light. Totally cleansed from top to bottom, he was now purer and more unfettered than he'd ever been during his lifetime.

He turned around and began walking toward the river's edge from whence he'd come.

As his head peeked out above the surface, Jackson asked, "What just happened?"

"It was a final purging. Nothing impure is allowed into heaven."

Jackson returned to the same spot in the tunnel from which he'd left. He strolled toward the end and, upon exiting, was stunned to find cheering crowds standing before him. He hesitated to move forward at first. Why all the fuss? Several smiling men he didn't know beckoned him forward, guiding him toward the golden pathway before him. Other people he'd never seen before were pressed in close to the path, congratulating him and patting him on the back as he passed by. It reminded him of nearing the finish line of a road race, except the people who were cheering here actually knew his name.

Everyone was wearing white linen robes, many with different

colored sashes. They looked young and beautiful and were beaming from ear to ear, exuding tremendous inner joy. Men and women of all races were represented. They were all singing "The Majesty and Glory of Your Name," which was his favorite choral work.

Everything beside the path was illuminated. Lightning-bright light burst outward from within every item—cobblestones, flowers, grass, and even buildings. He squinted as he looked upward. Angels were circling overhead like eagles.

City buildings jutted upward from behind the crowds as far and as high as he could see. The clarity of his vision was now amazing, far exceeding anything he'd ever experienced before. The buildings were made of gold and adorned with thousands, perhaps millions, of precious jewels.

He continued walking and encountered a magnificent flower garden on his right. The plethora of colors was astounding—so many vibrant shades. Not only could he see the colors; he could feel them as well. It appeared God's love permeated everything in his heavenly creation, even the flowers. Their light seemed to intertwine with the light that was now him. Perhaps the ultraviolet and infrared color bands, previously invisible to the human eye, were no longer hidden in the heavenly realms. He could not only zoom in and analyze the intricate detail of each petal from thirty feet away but could also look off into the distance, clearly seeing details on a mountain slope many miles away.

As he strolled toward the garden, the grass crumpled beneath his feet but bounced right back into place. The blades shimmered as light radiated outward from them. Light burst forth from the flowers and trees as well, many of which he didn't recognize. A rhythmic chiming filled the air as tree leaves swished against each other, reminiscent of Jesus's reference to even the rocks crying out with praise to God.

After roaming several more minutes in the garden, Jackson returned to the pathway that now ran directly parallel to the river and meandered toward a great room. Its massive cedar doors were open. In the distance, a huge throne was set atop an elevated landing and was exploding with light. Like the Lincoln Memorial in Washington, DC, it was accessible on all sides via a long set of white stone stairs, only it was far grander.

Two angels guarded the throne room entrance, each brandishing enormous spears. Swords encased in golden scabbards were strapped to their waists. They bowed, then stepped aside, allowing Jackson to enter. He turned around but didn't see Mekoddishkem or anyone else by his side or behind him. Who were these mighty angels bowing to?

Jackson trembled as he walked through the doors. A long set of steps loomed before him. He kept his eyes down as he climbed upward, afraid to catch a glimpse of the Holy Ones seated on their thrones. There were many Old Testament warnings that anyone looking directly at the living God would die because the shock would be so great. Seeing God the Father and the Lord Jesus now would obviously not kill him, but it would certainly shock him. There was nothing he could do to prepare for it. He just had to put one foot in front of the other. Light from the throne permeated his body, warming him as if he were moving closer and closer to a bonfire.

He reached the last stair, and as he stepped onto the landing, a thundering voice cried out, "Jackson!"

He collapsed forward onto the floor, covering his face with his hands and arms, trembling like a leaf, afraid to look directly ahead or upward. There was a gentle rustling. Someone was coming toward him. His heart pounded like a timpani drum.

"Jackson. Come up here!" The voice was powerful and authoritative, like that of a Marine Corps general.

This was not a request. It was a command. He must obey. He got to his feet but covered his eyes with his left hand, remembering that the seraphim did the same with one pair of their wings whenever they were in the presence of God. Weak and trembling, he could barely breathe. Someone touched his shoulder. The fear poured out of him, and pure energy infused his every cell, as if the batteries that had supplied energy to his body for his whole life were now fully charged.

Jackson kept his head lowered out of respect. A pair of hands reached into his field of vision. They were big and powerful, with gaping holes in them. Light poured out of the holes. Jackson finally looked up. He'd waited for this moment ever since he'd become a Christian. Every fiber in his body came alive. Before him, the person was dressed in a robe that reached down to his feet with a golden sash fixed around his chest. His head and hair were white like wool, as white as snow, and his eyes were like blazing fire. His feet gleamed like bronze glowing in a furnace, and his voice had the power of rushing waters.

"I am Jesus." His Savior moved closer, wrapped his arms around Jackson, and twirled him up in the air like a toddler. He pulled Jackson closer, hugging and kissing him on his cheeks. "I've been waiting for you, Jackson. Welcome home! I love you. I'm so proud of you."

Jackson began sobbing like a baby. He'd never received such love or acceptance before. His fear was completely gone.

Jesus leaned back and peered into Jackson's eyes, reading his thoughts like an open book. Everything in Jackson's past suddenly became present. Tiny details he'd forgotten long ago raced through his mind. Every good or bad deed he'd ever done, every kindness he'd ever rendered or failed to render, every harsh word or word of praise he'd ever given, was projected in 3D before him in his mind. The faces of the men he'd killed as a marine in Afghanistan were displayed, along with the women he'd slept with before marrying McKenzie. Every good and bad thought came directly into the light without first being filtered by his mind's defenses. The life review seemed to take only seconds, but nothing was kept hidden; everything was in full view before the Lord.

Jackson slipped from Jesus's embrace and fell to his knees, overcome by emotion as his psyche was confronted, then pummeled, with the rippling effects that each of his decisions had on others. But he kept looking at his Savior. Jesus winced whenever it came to mind that Jackson had said or done something particularly hurtful but smiled whenever Jackson had done something particularly unselfish, such as when he helped the homeless person while on a date with McKenzie, or when he confronted Jaime with her sin after she poisoned Pam, or when he reached out to Pam with God's love even though she was gay, and of course, above all, when he took a bullet for Monica so she wouldn't have to go to hell. Jesus had wept earlier when Jackson received him as Lord and Savior.

The only thing that seemed to matter to Jesus was Jackson's relationship with God and his relationships with others. There was no mention of his many accomplishments in life, like hitting the walk-off home run against Fairfield University during a college baseball game, graduating from college with honors, or earning the Silver Star, Bronze Star, and Purple Heart as a marine officer in Afghanistan. The only thing that mattered to Jesus was how he'd treated other people.

If he'd only understood… he would have lived his life so much differently. His deepest darkest secrets were now on display before a holy God, and there was nothing he could do about it. Disgusting thoughts that no one else knew about were fully revealed. What could he say in his defense? Nothing. He was guilty. He could have done better. He could have done more to help others. Instead, he'd disappointed his Lord and Savior by not living up to his full potential.

Surprisingly, at the end of the review, no judgment or condemnation emanated from Jesus, only love—pure love. A verse came to mind: *Love covers over a multitude of sins.*

Jesus proclaimed, "Well done, good and faithful servant! Well done!"

Suddenly, Jackson looked down. He was shining brighter now as if his internal high beams had just flashed on. Jesus was in him and was now radiating out of him to others.

Jackson tried to reconcile his life's many failings, as so clearly revealed during his life review, with this generous admonition from Jesus. Jesus's perfect work on the cross had wiped away Jackson's sins, rendering him pure, holy, and fully accepted in God's sight. His life review was just a foretaste of the formal judgment seat of Christ to come, during which Jesus would reward Jackson and all Christians for the things they'd done while on earth.

Jesus wiped the tears from Jackson's face with his robe.

"Thank you, Lord Jesus, for all you've done for me. I know I'm only here because of what you did for me on the cross. Thank you so much." His heart swelled with confidence. He was totally accepted by God even though he'd disappointed him so many times, in so many different ways.

Jesus nodded. "You are most welcome, Jackson!" Jesus turned toward those in his court. "This is my brother, Jackson, whom I love."

Jackson bowed and then fell to his knees. "I'm only here because of God's work in me."

Jesus smiled and helped Jackson to his feet. He looked around the throne room. God the Father sat nearby. He was huge. He had the appearance of jasper and ruby. A rainbow that shone like an emerald encircled the throne. Surrounding the throne were twenty-four other thrones and seated on them were twenty-four elders. They were dressed in white and had crowns of gold on their heads. From the throne came flashes of lightning, rumblings, and peals of thunder. In front of the throne, seven lamps were blazing for the seven spirits of God. Also, in front of the throne, there was what looked like a sea of glass, clear as crystal.

In the center, around the throne, were four living creatures, and they were covered with eyes in front and in back. The first living creature was like a lion, the second was like an ox, the third had a face like a man, and the fourth was like a flying eagle. Each of the four living creatures had six wings and was covered with eyes all around, even under its wings.

God the Father said to Jackson, "You are my son, whom I love; with you I am well pleased."

Jackson broke into an uncontrollable grin. Jesus had transferred *his* righteousness to Jackson's account. What could he say? Perhaps it would be better to say nothing—after all, that was what Job concluded after his encounter with God. But he couldn't let Jesus's sacrifice stand without acknowledgment. "Thank you, Father, for sending Jesus, your one and only son, to pay the penalty for my sins by dying a horrible death on the cross for me. What incredible love you have shown to me, and to all people."

Jackson then fell prostrate and covered his face with his hands. Nothing seemed to matter now except lying there in perfect peace in God's presence.

Time passed. At least it seemed like time had passed. How much time was anyone's guess. He pulled himself out of his stupor. What about the Holy Spirit? He hadn't thanked him yet. He stood up and stared at Jesus.

Jesus communicated with Jackson telepathically. *The Holy Spirit is my Spirit, Jackson. He lives within you.*

Jackson looked directly at Jesus. "I didn't say anything." *Oh, that's right; God knows my thoughts.* "Thank you, Holy Spirit, for all you've done for me."

Surrounding them, there were thousands upon thousands of people prostrate before the throne, praying, just as he had been. Their brightness varied by individual, but none were anywhere near as bright as Jesus.

A short distance away, in front of the throne and beside the sea of glass, were vast multitudes of people dancing, singing, and praising God with all the joy and gusto they could muster. There was no rush, no schedule to follow, no timetable. They were all singing "A Mighty Fortress Is Our God" in different languages, yet in perfect harmony with each other.

Jesus called out in a thundering voice, "Mekoddishkem."

A voice came from behind Jackson. "Yes, Lord."

Jesus then placed his hand on Mekoddishkem's shoulder. "You did an excellent job watching over Jackson throughout his life. Well done, Mekoddishkem!"

"Thank you, Lord."

Mekoddishkem took Jackson to a throne far away and said, "This is your throne, Jackson, prepared for you from before the beginning of the world."

Jackson shook his head. It was all too much to take in.

Chapter 3

Payback

DEMON LIEUTENANT BOTIS followed the two other demons as they climbed a hundred feet or so into the air—with a screaming Ronaldo Espinosa dangling between them—on their way to hell. Enraged, Botis shoved his sword through Ronaldo's back and out his chest.

"Urgh!"

Botis twisted the sword, striving to inflict as much pain as possible, then withdrew it. "Coward! I should have gotten someone else to do the job. You were supposed to kill Monica Baker, not Jackson Trotman, you idiot." Botis stabbed Ronaldo again. "You killed the wrong person!"

Botis returned his sword to the scabbard dangling from his waist. *No Monica in tow. Lord Agliarept is going to kill me. How did I get into this mess? I could've been living in bliss right now. Why did I listen to that liar, Satan? He makes one empty promise after another. Nothing I can do about it now. Lie low, do what I'm told, don't get on Satan's bad side.*

But I also must do everything I can to harass and kill the chosen ones. It's the only way to stop the resurrection of the enemy army. Failure means the Abyss, then the lake of fire… forever.

The group traveled over the Atlantic Ocean, the Mediterranean Sea, and the Euphrates River, then landed on a mountaintop. They plunged into a cave and passed through about ten feet of solid rock at the rear of it. They were soon hovering near the ceiling of an open cavern. Hundreds of feet below, in the center of the subterranean area, was a hole about fifty yards in diameter. A glowing red light and tremendous heat emanated from it. They passed over the Abyss and looked down but could see only a tiny red dot of percolating lava at the bottom.

Five to ten thousand people stood in line on a ledge surrounding the Abyss. They were all naked. Botis never tired of the cacophony of screams, the stench of rotting flesh, feces, and vomit, and the look of primordial fear on the faces of those lined up on the worst day of their lives.

Botis grabbed Ronaldo by the scruff of his neck and brought him to the head of the line. The being seated behind the old wooden desk studied Ronaldo, then turned and issued a command to a nearby demon. The demon wrote a figure on Ronaldo's forehead, then pushed him toward the Abyss.

"Wait!" Botis grabbed Ronaldo by the arm, pulled him close, and got right in his face, eyeball to eyeball. "I don't usually do this, but because you're so special, I'm going to escort you to your new home personally."

Ronaldo's eyes practically burst out of their sockets.

Botis leapt into the Abyss with Ronaldo in tow, as if they were diving off a cliff. Superheated air buffeted their faces as they fell. The farther they dropped, the hotter it became. As they continued their descent, nine-foot-high chamber openings began appearing in the Abyss's solid rock sides. A single demon stood at the entrance to each.

They soon passed other condemned souls tumbling downward, screaming and flailing as they went. About twenty yards ahead of them, a demon reached out, grabbed one of the lost, and pulled him into his chamber. A bloodcurdling cry followed behind them as they continued their downward fall.

Ronaldo shrieked, causing Botis to chuckle. "We've still got a long way to go, slave. I've got something extraordinary planned for you."

The lava at the bottom of the Abyss no longer appeared as a dot but had become the size of a red fiery basketball. The cacophony of screams increased exponentially while they fell, as did the intensity of the putrid stench.

The bubbling lava was now clearly visible. Botis turned and studied his captive, whose guttural cries of anguish drew no sympathy. Ronaldo's hair and eyebrows had been burned off, and his skin was now black and red with blisters all over it. Such agony. Botis smiled. This was just the beginning of his pain.

At the last second, Botis let go of Ronaldo's arm and watched as he fell directly into the molten lava. His victim dipped under, then burst upward out of the thick red fiery slop, screeching at the top of his lungs.

A massive reptilian demon appeared from a nearby chamber and struck Ronaldo through his torso with a pitchfork, lifting him out of the lava and carrying him, still impaled and squirming, toward a nearby chamber.

Botis cried out to the demon. "Give him the works."

The demon smiled and nodded, then disappeared into the chamber with Ronaldo.

Satisfied, Botis rocketed back up the Abyss toward the opening, banging into falling souls as he went, unconcerned as they were propelled into the walls like Ping-Pong balls.

Botis finally exited the Abyss opening and stood on a landing. Revenge was so sweet.

A demon approached him. "Lord Agliarept wants to see you right away!" Fear shot through Botis's body.

He passed through a nearby tunnel to another, much smaller

cavern. At the rear was a grotto with a nine-foot-high opening, framed on either side by a burning torch. Botis passed under the torches down a dark hallway, then entered a chamber extending about twenty yards ahead of him. At the rear of the chamber, illuminated from behind by about twenty torches, was a brownstone throne with a well-groomed demon seated upon it. Botis trembled like a leaf as he approached.

Agliarept sat grim-faced. He looked like an ancient Viking, massive in stature, muscular, and white-skinned with shoulder-length brown hair and horns stretching out from either side of his head, the tips meeting above it. "Bring him to me."

His stomach clenched. *This will be painful.*

Two nearby demons held Botis while a third plunged a foot-long meat hook into his side that was attached to a chain. Botis wailed in agony as they hoisted him up toward the ceiling, then slid him along a metal guide rail toward the throne.

Agliarept glared at Botis as he dangled and squirmed above him. "You failed me! What should I do with you?"

The pain was excruciating. Botis struggled to speak. "It's not my fault, master. A man jumped in front of the woman and blocked the bullet from my slave's gun. Then someone else shot my slave."

Agliarept straightened. "Don't give me excuses, you scum! Monica should be with me right now, serving as my queen. She's not... and it's because of your failure."

"Master." Botis writhed on the hook and gasped for air. "It will never happen again. I swear it."

Agliarept shook his head. "If you do fail me again, Botis, things will not go well for you. You will experience much worse suffering than hanging from a meat hook. Do you understand me?"

"Yes, master."

"Very well. Find another way to kill her."

Agliarept motioned to the other demons. "Take him off the hook."

Botis was lowered, and he screamed as the hook was extracted. He then stood hunched over, moaning before his lord.

"Stop sniveling. I want my new queen. I want her now! Do you hear me?"

Botis nodded. "Yes, master."

"I don't care what you have to do. Get her here. And find out who the man was that stopped you. I want him killed too."

"He's already dead, master. I saw him standing next to an angel after he was shot."

"An angel?"

"Yes, master. It was Mekoddishkem."

Lord Agliarept leaned forward, then stood up. "Mekoddishkem? Hmm. Oh, how I hate him."

"I know, master."

"There's no one I hate more in the universe."

"Yes, master."

"Well, I can't kill the man—he's already dead—so I'll need to figure out some other way of hurting him." Agliarept sat and leaned back against his throne. "Any ideas?"

Botis looked up. "The man had a wife, master. They were married the day before he died. The wife is Monica Baker's sister. Her name is now McKenzie Trotman."

Agliarept smiled broadly. "A wife. How wonderful. Go and kill her too. The sisters will die together, and they'll both serve me in my harem, forever."

Chapter 4
Discipleship

MCKENZIE TROTMAN STOOD on the front porch of Sally Tolbert's Cape Cod-style house in Simsbury, Connecticut, and knocked on the door.

A moment later, the deadbolt clicked, the door creaked open, and Sally appeared. She was wearing an orange pleated midi skirt with a white blouse. Hardly a regular outfit for a busy mom with three young children and two on the way, but it signaled their meeting must be important. Sally's black skin was smooth, her hair sassy-short and curly, and her smile contagious.

"Come on in." Sally reached out and hugged McKenzie as she stepped over the threshold.

McKenzie leaned back from the embrace and clasped her hands in Sally's. "Thanks again for calling and for being willing to disciple me."

"A promise made is a promise kept. Let's go into the kitchen."

Sally moved over to the stove and lifted a copper kettle. "Would you like some tea?"

"Yes, please. How are you feeling?"

"My last checkup went well, and the twins are baking just fine in Mama's oven."

McKenzie couldn't help but chuckle.

Sally brought over a white porcelain jar containing an assortment of teas, along with two matching black mugs, and placed them on the rectangular oak table. McKenzie sat in one of the chairs with a view out the bay window into the backyard. The trampoline was set up in the rear near the woods. Sally's kids we're jumping on it the first time McKenzie visited with Jackson. Would she ever have kids?

Sally filled McKenzie's cup with hot water. "How have you been doing since Jackson passed away."

Her directness was more than McKenzie could bear, so she burst into tears.

Sally put her hand on McKenzie's shoulder.

"It's been awful. I miss him so much. Our wedding day was the greatest day of my life. I couldn't have been happier. Then everything went haywire at the wedding reception, as you know."

"Actually, I was occupied with the kids, so I only know snippets of that day. Can you tell me how you feel about what happened?"

"Well, I thought I was safe when Dexter was put in prison—that was the man who raped me in college and tried to rape me again a few months ago—but he escaped. Fortunately, Mike killed him before he could hurt anyone else.

Sally nodded.

"It should have been over, but the next morning, my sister's ex-boyfriend tried to kill her. Jackson gave his life for her." A tear escaped from the corner of her eye. "I never imagined such horrible things could happen to me. I don't think I'll ever feel safe again."

Sally shook her head. "I'm so sorry. I don't know how you're doing it."

"It's Christ living in me who gives me strength. If I didn't have Jesus in my life, I'd be dead or in an insane asylum right now."

"You're a very wise young woman, McKenzie."

She scoffed. "Thank you, but the truth is I've only been a Christian for three months. I hardly know anything. I've read the Bible, but there is still so much I don't know. Will you please teach me?"

"Of course. That's why we're here today."

Sally handed her a small booklet and a pen. "We're going to review the gospel of John together for the next fourteen weeks, assuming my babies don't pop out first. Here are the materials you'll need."

McKenzie was a little taken aback by Sally's authoritative tone but made herself smile. Sally meant well.

"You'll follow the plan in the booklet, reading passages five days per week. For each day, you'll record your thoughts in the booklet using the STAR method."

"The STAR method?"

"Yes. It's an acrostic. S is for the Scripture reference, T is for the thought conveyed, A is for the application to your life, and R is for the response—meaning what will you do with the information. We'll meet once a week to review your thoughts and answer any questions you may have."

McKenzie took a sip of her tea. "Sounds good."

Sally held up another booklet. "Sometime after that, we'll work through another discipleship study together. It's thirteen weeks long. There's a different topic for each week. You'll memorize a key passage of Scripture, write answers to various questions about related Scripture passages in the booklet, then review your memory verse and responses with me at the end of each week. How does that sound?"

"Great! But why are we going through *two* discipleship programs together?"

Sally sat up straight. "The first study focuses on strengthening your personal relationship with Jesus, while the second focuses on gaining knowledge of him through his Word. My goal is not to fill your head with Bible knowledge, although that's important. My primary purpose is to get you closer to God. Eventually, the Holy

Spirit will fill you and radiate out of you, causing others to want to know Jesus too."

"That sounds wonderful, Sally. I can't wait to get started. I want to know Jesus and understand every verse in the Bible. I also want to do everything I can to serve him while I'm still on earth."

"Fantastic! I'm looking forward to helping you along your journey. Does this time and day of the week work for you?"

"Wednesdays at 10:00 a.m. are perfect. I guess it works for you too since the kids are in school."

Sally nodded. "Exactly. We'll start with the gospel of John next week."

"Sounds like a plan." McKenzie shrugged. "What should we talk about now?"

"Anything you like."

Suddenly, something crashed into the front door. McKenzie screamed and placed her hands over her mouth.

Sally placed a hand on McKenzie's forearm. "I'm sure it's nothing. I'll go take a look."

McKenzie's breathing became more rapid.

Sally opened the front door and called back. "It's a package I was expecting."

Sally returned to the table. "I can see you're really struggling, McKenzie, and that's okay. It will take time to heal, but you'll get better. God will help you through this. I guarantee it."

McKenzie looked up. "I know you're right, but I'm not there yet."

Sally stirred her tea.

McKenzie shifted in her seat and took a deep breath. "Okay. One thing still bothers me. I discussed it with Jackson, and he gave me a book to read about it, but I still have questions."

"What's the subject?"

"Evolution."

Sally smiled. "That's right up my alley, McKenzie. I was a biology major and took a few geology courses in college, so I'm very familiar with it."

"Great!"

Sally reached across the table, took McKenzie's hands into hers, and peered into her eyes. "I know this is really hard for you because, like everyone else, you've been taught your whole life—during elementary school, middle school, high school, and college, and bombarded with it daily by the media—that there is no God and we all got here by accident through evolution."

"Right."

"Well, let's start at the beginning. Proponents of evolution believe that over long periods of time, fish, wherever they came from, turned into amphibians, amphibians turned into reptiles, and reptiles turned into birds and mammals through random, fortuitous increases in genetic information.

"Human DNA contains three billion base pairs made up of two strands, which form a double helix. DNA is vastly more complex and compact than any computer chip. The amount of information contained in one square inch of DNA is equivalent to the information contained in seven billion Bibles.

"Here's the bottom line. For a fish to grow legs, specific DNA instructions would have to be provided. For an amphibian to grow reptilian scales, specific DNA instructions would have to be provided. For a reptile to grow feathers, specific DNA instructions would have to be provided. You see where I'm going with this?"

"Yes. You make it pretty easy to understand, even for an English major like me."

"Good. Evolutionists would have you believe this happened by accident, through chance mutations, which are errors that occur while genetic information is being transferred during reproduction. The problem with this argument is that virtually all genetic mutations result in a loss of or reorganization of information; mutations don't add the information required to modify creatures from one kind to another."

"What's an example of a mutation?"

"Individuals with blond hair have lost the ability to produce melanin in their hair. The human body is enormously complex. It contains sixty trillion cells, all organized into systems and organs that perform specific functions in perfect harmony. The human body includes twenty-five thousand miles of capillaries, twenty to thirty trillion red blood cells that transport oxygen throughout the body, one hundred billion white blood cells that fight invaders, eyes and ears that are more complex than anything ever created by humanity, and a brain with one hundred trillion connections.

"No scientific observation has ever demonstrated how DNA molecules originated from lifeless chemicals and organized themselves into a highly sophisticated single cell, let alone a complex living human being with a free will, a conscience, and a capacity for loving others.

"There are many other arguments against evolution, but the challenges regarding the increase in genetic information required to create new kinds is, in my opinion, the strongest."

McKenzie sipped her tea. "Wow! You really know your stuff, Sally. That was a compelling argument."

Sally smiled. "Thanks. I've done a lot of reading about this over the years. You can too if you like."

"Maybe someday. As I said, science isn't my forte."

McKenzie placed her teacup on the table and stood up. "Thank you very much for all the information. It's quite a bit to process. Thanks for the discipleship materials too. I think I'll head out now. My brain is full. I'm looking forward to meeting with you next week."

Sally stood up too. "I'm looking forward to seeing you next week too. Maybe we'll run into each other on Sunday."

They walked to the front door, hugged, and McKenzie navigated down the gray slate steps to her car.

A calm certainty settled over her. This session had confirmed that what the Bible said about creation was true. She would have to unlearn a lot of what she'd been taught in school. Going against the world system might have repercussions, but as Jackson would say, she should never be afraid of the truth.

Chapter 5
Spiritual Attack

MCKENZIE'S FAMILY HAD stayed to support her after Jackson's death, but the Blue Back Square condo seemed crowded. She needed a break. She escaped to the New York Sports Club gym located in the building next door. The facility had plenty of modern exercise equipment, nice clean locker rooms, friendly staff, and a lap pool.

She first ran three miles on the treadmill to blow off steam, followed by a fat burn routine. After grabbing a face towel, she went over to the free weights section and picked up a medicine ball and a mat. She laid the mat on the floor, then sat on the ball and leaned back, placing her hands on the mat and arching her legs upward. She then moved the medicine ball from side to side, trying to work her core hard.

McKenzie left the workout area for a quick bathroom break. On her way back, she peeked into the nursery through a window. A little boy with eyes and hair just like hers was playing with a tractor. She swallowed past a lump in her throat. With Jackson gone, she'd never get the chance to have a cute little child like that.

Her heart was heavy as she returned the medicine ball and mat to their stations and jogged back to the condo.

No family was there when she arrived home. *They must have gone out to dinner.* She took an organic vegetarian burrito out of the freezer, placed it in the toaster oven, and set it to bake for a while.

She walked down the hallway to the master bedroom and retrieved her Bible, along with the STAR journaling booklet. She completed the assigned reading in the book of John for that day and then recorded her thoughts in the journal.

❧

The demon Botis hovered nearby. Fortunately for McKenzie, he was restrained by her guardian angel. However, that didn't stop him from whispering thoughts into her mind from a distance. He spoke in the first person, hoping to deceive her into thinking the thoughts were her own. *How could I have had that abortion? It was an innocent child. How could I have done such a terrible thing? I'll never escape the fact that I'm a murderer.*

He scowled at the guardian angel. The angel might be able to keep him away, but Botis had experience with humans. McKenzie's guilt would be activated by his comments, and then she'd run with his comments and add her own shameful words.

❧

With trembling fingers, McKenzie read a passage about being like a child before God. She sucked in a shaky breath. *It wasn't my choice to have a baby. I was raped. I didn't know what to do. No father around to help. I was too young, still in college, and had my whole life ahead of me. Maybe I should have given the baby up for adoption, but there's nothing I can do about it now.*

All I can do is ask God for his forgiveness and move on... Actually, I've already done that, many times, so why am I revisiting the past now?

She should be grateful for her amazing wedding night with Jackson. How wonderful and fulfilling it was. She'd probably never have that kind of experience again. Would she ever be in a romantic relationship in the future?

What am I doing? Why am I thinking like this? Jackson has only been in the ground a short time. Enough of this! I need to call Sally.

She went into the kitchen, retrieved her phone from the counter, and texted Sally. *Hi, Sally. Please give me a call when you have a few minutes. Thanks.*

The phone rang thirty seconds later. "Hey, McKenzie. What's up?"

"I don't know. I'm having all these terrible thoughts about my past sins and even fantasizing about… other stuff. It all started happening while I was doing my discipleship training."

"Hmm."

"What does that mean?"

"Well, I'm not surprised. Don't worry, McKenzie. You're not alone. Every Christian goes through this, often for their entire lives."

"What?"

"Spiritual attacks."

"From whom?"

"Who do you think?"

"Satan?"

"Right, or one of his minions."

"What can I do about it?"

"Two things. First, put on the armor of God, as outlined in the sixth chapter of Ephesians. We're in a war against the 'spiritual forces of evil in the heavenly realms.' The passage talks about defensive armor to protect you from the darts of the evil one and offensive weapons to force the evil ones back on their heels."

"Okay. I'll take a look at that passage later. What else?"

Sally sneezed. "Sorry. It must be my allergies. The next step is to command the forces of evil to leave."

"How can I do that? I'm only a person? Why should they obey me?"

"They're not submitting to you, McKenzie, but they're submitting to the Word of God. Take a look at Matthew 4:10 for an example."

"Okay. Give me a minute… 'Jesus said to him, "Away from me, Satan!"' You mean, I can just tell him to go away?"

"Jesus commanded Satan to go away, so we can too."

"Okay. Anything else?"

"Yes. Quote Scripture. If you hear a thought in your mind that's contrary to God's Word, quote God's promises back to whomever or wherever the thought came from. For example, if you hear a thought about a past sin, quote 1 John 1:8–9. 'If we claim to be without sin, we deceive ourselves and the truth is not in us. If we confess our sins, he is faithful and just and will forgive us our sins and purify us from all unrighteousness.' So, you don't need to dwell on your past sins. In fact, it's not healthy. God wants you to press on and move forward with your life, as noted in Philippians 3:13–14."

"Thank you so much. You sure know a lot of Scripture."

"I've been a Christian for twenty years, so I've got a head start on you. I've memorized a lot of Scripture along the way. Did you write down all the passages I referenced?"

"No. Sorry. Let me get my notebook and a pen. Okay, what were they again?"

"Ephesians 6:10–17, Matthew 4:10, 1 John 1:8–9, and Philippians 3:13–14."

"Got it."

"Read those passages, pray about them, ask God to help you, and you should be much more effective in fending off these attacks. We can follow up about this at our next meeting. I'll be praying for you. Okay?"

"Yeah, I'm good. Thanks a lot, Sally."

"You're welcome. Oh, and don't base any decisions solely on your feelings. Feelings can lie to you."

"Got it. Thanks." But even as she assured Sally that she could handle it, doubts crept in. It would be hard not to agree with the condemning words, no matter whether they originated in her mind or not.

CHAPTER 6

UNWELCOME VISITOR

JACKSON STOOD BESIDE Mekoddishkem near the entrance to the throne room. Someone was being escorted in, guarded by perhaps fifty angels. "Who is that?"

"Satan."

Satan was perfect in beauty and proud in bearing, looking much like the other angels, but betrayed a haughty expression.

The Lord said to Satan, "Where have you come from?"

"From roaming through the earth and going back and forth in it."

Then the Lord said to Satan, "Have you considered my servant Jackson? He sacrificed his life for Monica Baker, whom your underling tried to murder yesterday."

Jackson leaned forward in his chair. Was this for real? Would he be the subject of an epic conversation between Jesus and Satan.

Satan guffawed. "Do you mean Jackson the murderer, the fornicator, and the drunkard? Is that the Jackson you're talking about?"

That was a low blow, but not a surprise, coming from Satan.

Jesus straightened and said, "Satan, you are a murderer and the father of lies. Jackson is a new creation. He is my brother and my friend and is now a member of my household. Although his sins were like scarlet, they have become as white as snow."

Wow! Jesus defended me. How wonderful he is, and so filled with love and compassion. I'd do anything for him. What a privilege it is to be here and witness a portion of the ancient battle for God's glory and renown.

Jesus looked up and said, "Jackson, come over here."

He immediately complied and stood before the heavenly court. He glanced briefly at Satan, who was now snickering at him. No light emanated from Satan, only an eerie flatness. Jesus walked over and placed his hands on Jackson's shoulders. Jesus then looked over at Satan and said, "You see, Satan. Jackson is as white as snow, as if he'd never sinned."

"It's only because you intervened on his behalf and put a hedge around him his entire life. Let me kill his friends and family, including his precious little wifey, his sister-in-law, and even his child. We'll see how white as snow he is after that."

Anger welled within him. "The Lord rebuke you, Satan! You murderer. How dare you ask for permission to kill my family? A thousand years in the Abyss and an eternity in the lake of fire await you."

Had he sinned in lashing out at Satan with his angry words? Could people sin in heaven? Jesus didn't rebuke him, so what he said must have been okay.

Satan glared at Jesus and said, "Ha! White as snow? I think not. I could turn him if given a chance."

Jackson screamed at him, "Never!"

Jesus patted Jackson on the back and glared at Satan. "Nonsense, Satan. He has been tested and proven worthy. As usual, you are lying."

Satan scoffed. "We'll see."

Jesus turned to the leader of the guard. "Michael! Escort Satan out."

A mighty angel bowed. "Yes, Lord." He gripped his spear with two hands and pressed the shaft against Satan's torso.

Satan roared and shoved it back at him. "Back off!"

The entire angelic guard crouched into a fighting position, spear or sword at the ready.

Satan laughed, turned, and sauntered back toward the throne room doors.

Jackson gazed into Jesus's eyes. "Why would Satan want to kill my family?"

"Because you brought glory to God by sacrificing yourself for Monica. Satan wants all the glory to go to himself, not God. He knows his time is short, and he will do anything to subvert God's plans for the world and his individual saints. We must be alert. I have important plans for your family back on earth."

"Important plans? What sort of plans?"

"That is not for you to know at this time, but they are far-reaching. You may pray that God's will be done on earth and in the lives of your family members."

"Will do." *What kind of plans could be so important? Why my family?*

"You may leave us now, Jackson."

He took a deep breath and nodded. "Yes, Lord." He looked toward the entrance to the throne room. Satan stood there, glaring at him for a moment, before he left. *Did Satan hear what Jesus just told me about my family?*

Jesus leaned forward. "Was there something else you wanted to ask me about, Jackson?"

"Oh, I almost forgot. I guess seeing Satan distracted me from my original reason for coming here. May I visit McKenzie on earth?"

"Don't you want to stay here in heaven, Jackson?"

"Of course. I love it here. But I miss my wife. I want to see her."

"You can see her from heaven, like everyone else."

"Yes, Lord, but I want to be near her."

"I understand, Jackson. We do not normally permit such visits. Don't you want to leave your old life behind?"

Jackson inhaled deeply. "Of course, Lord, but how can I remain behind these massive walls of safety, peace, tranquility, and joy while the evilest force in the universe wants to kill my family?"

"Angels will fight those battles for you."

"Yes, Lord. But I want to help."

"Very well. Mekoddishkem! Escort Jackson on a visit to see his wife. Ensure he learns how to defend himself before you leave."

"Yes, Lord."

Jackson prayed for God's protection over McKenzie, Monica, and his friends. What had Satan meant when he'd said "even his child?" Perhaps it was the fruit of some other one-night stand he'd had.

Jackson looked at Mekoddishkem. "May I see McKenzie now?"

The angel shook his head. "No, Jackson. You need to prepare yourself for battle first."

"Battle? What sort of battle?"

"You will see. Wait here. I will come back for you shortly."

When Mekoddishkem returned, he took Jackson to what appeared to be an ancient gymnasium, about the size of a basketball court. Swords of various lengths, along with shields and spears, were prominently affixed to the chiseled limestone wall in front of them and were also stored in racks interspersed on the wooden floor around the sides of the room.

A powerful-looking angel stood before them. "Welcome again, Mekoddishkem." The angel looked at Jackson. "This must be your young protégé, Jackson Trotman."

"It is."

"Welcome, Jackson. I am Raphael. I will be your sword fighting instructor. Mekoddishkem told me you were a United States Marine infantry officer with combat experience. He also said you earned a second-degree black belt in karate and that you used this training on several occasions to defend yourself or others. Is that correct?"

"Yes."

"Excellent."

Jackson turned to Mekoddishkem. "I'm very excited to be here, but *why* am I here?"

"Do you remember fighting the demons on Devereaux Beach in Marblehead?"

"Of course."

"How did you do?"

"Not so great. I had to call on you to save me."

"Actually, you fought very well for someone who never had any training. The reason you are here is that I may not be available to save you next time. You need to be proficient with the sword so you can take care of yourself. Pay close attention to your instructor. You will be called upon to use these skills very soon… perhaps even today."

Jackson gulped, then glanced at Raphael.

Raphael walked over to the wall, put on white protective gear that covered his head, torso, and arms, then put on matching gloves. After that, he went to one of the racks and selected two swords.

Raphael addressed Jackson. "We prepare the redeemed for the final battle. We rarely train someone for a visit to the earth before then."

He handed Jackson a sword. "We'd normally start with wooden swords, but we don't have time for that."

Jackson gulped again.

"You're holding what's called a Xiphos sword. It was used by the Greeks several thousand years ago and is ideal for training."

Jackson twisted it from side to side, studying it.

"We don't have time for you to train with that sword right now. I just wanted you to get a feel for it." Raphael took the Xiphos sword from Jackson and handed him the other sword. "I'd like you to train with this broadsword instead. These were used in Europe, starting about five hundred years ago.

"Start with your left foot forward and your right foot back. Grasp the sword with both hands and point it upward on your right side. Distribute your weight evenly on both feet as you face your opponent, which in this case, is me."

Jackson complied.

"Very good. Now bring your sword forward, pointing it at a forty-five-degree angle toward me… Good. Now bring your right foot forward toward me, always keeping your hips facing me… Good. Now strike downward on my left shoulder near my neck… Excellent. Keep your sword firmly in place as I counterattack… Good. You have now learned the most basic move of sword fighting. Let's try it again, only faster."

Raphael taught Jackson several other sword fighting techniques. Each was repeated multiple times to make sure he got it. He caught on quickly. Much faster than when he'd begun learning karate back on earth. It must be because of the greatly enhanced mind he now had in heaven.

As he trained, Mekoddishkem's words echoed in his head. He might need to use this training *very soon… perhaps even today.*

After his training session, Jackson and Mekoddishkem wasted no time in visiting McKenzie. They immediately transported themselves to The Wall.

Facing The Wall, Jackson said, "Take me to McKenzie Trotman's portal in the present." Invisible to McKenzie, they entered the condo Jackson had owned in West Hartford, Connecticut. He glanced out the window. Light flurries were falling outside.

His wife was sitting in the living room on the cordovan leather couch with her mother, sister, and brother, among the wedding gifts that hadn't been stored away yet. He marveled anew at her beauty—trim and athletic, pale white complexion, high cheekbones, and shiny, shoulder-length, straight brown hair. At five feet six, she was the perfect height for him. Odd. She was wearing the yellow sundress she'd worn on their second date in Connecticut, even though it was practically winter. He loved that dress. She always looked great in it.

McKenzie began to weep. Jackson reached out to her, but his hands passed right through her upper body. Her mother came over and softly put her hand on her daughter's shoulder. Jackson knelt beside his wife and cried with her for a long time. If only they'd had more time together.

He looked over at Mekoddishkem. "She really loved me, didn't she? I feel so bad for her. Oh, how I wish I could hold her again."

"She knows you are in a better place, Jackson. You will be reunited one day."

Jackson moved to envelop his body over McKenzie's. Maybe she would feel something, anything.

"She does not know you are here."

He sulked. Then he looked more closely at her. A golden cross was emblazoned on her forehead. It was glowing. He surveyed the others in the room—none of them had one.

"Wow! I had no idea. The cross on her forehead must mean she's a true Christian."

"Yes, Jackson. Although you have been separated for a time, you will get to spend all eternity together."

That cross on McKenzie's forehead must be how God's angels will be able to separate the wheat from the chaff on the last day.

An angel passed through an adjacent wall and hovered over McKenzie.

Jackson asked, "Is that her guardian angel?"

"Yes."

Jackson smiled and nodded at the angel. "Good. What about the others?"

"They do not have one."

Jackson glanced at Monica, the woman he had died for. The woman who had tried to seduce him shortly before his engagement to her sister. She looked the same—a blue-eyed buxom blond with brilliant blue, turquoise, and purple highlights in her hair. She was beautiful, but the absence of a cross on her forehead weighed on him. When would she come to her senses and turn her life over to God?

Botis suddenly appeared with five other menacing demons. They hovered over Monica, but didn't initially notice Mekoddishkem, Jackson, or McKenzie's guardian angel standing nearby.

One of the demons said to Botis, "Whoa. She's hot! No wonder the master wants her. Should I kill her now?"

Jackson instinctively removed his sword from its scabbard and pounced toward the demon who had just spoken, striking him right where the left shoulder meets the neck, just as he'd been instructed. The demon split like a half-opened corn husk. The others immediately turned on Jackson. He fought them off briefly on his own, using the defensive moves he'd just learned, but was quickly joined by Mekoddishkem and the other angel.

A fierce battle ensued. Another one of the demons who had accompanied Botis was struck down by Mekoddishkem. The rest fled, followed by Botis.

Jackson caught his breath. "We need to get a guardian angel for Monica. She's totally defenseless. Satan said he wanted to kill her and the rest of my family!"

He gaped at McKenzie and her relatives. They were oblivious to what had just happened. "The apostle Paul was right. The battle really is not against flesh and blood, but against the spiritual forces in the heavenly realms. I need to help them more. Exit portal."

❧

Jackson and Mekoddishkem reentered God's throne room. He should probably wait until called upon, rather than approach Jesus directly. After all, that was what Queen Esther did when she desperately needed to talk with her king.

However, a moment later, a passage in Ephesians came to him that stated he could boldly approach God with *freedom and confidence*. Jackson took a deep breath, walked forward, and knelt before Jesus, who was seated on his throne at the right hand of God the Father. He kept his gaze on Jesus, hesitant to look at the Father.

The throne room shook as the Father spoke. "What do you seek, my child?"

He trembled with reverence. "Father, I seek angels to guard my friends and family on earth. Five demons just attacked them."

"I know."

Jackson paused. A Bible verse came to mind: *Your Father knows what you need before you ask him.*

Light and warmth radiated from the throne, permeating every aspect of Jackson's being. The Father was not distant or unapproachable, but filled with love, just like Jesus.

"I ensured that you and Mekoddishkem were there at just the right time to prevent her from being harmed."

A shiver of awe went down his spine. The Father could see the future and orchestrate events to comply with his will.

"Jackson, Monica is not under my protection because she has not accepted my offer of forgiveness through my Son, Jesus."

Jesus leaned over toward the Father. "Let us give her more time to repent."

Jackson furrowed his brow. "How do we get her to repent and turn to you?"

Jesus said, "No one can come to me unless the Father draws him."

Jackson returned his gaze to the Father. "What makes that happen?"

The Father said, "She must respond in faith to my call. If she does not, whatever faith she had will be taken from her, and her heart will become hardened. She cannot enter my presence until her sins have been paid for."

His heart sank.

The Father said, "So that you will not fret, Jackson, I will send a powerful angel to protect her for a while to give her more time to repent. If she refuses, I will withdraw my protection again."

He breathed a sigh of relief. "Thank you, Father." He fell forward onto his face, basking in God's glory.

C HAPTER 7

BOY IN A WHEELCHAIR

MCKENZIE LAY IN bed reading Revelation 12:

A great sign appeared in heaven: a woman clothed with the sun, with the moon under her feet and a crown of twelve stars on her head. She was pregnant and cried out in pain as she was about to give birth. Then another sign appeared in heaven: an enormous red dragon with seven heads and ten horns and seven crowns on its heads. Its tail swept a third of the stars out of the sky and flung them to the earth. The dragon stood in front of the woman who was about to give birth, so that it might devour her child the moment he was born.

The study notes in her Bible stated that the woman represented the nation of Israel and the child was the baby Jesus whom Satan wanted to kill. Would she ever have a baby? If she did, she'd protect it from all the evil in the world. McKenzie placed her Bible on the nightstand, then dozed off.

She dreamed she was in a hospital room. To her surprise, she looked down and discovered she was very pregnant. Pain hit her midsection as contractions began in earnest.

The nurse standing beside her had a kind face. "That's it, McKenzie. Good work. You're almost there. Now, I want you to stop pushing for a minute. The baby is almost crowning. I'm going to fetch the doctor, so sit tight."

She cried out in pain as the pressure kept building. Why had the nurse left her alone? What would happen if the baby came out without her or the doctor being there?

Six hideous creatures suddenly appeared at her bedside. They were about seven feet tall with greasy, scraggly hair, yellow teeth, and eyes of death. The beings hovered in front of McKenzie with swords drawn, staring at the crowning baby. They must be demons.

She screamed, "Jesus, help me!"

Angels abruptly appeared and clashed with the demons, causing them to flee.

McKenzie woke up in a cold sweat, thanking Jesus. But did the dream mean something? Or was it a product of her imagination?

She drifted back to sleep. This time, she dreamed of looking down a dirt road that passed through fields of fully grown corn, ready to be harvested.

Twenty feet or so down the road, a man stood beside a boy in a wheelchair. The man had his hand on the boy's shoulder. Both had their backs to her, so she couldn't see their faces.

About forty demons stepped out from either side of the cornfields onto the road and maneuvered toward the man and the boy. They drew their swords menacingly as they walked.

She cried out, "Lord Jesus, please help them!"

Angels instantly appeared and fought off the demons.

She woke up again with sweat dripping from her brow. What could these crazy dreams mean?

THE MANSION

AS JACKSON STROLLED among the residents of heaven, accompanied by Mekoddishkem, he kept staring at their faces. A radiant glow lit up their skin. This must have been what Moses's face looked like after speaking with God for forty days on Mount Sinai.

He glanced at his guide. "How big is heaven?"

"The surface is about half the size of your United States. It extends upward, backward, and sideways the same distance, forming a perfect cube."

Jackson surveyed the buildings again. One of them extended so high that the top wasn't visible. "How tall is *that* building?"

Mekoddishkem looked up. "Twelve hundred stadia."

"What's that in miles?"

"Fourteen hundred miles."

"A building fourteen hundred miles high?"

"Yes."

"That's huge. How many stories is it?"

"This particular building contains 396,000 stories, each twenty feet in height. Each level houses people groups from different earth time periods. You can view the homes of the Israelites from four thousand years ago, or the early church from two thousand years ago, or even Christians who lived in Europe during the 1700s, 1800s, or 1900s."

"Fascinating! How will we travel to the expansive areas within the different levels? Are there any elevators?"

Mekoddishkem shook his head. "No. Just think where you want to go, and you will be transported there."

"Cool! Where should we go first?"

"Your new home."

"My new home?" How exciting. What would it look like? He was instantly whisked upward and arrived with Mekoddishkem at the designated level. The ground below was so far down that it was nothing but a gray area. A clear, glistening door, about ten feet in height, stood before them, encased within a golden frame. Mekoddishkem opened the door and smiled. Jackson walked in and closed the door behind them, then looked back. "What a beautiful glass door."

"Actually, the transparent portion you're looking through is made of a single slab of solid diamond, and the framing around it is made of pure gold."

"Diamond? That big? Incredible! The door alone would be worth billions of dollars on earth."

Jackson entered a small apartment with a pure white ceiling, floor, and walls. There were no pictures on the walls or furniture, except for a plain wooden chair, a nightstand, and a single bed covered with a white linen bedspread.

"This is your apartment in the heavenly city, Jackson."

It was very plain. Sparse even. But what did it matter? There was no reason for jealousy here. It was a privilege to dwell for all eternity in heaven with the living God.

In the right rear of the apartment was a door that glistened. "Where does this door lead, Mekoddishkem?"

"Enter it, and you will see."

He walked through the door and found himself standing on the edge of an ancient forest. Before him was a chalk-white pebble path advancing through the center of it. The beech, oak, sycamore, and maple trees that dotted the forest all had enormous trunks. He'd never seen an old-growth forest. Though wild, everything in the grove was in pristine condition—no dead leaves or rotting tree trunks could be seen anywhere along the grounds. Light burst forth from every leaf, every blade of grass, and every flower.

He approached a bend in the path. As he made the turn, a magnificent mansion came into view. It had a white stone façade, the same hue as the pathway. He counted three floors, with floor-to-ceiling windows and wrap-around porches on the first two and six grand columns supporting the third-floor overhanging roof on each side of the building. The top floor had three intricately crafted dormer windows jutting out from the slate roof facing them, complemented by redbrick chimneys on either side of the home. A dozen perfectly spaced ancient oak trees framed either side of the driveway leading up to the building, their branches intertwined above the path.

"Is all this for me?"

"Yes."

"Wow! It's so beautiful, Mekoddishkem. Greater than I'd ever imagined."

The angel looked around and nodded. "Yes, it is."

Jackson flung open the wide mahogany front door and strutted into a large foyer. Alternating diagonal black-and-white marble floor tiles dominated the room. A marble statue, rivaling Michelangelo's *Pieta*, stood in the center. Original Baroque paintings he didn't recognize, set in golden frames, covered each white wall. A Chippendale-like chest rested in the rear.

He gaped at the statue as he passed by it. "This room is amazing, Mekoddishkem!"

"This estate was specifically designed and built for you, Jackson."

"By whom?"

"Jesus."

"Wow!"

Mekoddishkem prepared to leave. "There will be a welcome dinner for all new arrivals with the King. I will come by to pick you up in a little while. You may explore your new home if you wish."

"Will do."

Jackson remained in the lobby, studying the paintings for some time. One looked very much like a Caravaggio he'd recently viewed at the Wadsworth Atheneum in Hartford, but it wasn't the same one.

He twirled around, then walked into the dining room. The mahogany table could comfortably seat fifteen and was embellished with stenciled designs similar to the Hitchcock furniture he'd seen in Connecticut. The matching chairs were also made of mahogany and covered with gold and off-white velvet cushions. An oak chest with a solid silver top sat against a wall. On it was the most opulent porcelain bowl he'd ever seen. French Impressionist paintings dotted the walls. He could spend hours looking at just one of them. Renoir had likely painted the one above the chest. But how could it be? He'd never seen it before. He walked right up to the painting and studied it closely, then stepped back to the other side of the room, leaning over one of the dining room chairs, and gazed at it again. The characters seemed to jump off the canvas at him. *Magnificent!* Could Michelangelo, Caravaggio, Renoir, and others have actually created these works of art for his home?

He moved on to the bedroom, which contained a king-size four-poster mahogany bed. It was covered with a white linen bedspread, which was embroidered with intricate gold designs. An incredibly lifelike portrait of Jesus hung above the bed, perhaps by a seventeenth-century painter like Vermeer.

The library contained floor-to-ceiling shelves of books. He picked up, what appeared to be, an original copy of John Bunyan's *The Pilgrim's Progress* sitting on a table next to a cordovan leather sitting chair. The document was in mint condition. He opened the front cover and found a salutation inside, addressed to him and signed by the author. Jackson shook his head in awe. What a thoughtful act by his wonderful Lord and Savior.

The back wall consisted of white French doors with floor-to-ceiling windows on either side. A fresco of *The Last Supper* covered the arched vaulted ceiling above.

The French doors opened to a garden with a large reflection pool that was flanked on either side by Blue Moon wisteria, all neatly aligned. Rectangular flower beds containing various flower types—Canterbury bells, foxgloves, snapdragons, tulips, Laeliocattleya orchids, and rose of Sharons—were set perpendicular to the wisteria. Once again, perfect symmetry.

The French doors closed behind him. Jackson turned around. It was Mekoddishkem. "It is time for the welcome dinner, Jackson. Get your sash. It is time to see the King."

⌘

Jackson, escorted by Mekoddishkem, entered a grand ballroom the size of several football fields. Intricately designed crystal chandeliers hung from a vaulted frescoed ceiling perhaps thirty feet above. About two hundred rectangular tables were neatly arranged in rows perpendicular to him. At the rear of the room, on an elevated platform, was the head table.

The crimson red walls were accented with golden floor and ceiling molding. The tables were all covered with pressed white linen tablecloths, each hosting silver candelabras interspersed between white rose arrangements. It reminded him of a picture he'd seen of a formal dinner party at Chatsworth House, an elegant English country estate.

He gaped at all the finery for a minute, then asked, "Where should I sit?"

"Wherever you wish."

The parable of the lowest seat at the feast came to mind. To keep from being humiliated on his first day in heaven, he asked, "Where is the lowest seat?"

"Those that are the farthest away from the head table."

Jackson sat down in a chair at the end of one of the rows of tables. "Will you join me?"

"No, this feast is just for the redeemed." Mekoddishkem nodded, then turned and left.

Hundreds of people began walking in; their eyes aglow with wonder. All were dressed in white linen robes.

Jesus walked into the hall amid clapping and cheers. Jackson stood and joined them. Jesus smiled and acknowledged the crowds, then walked directly to Jackson's table. Had he done something wrong?

"Jackson, Azizi, come with me."

Jackson and presumably Azizi followed Jesus as he slowly walked past the cheering people. Jesus knew every person he spoke to by name.

They walked with Jesus behind the head table. Jesus bid Azizi sit on his right, then he motioned for Jackson to sit on his left.

Jesus leaned over to him. "How do you like your new home?"

He smiled from ear to ear. "I love it. It's so lavish. More than I ever imagined. Thank you so much, Lord. It's perfect. The architect and builder are God, so how could I not love it?"

Jesus smiled broadly. "You are welcome, Jackson. Did you like the Caravaggio?"

His jaw dropped. "I *thought* it was a Caravaggio, but I'd never seen it before."

"That's because it is an original. I had it commissioned for you."

"Commissioned?"

"Yes. I had Caravaggio paint it for you."

Jackson slumped back in his chair. "Wow! That's fantastic."

Jackson let the unreality of the moment soak in. The God of the universe was talking directly to him. Every word that came out of his mouth was the Word of God.

How is Jesus able to talk to me, to be in this room surveying hundreds of people, to hear the prayers of millions, and to run heaven and earth from the throne room all at the same time?

Jesus placed his hand on Jackson's shoulder, amid all the chatter in the background, and said, "I am, in the words of your theologians, omnipresent. I can be at many places at the same time. I am not finite like you, Jackson. I know and can do all things."

He hadn't verbalized his thoughts, and yet Jesus knew them telepathically. Of course, he did.

"Caravaggio used his talents for God to impact the world. But the greatest impact on the world is made by those who teach and disciple others, a few people at a time. You influence one, then they influence another, and then that person influences someone else. It's God's plan for changing the world."

"The Great Commission."

"Exactly." Jesus sat upright in his chair. "Mekoddishkem will give you a tour of heaven tomorrow. There is no limit to the exploring and experimenting you can do here. Perhaps you'd like to try a little painting."

"I've never painted before, but sure. I'm up for a new challenge."

"I've arranged a painting lesson for you—with Caravaggio himself."

"What? The Baroque master?"

"Yes, don't you remember wishing you could paint like Caravaggio?"

Jackson searched through his memory.

Jesus put a hand on his shoulder. "It was during your tour of the Wadsworth Atheneum with McKenzie and Monica."

"Oh, yes. I do remember saying that. It was more of an off-hand remark."

Jesus smiled. "Yes, but it came from the heart."

"But Lord, I don't have any talent."

"I know. Do not worry, Jackson. I will equip you. You may train with Renoir too if you wish."

"Wow! What an honor, I'd love to. Thank you, Lord Jesus."

Jesus nodded.

Angels served the dinner, which included the finest meats and vegetables he'd ever sampled. His taste buds were launched into an explosion of flavor. He stared at his goblet, filled with wine. Should he partake of any of it since he'd given up drinking later in life? Maybe just a sip; after all, it would probably be the best glass of wine he'd ever had. He hesitated. Would he ruin a wonderful evening by sliding back into his old ways? Better to play it safe. He looked over at Jesus, who returned his gaze and said, "You're free, Jackson. Have a glass of wine, if you wish, or don't have a glass. It's up to you."

Jackson picked up his glass, then put it back down. He didn't trust himself.

After finishing his dinner, Jesus got up and walked among all the tables. Again, Jesus knew everyone by name, even though over a thousand people were here. Not only that, but he commented on something he knew about each of them. Jackson's admiration for Jesus grew deeper and deeper as he watched his King engage the guests.

After greeting each person, Jesus walked toward the door, turned, and waved to everyone, then left to thunderous applause and cheers.

Jackson transported himself back to his bedroom, changed into the pajamas provided, and lay on his bed under the covers. "Wow! What a day."

He'd done a lot but wasn't tired. Why? It seemed he didn't need to sleep. How could he sleep after a day like this anyway? Nevertheless, the bed was so comfortable that he soon drifted off to sleep.

Jackson awoke to a doorbell ringing. His first day in heaven had been amazing. He popped out of bed and strode straight to the front door. He'd never felt so rested or had so much energy in his entire life. He could probably function at full capacity from now on with a lot less sleep, perhaps no sleep at all. *Carpe diem*, time to seize the day.

Jackson thrust the front door open and found Mekoddishkem standing there. The angel said, "Come on, Jackson, we need to get going. You have an appointment with Brother Caravaggio."

"Great! I can't wait."

After Jackson changed clothes, he and Mekoddishkem were instantly transported into a painting studio. Many unframed canvases leaned against the cedar-paneled walls. Jackson carefully examined several of them while he waited. Each took his breath away.

The subjects for many of Caravaggio's paintings on earth were biblical stories. However, the painter didn't always follow biblical principles. He'd had many brushes with the law during his lifetime—arrested at least eleven times and once killed a man in a duel. The fact that Caravaggio was in heaven spoke to God's awesome forgiveness.

A large unfinished painting of a man seated on a horse rested on an oak tripod easel in the room's center. A man standing on a platform was working on it, quickly and effortlessly applying brush strokes. Beside him, an assistant stood with his hand leaning on a nearby wooden table that was covered with brushes and paints. Another assistant sat at a different table, mixing paint. In one corner of the room, a woman sat in a regal chair for a portrait. The man painting the portrait had his back to them.

Mekoddishkem approached him. "Brother Caravaggio, this is Jackson."

Jackson moved forward and shook the man's hand.

"Jackson, this is Michelangelo Merisi, otherwise known as Caravaggio."

"It is an honor to meet you, sir."

"The honor is all mine, Jackson. It's not every day I get to meet a martyr for the faith."

"Martyr? What do you mean?"

"It's the red sash you're wearing. It means you gave your life to further God's kingdom."

"Oh, I didn't know that."

Mekoddishkem placed his hand on Jackson's shoulder. "It is a great honor, similar to the Medal of Honor granted to those who served gallantly in your American military."

Jackson paused for a moment, not sure how to process this information. He hadn't thought about his life on earth since he'd arrived. And why should he? Heaven was the most wonderful place he'd ever been. He spent time with people like Jesus, Mekoddishkem, and now the Baroque master, Caravaggio.

"Did you like the painting I completed for you?"

"Very much. It was nice of Jesus to commission it for me, and kind of you to complete it."

"You are welcome, Jackson. I paint for God's glory, not my own. He's the one who equipped me to do this. I am ready to serve him whenever he calls."

"I saw your stigmata painting of Saint Francis of Assisi while on earth. It was a great blessing to me."

Caravaggio took Jackson's hand. "I'm glad. Do you have any painting experience?"

"I do not."

"That is not a problem. I will have one of my assistants help you get started with the basics."

"Jesus said he would equip me."

"Of course."

"Are you speaking to me in Italian, Brother Caravaggio?"

"Yes."

"What language are you speaking to me in, Jackson?"

"English."

"Nothing is too hard for God."

"Amen. It's like Google Translate has been enabled here in heaven."

Caravaggio's eyebrows narrowed. "What is 'Google Translate'?"

"Never mind. I am sorry to burden you with my lack of talent and experience."

"God has gifted you with special talents and abilities. Painting will come easily to you. You will see. But you must work hard if you are to bring glory to God through it."

He was escorted to a section of the studio where no one else was working. Caravaggio gave him a charcoal pencil and sketch paper and asked him to draw a nearby sculpture. Jackson became totally absorbed in his work. In just a few hours—at least that was how much time seemed to have passed—he was able to complete the best drawing of his life with minimal effort.

He gave the drawing to Caravaggio's assistant to review, who later gave it to Caravaggio.

"This is an excellent start for a beginner." He explained several things that could be improved, then said, "That's enough for today, Jackson. Come back tomorrow to continue your lessons."

"Thank you for your time, sir. I'll plan to see you tomorrow if the Lord wills it." Jackson felt a twinge of hunger. "Where should I eat tonight? I imagine the banquet I attended last night was just for new arrivals."

"You are correct. As you know, there will be a wedding feast. Until then, you are free to eat with any friends or family you wish tonight."

"I think I'll eat at my grandmother's house. I'd love to have some of her special cookies and Junket pudding again."

◆

Jackson transported himself to his maternal grandmother's home in heaven. He knocked on the front door. His grandma smiled and threw her arms around him.

"Jackson! What a wonderful surprise. Please, come in."

She was so much younger now—none of the gray hair or wrinkled skin he remembered. Her hair was light brown with thick curls, cut just below the ears. She seemed taller, maybe five feet three, and appeared to be about thirty years old, vibrant, and full of energy.

"Grandma! You don't have a walker anymore."

"I'm free of that old, decrepit body, Jackson. Jesus gave me a new temporary body for our time here in heaven, and he will give me a new permanent body when he returns to earth to rapture his people."

Her residence was much like her home on earth. Beige textured wallpaper, hardwood floors, oval multicolored area rugs, a tan easy chair, and cherry dining room furniture door. The same James Tyler painting, which captured waves crashing on a rocky coast during a storm, hung over an old clock positioned in the center of the mantel. The clock ticked and tocked just as it had when he was a little boy and when he'd surreptitiously visited her earthly home via The Wall.

"Let's go into the kitchen, Jackson. I have something for you."

Jackson whooped. "I've been waiting twenty years for this."

The smell of freshly baked cookies filled the air. With royal-blue edging along the cover, a white metal container sat prominently in the center of the kitchen table. Jackson lifted the top, reached in, and grabbed a cookie from the mound within. He inhaled the first one. It was so supple, loaded with butter, sugar, walnuts, and of course, chocolate chips. He grabbed another and ate that one quickly too. *So good.*

Two freshly chilled glass goblets of Junket pudding rested on the counter beside the cookie container. It was all just as he'd remembered. Heaven was wonderful, not just because of what was new, but because of what was old.

His grandma was beaming from ear to ear. "How do you like heaven so far, Jackson?"

"It's fantastic, greater than I'd ever imagined. Where's Grandpa?"

"He has his own home too. There's no marriage in heaven, as I'm sure you know, but we're still the best of friends. He'll be coming over for dinner soon."

Jackson's sister and daughter burst into the room. He knelt, and both of them jumped into his arms. He held them close to his chest and kissed each on the forehead. He briefly lost his composure, then stood up, holding them by the hand, and walked toward Grandma.

He gazed into Susan's eyes for a moment. She still looked like a seven-year-old, even though she'd been in heaven for twenty-two years. Her blue eyes and golden-brown hair, complete with pigtails tied with white scrunchies, shimmered in the light.

Although she only lived for a day or so on earth in her mother's body, his daughter appeared to be about two and a half years old in heaven even though she'd been here for ten years. Cute as a button, she had jet-black hair, just like her father. It was tied back in pigtails with red scrunchies. She was wearing a white linen robe, along with silver-colored sandals.

The doorbell rang. Jackson's paternal grandmother arrived. She had died when he was very young, so he didn't know her while he was on earth. However, he remembered his paternal grandfather very well. "Where's Pappi?"

"He's not here, Jackson." His grandmother choked up. "He decided he didn't want to come to heaven." She bit her lip and looked away.

Jackson collapsed into a nearby chair. He had been very close to his grandfather growing up. He'd cried and cried when his grandfather had died. It was hard back then, but this was worse. Jackson had been to hell. His grandfather must be suffering terribly with no end to the torment. "I'm so sorry to hear that, Grandmother. I loved Pappi very much."

He walked toward her and held her close.

"It was his choice, Jackson."

"I know, but I bet he would have made a different choice if he knew where he'd end up and what he'd be missing."

Grandma nodded solemnly as they sat at the table, then she smiled. "We were thrilled to watch you get married last week. It was a beautiful ceremony. McKenzie seems like a wonderful girl. The rest of the weekend was great too… until those evil men arrived."

Jackson's fork slipped out of his hand onto his plate. "How were you able to see it?"

"You'll see."

Chapter 9
Horror in Her Eyes

MCKENZIE WENT BACK to work. Her boss told her to take it slow at first. She stepped into the elevator and pressed the button for her floor. It was the same elevator where Jackson tried to kiss her. She smiled. What a wonderful moment that was.

McKenzie sat in her cubicle and turned on her laptop. Her coworkers kept their distance at first. She could hear them whispering. It was understandable. She wouldn't know what to do in this situation either. Gradually two of them came over and hugged her, telling her how sorry they were. McKenzie fought back her tears.

A few minutes later someone approached from behind and tapped her on the shoulder. It was Anabelle and she was all smiles.

"Hey McKenzie. I just got back from Barbados. How was your honeymoon in Bermuda?"

McKenzie burst into tears. This wasn't going to work. She'd come back too soon.

⚘

McKenzie lay in bed that evening reading Luke 16:

There was a rich man who was dressed in purple and fine linen and lived in luxury every day. At his gate was laid a beggar named Lazarus, covered with sores and longing to eat what fell from the rich man's table. Even the dogs came and licked his sores. The time came when the beggar died and the angels carried him to Abraham's side. The rich man also died and was buried. In Hades, where he was in torment, he looked up and saw Abraham far away, with Lazarus by his side. So he called to him, "Father Abraham, have pity on me and send Lazarus to dip the tip of his finger in water and cool my tongue, because I am in agony in this fire." But Abraham replied, "Son, remember that in your lifetime you received your good things, while Lazarus received bad things, but now he is comforted here and you are in agony. And besides all this, between us and you a great chasm has been set in place, so that those who want to go from here to you cannot, nor can anyone cross over from there to us."

McKenzie fell asleep and dreamed she was standing beside Jesus, looking across a large canyon into hell. Souls on the other side moaned continually, void of any hope.

Why was she here? She scanned the faces visible across the way. A familiar voice registered in her mind, focusing her. She scanned the other side a second time and saw Monica. Her sister was screaming in agony.

How could her sister be in hell? Why hadn't she received Jesus as her Lord and Savior right away when she'd had the chance? Now it was too late.

Monica glanced in McKenzie's direction. Recognition flickered in her eyes. "McKenzie. Is that you? Oh, God, McKenzie. Get me out of here!"

Monica trembled as an enormous reptilian demon approached

her. She looked back at McKenzie and cried, "Save me, McKenzie! Save me from this horrible place."

The demon dragged Monica off by her hair.

McKenzie woke in a cold sweat, horrified. She had to save Monica.

She knelt beside her bed and prayed. "Oh, Lord, please draw Monica to yourself. In Jesus's name, I pray, amen."

CHAPTER 10

THE MUSEUM

THERE WAS A knock at the door to Jackson's home. It was probably Mekoddishkem. He opened it, and Jesus stood before him. Jackson gasped and fell to his knees.

"What a great honor to have you here. Please come in, Lord."

Jesus reached out his hand.

Jackson took hold of it and stood up, noting the hole in his Savior's hand. "What can I do for you, Lord?"

Jesus spoke to him telepathically. *I came for a visit, Jackson.* He looked around the foyer at the floor, walls, and ceiling. *How are you enjoying your new home?*

"It's more than a home. It's an incredible estate, more than I ever imagined or hoped for. Thank you so much for preparing it for me."

Jesus smiled. "You're very welcome, Jackson. It was my pleasure to give this to you. I'm keeping a promise that those who follow me will be rewarded. What would you like to do today?"

"What do you mean 'today?' Don't you have to run the universe?"

Jesus laughed. "While on earth, I took on the form of a human body, but here in heaven, I can be in multiple places and do multiple things at the same time."

Jackson pondered that for a moment. "Then, what is the role of the Holy Spirit?"

"The Holy Spirit is my Spirit living in you and all others who follow me. What would you like to do today, Jackson?"

He shrugged his shoulders. "I'm new to heaven, so I don't know what we should do. Do you have any suggestions?"

"You like museums, don't you?"

"Of course."

Jesus motioned with his arm. "We have many museums in heaven, but there's one, in particular, I think you'd like."

Jackson nodded. "I know how busy you are. Are you sure you don't want Mekoddishkem to take me?" His lip stiffened as tears formed in his eyes.

Jesus wiped away Jackson's tears with the sleeve of his robe, then pulled him close. He kissed Jackson on the cheek and said, "Your earthly father was busy running a car business, wasn't he?"

"Yes, Lord."

"He wasn't able to spend very much time with you when you were a boy."

Jackson sniffled. "Yes, Lord. You know. I forgave him. He did the best he could."

Jesus released his embrace, stepped back, and gazed into Jackson's eyes. The complexity and variety of colors in Jesus's eyes overwhelmed Jackson with awe and wonder.

"I'm not too busy for you, Jackson. I love you so much. I want to spend the whole day with you. Just the two of us."

Jackson let out a cry of surprise. He couldn't help it. Joy tingled through every inch of his body. He was completely loved and accepted by the greatest being to ever have walked the face of the earth. "I'm all in, Lord Jesus."

Jesus smiled. "I know you are, Jackson. You are my very precious creation. I love you."

He bowed his head. "I love you too, Jesus. I didn't know there were museums in heaven. I can't wait to spend the whole day with you."

"Great! Let's go."

Jackson was transported with Jesus to a gold cobblestoned courtyard in front of a sparkling multicolored stone building with three side-by-side doorways, the middle of which was wider and higher than the others. Each doorway had a triangular-shaped archway above it, reaching perhaps a hundred feet upward that merged into three triangular-tipped towers.

As they walked toward the center doorway, many people and angels bowed low, then raised their heads and gazed at Jesus. Little children ignored all protocol and sprinted directly toward Jesus, hugging him around his thighs. With his face filled with joy, Jesus placed a hand on the head of every child, called them by name, and embraced them.

Jackson walked with Jesus into the narthex. The light of Jesus filled the building as if a spotlight were being shined into every nook and cranny. The ceilings were about a hundred feet high. The walls were adorned with intricate stone carvings, perhaps of biblical characters, each reminiscent of Michelangelo's *Madonna of Bruges*. Elegant paintings depicting various biblical events hung majestically on the walls. Jackson glanced at one of them and quickly became captivated. It was Noah and his family preparing to enter the ark. The people portrayed in the painting seemed so lifelike, so real, ready to jump off the canvas at him.

The vaulted ceilings hosted brilliantly colored frescoes depicting biblical scenes. Jackson examined every scene in great detail, given the amazing upgrade his eyes had received upon entry into heaven. He particularly admired the scene depicting Jesus delivering a sermon from a boat in the Sea of Galilee. It struck him that these scenes were not the products of an artist's imagination but were real-life portrayals. He could stand there all day, just staring at the pictures.

Jackson peered down the nave and observed a small limestone hill with three life-size crosses standing upright at the end of it. The hill became more and more encapsulated by light as Jesus approached with Jackson by his side. "Lord, is this what I think it is?"

"Yes, Jackson. These are the actual crosses used at the site of my crucifixion."

What could he say? "Amazing" was all he could think of.

Jackson drew closer. Hammers, spikes, ropes, and spears lay on the ground. The limestone was covered with dried blood.

He squared off in front of Jesus. "May I hold your hands?"

"Of course, Jackson."

He took both of Jesus's hands in his and knelt before him. "Thank you so much for what you did for me."

Jesus pulled him up to his feet. "Greater love has no one than this, that he lay down his life for his friends… I call you *friend*, Jackson."

"What a great honor, Lord. Thank you."

Jesus gazed deeply into Jackson's eyes. "Do you really understand what I did for you?"

He could have said, "Of course," but stopped himself. Jesus understood things at a far deeper level than he ever could. Jesus knew exactly what he was thinking at that very moment. "I think so… but perhaps I don't?"

Jesus pointed to his right. "Press that button over there."

Jackson approached an iron lectern with a red button encased on the surface. "Okay."

He was transported from the museum to a limestone hill with Jesus by his side. It was a cloudy day. Roman soldiers were standing nearby, but they did not startle at the arrival of Jackson and Jesus. They must be invisible to the soldiers. Various metal tools and weapons lay on the ground.

A procession of people, walking behind another contingent of Roman soldiers, was approaching. Some of the civilians wore rich, colorful flowing robes, while others wore sackcloth. The hair of most looked dirty and disheveled by today's standards. A man at the center of the procession was nearly naked. Blood streamed down his face, and fresh, horrific wounds were visible all over his body. Shreds of torn skin flapped as he stumbled off-balance the remainder of the way. A primitive crown of thorns had been set upon his head. Another man, who was clothed and much larger and stronger, helped the man carry the cross. One of the Roman soldiers shouted a command, and the two of them dragged the cross a little farther, then dropped it to the ground.

Jackson swallowed hard. He was witnessing the actual crucifixion of Jesus, one of the greatest events in human history. A lot of people were in attendance. Herod's Temple sat on the Temple Mount in the distance. Some women were wailing nearby. One of them must have been Mary, the earthly mother of Jesus and perhaps the holiest woman who ever lived.

The Roman soldiers moved the cross to align with a hole in the ground. Jesus was brought over and forced to lie down on the cross. His arms and legs were lashed to the cross with rope, then large spikes were driven through the palms of each of his hands and then through each of his feet. Jackson winced with each blow. It was disgusting to watch but must have been far worse to experience.

How could they do such a horrible thing? It was unconscionable. The sight of the spikes ripping through flesh and bone made Jackson nauseous. The two other victims cried out in agony as the spikes were driven into their bodies.

The three crosses were then lifted with ropes so that the base of each cross slid into the hole directly in front of it. Jesus grimaced as his cross was slid into place.

Jackson stood there, watching helplessly, as Jesus hung on the cross, his face sweaty and bloodied and contorted with agony.

After what seemed like seconds, Jesus on the cross cried out,

"*Eloi, Eloi, lama sabachthani?*" which Jackson understood to mean "My God, my God, why have you forsaken me?"

The Father then laid the sins of all humanity—past, present, and future—on Jesus.

On the cross, Jesus opened his eyes and seemed to be staring directly at Jackson. It wasn't possible, of course, that Jesus on the cross could be looking directly at him or that he would even have any idea Jackson would be standing there, watching from a different time and dimension. It must be coincidental.

Jesus by his side then said, "I was looking into the future; toward all the people who would one day benefit from my obedience to the Father's will. I did this for all my friends, every one of them, including you, in obedience to my Father."

Jackson shook his head. "Astounding."

Jesus said, "I've shown you what I did to save you. Now I'm going to show you what I saved you from."

Heat and a putrid odor assaulted his senses. They had been transported to hell. It was just as he remembered it from his previous trip with Mekoddishkem. This time, however, it was worse. They were in an underground cave that was pitch black, except for some nearby percolating lava pits. He could barely breathe. The heat was far more oppressive than anything he'd experienced in Afghanistan. The stench was gut-wrenching—vomit, rotting flesh, and feces all rolled into one. The jarring mixture of moans and screams was deafening and overwhelming. The people here knew great suffering. The worst part was that it would never end.

Jackson's earlier arguments with Mekoddishkem about why there was a hell and why people who weren't that bad were sent there was just a distant memory now. This is God's world, not man's world, and humans have to abide by *his* rules, not the ones they make up. While most people see the justice in sending mass murderers like Hitler and Stalin to hell, they never seem to think *their* sins are bad enough to send *them* there. This is a fatal error. God's standard for entrance into heaven is perfection. No one can meet that standard alone, no matter how pure they think they might be or how many good works they perform to atone for past misdeeds. Their sins are encased in concrete and can't be removed from the record by anything they do, except for reaching out and grabbing hold of the forgiveness offered in Jesus Christ's atoning death on the cross as payment for those sins. God is just, and sin must be paid for. Gratitude swelled inside Jackson's heart. Jesus had paid for his sins on the cross, so he wouldn't have to pay for them himself in hell.

"Why did you bring me here, Jesus?"

"I have something to show you."

They came upon a large naked man strapped down on a slab of stone perched at a forty-five-degree angle. Two enormous, scragglyhaired demons, reptilian in appearance, tortured the man without mercy using red-hot tipped iron poles.

"They can't see us, Jackson. This is Dexter, the man who raped McKenzie at the Brown Sigma Chi fraternity house before you carried her to safety. Years later, he tried to kill you at the Farmington River while you were tubing with McKenzie. Several months after that, he killed an FBI agent and then tried to kill you and McKenzie at your wedding reception. He has been sent to one of the worst parts of hell as the penalty for his sins."

"Dexter should have turned away from his sinful life while he had the chance. I remember warning him as he sat in the police car after he had tried to kill me. Now, look at him. It's horrible. I wouldn't wish this on my worst enemy, which he probably was."

"The Holy Spirit is not actively working here to restrain evil." Jesus placed his hand on Jackson's shoulder. "You did warn him, Jackson, and I commend you for that, but don't ever get the idea you were any better than him because you didn't rape or murder someone. You would have been right here, on this very slab, if you hadn't repented of your sins and turned to me for forgiveness."

He was stunned, but Jesus was right. His life review was awful. True, he hadn't raped or murdered anyone, but he'd certainly broken all the Ten Commandments, either directly or indirectly, in thought or deed. He'd valued money and sex more than God, and he'd taken the Lord's name in vain too many times to count, especially in the marines. He'd ignored the Sabbath, dishonored his parents, been angry at others in a way that qualified as murder, slept around with various women, been an unwitting party to an abortion, stolen things when he was young, lied, and coveted things other people had. His mutilation of an enemy soldier's body with a pistol came to mind. The list of his sins went on and on.

"Thank you for showing me what you saved me from, Lord."

"You are very welcome, Jackson."

"During my last visit to hell, I noticed many people sat alone in prison cells while others were being tortured. Why is that?"

"If a person is found guilty of committing a crime, a just judge would send them to prison for a time proportionate to the severity of their offense. Likewise, people in hell are treated in a manner commensurate with their offenses. God is just, Jackson. Some people are punished more severely than others, but sin must be paid for.

"Heaven is the presence of God at its fullest, while hell is the absence of God at its fullest. The mercy of God, offered to each person while they are still alive on earth, ends once they die if they reject it."

Jackson covered his mouth with his hand and sighed. "So tragic. May I ask you a question? It will sound strange."

"You may, Jackson."

"You already know what my question is, don't you?"

"Yes, Jackson, but I still want you to ask it. Don't you see? I love you and want to deepen my relationship with you."

Jackson choked up for a moment, then asked his question. "What is it like to see a couple hundred thousand people die every day with most of them going to hell?"

Jesus teared up. "It grieves me deeply, Jackson. And it grieves my Father very deeply as well. These are my children, each of whom I've known and cared for before creating the world and throughout their entire lives. Of their own free will, they've rejected me, refusing to turn away from their sins and turn to me for forgiveness. As you know, God is not willing that any should perish, but that all would come to repentance."

"How are you able to bear such a terrible burden?"

"Because I love people so much, I give them free will—the ability to choose to be with me forever in heaven or apart from me forever in hell. The choice is theirs."

Jackson shook his head and exhaled. *What tremendous suffering Jesus underwent on our behalf, and what tremendous suffering he endures for us each day as he sees his children reject his mercy and turn away from him forever.*

"Would you like to return to the museum now, Jackson?"

He nodded. "Yes, Lord."

They arrived at the museum and headed down the hallway.

Jesus asked, "What is your favorite passage of Scripture, Jackson?"

He didn't hesitate. "You know, Lord. The Sermon on the Mount."

"Would you like to see me deliver it?"

"Wow! Can I? That would be incredible."

A second later, he stood with Jesus on a grassy hill overlooking a large lake. Several wooden boats, occupied by fishermen with nets, were visible just offshore. "Jesus, is that the Sea of Galilee?"

"It is, Jackson."

Thousands of men and women, dressed mostly in plain brown robes, were mingling below beside the lake. "Are those your disciples?"

"Yes."

One of the people trudged up the grassy hill toward them. It was Jesus in human form. He walked right up to where Jackson was standing with his Lord, then turned and sat down, facing his disciples below.

"Jesus, can you point out Peter and John?"

"Of course." Jesus pointed with his right index finger. "Peter is the man with the black beard over to our left."

Jackson whooped. "Wow! He looks strong… I guess that makes sense since he was a fisherman."

Jesus then pointed to another man. "John is the man with the long auburn hair and beard, sitting to our right."

"He was a man of great intelligence and faith, a man filled with compassion for others."

"These were two of my closest friends while I walked the earth as a man."

Jackson hadn't had many close friends when he walked the earth. But none of that mattered now. All that mattered was that he had the closest friend in the universe, and he was standing right next to him. He'd like to visit with the apostles at some point.

Jackson listened as Jesus at the Sea of Galilee began speaking:

Blessed are the poor in spirit,
for theirs is the kingdom of heaven.
Blessed are those who mourn,
for they will be comforted.
Blessed are the meek,
for they will inherit the earth.
Blessed are those who hunger and thirst for righteousness,
for they will be filled.
Blessed are the merciful,
for they will be shown mercy.
Blessed are the pure in heart,
for they will see God.
Blessed are the peacemakers,

for they will be called children of God.
Blessed are those who are persecuted because of righteousness,
for theirs is the kingdom of heaven.
Blessed are you when people insult you, persecute you and falsely say all kinds of evil against you because of me. Rejoice and be glad, because great is your reward in heaven, for in the same way they persecuted the prophets who were before you.

Jackson was speechless. He'd spent years of his adult life reading and memorizing God's Word. It was overwhelming to hear it live, originally delivered by the Son of God thousands of years earlier. It was exactly as recorded in the Bible.

Jesus continued to discuss the true meaning of murder, adultery, divorce, loving your enemies, giving, prayer, fasting, and other topics as recorded in Matthew 5–7. Jesus was instructing his disciples how they should live—at a level of righteousness practiced internally, not merely externally, which God required and could not be achieved without divine help.

After finishing his sermon, Jesus walked down the mountainside. The crowds followed him. A man with leprosy approached him and said, "Lord, if you are willing, you can make me clean."

Jesus reached out his hand and touched the man. "I am willing," he said. "Be clean!"

Immediately, the man's leprosy left him. The man's skin transformed from blotchy and red to smooth and clear in a split second.

A thought occurred to Jackson that he hadn't fully processed before. He turned to his time-traveling companion. "Isn't that the ultimate meaning of the Sermon on the Mount? We are all lepers, and only you can make us clean."

Jesus gave Jackson a proud father smile.

Jackson walked with Jesus to the museum entrance. "I've had a wonderful time with you today, Lord Jesus. Thank you for the fascinating journey through biblical history at the museum. It was the most thrilling experience of my life."

"You are welcome, Jackson. There is so much more in heaven that you haven't seen yet. There are other museum exhibits such as Noah's Ark, Jonah and the Whale, the Tabernacle, and many others. But don't worry, you'll have all eternity to explore this city and the universe. We'll have to do it again very soon."

"Yes, Lord. I look forward to it."

Jesus pulled Jackson near to him and hugged him. "Call out to me any time. I will be there for you. I love you, Jackson."

He teared up yet again. "I love you, Lord."

Jesus released his embrace, then began walking away from the museum entrance. As he walked, the image of him faded, then disappeared.

Several children ran around in the fresh air. *Children.* He hadn't spent much time with his daughter… or his sister. He needed to find out from Mekoddishkem where they lived.

CHAPTER 11
JACKSON'S GIRLS

JACKSON ARRIVED AT a classic three-story Georgian brick mansion. It had a slate roof topped with a white wooden cupola, white trim around the windows, and black shutters. Off to the side was an in-ground swimming pool, tucked behind perfectly manicured green hedges, where children were playing Marco Polo. He rapped the golden knocker on the large black door. A woman with a kind face appeared.

"Hello. I'm Jackson Trotman. I'd like to see my sister, Susan."

"Oh, I've heard so much about you, Jackson. My name is Rachel. I've been taking care of your sister since she left you."

He gasped, then reached out and hugged her. "That was twenty-four years ago."

She smiled. "Oh, it seems just like yesterday. We don't really keep track of time up here."

Jackson lost his composure for a moment, then he stepped back. "On behalf of my parents and me, thank you so much, Rachel, for taking care of my sister. I don't know how we can ever repay you."

Rachel just shook her head. "During my life on earth, I never had any children. It's been my pleasure and joy to take care of Susan."

Rachel invited him inside and took him into Susan's room. It was covered with several dinosaur paintings, each of which was quite exquisite in detail. He laughed. "I'm not surprised at her artwork selections. She loved dinosaurs when she was a kid. I saw her playing with them a few months ago while watching her through her portal. It was very reassuring that she was well cared for."

"I don't know what you're referring to, but I'm glad you got to see her."

Susan walked in, wearing a bathing suit, and her face lit up when she saw Jackson. She ran over to him and flung her arms around his waist.

He held her tight for a moment, then bent down to her eye level. "Hey, Susan, how are you, and how are your pet dinosaurs?"

Susan tilted her head. "First of all, let me just say it's a little weird looking up to my baby brother."

He chuckled. "I was five when you went to heaven, so I wasn't *exactly* a baby."

"True... How did you know about my *Apatosaurus* and my other dinosaurs?"

"My guardian angel took me to heaven a few months ago and showed them to me. He also showed me you."

"Really? I had no idea you were watching me. I got to watch you a few times too."

He made a mental note to ask Mekoddishkem how people in heaven could see people on earth, apart from The Wall.

Jackson took Susan by the hand. "I want to spend time with my daughter too, but I don't know her."

"It's okay. I see her all the time. Her room is right down the hallway. I'll take you to see her."

He sighed, then turned to Rachel. "You've been taking care of my daughter too?"

"Yes, Jackson."

"Why didn't you tell me?"

"You didn't ask."

"Then a double *thank you* to you."

"You're welcome. It was my pleasure. I will miss them."

He motioned for Rachel to step outside into the hallway with him. "Do they need to leave?"

"Why yes if you want them to. I assumed they would go live with you."

"I suppose you're right, Rachel. I never thought about that." How would he juggle worshipping God, watching the kids, attending painting classes, and checking in on McKenzie?

Rachel placed her hand on his shoulder. "There's no rush, Jackson. You can take some time to think about it. Just let me know what you'd like to do."

Rachel must have read his mind. "I will. Thank you. You've been so incredibly kind."

They went with Susan to his daughter's room, but she wasn't there. A bout of insecurity hit him. What would his daughter think of him since he hadn't even known she existed until Mekoddishkem told him?

Susan said, "She must be at the playground. I'll take you there."

With merely a thought, they arrived at a playground that was about as big as four football fields. It had a flat, rectangular strip of gold, the size of a basketball court, from which streams of water randomly spurted into the air out of hundreds of nozzles. Kids, from toddlers to teenagers, were shrieking and frolicking there with glee. Solid silver slides, swing sets, and jungle gym monkey bars abounded nearby. There didn't appear to be much adult supervision, which must have thrilled the kids.

Jackson had to ask his sister a fundamental question. There was no delicate way of doing it, so he just blurted it out. "Susan, what is my daughter's name?"

She chuckled. "You never named her, Jackson, so we call her Joy."

"Joy! That's a wonderful name. Thank you for doing that."

They wandered around the playground, looking for his daughter.

Finally, Susan found Joy sitting atop a slide with her face gleaming. She pointed her out to Jackson.

He paused, waiting for their eyes to connect.

Joy shrieked, "Daddy!" and ran toward him.

He dropped to his knees and enveloped her in a bear-hug, then picked her up. He broke into a huge smile as the tears trickled down his face.

Joy squirmed, a clear indication she wanted to be put back down on the ground. When her feet touched down, she ran over to Susan and hugged her, then she tugged on Jackson's hand. "Push me on the swing, Daddy. Please?"

Jackson choked up. He couldn't speak.

"It's okay, Daddy. I love you."

Jackson worked hard to fight back the tears but couldn't any longer. He got down on his knees and hugged her with all his might, crying like a baby. "I love you too, Joy."

"Daddy, when is Mommy going to get here?"

"I don't know. Only God knows."

"Let's pray for her."

"Okay." The three of them got down on their knees in the middle of the playground. Jackson put his arms around both of them. No one seemed to notice as the chatter continued around them. The mother's name came to him. "Lord, I thank you for my precious little daughter, Joy, and my sister, Susan. Thank you for all you've done to save us and welcome us to live with you in heaven. We lift up Cassandra Alvarez to you and pray you would turn her heart toward God so she can be in heaven with us one day. In Jesus's name, we pray, amen."

Jackson touched Joy's knee. "Would you like to go see your mother?"

"Sure, Daddy."

The three of them stood up and held hands. Jackson hesitated. How would he get to The Wall? He closed his eyes and just willed they would all be transported there. Soon, they stood together on the gangplank facing it.

"Daddy, what is this place?"

"It's called The Wall. It allows you to go into the past, present, or future of anyone who ever lived."

Jackson took a step forward then stopped. This could be dangerous, and he hadn't brought a sword. "Just a minute, girls. I forgot something. I'll be right back."

With a quick wish, he arrived at the training center. His sword-fighting instructor happened to be there, teaching someone else. "Raphael, may I borrow one of the swords? I want to visit someone with my sister and daughter."

"Sure, Jackson. Take one from the rack over there. They are very sharp, so be sure to put it in a scabbard when traveling."

"Will do."

"Oh, take one of those shields with you too. You never know when you might need it."

"Thank you."

"That is alright, Jackson."

He slid a broadsword into the scabbard portion of the leather harness, then strapped it onto his back so it was accessible by simply reaching over his shoulder. He then picked up the golden shield. It was circular with a red cross embossed over the front of it.

He willed himself back to The Wall.

Jackson took his sister's and his daughter's hands. "Take me to the portal of Cassandra Alvarez in the present."

It had been nearly a decade since he'd last seen her when they'd only spent one drunken night together. Jackson instantly recognized her but was shocked by her appearance. Cassandra was sitting in a wheelchair, her neck held in place by a brace that extended up from the back of her wheelchair.

Joy looked up at Jackson. "She got hurt in an accident, Daddy. She can't walk anymore."

"That's very sad, Joy. I'm so sorry."

He asked Susan, "Is Cassandra a Christian?"

"I don't think so. She was furious after the accident. She blamed God for allowing it to happen. I even heard her curse God once."

He studied Cassandra's forehead—there was no golden cross on it like on McKenzie's. "We need to pray very hard for her, girls. We want her to come live with us in heaven one day, don't we?"

Susan and Joy nodded in unison.

There was a knock at the front door. Cassandra maneuvered to the door and called out, "Who is it?"

"Becky."

Cassandra smiled and unlatched the door. "Come in."

A slim woman with a broad grin on her face, wearing navy-colored scrubs, walked in. "Well, good day, Miss Cassandra! How are you doing today?" Becky had a cross on her forehead.

He pointed. "Look, girls. That woman is a Christian. I hope Cassandra listens to her."

Susan and Joy nodded.

Joy approached and tugged persistently at his robe. "Will Jesus give Mommy a new body when she gets here?"

"If she becomes a follower of Jesus, she'll be able to stand up again and run just like you and me. Before that can happen, she must believe in Jesus and be willing to turn away from her old way of life and follow him."

Joy continued, "How can she not believe in Jesus?"

He paused. How should he phrase it to communicate this truth to a toddler? "People on earth can't see Jesus like we can, Joy. They must *believe* he exists instead. People are born not wanting to obey

God. You wouldn't know about that because you came to heaven before you were fully grown and out of your mommy's tummy. People living on earth want to live their lives their own way and sometimes do bad things. They don't want to follow God's ways. Jesus would like everyone to live with him in heaven one day, but most won't because they don't want to listen to him or believe in him."

"That's too bad, Daddy. Let's go get ice cream!"

He chuckled, then stopped himself. This was no laughing matter. He prayed silently. *Father, please help Cassandra get through her physical trials on earth and give her purpose and meaning in life. Also, please save her so she can be with us in heaven one day. In Jesus's name, I pray, amen.*

Both Susan and Joy said, "Amen."

"You heard my prayer?"

Susan nodded. "Uh, yeah. Thoughts can be public or private. Prayers to God are always public in heaven."

He inhaled deeply. "Good to know."

The home health aide took a Bible out of her bag. "I read a very moving passage about heaven this morning. Would you like me to share it with you before I start dinner?"

Cassandra scoffed. "We've been through this before, Becky. I don't want to have anything to do with the Bible or God. I know that stuff works for you, and I'm sure you mean well, but I'm not interested."

Jackson shook his head. "That's not good. There's nothing else we can do right now, girls. We'll just have to keep praying. Let's go back now. Exit portal."

❧

Botis tapped his chin after interviewing a demon who said Jackson Trotman showed up at a paralyzed patient's house. Of course, the demon could have been mistaken. Everyone knew of Satan's order to kill any of Jackson's offspring. Perhaps this demon was overzealous.

But Botis couldn't take any chances. He had to send this up the chain of command. Besides, it was past time for him to confess that his latest attempt to kill Monica had failed.

Botis approached Agliarept's throne room and waited for him to make eye contact. Best to start with the helpful info. "Master, I have something to report about the traitor Jackson."

Agliarept leaned forward. "Proceed."

"I learned that Jackson has a sister and a daughter in heaven."

"Why does that matter to me, you fool?"

"The daughter is the fruit of a sexual liaison between the traitor and someone named Cassandra Alvarez. She is paralyzed and confined to a wheelchair."

"Very well. I will report this to Satan, and we shall see what he wants to do." Agliarept got up, strode over to Botis, and spoke directly into his face. "But that's not all you have to tell me, is it? You failed me again, Botis."

Within minutes, he was gored with a meat hook that was attached to a chain dangling from the ceiling. Agliarept cranked a lever and strung Botis up before the throne. Botis writhed in agony as he waited for his master to speak again.

Agliarept was maddeningly silent.

Barely able to breathe, Botis grimaced and said, "Master, there were two angels and a man opposing us. We didn't know they would be there. They bested two of my warriors."

"Excuses, excuses—that's all you ever give me, Botis. Where is my new queen?"

Botis, knowing his master's revulsion toward one of the angels, mentioned him by name again to deflect attention from himself. "One of the angels who fought us was Mekoddishkem."

Agliarept retreated to his throne. "Mekoddishkem. Oh, how I hate him. I'll need to think about this." Agliarept gritted his teeth, then strode toward the door. "While you're hanging there, Botis, you'd better come up with a better plan for bringing Monica to me."

⤚

Agliarept trembled with fear as he approached Satan's throne. He would be extremely cautious this time, carefully evaluating every word that came out of his mouth. The memory of one golden lion ripping the flesh from his right leg and another ripping his left arm out of its socket was still fresh in his mind. He *never* wanted to go through that again.

Satan glanced up at Agliarept from his throne. He lifted both arms in the air. "Awaken!" All the golden lions on either side of him came to life, fourteen in all, and sat in place, growling. "What do you want, Agliarept? It had better be good."

He fell to his knees. Being ripped limb from limb by an entire pride of lions would be even worse.

"Speak, you idiot!"

"Yes, master. I discovered the traitor Jackson had slept with a woman named Cassandra Alvarez before meeting his wife."

"So?"

"She conceived. A morning-after pill killed the child, but the mother still lives."

"Kill her!"

Agliarept hesitated. His master would normally obtain permission from the God of Abraham, Isaac, and Jacob before slaying anyone ahead of their appointed time. If he followed Satan's orders directly, without question, he would be in trouble with God. If he didn't, he'd be in trouble with Satan.

"What is it, you imbecile?"

"Master, you normally ask for God's permission before ordering me to kill someone." As soon as he'd uttered those words and observed the expression on Satan's face, he cowered in fear.

"That is correct, Agliarept, but these are not normal times." He looked to his right. "Guard, come here."

An enormous, hooded demon dressed in a ruby-red robe appeared from the shadows, carrying a spear about ten feet long. Agliarept eyed the serrated tip at the end of the shaft. The guard stood on the right side at the base of the throne.

"Hand me your spear."

The guard tossed the spear sideways to his master so that the center of the shaft landed in his master's hand. Satan then stood, cocked the spear backward with his right arm, and launched it through the air toward Agliarept, striking him through the heart. Agliarept fell to the floor, gasping for air and screaming in agony.

Satan yelled from his throne, "You didn't learn much from your last lesson with the lions, did you Agliarept! Guards!" Three other guards appeared. "Stand the spear up in the casing over there, so I can view Agliarept impaled on it for a time."

The guards forced him to his feet, then dragged him toward the side of the throne room. Pain sliced through him with every move-ment. A foil with a hole in the middle was placed over the spear's base, slid up the shaft of the spear next to his body, then tightened in place with a built-in lever. Two of the guards lifted his body into the air, while the other two maneuvered the spear's base into an iron stand specifically designed for this circumstance. Agliarept hung in the air, impaled on the top of the spear, squirming, and crying out in agony.

Sometime later, Satan approached Agliarept, who was still impaled on top of the spear. "What am I going to do with you?"

Agliarept continued wailing and thrashing about. It was the worst pain he'd ever experienced.

"Don't ever question one of my orders again! Do you under-stand me?"

He struggled to get the words out. "Yes, master."

Satan turned toward the guards. "Take him down."

The four guards lifted the spear into the air, with Agliarept still impaled on it, then threw him to the ground. They removed the foil from the shaft. One of them placed a foot on his chest and forcibly extracted the spear from his body, causing him to scream even louder.

"You know what you need to do now, don't you, Agliarept?"

He could not get up, but with all the energy he could muster, he lifted his head, and said, "Yes, master."

Satan repaired Agliarept's chest wound by touching it.

Slowly he got up. He bowed very low as he walked backward from the throne and left.

Botis waited in agony, shifting to take the pressure off his burning chest. Finally, Agliarept returned with a scowl on his face.

"We have orders from Satan to kill everyone associated with Jackson Trotman's family," Agliarept said. "They could be the key to stopping the resurrection of the enemy army."

"Yes, master. Don't we need to get permission from Yahweh before killing them?"

Agliarept grabbed Botis's torso and spun it around the meat hook, then twisted it back and forth.

Botis screamed at the top of his lungs.

Agliarept returned to his throne. "I've just come from seeing Satan. He impaled me on a spear for saying what you just said."

"Oh, master. I will do anything you ask."

"Give me Monica."

"Yes, master."

"I also have another assignment for you."

"Yes, master."

"I just spoke to Satan about Cassandra Alvarez, the woman you reported was Jackson's whore. Satan gave me a direct order to have her killed. Kill her now. You shouldn't encounter any opposition—she is unprotected. After that, kill Monica Baker. Do you understand?"

"Very well, master."

Agliarept pulled a lever to release the meat hook cable, then left the room without another word. Botis lay on the floor, trying to wriggle the hook out of his torso as gingerly as he could. It wasn't working, so he took a deep breath and ripped it out. "Urgh."

Someday, he'd pay Agliarept back for all the harm he'd inflicted on him over the centuries.

CHAPTER 12

TORN BETWEEN TWO WORLDS

JACKSON LAY ON his bed, thinking. On the one hand, being in heaven with God, seeing his redeemed family members, and meeting the wonderful people here was everything he'd dreamed of. On the other hand, he had an intense need to see McKenzie again—now! He got out of bed, strapped his leather scabbard harness complete with sword onto his back, and transported himself to The Wall. There, he asked to be taken to McKenzie's portal in the present.

He arrived at Valley Community Baptist Church, invisible to those in the sanctuary. McKenzie was sitting in their old pew in the balcony with Monica by her side. A golden cross shone brightly on McKenzie's forehead; conspicuous to Jackson was the absence of one on Monica's forehead. He surveyed the audience. Most of those he'd once worshipped with had crosses on their foreheads, but a few did not, including a church staff member, a choir member, and a deacon. He cringed at the thought of them being carted off to the lake of fire, dumbfounded, and crying out to God, "Lord, don't you know me?"

Many guardian angels hovered overhead. He maneuvered around the sanctuary. Most people were attentive, but several struggled to stay awake. Still others were chitchatting or texting. *If they knew such a great cloud of witnesses was watching them from the heavenly realms, they would behave differently.*

A verse of Scripture filled his mind: *For your ways are in full view of the Lord.* What must God think when he observed his church worshipping in this way?

After the service, Jackson stood alongside McKenzie and Monica as they chatted in the lobby. Each was holding a white Styrofoam cup of coffee. McKenzie wore a tan barn coat and yellow duck boots, while Monica wore a navy-blue Red Sox jacket, tight-fitting blue jeans, and white Converse sneakers with fire-engine-red laces.

McKenzie asked, "What do you think of the coffee?"

"Not bad, but I've gotten pretty spoiled working at Starbucks." The Boston accent was still pretty thick but seemed to have faded a bit since she'd started living in Connecticut with McKenzie.

Jackson's old friend Mike Tolbert sat alone at a table in the lobby across from the coffee area. Jackson floated in that direction. Mike was wearing a light-blue collared shirt, admiral-blue cardigan sweater, gray slacks, and black wingtips. Mike's elbows were on the table with his black hands propping up his head. He was staring into space. Jackson slipped in closer to eavesdrop.

Why, Lord, why? Why did you allow my mother to die? She was so young. Mike shook his head and sighed. *And why did you allow Jackson to die? He was my best friend!*

Sally arrived impeccably attired as always. She stood behind Mike and placed her hands on his shoulders. She was wearing a classic light black L.L.Bean insulated coat with a drawstring at the collar and pressed black slacks. "A penny for your thoughts?"

"I was just thinking about Jackson. It's so sad he's gone. I feel awful for McKenzie. They were only married for one day."

"Yes, it was a terrible thing. I'm helping her all I can during our discipleship meetings. Having her bury her mind in Scripture should help, but she'll never get over it. She just has to learn to live with it. Is anything else bothering you?"

Mike straightened. "What else could be bothering me? Isn't that enough?"

Sally paused and studied him. "Think!"

Mike folded his hands and put them on his lap. Sally kept staring at him. About twenty seconds passed. "Do you mean the two people I shot and killed?"

"Yes."

Mike frowned. "What about it?"

"How does it make you feel?"

Mike sighed. "I don't know how I feel."

"That's totally understandable, but if you hadn't killed the first guy, then Jackson, McKenzie, and who knows who else would have died at the reception. They would never have been able to spend their wedding night together. And if you hadn't killed the second guy, Monica certainly would have died. So, you saved your best friend's wife and sister-in-law from certain death. You did a righteous thing, my husband. I'm so proud of you."

Tough-guy Mike fought back the tears as Sally wrapped her arms around him.

Mike sniffled. "I know you're right, but it doesn't feel righteous. I've never killed anyone before. Even though they were evil, they were still someone's son, brother, or friend. I've got to assume they weren't Christians, so they must be in hell right now, suffering terribly because I put them there."

Sally scoffed. "They put themselves in hell, Mike. You didn't. They probably would have ended up there anyway. Don't let that bother you. You did what you had to do."

"I guess you're right, but I still have to process what I did."

"Understood. Take all the time you need." Sally pulled Mike

off the chair and held his hand. "Let's go pick up the kids from Sunday school."

As they walked off, Jackson floated back to McKenzie. A man and a woman approached her in the church lobby. McKenzie glanced at the name tag on the man's lapel. It read *Usher*.

The man reached out his hand. "Hi, McKenzie?"

She returned his handshake with a furrowed brow. Obviously, she didn't know the man.

"I'm Timmy. I'm an usher here at Valley."

"Hi, Timmy."

Timmy turned to the woman beside him. "I'd like you to meet Pam Shuster. She asked me to point you out."

McKenzie reached out her hand. "Hi, Pam."

Pam's bleach-blond pixie haircut, combined with a chestnut-brown pantsuit and multicolored scarf, gave her a distinctive look.

Timmy smiled. "Well, if you'll excuse me."

McKenzie pointed with her arm. "This is my sister, Monica."

Pam nodded. "You're probably wondering who I am."

McKenzie laughed. "Yes, as a matter of fact, I am. I don't believe we've met."

"We haven't. I worked with your husband, Jackson, at Aetna."

McKenzie's face fell. "Oh."

"Your husband was a great man. He told me about Jesus, even though I was Jewish and gay. I was initially nasty to him. I wanted nothing to do with him or his 'triune' God. But I realized he had something I didn't have, and I wanted to learn more. I'm not sure if you know this, but he invited me to this church shortly before he died… Well, here I am."

Tears welled in McKenzie's eyes. "That's so nice of you to say, Pam. I'm glad you're here, and I'm glad Jackson had a positive impact on you."

"You're welcome. He told me about a class being conducted here called Alpha. The people at the front desk said another class will be starting in two weeks. I just signed up."

"That's great. I was thinking about taking that class too."

"You're welcome to join me if you like."

McKenzie tapped a finger on her chin, then looked at Monica. "Maybe we will."

After a few more minutes of chatting with Pam, McKenzie and Monica walked out to the church parking lot and hopped into McKenzie's car. Jackson settled in the back seat, invisible to both.

Botis suddenly burst through the windshield with sword drawn, roaring. Jackson yelled and managed to jump out of the way just as Botis thrust his sword at him. Jackson positioned himself outside the car and drew his sword. He attacked the demon, slashing wildly at first, but after a moment, he gathered himself and began using the techniques Raphael had taught him. The beginning of the skirmish went well, but toward the end, he was about to be bested.

Jackson cried out for help, "Mekoddishkem!"

The demon quickly departed when Jackson's guardian angel arrived.

He gave Mekoddishkem a grateful look. "Thank you."

"You are welcome. It was Botis, the servant of Agliarept, demonic lord of New England."

"Are there demonic lords over all the states and major cities in America?"

"Demonic lords are reigning over all the principalities of the world."

Jackson shook his head. "I guess I read about that in the Bible but had no idea they were organized in that way."

"They all report through a chain of command to Satan himself."

Jackson paused. "My one-on-one battle against Botis did not go well."

Mekoddishkem placed a hand on his shoulder. "Cheer up, Jackson. You need to keep this in perspective. On the positive side, you did well to depart a sword fight unscathed with a demon who has several thousand years more experience than you. On the other hand, it would not have gone well had I not arrived to assist you."

"Agreed. I need to get better. Can I train with Raphael again?"

"Of course. I will arrange it."

᳀

Back in the training center, Jackson addressed the angel Raphael. "Thank you for agreeing to see me on such short notice."

"It is my pleasure, Jackson. How can I help?"

Jackson recounted the sword fight, including his need to call in Mekoddishkem.

Raphael smacked Jackson's shoulders. "Why do you think Botis fled?"

"Because Mekoddishkem is so strong and powerful."

Raphael nodded. "What else?"

Jackson had to think for a moment. "Because he knew he would lose."

Raphael made a fist. "Exactly. That's the kind of attitude you need to bring to your next fight. You must be so confident in your skills that you know your opponent will lose."

"How do I achieve that?"

"You already know the answer."

What did he mean by that? Jackson had been involved in a few fights in Amsterdam and at the Connecticut pub, both of which he'd won. But how had he won? With overwhelming force and skill. His opponents had been no match for him. How had he gotten to that point? Raphael was right. The answer was obvious. "Through good training, lots of practice… and sparring."

"Correct. We'll begin immediately."

Raphael walked over to a cabinet and withdrew two wooden

longswords, two helmets, two vests, and two pairs of heavy gloves. Jackson removed the scabbard from his back and laid it on a nearby table.

Raphael first had Jackson demonstrate the drills he learned during their previous session. After these exercises, Raphael said, "Your execution was flawless, Jackson. I've never seen anyone learn and retain instruction as quickly as you. Good work. I want you to keep practicing these drills on your own."

"Yes, Raphael."

"Now, let's add some opposition. I will spar with you."

His chest tightened. Like Mekoddishkem, Raphael was nearly seven feet tall, muscular, and well-versed in the art of sword fighting. Jackson was just a beginner. The best he could hope for was a draw.

They began sparring, initially with Jackson as the aggressor, then Raphael. Raphael did not go easy on him. Jackson had to adapt to his opponent's quickness and brute strength immediately. In the end, he was no match for his teacher. He could not fight off the blows to his arms and torso, but he kept at it.

At times, Raphael would pause and tell Jackson what he was doing wrong, then they would start sparring again. This went on for about two hours before Raphael finally concluded the session. "That is enough for today, Jackson. Although you have a lot to learn, you demonstrated one quality that surpasses all others in becoming a great swordsman."

"What is that?"

"You never gave up."

⚬

McKenzie walked into Monica's room wearing a gray sweatshirt and sweatpants, along with black flip-flops. She pushed aside a Red Sox jacket and sat on the bed. "You know I love you, Monica, and I really appreciate you coming to live with me after Jackson's death, but I want you to know you're free to leave whenever you want. I'll be fine."

Monica turned around. "I know you'll be fine, sis, but a tragedy like this will take time to heal from. It's hard to believe it's already been a month since the wedding."

McKenzie teared up. No one could understand how painful the last month had been.

Monica reached over and held McKenzie's elbow. "I'm so sorry."

"It's okay. It was a wonderful wedding, wasn't it?"

Monica nodded. "Oh, yes. The best I've ever been to. It was perfect."

McKenzie smiled.

"The reception was wonderful too, up until that monster Dexter showed up, but he got what he deserved." Monica went quiet for a moment. When she spoke again, her voice sounded strained. "Hey, I was thinking about getting a job at one of the nearby Starbucks, like the one I worked at back in Massachusetts."

"Why?"

"What do you mean, 'Why?'"

"Why do you want to go back to working at Starbucks?"

Monica clenched her jaw. "Is there something wrong with that? Not everyone can be an Ivy-leaguer working in a glitzy corporate job."

McKenzie sat up straight. "Wow! Where did that come from?"

"You shouldn't put me down for the work I do."

"I wasn't putting down the work you do. I just thought you might have other hopes and aspirations."

"You mean, like doing communications work at an insurance company?"

McKenzie huffed. "Touché." *Better let it go.* "What I mean is, what do you want to do with your life?"

Monica paused, then sighed. "I don't know."

"I'm just saying, why do the same thing you were doing before?

Why not try something different? What did you dream of becoming when you were a little girl?"

Monica breathed in deeply. "A fashion model. I wanted to be like my Barbie dolls."

"Hmm. Why not do that?"

"Do what?"

"Why not become a fashion model?"

"Me?"

"Well, yeah. You're gorgeous. You could do it. I could help you get started."

Monica shook her head. "I don't know. I mean, I don't know anything about it."

McKenzie lifted both hands. "Neither do I. Let's find out together. What do you have to lose?"

Monica bit her lower lip for a moment. "Let me think about it."

"What's to think about?"

"Well, it's a big move."

"Look. You're twenty-three, no attachments, you have a place to live, you don't have to go back to work at the moment. Why not give it a shot? You have your whole life ahead of you. You can do anything you want."

"You know, I never even heard of the word 'barista' when I was growing up."

"Nothing against baristas, but let's switch from that life path and start a new one."

Monica shrugged her shoulders. "Why not? I'm in."

"That's the spirit. We'll start working on it tomorrow."

"Great! This is so exciting—and kind of scary. What about you? Will you be going back to work soon?"

"I don't think I'm ready yet."

Monica got off her chair and sat next to McKenzie on the bed. "Understood."

"Just so you know, Monica, I don't have to go back to work."

"You don't? Why?"

"Jackson had a lot of life insurance."

Monica smiled. "That was smart. What a wonderful gift. It shows how much he loved and cared about you."

A pang of nausea hit McKenzie. She stood up and ran into the bathroom where she began throwing up in the toilet. Monica followed, flicked on the bathroom lights and fan, then walked out and closed the door behind her. McKenzie remained inside for a few minutes, until her stomach was empty, then she gargled with mouthwash and came out.

"What's wrong? Did you get food poisoning?"

"I don't think so. I'm just nauseous."

"When did it start?"

"Earlier this week."

"You've been nauseous for nearly a week?"

"Yes."

Monica placed her hand on McKenzie's upper arm. "Maybe there's something else going on."

"Like what?"

"I don't know. Maybe you should go see a doctor."

"Okay."

Monica's eyes lit up. "Wait. Come with me."

McKenzie and Monica walked to a pharmacy a few blocks away. They went inside and stood in front of the registers.

Monica pointed at McKenzie. "Wait here."

What in the world is she doing?

Monica returned a few minutes later, holding a small box in her hand. She paid for it, and they walked home.

Back at the condo, McKenzie asked, "What did you just buy?"

"A pregnancy test."

"A pregnancy test? Are you crazy? We were only married for one night."

"Stranger things have happened."

A huge smile came over McKenzie's face. "Could it be? That would be so exciting."

She went directly to the master bathroom and took the test. After an excruciating wait, she glanced at the display. She yelped.

Monica burst into the bathroom. "What's wrong?"

McKenzie showed her the test kit.

Monica's eyes narrowed. "It's showing a blue cross. What does that mean?"

McKenzie beamed. "I'm pregnant."

Monica hugged her. "You are? That's fantastic! I'm so happy for you... You are happy, aren't you?"

"Of course I'm happy. I'm ecstatic! Praise God," said McKenzie. She looked up to heaven. "You're going to be a father, Jackson!"

Jackson jumped up and down, hugging Mekoddishkem. "I'm going to be a father. I'm going to be a father. I can't believe it!"

He rushed over to hug her, tears streaming down his face, but his body just passed through hers. "I know, McKenzie. I know. I'm right here with you."

Mekoddishkem showed Jackson the tiny baby developing in McKenzie's womb. The image was clear as if there were no flesh surrounding it. Not at all like the fuzzy ultrasound images he'd seen in the past.

Jackson shook his head. "Wow! I can't believe it. All it took was one night..." He looked up at the angel. "Won't it be hard for McKenzie to raise the child alone?"

"God, her family, and friends will be there to help. You heard her, Jackson. She's thrilled that a part of you has been left behind."

He sighed. "I'm thrilled too. I'm so relieved she's going to be okay."

"Yes. It won't be easy, but she can do it. Remember, you can pray for her anytime you wish."

"You're right. I'll plan to do that."

Family, friends, and coworkers came to Jackson's mind. If only he could share all he'd learned and experienced in heaven with them. It would be left to McKenzie to do that now.

Agliarept sat on his throne, enraged that his new queen was still not by his side. Time to take it out on Botis who had just arrived. But then, a demon entered the room and whispered something in Botis's ear.

Botis approached Agliarept's throne. "Master."

"Yes, Botis. What do you have for me?"

"In my foresight, I assigned a warrior to watch the home of the traitor McKenzie, former wife of Jackson Trotman. My warrior reports she is pregnant."

"She is with child? How can that be? The traitor Jackson is dead."

"Yes, master, but they were married for one night."

"Have you confirmed this?"

"Yes, master. My warrior reports the traitor McKenzie took a pregnancy test, and the results were positive."

"Very well, I will take this matter to Satan himself. Do not tell anyone else about this."

"Yes, master."

Moments later, Agliarept approached Satan's throne.

"What do you want, Agliarept?" Satan yelled at the top of his lungs.

Agliarept cowered before him. Memories of being mauled and impaled flooded his mind. "Master, the traitor Jackson's wife is pregnant."

"What?" Satan sprung off his throne and began pacing. "This is not good. Not good at all. Have the wife killed immediately! We need to make sure the Nazarene doesn't come back to resurrect his enemy army, as foretold in the prophecy."

Satan studied him with a penetrating gaze, probably wondering if Agliarept would obey his orders without question this time. Agliarept had learned the hard way not to ask his master if God had approved. Better to take the safe route and tell Satan precisely what he wanted to hear. "Yes, master." He'd get Botis to do it.

"Oh, and Agliarept…"

"Yes, master."

"Tell Botis to let Jackson win their next swordfight. I want him to think he's invincible."

"I will do it, master."

Chapter 13
Reunion

BOTIS TRANSPORTED HIMSELF back to the earth's surface. He entered the apartment of Cassandra Alvarez, who was seated in a black wheelchair at a speckled white Formica kitchen table. She was being fed by her home health aide, Becky. Cassandra was dressed in a white blouse with navy-blue pants. Her black hair was curly and disheveled.

Becky was feeding Cassandra from a plate of spaghetti and meatballs with tomato sauce. Botis checked the area. Just as his master had said, there was no guardian angel nearby to protect her. Botis approached Cassandra and touched her throat.

She immediately began choking. The home aide got behind her and began the Heimlich maneuver. After several unsuccessful tries, she picked up her phone and dialed 911.

"Nine-one-one, what is your emergency?"

"A woman is choking. The Heimlich is not working. We need an ambulance right away."

The home aide gave their location, then kept trying the Heimlich maneuver on Cassandra.

The ambulance arrived about four minutes later. But that was two minutes too late. As they were moving Cassandra onto the gurney, two demons arrived and took her to hell.

◈

Jackson left the playground with Susan and Joy and walked with them down a magnificent boulevard made of gold. He twirled around. "It's just like the Bible says. The streets of heaven really are paved with gold."

Joy faced him and lifted her arms straight into the air, indicating she wanted to be picked up. He gladly complied, then turned to Susan. "Where do we get the ice cream?"

"It's just up here on the left."

They walked into an old-time soda fountain shop that looked much like the drugstore in the movie *It's a Wonderful Life*. A smiling, older gentleman, wearing a white paper soda jerk hat, greeted them. "Hello, folks, what can I get for you?"

They each ordered a scoop of ice cream on a sugar cone. Joy ordered chocolate, Susan ordered vanilla, and Jackson ordered strawberry. Each was topped with rainbow sprinkles. He took a bite. His taste buds exploded. "Wow! This is the best ice cream I've ever had."

The gentleman smiled and nodded.

As Jackson walked out the door, he was greeted by the most beautiful-sounding choir he'd ever heard. "Where's that singing coming from?"

Susan pointed to an auditorium at the end of the boulevard. They walked that way.

A concert was in progress. The cut-diamond arched entranceway, perhaps fifty feet high and forty feet wide, sparkled in thousands of directions as they strolled under it. The concert hall itself was massive, seating at least two hundred thousand people. The walls were made of transparent gold, complemented by silver molding, and adorned with every possible jewel. The vaulted ceilings were painted with frescoes detailing biblical stories.

A huge organ and full orchestra accompanied the choir perfectly. It sounded like Bach, but Jackson had never heard this piece before.

An usher approached them.

Jackson asked, "Sir, what is being played today?"

"Brother Bach is composing a new oratorio."

"*The* Johann Sebastian Bach?"

"Why, of course."

"Wow! Is that him at the organ?"

"Yes."

"So, he's been up here in heaven composing music for the past two hundred and fifty years or so?"

"Two hundred and sixty-one to be exact, sir. Are you new to heaven?"

"Yes, I am."

"Welcome! You will see many other incredible things during your stay. There is no end to the wonders of God."

"Great! I'm looking forward to it."

The concert stopped abruptly. Brother Bach stood up, walked over to the violin section, and began giving the concertmaster instructions. Jackson addressed the usher again. "So, this is just a rehearsal?"

"Yes."

"How many people are here?"

"About one hundred and fifty thousand."

"For a rehearsal?"

"Yes."

"Why would so many people come to a rehearsal?"

"Wouldn't you, if you could hear Brother Bach creating some of the most beautiful music ever written?"

"Yes, I see what you mean."

Suddenly, all the people stood up with their arms raised and eyes closed, crying out to God individually, yet in a way that seemed, somehow, harmonious. Jackson listened to an older black gentleman seated nearby. He spoke in a loud, clear, and melodic baritone voice. "Oh, thank you, Father, for allowing me to come to this wonderful place. Thank you, Father, for making me a part of your family. Oh, Father, how can I ever repay you for all your kindness to me. Oh, Jesus, thank you for all you did for me, dying on that old rugged cross and making me clean so I could come into this place and be with you. Oh, Holy Spirit, thank you so much for quickening my heart and turning me from a dead man to a live man. Oh, thank you, God, for making a place for me here in heaven with you. So much joy, so much joy, praise God almighty, so much joy. Hallelujah! How can I ever thank you enough, God? Thank you, Father; thank you, Jesus; thank you, Holy Spirit. Amen and amen."

It was the finest praise soliloquy he'd ever heard. Instinctively, he raised his arms and exclaimed, "Oh, Lord, I agree with all the praises lavished on you by this brother standing beside me. I can never repay you for all your kindness to me. Thank you for allowing me to be here with my daughter and my sister. Thank you that I get to hear Brother Bach himself play the organ right in front of me. What a blessing. What an inspiring place to be. What joy you have given me. Oh, thank you, Father, for lavishing your love on me."

Jackson looked to his right, then to his left. Susan and Joy were also praising God. What a privilege it was to be here. As a result of his praises, he was filled with inexpressible joy. There was no hurry, no agenda, no schedule to follow. He was simply in awe of God and thankful for God allowing him to experience the never-ending high of being in his presence. Worship on earth had never been like this.

Sometime later—who knew how much time had passed—the rehearsal ended, and everyone in the auditorium began heading home. As they were walking out, a familiar face caught Jackson's attention. He edged closer to make sure he recognized the man, dragging his sister and daughter in tow.

It was George Washington, commanding general of the Continental army and first president of the United States.

Jackson approached the general and extended his hand. "Mr. President, I'm Jackson Trotman. This is my sister, Susan, and my daughter, Joy."

The president nodded his head and shook Jackson's hand. "Nice to meet you, Jackson." There was a commanding tone to his voice. It was similar to recordings he'd heard of President Dwight D. Eisenhower talking on Normandy's beaches with CBS reporter Walter Cronkite. They were reflecting on what the world was like twenty years after World War II. General Washington squatted down to be at eye level with the girls and smiled. "Nice to meet you, Susan and Joy."

The president returned his attention to Jackson. "Trotman. Are you *the* Jackson Trotman?"

What does he mean, 'the' Jackson Trotman? Nothing special about me. "That's my name, sir, but perhaps there's some other Jackson Trotman you're thinking of."

"Did you give your life the other day for a young lady named Monica?"

"Yes, sir."

"Then you're the one. That was a courageous thing you did."

"Thank you, General, but I was just scared to death she'd go to hell, so I had to stop it."

"Admirable. I could have used more people like you in the battles I led."

"It would have been a great honor to serve under your command, sir."

"The honor would have been mine, Lieutenant Jackson."

How does he know I was a lieutenant? "Speaking of battles, I saw you at Fort Duquesne in 1755, during the French and Indian War. One of my ancestors fought beside you."

"Oh really, what was his name?"

"He was on my mother's side, so his last name must have been Wright. He was a foot soldier in the infantry, most likely a private."

"Hmm. Private Wright. I believe I do remember him. Is he here?"

Jackson huffed. "I never thought to ask, sir. I'll have to find out. He was one of the few soldiers who was not killed or wounded that day. I was amazed at how you remained at your post throughout the battle. You were in an open field, sitting on your horse, as the Native Americans fired round after round at you."

"I didn't want to let my men down. I had to set a good example for them."

"You certainly did, sir. You know, we don't fight that way anymore."

"Yes, I know. I saw some of the battles you were involved in while serving in Afghanistan. The weaponry you used was much more advanced than what we had."

General George Washington saw me in combat? "Agreed, sir. But I wouldn't have wanted to be involved in the type of hand-to-hand combat your troops had to engage in. I never had to thrust a bayonet into someone's chest at close quarters. Rarely got that near the enemy. What did you think when you got back to your base camp and found several bullet holes in your blouse?"

"God protected me. It gave me great confidence in the many clashes ahead that God was with me. How do you know all these details about me?"

"My guardian angel showed me how to use something called The Wall, which allowed me to travel into the past, and I saw you at that battle. How do you know so much about me?"

"I was there for your life review."

Jackson gulped. Other people knew everything about him? Even the stuff he'd rather keep hidden?

"Everything is very transparent here in heaven, Jackson. That's why God has to make sure we're clean before he lets us in."

❧

Later that night, Jackson returned Susan and Joy to Rachel's home and put Joy to bed.

He took Rachel aside. "Joy is so happy here!"

"Yes. But she's your daughter, Jackson." Tears welled in her eyes. "I will miss her, of course. My house is the only home she's ever known. I suggest we give her some time to adjust."

Jackson nodded. "I agree. Thank you again for all you've done for her."

"You're welcome, Jackson. It was my pleasure."

After giving her a hug, Jackson left and closed the front door. As he was coming down the sidewalk, he was approached by Mekod-dishkem. His angelic friend had a grave look on his face. "Jackson, I'm afraid I have some sad news."

"What happened?"

"Cassandra, the mother of your daughter, Joy, has died."

"Oh, no. That's terrible. She wasn't a Christian yet, was she?"

"No, she was not."

"But we just prayed for her to become one."

"Yes. She made her choice. She was just murdered by the demon Botis on orders from his master, Agliarept."

Jackson yelled, "Botis! That monster. He's so evil. Why did God allow it? She needed more time to repent."

"Apparently, more time would not have made any difference in Cassandra's case. Ultimately, she made a dreadful decision to be separated from God—forever."

"That's horrible. Does Joy know?"

"She does not."

"I just put her to bed. I'll tell her in the morning."

"That is up to you, Jackson, but you do not want her to find out from someone else, do you?"

He sighed. "I suppose you're right." He went back to the front door and knocked.

Rachel opened it. "Oh, hello, Jackson. Back so soon?"

"Yes. I need to talk to Joy. It's an emergency."

"What happened?"

"You'll find out in a minute. Please, come with me."

He walked into Rachel's home and waited in the foyer. Mekoddishkem remained outside.

"Very well." Rachel called up the stairs, "Joy, your daddy is here."

Jackson walked up the stairs and down the hallway leading to Joy's room. Rachel followed behind him.

The door opened just as he approached. "Hi, Daddy." She ran forward and hugged him, as she usually did, around his thighs. "Why did you come back?"

"I just learned some terrible news."

"What is it, Daddy?"

"Your mommy won't be coming to live with us in heaven."

"Ever?"

"No. I'm very sorry, Joy. She died."

Joy burst into tears. "Does Jesus know?"

"I'm sure he does, sweetheart."

Joy vanished, leaving him hugging empty air.

He asked Rachel, "Where did she go?"

"To see Jesus, I imagine."

He immediately arrived at God's throne room. Joy was already there, sitting on Jesus's lap and crying. "My daddy said my mommy won't be coming to live with us in heaven."

Jesus wiped away her tears with the sleeve of his robe. "Your mother didn't know about you, Joy. But if she did, she would have loved you very much. The Holy Spirit asked her many times to give up the bad things in her life, but she refused. So, she will not be coming to live with us in heaven."

"Oh." Joy began crying again.

Jesus pulled her close and wept with her, then he set her down on her feet facing him. He looked into her eyes. "Someone extraordinary will be coming to heaven soon. They will be thrilled to take care of you. They will love you, just like your mother would have."

Joy looked up into Jesus's eyes. "Who?"

"You will find out very soon."

Jackson rumpled his brow. Who was Jesus talking about? It might be better not to ask, at least not now.

Joy ran to Jackson. He lifted her, and she instantly buried her face in his shoulder.

He looked over at Jesus. "Thank you for explaining everything to us, Lord Jesus. I'll take her home now."

Jesus nodded.

Mekoddishkem grasped Jackson's elbow while they were leaving. "I am planning to take you somewhere in the morning."

"Where?"

"You shall see."

※

Jackson slept on the couch in Rachel's house that night, just in case Joy needed him. The next morning, Mekoddishkem arrived and took him to The Wall where he was transported to the front yard of an elegant two-story colonial in an upscale neighborhood on earth. Jackson gasped. "It's my old house! I grew up here, Mekoddishkem."

The angel raised his eyebrows in mock insult.

"Oh, since you're my guardian angel, I guess you already knew that."

"That is affirmative, Jackson."

"Why are we here?"

"You will see. Follow me."

They ascended about fifteen feet into the air and passed through the clapboards on the house's front into an upstairs bedroom. His mother was lying on an exquisite mahogany four-poster bed, replete with intricate carvings on the headboard. She was propped up with lots of pillows. A nurse in an all-white outfit sat beside the bed, reading a book. His mother's face was jaundiced, and her eyes yellow. She'd lost a lot of weight, and it looked like she'd lost much of her hair too. Her head was tilted back with her mouth wide open. Her breathing was slow and labored. A cross shone brightly on her forehead.

Jackson nodded slowly. "She's got a cross on her forehead. That's fantastic. I guess I already knew that, but it's a relief to see anyway. Mekoddishkem, she looks terrible. What's going on?"

"Pancreatic cancer. She didn't know she had it until three weeks ago. She will be departing this life very soon."

The nurse checked her vital signs. "Looks like you'll be going to heaven soon, Mrs. Trotman." There was no response. The nurse continued voicing her thoughts out loud. "So sad. She lost a daughter to a traffic accident and a son to a bullet."

The nurse bowed her head and began to pray. She had a cross on her forehead too. "Father in heaven, please give Mrs. Trotman the strength to endure this final trial and give her a rich welcome into your kingdom when her time on earth has ended. In Jesus's name, I pray, amen."

Jackson was at a loss, so he simply said, "Amen."

Should he be happy or sad? Should he pray for her to get better or not? After all, he only had one mother. It was awful to see her lying there, suffering and wasting away. On the other hand, she would be meeting Jesus soon and seeing many of her deceased relatives, including her mother and father, her long-lost daughter Susan, and, to her great surprise, a previously unknown granddaughter named Joy. And of course, Jackson would get to be with her too.

The nurse stood up, bent over the side of the bed, and studied his mother very closely. She walked out of the bedroom and into the hallway. From the top of the stairs, she called out to the first floor, "Mr. Trotman. I think you'd better come up here."

How would his father react to his mother's death? After all, they'd been married for thirty years. Would he go back to the young blond woman he'd rendezvoused with at the hotel about six months earlier? Time would tell.

Mekoddishkem placed his hand on Jackson's shoulder. "Let's go, Jackson. You want to be a member of her welcoming party, do you not?"

"Of course."

✦

Mekoddishkem and Jackson were transported to an area directly outside one of heaven's twelve gates. His two grandmothers and his grandfather were already there, along with Susan and Joy. They all smiled at Jackson as he arrived.

Joy was jumping up and down. "Grandma's coming! Grandma's coming!"

Susan ran to Jackson and grabbed him around the waist. "I can't believe it. Mommy's finally going to be here. This is so exciting!"

He looked down at her. "I can't wait to see the surprise in her eyes when she sees us."

A few moments later, three figures appeared far in the distance. Jackson focused on them, then announced, "It's Mom with two angels guiding her."

He glanced around at his close relatives. A lot of other people had joined their group, many of whom he didn't know. They were all dressed in white robes and beaming broadly.

His own experience of arriving at heaven had been overwhelming. The light was so bright he couldn't see, which terrified him. "Father in heaven, please be with my mother and help her not to be afraid like I was."

Two angels arrived with his mom and set her down before the welcoming party. She'd placed her hands over her eyes because of the bright light. She was wearing red, Scotch-plaid pajamas. The welcome party moved closer, not saying a word.

Evidently, Susan couldn't stand it anymore and raced toward her. "Mommy! Mommy!"

Mom removed her hands from her face. The jaundiced skin tone was gone, along with the wrinkles. She looked forty years younger. She squinted at Susan rushing toward her. Mom shrieked, bent down, and swept her daughter up into her arms. "Susan? Oh, Susan! I can't believe it. My little girl. It's been so long. I've missed you so much." Mom pulled Susan close and didn't stop kissing her. "How are you? A day never went by that I stopped thinking about you, honey."

"I'm fine, Mommy. Heaven is a wonderful place. You'll love it here."

"Heaven? I'm in heaven?" A huge smile came over her face.

"Of course. The entrance is right over there. Don't you see the gate?"

Mom looked around. Recognition of other people she'd known in life was crystal clear on her face.

Joy ran up to Mom and grabbed her around the thighs. Mom bent down to her knees and faced her. "And who are you, my little friend?"

Susan said, "She's your granddaughter."

Mom's jaw dropped. "Granddaughter? I didn't know I had a granddaughter."

Mom smiled and gazed into her eyes. "What is your name, sweetheart?"

"My name is Joy. Jackson is my daddy."

Mom wrapped Joy in her arms, stood up, and looked at her. "Oh, I'm so happy to meet you, Joy." She turned to Susan. "One of the greatest regrets of my life was not having any grandchildren to love. Now I get to spend all eternity with you, Joy, just you. Hallelujah!"

Mom studied the other faces in the audience, searching. "Is your daddy here?"

Joy chuckled. "Of course, he's here. Daddy, come over and see Grandma."

Mom set Joy down and rushed toward Jackson as he approached. Tears streamed down her face as they embraced. "Oh, Jackson, my boy. My baby boy! It's so good to see you. How are you? I'm glad you're alive again. I've missed you." She squeezed him tightly and lost her composure. "It feels good to hold you in my arms again. It was just awful what happened right after your wedding, but now, I couldn't be happier."

Jackson raised his right index finger and pointed it upward. "Praise God."

"Yes, praise God!"

Mom took a panoramic view of the welcoming party. "We're a family again. Hallelujah! We'll be together forever."

Jackson raised his arms in victory. "We certainly will."

Mom's mother and father approached. She fell to her knees. "Oh, my. Wow! Mom and Dad. You're alive. You look so young. This is fantastic. Oh, God is so good, isn't he? Hallelujah! He said he would wipe away every tear, and he has."

"Amen."

CHAPTER 14

HIGH STAKES

JACKSON TRAVELED WITH Mekoddishkem to his former boss's office in the Aetna home office building. Fred had rebuffed Jackson's earlier warnings about hell, and now a demon hovered over him, whispering things into his ear. Jackson removed his sword from its scabbard and attacked the demon. After seeing Mekoddishkem, the demon fled. Jackson spoke to Fred about his destiny, but Fred couldn't hear him.

"You must pray, Jackson. Pray that God will open Fred's heart to receive his offer of forgiveness."

Jackson bowed his head. "Father in heaven, please allow Fred to choose life with you in heaven, over life without you for all eternity in the lake of fire. In Jesus's name, I pray, amen."

Instantly, a halo of light appeared and enveloped Fred. He began whispering things into Fred's mind. Jackson fell to his knees, in awe of his God's holiness and majesty.

Fred walked over to two boxes located in the corner of his office.

Jackson asked, "What's he doing?"

"The Holy Spirit prompted Fred to look for something in one of those boxes."

"What's in there?"

"Your personal belongings—from your cubicle."

Jackson frowned. "He should have given them to McKenzie weeks ago. It's been a whole month since I passed away."

"You are right, Jackson. He should have given McKenzie the boxes by now."

Fred opened the box and pulled out a Bible tract. It was the same booklet Jackson had tried to give him months earlier while sitting in his office.

Fred read the first few pages, then threw it back in the box. "Who can believe this garbage? It's just a bunch of myths and fairy tales. When you die, you die, and that's the end of it."

"That's not good."

Mekoddishkem shook his head. "Not good at all."

"What will happen next?"

"You will see."

Jackson breathed deeply. "Will he be given more time to repent?"

"No. That was his last chance. The god of this age has blinded the minds of unbelievers so that they cannot see the light of the gospel."

"Jackson, come here!" a voice called out.

It was Jesus.

Jackson transported himself to God's throne room with Mekoddishkem by his side and fell to his knees.

"Satan ordered Agliarept to kill McKenzie because she is with child. Agliarept will have Botis do it. She is under my protection, but I wanted you to be aware."

"Thank you, Lord." *Botis again. Pure evil. He must be destroyed. I will protect my family with every fiber of my being. Must prepare myself for battle. Must become so ready I cannot lose.*

⁓

McKenzie sat next to Monica on the living room couch and placed her laptop on the coffee table. "I've been doing some research."

"About babies?"

"No, about modeling."

"Modeling? Oh, great. What have you found?"

McKenzie folded her hands. "First, you need to figure out what kind of model you want to be—fitness, high fashion, runway, commercial print, or whatever other types of models there are. Then you need to find a modeling agency that specializes in your type. After that, you need to enter competitions, open calls, and castings to get discovered. You'll need to be prepared for lots of traveling to different locations on short notice.

"We'll need to get professional pictures taken—front, left side, right side, three-quarters view, full view, and headshot. Then we'll need to have flyers made that include the pictures, your various measurements, and your contact information. We should also put together a cover letter that tells something about you and what you're interested in."

Monica stared at some of the headshots on the computer while McKenzie spoke.

"We're also going to have to do some shopping. You're supposed to wear a white T-shirt or tank top, black high-waisted jeans, and heels, all of which are designed to accentuate your body's features. They want natural-colored hair, too, so you're going to have to lose your highlights. You're not supposed to wear a lot of makeup or colorful clothing either. The modeling agents and scouts want to be able to visualize if they can dress you up and sell the image you present to the customer."

Monica leaned forward on the couch. "Sounds very exciting."

McKenzie began to process the implications of what she'd been saying. "I know I'm the one who said you should follow your dreams, but I hope this modeling stuff doesn't get too sleazy."

Monica chuckled. "Don't worry, sis, I can handle myself. I'm not going to let those guys push me around. I won't do anything I don't want to."

McKenzie sighed. "That sounds like a great attitude, but be careful not to compromise who you are. It's more important to be beautiful on the inside than on the outside."

Monica smirked. "Yes, Mother, I mean, McKenzie. I'll be careful."

"Good." McKenzie began typing on her laptop. "One of the websites I reviewed said people who are just starting out in modeling should arrange test shoots with photographers who are also starting out. They'll get experience photographing you and building *their* portfolio, while you get experience modeling and building *your* portfolio. So, it looks like there are three major modeling agencies in the Hartford area. I'll determine what their submission requirements are, then we can go from there."

Monica smiled, then shifted to hug McKenzie. "Thank you very much for all the research you did."

"My pleasure."

Two weeks later, McKenzie stood by the front door of the condo with her winter coat on. "Monica, we'd better leave soon. The open call starts in an hour, and it will take us at least forty minutes to get there."

Monica called from her bedroom. "Here I come."

"Stunning" was the first word out of McKenzie's mouth. Monica had followed her directions to a tee. Gone were the multicolored highlights. Her hair was now fully blond and a little curly. Her makeup was light, and the tight-fitting white tank top and black pants revealed a perfect figure. "You look great, Monica. I really mean it."

"Thanks."

"Do you have your heels with you?"

"Yes. They're in the bag over there. I don't want to put them on until we get to the agency. They might get wrecked by the salt in the parking lots. Is it okay if I wear my Converse sneakers for now?"

"I'd wear your black flats instead."

"Okay."

"Do you have your personal planner, your photoshoot book, and the flyers?"

"They're in the bag too."

"Oh, I almost forgot. Do you have your swimsuit?"

Monica gasped. "Oh, no, I don't." She ran back to her room to get it.

She returned a minute later, wearing her black flats, and threw her bikini into the bag. "Thank you so much for reminding me."

"You're welcome. This is so exciting." McKenzie held the door open for Monica on their way out.

❧

Monica walked into the lobby of the McGregor Modeling Agency. The white walls were covered with pictures of famous models strutting their stuff on runways and adorning magazine covers.

The receptionist greeted her. "Are you here for the open call?"

"I am."

The receptionist handed her a clipboard with some papers on it. "Just fill out the forms and sign at the bottom of each page. Someone will call for you when we're ready."

Monica sat in a chair in the reception area. She sized up the twenty or so other young women and girls in the room. Stiff competition.

Promptly at two o'clock, a man with oversized, black-rimmed glasses and silver hair called everyone into a large room. They lined up with clipboards in hand, and one by one, their heights and weights were recorded on their sheets. A photo was taken of each of them holding their clipboard over their chest.

Monica then approached a woman seated behind a table.

"Clipboard, please." The woman looked up as she took the clipboard. "Hi, Monica. Do you have any modeling experience?"

"I'm just starting."

"Do you have any pictures of yourself?"

Monica handed the woman her portfolio book and a flyer.

The woman glanced through it. "May I keep the flyer?"

"Of course."

"Did you bring your bathing suit?"

"I did."

The woman handed the book back. "Thank you for coming in, Monica. Have a seat over there, and we'll let you know shortly if we can use you."

"Thanks."

After everyone had been interviewed, the agency employees departed for another room.

Five minutes later, they returned. The man with the oversized glasses spoke. "Thank you all very much for coming. You've been a good group. If your name is called, it means we won't be needing you today. Please be sure to pick up your belongings as you leave."

Monica's heart raced. One by one, each wannabe model got up and walked out as her name was called. Before long, only Monica and one other young lady were left. The man waited for the other applicants to leave the room.

"Monica, Chelsea, congratulations on getting this far. Please switch into your bathing suits in the changing rooms over there."

After a quick change, both women returned. The agency personnel looked them over, then went to another room again.

A minute later, they returned. "Chelsea, thank you for coming

in. You made a good impression. We'll consider you for future work."
Chelsea teared up and left.

"Monica. We have a pool shoot coming up with a client in a few weeks. Mrs. Cavanaugh here will have you fill out some paperwork and tell you what to expect. Any questions?"

Joy swelled in her heart. They thought she could do this. She couldn't believe it. "No. Thank you so much for this opportunity."

❧

A week later, McKenzie sat at the kitchen table in Sally's house for their weekly discipleship session. They were studying John 6:19–21:

When they had rowed about three or four miles, they saw Jesus approaching the boat, walking on the water; and they were frightened. But he said to them, "It is I; don't be afraid." Then they were willing to take him into the boat, and immediately the boat reached the shore where they were heading.

"McKenzie, what's the thought conveyed in this passage?"
"It's about Jesus walking on the water."
"What else?"
"Well, only God could do that. Some people might think this was just a made-up story for children, the figment of some writer's imagination, but to me, it's one of those passages that proves Jesus is the Son of God."
"Very good, but what else about the passage is amazing."
McKenzie carefully reread it and didn't notice anything unusual until the last sentence. "Oh, I missed it last time: *Immediately the boat reached the shore.*"
"That's right. What does that phrase tell you about God?"
"The disciples had rowed three or four miles, then Jesus got them

to shore immediately. That's amazing. It tells me that God is outside of time. He can speed things up, or he can slow things down. He can fall back into the past or leap forward into the future. He's incredible! He can do anything. Nothing is too hard for him."

Sally smiled. "You have a strong faith, McKenzie."

She shrugged her shoulders. "Faith comes by hearing and hearing by the Word of God."

Sally looked down at her discipleship booklet. "How will you apply what you've learned to your life?"

McKenzie folded her hands. "Whenever I have a problem, I can trust God to solve it or at least help me get through it."

Sally nodded. "What is your response to God as a result?"

McKenzie bowed her head and closed her eyes. "Father in heaven, I know you hear my prayers and will help me overcome any obstacle or crisis that comes before me. Please help me to trust in you completely at all times. You can do anything!"

"Amen. I think that concludes our lesson for today. Did you have any other questions?"

"Yes. I was reading in the second chapter of Ephesians earlier this week. It says we're seated with Christ in the heavenly realms. What does that mean?"

"God will give us a throne in heaven. After the judgment seat of Christ, we'll receive a crown if we're found worthy. We also may be called upon to rule with Jesus during his thousand-year millennial kingdom. We don't know all the details now, but we'll find out more once we get there."

"Fascinating."

As McKenzie drove home from Sally's, her mind stewed over what could have been. *Life would be so much better if Jackson were here. I wouldn't be so lonely. Why can't I have an abundant life and be married with kids like Sally… Wait a minute. Where did those thoughts come from? Of course, I wish Jackson were here, but that doesn't mean*

God doesn't love me. He's been helping me every day. He's molding me to be more like Jesus and using my suffering to make me worthy of heaven. Oh, Lord, please fill me with your Holy Spirit. What was it that Sally told me to do when under spiritual attack?

She shouted, "Satan, or whatever your name is, in the mighty name of Jesus Christ, the Holy One of God, I command you to get behind me and leave!"

McKenzie's guardian angel shot a smirk at the demon Botis who stood on the other side of her. Faith, even as small as a mustard seed, was more than a match for this evil creature.

Botis grimaced and said, "This one is more perceptive and powerful than I thought, I will find another way to drag her down." Then in an instant, he disappeared.

Good riddance. The guardian angel smiled down at McKenzie. "She's learning."

Chapter 15

Amazing Creation

JACKSON RETURNED TO The Wall with Mekoddishkem after visiting McKenzie. "I'm not sure this modeling stuff is the best thing for Monica. So much of that business is superficial. Young women are sometimes exploited and viewed as objects to arouse men. I don't see how this is going to point her toward Christ."

"She has to follow her own path, Jackson. Perhaps she'll realize, over time, that this career is not as satisfying as she'd hoped, and then she'll turn to God."

"Understood. Maybe she'll only take modeling jobs that don't involve selling sex." He touched Mekoddishkem's elbow and sighed. "I've always loved all the stars and galaxies visible behind The Wall. Isn't it amazing? What an incredible universe God has created!"

"Would you like to visit one of them?"

"What do you mean?"

"Which star system would you like to go to?"

Jackson ran his hand through his hair. "Those places are hundreds, thousands, and perhaps even millions of light-years away. How could we possibly get there?"

Mekoddishkem put his hands on his hips and looked down at Jackson. "Very quickly, in the blink of an eye, in fact."

"What? I don't understand how that's possible. The speed of light is 186,000 miles per hour. Can anything go faster than the speed of light?"

"As McKenzie noted, nothing is too hard for God."

Jackson took the angel at his word. He surveyed the sky and pointed in a particular direction. They were immediately transported to a spot above the atmosphere of a planet, hovering over it like twin kites. "Where are we?"

"We are about fourteen hundred light-years away from the earth above the planet Kepler-452b in the Cygnus constellation."

"How did we get here so quickly?"

"We thought our way here."

"Doesn't thought have mass?"

"Not in our dimension."

Jackson surveyed the planet directly below them. "This is absolutely incredible! Not in my wildest dreams did I ever imagine doing this." He glanced over at the nearby sun. It looked like the photographs taken by astronauts in space. Nothing could compare, however, to actually being here. It was like studying an original Renoir in a museum—infinitely better than viewing it online or in an art book.

Jackson asked, "Is this the planet scientists refer to as Earth 2.0?"

"Excellent, Jackson. You remembered that from your college astronomy class. I guess you did learn something. I know you only took the course because you thought it would be an easy A."

Jackson motioned with a thumbs-up. "It seems larger than the earth, but of course, I have no way of knowing that." Empty space spread hundreds of feet beneath him down to the fluffy white clouds of the atmosphere. He was actually hovering over a planet. He glanced at Mekoddishkem whose brow was furrowed. "What's wrong?"

Mekoddishkem took hold of his arm. "We must return quickly."

Instantly, they stood before The Wall. Within another fraction of a second, they were transported to earth and stood in the driveway of a suburban home. Someone came out of the house and got in their car. Could be either a man or a woman. It was too dark to tell, and the person kept their back to him.

They heard a crack, and a massive limb broke off a nearby tree, crushing the roof of the car parked in the driveway directly in front of them.

Jackson stepped back, startled. "Oh, no. That poor person. No one could have survived that." He looked up and saw two demons perched in the tree next to where the limb had just broken off. They were smiling.

Mekoddishkem said in a sad voice, "Fred was in that car."

Jackson gasped, then shook his head and sighed. "Poor Fred."

They watched as the two demons slithered down the tree to retrieve Fred's soul from his body.

Jackson clenched his teeth. "We're too late."

"No, God allowed it to happen."

Fred's soul was retrieved from his body. His eyes went wide when he saw the demons, then he screamed. Each demon clasped one of his arms. Fred looked over and saw Jackson. His eyes seemed about to burst out of their sockets. He shouted at the top of his lungs, "Jackson! You're alive!" He tried to break free but couldn't. "Jackson, what are they doing? What's happening?" The fear in his voice escalated as he eyed the demons again. He continued struggling, then screamed, "Jackson! Do something!"

Jackson frowned and shook his head. "There's nothing I can do, Fred. It's too late. I'm so sorry."

The demons chuckled as they took off eastward into the air with Fred in tow.

Jackson put his hands over his face and couldn't stop shaking his head. "Was there anything else I could have done?"

"No, Jackson. You presented the way of faith to him, but he rejected it of his own free will. The saddest sight in the universe is the look on someone's face when they realize it's too late for them to receive God's offer of forgiveness."

❦

Monica was sitting with McKenzie in the kitchen at the condo. Chinese takeout containers littered the table and chopsticks rested beside their plates. Monica tried to listen as McKenzie rambled on about the sermon from that week. Seriously, all she seemed to talk about was God lately.

Monica said, "Look, I like going to church with you. The people are nice, but what do I need God for? I mean, I'm doing just fine on my own. Besides, how can you be sure there is a God anyway?"

"It's obvious from the creation."

"What's that supposed to mean? What's so 'obvious' about it. I don't see God walking around introducing himself to everyone."

McKenzie sat up straight. "It means it's clear that the universe got here by design, not by accident. Just look at the complexity and massive scale of the sun, moon, and stars, and how they orbit around each other in perfect harmony, enabling life to exist. Everything is so fine-tuned it couldn't have been formed by accident."

"How is it so fine-tuned?"

"Well, I'm no expert. I just saw a video about this topic on the internet. The speaker said there are various constants in the universe and that if they were altered, even slightly, life would cease to exist."

"What's a constant."

"A factor that doesn't change. Three were mentioned in the video. One is the gravity constant. If gravity were slightly stronger or weaker, life would cease to exist."

Monica stood up. "I'm really not into all this science stuff. Okay?"

"I know what you mean. Let me give you an analogy I heard. Failure to maintain the universe's tuning would be catastrophic. It's is equivalent to an aircraft carrier being sunk by placing a penny on its deck."

"I'm going out for a walk." Monica put on her coat and gloves, grabbed her keys, and slammed the door behind her.

She tried to make sure she didn't step on any ice on the sidewalks as she walked. McKenzie was getting on her nerves. *It's fine that she's religious, but she shouldn't try to push it on me. I want to be left alone to enjoy my life. I don't want to dwell on death all the time. It's not healthy. I need to seize each day, not spend all my time thinking about my last one.*

The sound of tires screeching jolted her out of her daze. She looked to her left. A car had been rapidly approaching and the driver had just slammed on the brakes. She screamed and jumped in the air, hoping to minimize the impact. When she landed, she realized she was standing in the middle of a crosswalk. The car had stopped just on the left edge of it. *Man, that was close.* She waved at the driver, then pointed to herself and lipped, *My bad.*

❧

Jackson glanced at Mekoddishkem. "How much time does Monica have?"

"Not much. Satan will have his demons kill her the first chance they get."

"We've got to hurry. I don't want her to end up like Fred."

But to help her, he would need to go on the offensive. The training center was empty when Jackson arrived. He practiced his drills alone since there was no one to spar with. After a half hour, Raphael appeared in the doorway.

"Raphael, Satan has ordered my wife and sister-in-law back on earth to be killed. I need to defeat the demon Botis before he can carry out Satan's orders. Will you help me?"

"Of course. Get your gear on. Let's spar."

CHAPTER 16

NEITHER ARE YOUR WAYS MY WAYS

JACKSON RETURNED TO the throne room. He hadn't focused on it earlier, but before the throne, there was what looked like a sea of glass, as clear as crystal. Nearby, thrones were occupied by people dressed in white. Jackson looked upward. Thousands upon thousands of other occupied thrones surrounded him.

Images began appearing on the glassy sea. Jackson sought out Mekoddishkem and soon found him. "What are those images?"

Mekoddishkem said, "Those are events transpiring on earth. Everything is in full view of the Lord."

Jackson leaned forward. "There are so many people watching here in heaven. Is this what's meant by the 'great cloud of witnesses' referenced in the Bible?"

"Yes, it is, Jackson."

They watched as a man, dressed in a short-sleeved black shirt with a white clerical collar, knelt on the ground. Another man, wearing a traditional white Arabic thawb stretching down to his ankles, stood above him, pointing a gun at his head. They were in a desolate desert area about forty feet down a gully from a dirt road. An old, beat-up pickup truck was parked on the road above them. Two other men, also wearing thawbs, were standing nearby.

"What's going on, Mekoddishkem?"

"A Catholic priest, who is serving as a missionary in a Muslim country, is about to be martyred for his faith."

"Why doesn't God stop it?"

"Remember two principles, Jackson: first, people have free will, and second, everyone is going to die sometime unless the Lord returns to rapture his church beforehand. He allows such things, according to his will." The angel swept a hand toward the scene. "Many will come to faith and be saved because of this priest's bravery, including his killer."

The man holding the pistol addressed the kneeling Catholic priest. "Acknowledge that Allah is God, and you will be spared."

The priest tilted his head upward to gaze at the man. "I am a follower of Jesus, the Son of God. I will not deny my faith in him."

"Infidel!"

The priest took a resigned breath. "You hold Jesus to be a prophet, do you not?"

The Muslim man nodded his head. "Yes. Abraham, Moses, Jesus, and Mohammad are the great prophets of Islam. Of them, however, Mohammad is the greatest."

The priest shook his head. "I believe the prophet Jesus is the greatest. The prophet Jesus said, 'I am the way and the truth and the life. No one comes to the Father except through me.' So you see, my friend, Jesus is the only way to heaven. Mohammed was not sure he would go to heaven, but *you* can be sure you will go to heaven if you ask Jesus to forgive your sins and save you from hell."

"Blasphemy!" The Muslim pulled the trigger, and the priest toppled over. His soul was immediately retrieved from his body by two angels who were standing nearby. Great fear came over the priest's face, followed by great joy. The heavenly assembly all cried out, "Amen!"

Mekoddishkem said, "Precious in the sight of the Lord is the death of his faithful servants."

Jackson whispered to his guardian angel, "That doesn't seem very fair to the priest."

Jesus called out, "Jackson, come over here!"

Jackson stood before Jesus's throne. Before he could speak, Jesus said, "For my thoughts are not your thoughts, neither are your ways my ways. We all stood here several months ago, watching you dive in front of the bullet intended for Monica. When you sacrificed your life to save her from hell, the whole assembly cried out, 'Amen!' just like you witnessed here today with the Catholic priest. You brought great glory to God by your unselfish act and saved your sister-in-law from hell. Greater love has no one than this, that he lay down his life for his friends."

Jackson waited a moment longer, expecting a sharp rebuke, but none came. He certainly deserved it. He would have been chewed out big-time for saying something like that at OCS, but this wasn't Marine Officer's Candidate School. All he felt was love and acceptance, and no judgment. He sighed and said, "Yes, Lord."

Jackson turned to leave, but Jesus said, "Do you remember Jeremy Brown?"

"Yes, Lord. He's the young man who hit me with his car in the hospital parking garage, then fled the scene."

"Do you remember what you told Mekoddishkem about that accident?"

"That I forgave him."

"Yes, Jackson. That was a very kind thing for you to do. What else?"

Where is Jesus going with this? "Oh, sorry, Lord. I know you know what I'm thinking." He had to tell the absolute, unvarnished truth. "That he was only a kid and shouldn't have had to go to hell."

"That is correct, Jackson."

"And what was Mekoddishkem's response?"

"That Jeremy had plenty of opportunities to receive your offer of forgiveness through faith in you, but he declined to do so."

"That is correct, Jackson. Do you think I would allow Jeremy to be taken to hell without giving him a chance to receive my forgiveness?"

"Of course not."

"Would you like me to show you all the times I reached out to him through my Spirit, only to be rejected by him?"

"That is not necessary, Lord. I believe you. You are just and holy and cannot do wrong."

"Nevertheless, I will show you one instance."

A classroom came into view on the sea of glass. Jackson recognized it. The room was located on the first floor of his church's Sunday school building. A group of middle school students were seated around tables arranged in a horseshoe configuration. The youth pastor was standing at the front of the room. He looked much younger than the last time Jackson had seen him. Jeremy sat at the table. He was a foot taller than all the other middle schoolers but a foot shorter than when the accident occurred. "Jeremy came to my church?"

"Yes, when he was a boy. A friend invited him to a middle school event there."

"I had no idea."

"Of course."

The pastor held up his Bible and spoke. "Please turn with me in your Bibles to Luke, chapter seven, verse eleven." He waited a moment while pages flipped. "Does everyone have it? Good." The pastor began to read:

Soon afterward, Jesus went to a town called Nain, and his disciples and a large crowd went along with him. As he approached the town gate, a dead person was being carried out—the only son of his mother, and she was a widow. And a large crowd from the town was with her. When the Lord saw her, his heart went out to her and he said, "Don't cry." Then he went up and touched the bier they were carrying him on, and the bearers stood still. He said, "Young man, I say to you, get up!" The dead man sat up and began to talk, and Jesus gave him back to his mother. They were all filled with awe and praised God. "A great prophet has appeared among us," they said. "God has come to help his people." This news about Jesus spread throughout Judea and the surrounding country.

Jeremy turned to his friend and whispered, "That's just a bunch of bull. Nobody can raise someone from the dead. It's impossible."

His friend replied, "It's not impossible for God."

Jeremy shifted in his seat. "Maybe the man wasn't really dead. Maybe it was all a setup, trying to make it look like Jesus performed a miracle when he really didn't."

"No, it really happened."

"How do you know?"

The boy leaned over to Jeremy. "Because the Bible says it did. The Bible is God's Word. God doesn't lie."

The pastor spoke again. "Do you have something you'd like to share with the rest of the group, Jeremy?"

Jeremy shook his head. "No, I'm all set."

The pastor continued, "Does anyone not believe they're going to die someday?" He paused and looked around the room. No one raised their hand. "In the same way that Jesus raised that young man from the dead, he can raise you from the dead when it's your turn to die. All you have to do is tell God you're genuinely sorry for the bad things you've done, be willing not to do them anymore, ask Jesus to take away your sins, and be ready to follow him for the rest of your life. God will know if you really mean it. Would anyone like to do that today? Would anyone like to make sure they'll go to heaven when they die?"

Jeremy giggled.

"What's so funny, Jeremy?"

"Nothing."

"This is a grave matter."

"Yeah, whatever you say, pastor."

"It's not what I say that matters, Jeremy. It's what God's Word says that matters. I hope you'll realize that one day before it's too late."

Jackson returned his focus to God's throne room. "So sad. He was clearly given a chance, but he rejected the offer."

"He was given many other chances too. No one knows how long they have to live. Only God knows, and he is not willing that any should perish, but that all should come to repentance. However, some people, like Jeremy, realized that too late."

Jesus motioned to Jackson. "Jackson, come up here."

He climbed up the stairs to be at the same level as Jesus, just in front of his throne. "Yes, Lord."

"Sit with me on my throne for a moment."

"What?"

"To him who overcomes, I will give the right to sit with me on my throne, just as I overcame and sat down with my Father on his throne."

Jackson sat down next to Jesus and looked outward, surveying the hundreds of thousands, perhaps millions, of thrones surrounding them in the distance. Light burst forth like a searchlight from behind him. For that one moment in time, he was at the epicenter of the universe—the source of all wisdom, all truth, all knowledge, and all love. The light of the others in front of him paled when compared to the light he was enveloped in. He only sat on the edge on the throne with his back firmly upright. Over and over in his mind, he chanted, *unworthy, unworthy, unworthy*. He sobbed briefly, then collected himself and said, "Thank you, Lord Jesus, for this great honor."

Jesus nodded. Jackson slid off the throne as quickly as he could and stood beside Jesus.

Jesus smiled at him. "You are here not because of your own righteousness but because my righteousness has been transferred to your account. You are not intrinsically worthy, Jackson, but I have *made* you worthy. I did all this for you because I love you very deeply."

Jackson involuntarily collapsed to his knees and looked up to his Savior. A tidal wave of joy filled every fiber of his being. He'd focused so much on his unworthiness that he had missed the wonder of God's free gift of righteousness. That wouldn't happen anymore. The Lord of the universe was talking to him. Every word that came out of his mouth was the Word of God. What an incredible honor. "Thank you for all you've done for me, Lord Jesus."

CHAPTER 17

ALPHA

IT WAS A chilly Monday night in December. McKenzie strolled into the church's middle school room with Monica. There was a stage at the front of the room with a large white screen hanging directly behind it. A digital projector hung from the ceiling in the center of the room, pointing to the screen. An amber light blinked on the back of the projector.

McKenzie surveyed the room. The lighting was low. There were a dozen circular tables, each fashioned with a white tablecloth, a lit candle, a clear glass vase containing purple chrysanthemums, and eight place settings. Where should she and Monica sit? She was still fairly new to Valley, so she didn't know many people yet.

A voice called out from behind her. "Mrs. Trotman?"

McKenzie turned around and recognized Pam Shuster. Pam was dressed in a gray plaid wool skirt with black stockings, black loafers, a white blouse, and a navy-blue jacket. She must have come straight from work.

"Hi, Pam. Please call me McKenzie. You remember my sister Monica, don't you?"

"Of course. Are you ladies sitting at a particular table?"

"No, we just got here. Would you like to join us?"

"Sure."

After each chose a chair facing the stage, they sat down and passed the water pitcher, dinner rolls, and butter to each other. Servers then brought out bowls of brown rice and broccoli and platters of grilled lemon chicken and placed one of each at every table.

Pam asked McKenzie, "Have you ever been to one of these meetings before?"

"No, this is our first time."

Pam looked around. "This is really nice."

Monica smiled. "Agreed. I love the ambiance, and it looks like we're about to have a great meal."

A well-dressed man cruised onto the stage and flicked on the microphone. "Welcome to Alpha, everyone! My name is Bob, and I'll be your host for this evening. Before we start, I'd like to review the agenda. After having this wonderful meal and spending time getting to know each other at our tables, we'll watch episode one of the video series called *Alpha*. This series is designed for people who are not regular church attenders but have questions about God. After that, we'll break into small groups to discuss what we heard. No questions will be off-limits, and everyone's opinion will be respected, no matter how different it may be from your own. Enjoy your dinner, and thank you for coming tonight."

When dinner and the video were over, McKenzie, Monica, and Pam all moved to another classroom. There were five other attendees in the room, along with a facilitator who welcomed them as they entered. Their small group leader's name was Mark. He was a professor at a local college. After everyone introduced themselves, he opened the floor for questions.

Pam spoke first. "If Jesus were on earth today, what would he say about gay people?"

The professor shifted in his chair a little, then looked around. "What does everyone think? Trevor?"

A young black man of about twenty-five raised his hand. "I heard the Bible says homosexuality is an abomination, so I guess that summarizes how God feels about gay people."

Monica was next. "From my experience, many Christians hate gay people. A number of my friends from Massachusetts are gay and have no interest in getting involved in any kind of organized religion because of this."

A middle-aged woman with dirty blond, curly hair said, "God loves everyone, so I don't think he hates gays."

An older man chimed in. "I think gays are probably born that way. It might even be genetic. I don't think God would judge people harshly for being who they truly are."

McKenzie was hesitant to add her thoughts. The opinions being expressed were all over the place. "God does love everyone, but he's also just and can't allow sin to go unpunished."

Monica grimaced at McKenzie.

After a pause, the professor asked, "Are there any other opinions about this topic?"

Pam raised her hand. "My parents are Jewish. They disowned me when I came out as gay. Some of my friends, who called themselves Christians, disowned me as well. The only exception was Jackson Trotman." She looked directly at McKenzie. "Your husband saved my life. He gave me CPR while I was having a heart attack at work." She shook her head. "His boss would have let me die. Jackson treated me with respect and dignity and never judged me. May God rest his soul."

McKenzie nodded as the emotion welled within her. She'd lose it if she spoke, so she just kept nodding.

Pam eyed the professor. "What do you think?"

"I'd like to be certain no one else has an opinion first. I don't want to discourage anyone from sharing their views. Does anyone else have a comment?" He looked around for a moment.

A middle-aged, balding man spoke up. "There are many paths to God. I don't think we need to be limited to the Christian view on this. Gays have been oppressed for centuries, and it needs to stop."

After seeing no one else, Mark smiled. "Thanks to all who expressed their views. We certainly had a wide variety of opinions here tonight." He turned his attention to Pam. "Your question was 'What would Jesus say about gay people?' I think the best way to answer this is to see what the Bible says about it.

"First of all, there's nothing in the Bible that directly quotes Jesus's thoughts about gays while he walked on the earth. However, I can share some principles to help us understand what he might have said. Let me first give you some background before I answer your question directly. In the Sermon on the Mount, which is found in the book of Matthew, chapters five through seven, Jesus addressed judgment.

Do not judge, or you too will be judged. For in the same way you judge others, you will be judged, and with the measure you use, it will be measured to you. Why do you look at the speck of sawdust in your brother's eye and pay no attention to the plank in your own eye?

"This principle about not judging others is also addressed by the apostle Paul in 1 Corinthians, chapter five. He says we should not judge those outside the church. However, he says we may judge those inside the church. This is echoed in Matthew, chapter eighteen where Jesus says if a fellow Christian is involved in a sin, he should be approached about it one-on-one. If he doesn't turn away from it, a small group of fellow believers should confront him. If the person still refuses to listen, the matter should be brought before the entire church.

"The Bible teaches that gay, straight, or any other type of sexual activity outside of a marriage between a man and a woman is sexual immorality or sin. Sin is anything that is opposed to God's will for our lives."

Pam stopped him. "That's a pretty general statement. Do you have any specific references to back that up? I'd like to check what you're saying later."

"Sure. Off the top of my head, references include Leviticus, chapter eighteen and twenty in the Jewish Tanakh, or what Christians call the Old Testament. New Testament references, which begin after Jesus was born, include Romans, chapter one, Ephesians, chapter five, and 1 Corinthians, chapter six. Revelation, chapter twenty-one even says those who practice sexual immorality will be kept out of heaven. With that as background, Pam, I think the best place to find the answer to your question is in John, chapter eight, the story about the woman caught in adultery.

"Some Jewish leaders brought a woman before Jesus who had been caught in the act of adultery. They said the law of Moses required them to stone her and wanted to know what he had to say about it. They said this to try to trap him. If he said *not* to stone her, he would be violating the Old Testament law. But if he said they *should* stone her, he would be in trouble with the Roman rulers because only they had the authority to administer capital punishment at that time in Israel.

"Jesus drew something on the ground with his finger, then said, 'Let any one of you who is without sin be the first to throw a stone at her.' Slowly, the Jewish leaders began to leave, beginning with the oldest, until none were left. Jesus then spoke to her. 'Woman, where are they? Has no one condemned you?' The woman said, 'No one, sir.' So, Jesus replied, 'Then neither do I condemn you… Go now and leave your life of sin.'

"To summarize, I think Jesus would say the following about gays:

don't judge or condemn them. Let the Holy Spirit convict them to leave their life of sin."

Mark ran a hand through his hair. "Before we move on to the next question, let me offer a word of caution. These truths apply to anyone having sex outside the boundaries set by God, not just gays. The type of sin someone is involved in, whether sexual or not, is not what's important. What's important is that we acknowledge we're a sinner before God, be willing to turn away from our sins, and ask God to forgive us."

Mark surveyed the room with a sheepish grin as if he just realized how much he'd been talking. "That was a fascinating discussion, folks. What other questions do you have?"

The older man raised his hand. "May I speak?"

Mark leaned forward in his chair. "Of course. Go right ahead, sir."

The man gestured with both hands. "What about all the people who live in remote regions of the world—such as the jungles of Cameroon, Brazil, or Indonesia—who've never heard the gospel? How could God be considered fair and just if Jesus is the only way to God, but millions of people have never heard of him?"

Mark smiled. "Boy, you guys are tough. You've asked some really great questions tonight. Does anyone else have a comment on that question before I respond?" Mark looked around.

McKenzie wasn't sure how she would answer.

When no one spoke up, Mark tackled the question. "Take a look at Romans, chapters one and two in the Bible when you get home. Those passages argue that the existence of God the Father is obvious from the creation, and anyone who thinks otherwise will be 'without excuse' at the judgment. Psalms fourteen and fifty-three go even further

The fool says in his heart, "There is no God." So, even if a person has never heard of Jesus, God the Son, they will be required to have believed in God the Father.

"We know that God will be fair at the judgment because of his character. He is absolutely holy and righteous, perfect in every way. For those who never heard of Jesus during their lifetime, Jesus will still be the only way to heaven. However, judgment will be based on what they knew and what they did with that knowledge.

"We are all created with a conscience. Was the person who never heard of Jesus true to their conscience? Did they know they were a sinner, but didn't know how to remedy it? Perhaps they pleaded with an 'unknown' god to forgive them. Did they have the mental capacity to understand the gospel? Would they have responded to the gospel if they had heard it?

"There are many stories of Jesus appearing to Muslims in dreams and visions, apparently because there was no Christian witness where they lived, and God recognized they had enough faith to believe in Jesus.

"Only God knows how he will judge those who have never heard the gospel. We can trust that he will be fair. We must be cautious not to use this line of reasoning as an excuse for not believing the gospel ourselves. We have heard. Therefore, we are accountable for what we know and for what we do with that knowledge. Jesus said, 'From everyone who has been given much, much will be demanded.' I hope this answered your question."

"Yes, it did. Thank you."

"You are very welcome."

The leader then provided an overview of the great religions of the world and how many tenets of those religions contradicted each other, making it impossible for all of them to be true.

"That's it for tonight, folks. Thank you very much for coming. I look forward to seeing all of you again next week."

McKenzie shook Mark's hand as she was leaving. "Great job! You really know the Bible well. Thank you for the answers you provided."

"You're welcome. Was it too much."

"The section comparing the world religions was a little long, but it was still great. Thanks for all you did tonight."

McKenzie drove Monica home in her Volvo. It began raining hard about five minutes into the trip, causing her to turn the windshield wipers on.

McKenzie placed her hand on Monica's. "So, what did you think about tonight?"

Monica nodded her approval. "I really liked it. The food and atmosphere were great, the people were very nice, and I enjoyed the video and discussion afterward. It gave me a lot to think about."

McKenzie clicked on her high beams. "Like what?"

"The black guy said most religions are the same, and the old guy said there are many paths to God, but the discussion leader gave specifics on how the great religions of the world are very different from Christianity." Monica sighed. "How do I figure out what the truth is?"

McKenzie cleared her throat before speaking. "Jesus said, 'I am the way and the truth and the life. No one comes to the Father except through me.' So, Jesus was saying he is the only path to God."

"Hmm. Does it actually say that in the Bible?"

"Yes. It's in John, chapter fourteen, verse six. When you really understand what the world's major religions stand for, you'll realize they aren't all the same, and therefore, can't all be true.

"A common theme of non-Christian religions is that entry into heaven—if they believe there is one—is based on performance. Unfortunately, no mortal has ever been able to keep the Ten Commandments, the five pillars of Islam, the eightfold path of Buddhism, or even keep true to their own conscience. Christianity is the only religion that depends not on what we do but on who we know. God's standard for entering heaven is perfection. You'll never be good enough to get into heaven on your own. You need to believe that Jesus died on the cross to pay for your sins, so you won't have to pay for them yourself in hell." McKenzie scratched her head, then glanced at Monica. "Do you really think Christians hate gays?"

Monica squirmed in her seat. "Perhaps I was a little harsh and a little prejudiced. Sorry about that. Jackson certainly didn't hate gays, and you don't, so I guess there are exceptions."

McKenzie removed her hand from Monica's. "Some Christians zero in on attacking the gay lifestyle because there are specific passages against it in the Bible. This kind of talk is dividing rather than unifying. The fact is that we're all sinners and need a savior, and we all have to repent of our sinful way of living, regardless of who we are or what we've done."

A bright light, followed by a loud clap, startled McKenzie as she drove on the Avon Old Farms Bridge over the Farmington River.

Monica screamed, "What was that?"

McKenzie looked in her rearview mirror and saw a faint whiff of smoke rising from the bridge's steel guardrail. "It looks like lightning struck the bridge and just missed us. Weird."

Jackson strolled with Mekoddishkem through the construction site of an elegant home in heaven. Workers were applying marble trim along the grand stairway leading up to a landing, midway between the first and second floors. Nearby, scaffolding extended up about thirty feet. A man was at the top, lying on his back, painting frescoes on the ceiling. Plans were spread out on a piece of plywood, resting on two sawhorses, in the middle of the foyer.

Jackson gaped at the artwork. "Wow! This place is going to be gorgeous. Who's the architect?"

"The architect and builder are God."

"Who are all the workmen?"

"They are gifted master craftsmen specifically selected by Jesus for this project."

Jackson cocked his head at an angle. "Aren't people supposed to be resting in heaven?"

Mekoddishkem chuckled. "They love doing this, Jackson. It's not work for them. They love serving God and others."

Marble frames were already in place along the plaster walls for paintings, and pedestals were ready to support sculptures. "Who is this home for?"

"McKenzie."

"McKenzie? Good for her. She'll love it. Jesus really is preparing a place for us, just like the Bible says."

"Indeed."

Jackson tapped his chin. "Is Jesus preparing a place for Monica?"

"No, not yet."

He exhaled. "Isn't God able to see into the future? Doesn't he already know who will become Christians and who will not?"

"Yes. He has known before the creation of the world."

Jackson shook his head. "I don't understand."

"Monica has free will and must choose to accept the forgiveness of sins offered to her. That hasn't happened yet."

"I know, but I still don't understand."

Mekoddishkem paused. "What will happen in heaven if Monica repents?"

"There will be much rejoicing."

"God knows what Monica will decide, but the rest of heaven does not."

"Oh, I get it now. Thanks, Mekoddishkem."

"Jackson!" It was Jesus who called.

"Yes, Lord."

"Go to Monica right away and take Mekoddishkem with you."

"Yes, Lord."

THE BATTLE FOR ONE SOUL

JACKSON AND MEKODDISHKEM rushed to The Wall, then entered Monica's portal in the present. Monica was standing at the end of an indoor pool, which was about twenty-five yards long, with her hands on her hips. A middle-aged, balding photographer, dressed in black trousers and a black shirt, was on one knee making adjustments to his camera. His young, redheaded female assistant, also dressed in nondescript all black, had just finished adjusting the tripod's height and was now focused on positioning the lighting equipment.

Monica looked beautiful. She was wearing the same chartreuse bikini she'd worn at Devereaux Beach in Marblehead the summer before. The white cloth bracelet was still visible on her left ankle, as was the tattoo on the small of her back. She removed a golden chain from her neck, which had a blue amulet attached to it, and placed it on her towel resting on a nearby pool chair.

The photographer placed his camera on top of the tripod and looked through it. "My, you look beautiful today, Monica."

She smiled and nodded.

The photographer glanced at his assistant. "Melanie, we're going to need a scrim to block the light from coming in through the windows."

His assistant procured a silk screen from against the wall. It was about six feet long and four feet wide. She held it up in the air as she stood between the windows and Monica.

The photographer looked through his camera again. "That's better."

He now directed his attention to Monica. "Can you swim?"

"Of course."

"Okay, good. I want you to swim to the other end of the pool, then turn around and swim back. When you return, I want you to place both your hands on the metal exit ladder on the side over here, then look at the camera and slowly pull yourself up the steps, leaning back slightly as you let the water drip off you."

"Got it."

Despite her beauty, Jackson wasn't staring at her lustfully. What a change from the way he'd looked at her when he saw her lying on the beach with McKenzie. She swam the backstroke toward the opposite end of the pool, then switched to the breaststroke on her way back. She then sauntered through the water to the side and touched the in-pool metal exit ladder with both hands.

Botis appeared and spoke to Melanie. "Look at how beautiful Monica is. I wish I could be more like her."

The photographer called out, "Move the scrim to your left!" About five seconds later, he looked up. "Melanie! Wake up! Shift the scrim to your left."

Startled, Melanie complied without looking, causing her to trip over a chair. She fell, knocking one of the high-intensity photography lights into the pool with the wires still attached.

Monica screamed. Her body began twitching and shaking uncontrollably, then her face fell into the water. Jackson frantically looked around. There was no lifeguard on duty.

Several other demons snickered nearby.

Jackson cried, "No!"

He rushed at the demons, flailing his sword, with Mekoddishkem behind him. Botis and the other demons fled.

The photographer screamed, ran away from the pool to the door, and just stood there with his hand over his mouth. "I'm *so* going to get sued over this."

Melanie threw down her scrim and reached out to grab Monica by the hair but quickly reared back and yelled, "I just got shocked!" She looked around. "Help! Somebody, help!"

At the opposite end of the pool, a man bounced up from his chaise lounge chair, ran across the terracotta tile, and then grabbed the aboveground handrail still being held by Monica. "Ow! I just got shocked too." He looked over at Melanie. "The light must be electrifying the pool. Pull the plug from the wall, then call nine-one-one."

Melanie froze.

The man spoke in a loud, commanding tone. "Now!"

Melanie ran to the wall, ripped every plug out of their sockets, then scurried away from the pool area toward the front desk.

Jackson grabbed Mekoddishkem's arm. "No one is helping her."

The man paused for a moment, then ran to the opposite side of the pool and picked up a plastic pole with a net at the end of it. He placed it around Monica's head and dragged her to the end of the pool. He pulled her out and placed her on her back on the tile beside the pool.

A woman in a blue polo shirt and khaki slacks appeared at the entryway to the pool area, then ran over to them. The man grabbed her by the arm. "Did someone call nine-one-one?"

"Yes. Help is on the way. They should be here in four minutes."

"Good, but she doesn't have four minutes. She's not breathing. I'm going to start CPR."

"How can I help?"

"Do you have a defibrillator?"

"Yes."

"Get it."

"Okay." The woman returned about thirty seconds later with the device.

"Do you know how to use it?"

"Sort of."

The man shook his head and raised his voice. "I don't have time to train you. Take it out, set it up on her as best you can, then run to the front entrance and wait for the EMTs to arrive."

"Will do."

The man began chest compressions on Monica, followed a moment later by two quick breaths.

Jackson blurted out, "I feel so helpless."

"You're not helpless, Jackson. You can pray."

He bowed his head. "Father in heaven, please help Monica to survive this. In Jesus's name, I pray, amen."

Mekoddishkem nodded. "Good."

"As you can see, from a human perspective, this was an accident, but from our perspective, here in the heavenly realms, it was not."

The man grabbed a towel from a nearby chair and dried Monica off as best he could. He checked her bathing suit to make sure there was no wire in the bra, then connected the defibrillator pads, one below the right collar bone on the front of her chest and the other on the opposite side below the left breast on the back of her chest, creating a straight line between the pads so a bolt of electricity would pass directly through her heart.

The man pressed the Analyze button. It indicated a shock was needed, so he immediately pressed the Shock button. Monica's torso arched sharply upward, then settled to the tile.

The man continued CPR and applied another shock about two minutes later.

The ambulance workers finally arrived and took over from the Good Samaritan.

Jackson and the angel followed Monica as she was wheeled on a gurney toward the ambulance. He prayed for his sister-in-law as they entered the ambulance with her.

The group sped to St. Francis Hospital with the sirens blaring, arriving about ten minutes later. Monica was rushed into the ER. For half an hour, the doctors feverishly tried to revive her. Finally, they stopped.

Jackson shook his head. This couldn't be real. "It can't be. Not Monica. What's going to happen now?"

Two demons arrived and retrieved Monica's spirit from her body. Another demon stood by, smiling. It was Botis, the same one who had possessed Ronaldo and killed Cassandra.

Mekoddishkem cried out, "Botis!"

The angel assigned to guard Monica fought the demons. Jackson and Mekoddishkem unsheathed their swords and joined the fight for Monica's soul.

Botis's eyes bulged when he recognized Mekoddishkem. "Agliarept! Help!"

In what seemed like seconds, perhaps a hundred demons arrived.

Monica became aware of her surroundings and shrieked. Demons swarmed all around her guardian angel like piranhas on a fresh piece of meat. She reared back the instant she saw Jackson. "Jackson, I can't believe it. You're alive!... What's going on?"

Now wasn't the time to talk. Mekoddishkem and the other angel were fully occupied. What could he do to help more? Three of them couldn't fight off a hundred, could they?

About a dozen of the demons peeled off from the horde and headed toward Jackson. He wielded his sword with all his might, thrashing back and forth, doing his best to kill or dismember as many of them as he could. He was fighting well, as one after another succumbed to his sword, but there were just too many of them. He couldn't last much longer.

Monica cried out, "Jackson, what's going on? Can't you talk to me?"

He heard her cries, but there was nothing he could do. He continued fighting the demons. As he vanquished one more, he yelled, "Pray, Monica! Pray!"

"I don't know how to pray." Then Monica gasped. McKenzie had arrived in the hospital room. "Look at the golden cross on McKenzie's forehead. It's glowing!"

A second later, Monica screamed. Jackson glanced over. Two of the demons had grabbed her and were about to fly off with her.

Jackson cringed. He tried to get over to her but could not. There were just too many of them. "No! Not Monica!"

Monica looked back at her sister. "McKenzie, help me." There was no response. "Pray for me, McKenzie. Pray for me. I'm not dead yet."

As if on cue, McKenzie placed her hands on Monica's body and began to pray. "Father in heaven. You are mighty. Nothing is too hard for you. If you are willing, please bring Monica back. I don't care what the doctors say. You brought the widow's only son back to life, you brought Lazarus back to life, and you can bring Monica back to life too. Send a legion of angels if you have to but bring her back. In Jesus's name, I pray, amen."

A second later, a huge formation of angels, numbering in the thousands, suddenly appeared through a fold in space. The remaining demons surrounding Jackson squealed and fled. Jackson searched for Botis, and after locating him, lunged in his direction with sword arched upward, ready to strike.

Botis appeared momentarily stunned by the power and effectiveness of McKenzie's prayer. He regrouped when he saw Jackson bounding toward him. Rather than staying to fight, the demon turned toward McKenzie and touched her belly. Jackson caught up to Botis from behind as he fled and nearly severed his left arm at the shoulder.

McKenzie's body shuddered.

Monica's spirit immediately returned to her physical body. She gasped for air. McKenzie jumped back and shrieked. McKenzie edged back from Monica's hospital bed and studied her face.

Monica opened her eyes and breathed.

McKenzie hollered with delight. She reached across Monica's body, picked her up by her torso, and pulled her close. Tears streamed down her face as she hugged her sister.

Jackson jumped for joy. "That's incredible. I've heard about people being revived but have never seen anything like this. McKenzie's prayers really worked."

Mekoddishkem looked at him solemnly. "The prayer of a righteous person is powerful and effective."

Monica stared at her sister, puzzled. "Where am I? What am I doing here?"

"You're at the hospital."

Monica asked, "What? The hospital? How can that be?"

"You were electrocuted in a swimming pool during your photoshoot, then taken to the hospital by ambulance. The doctors tried to revive you but could not, so you were declared dead. The modeling agency called me. Fortunately, I was driving close by. I rushed to the hospital, came in and prayed for you, and you came back to life."

"I don't know what to say."

McKenzie smiled. "How about saying 'Thanks, sister,' for starters."

Monica wrapped her arms around her sister. "Thank you, McKenzie."

"You're welcome, but you should really be thanking God. He's the one who revived you."

"Okay." Monica looked upward. "If you're there, God, thank you very much for reviving me."

"What do you mean, 'If he's there'? What kind of prayer is that?"

"That's the best I can do."

McKenzie shook her head. "Okay."

Jackson bowed his head in prayer. *Please, Lord, open her eyes to her need for you and to the battle raging around her.*

Monica sat up and wrapped a sheet around her. "McKenzie?"

"Yes."

"I had a dream or vision. Or maybe it was an out-of-body experience like Jackson had. I'm not sure which, but everything seemed so real."

"Wow! What was it about?"

"I was hovering over my body, and demons and angels were fighting over me with swords. Jackson was there, shining brightly like the angels, battling against the demons."

McKenzie collapsed to her knees and slapped her hand over her mouth.

"What do you think it means?"

McKenzie cleared her throat. "I think the demons were trying to take you to hell, and the angels were trying to stop them."

"Maybe my mind was playing tricks on me."

McKenzie stood up, put one hand on her hip, and pointed with the other. "When are you going to realize what the stakes are here, Monica? Do you want to go to hell?"

"I don't know… I'm scared."

"You should be."

Monica looked away. "Thank you for praying for me. You are a true Christian."

"You're welcome. Why do you say I'm a 'true Christian'?"

Monica stared at her sister. "I saw you. You were praying for me and had a golden cross on your forehead. It was glowing."

McKenzie's jaw dropped again.

Jackson looked over at Mekoddishkem. "McKenzie has become such a strong Christian in such a short time. She has great faith."

"Yes, she does, Jackson."

"Is there anything else we can do to help Monica go to heaven?"

"Pray, Jackson. Monica has to decide for herself where she wants to spend eternity."

McKenzie sat beside Monica, holding her hand as she lay in a hospital bed. The doctors thought it best for her to remain overnight for observation after she had been revived.

A gentleman with pepper-gray hair, dark brown tortoiseshell glasses, and a white coat strutted into the room, followed by two men and two women in their twenties. A name was embroidered with blue thread over his left breast pocket.

The man reached out his right hand to Monica. "Miss Baker?"

She shook the man's hand and said, "Yes."

Monica pointed to McKenzie. "This is my sister, McKenzie."

The man reached over the bed and shook McKenzie's hand. "I'm Dr. Barnstable." He turned and motioned with his right hand toward his entourage. "These folks are interns from our department and are here to observe if you don't mind."

"I don't mind."

"I'm the attending physician who pronounced you dead earlier today." The man shook his head. "Frankly, I'm amazed you came back to life. I've never seen anything like it in all my thirty years of medicine. Your vital signs clearly indicated you were no longer with us. I'm very sorry I got it wrong."

"You didn't get it wrong, Doctor."

The doctor's head tilted to one side. "What do you mean?"

"You were right. I *was* dead."

"How do you know that?"

"At first, I thought it might have been a dream. But after thinking about it, I realized I must have had an out-of-body experience. I saw angels, demons, and McKenzie's deceased husband fighting over me."

The doctor guffawed. "Wow! That's quite a dream you had."

Monica gritted her teeth and pointed at the doctor. "How can you dream if your brain isn't functioning?"

The doctor remained silent.

"I saw McKenzie praying for me. She had a golden cross on her forehead."

The doctor chuckled. "Oh, a golden cross?"

"Yes. That's because she's a Christian. How else can you account for someone who is clinically dead coming back to life? Only God could do that."

One of the interns shifted his weight from one leg to the other.

Dr. Barnstable leaned forward. "I don't have an explanation, Miss Baker. Doctors don't know everything. You're just a very lucky young lady."

Monica huffed. "I can assure you, Doctor, that *luck* had nothing to do with it and that McKenzie's prayer had everything to do with it."

A swell of godly pride ran through Jackson's spirit. Her sister-in-law was certain of what she saw and wasn't about to let some doctor talk her out of it.

Chapter 19

More Than She Bargained For

MCKENZIE RETURNED TO her condo, locked the door behind her, and hung her barn coat in the closet. After placing her brown leather hobo bag on the kitchen counter, she sat at the kitchen table for a few moments. This day had been monumental. It was truly a miracle that Monica was still alive.

McKenzie needed to pray. She walked into her bedroom, knelt beside her bed, and extended her arms and upper torso over the bedspread. *Thank you so much, Father, for bringing Monica back to life. And thank you that I might have played a small part in it... Were angels and demons actually in the heavenly realms fighting over Monica? Was Jackson really there too, or was it all just a figment of Monica's imagination? Whether all that happened or not, I thank you for answering my prayer. I trust you're taking good care of Jackson up in heaven and that I'll see him again someday. Thank you again for being so kind and merciful and giving Monica another chance to turn to you. In Jesus's name, I pray, amen.*

McKenzie remained kneeling for a while beside her bed. Her thoughts drifted off to Block Island. She worked as a hostess that summer while Jackson was a lifeguard. He was so handsome when he'd walked up to the Spring House Hotel for the first time. She chuckled at how she'd scolded him about the two thirtyish-looking women he met at the bar, telling him they were too old for him. The following day, at the beach, he caught her staring at his abs. He was so gracious about it. A few days later, on their first date, he saved that little girl from drowning at the other beach. She sighed. It's too bad they hadn't spent more time together that summer, but his drinking was too much for her to handle.

McKenzie fast-forwarded seven years to her job at Aetna. The shock she felt bumping into him at the cafeteria still permeated her soul. He stood there, as handsome as ever despite the crutches, but he had somehow changed, and whatever he had, she wanted it.

Their first date after reconnecting—the train ride, the boat ride, dinner at the Gelston House, the musical at the Goodspeed Opera House—had been such a glorious day. After the show, he had tried to kiss her on the way to the parking lot, but the torrential rain forced a postponement.

When he finally kissed her, her insides melted. Only a few months later, he'd proposed at the Riverton Inn. She had no idea a marriage proposal would be offered that night. It was a complete surprise. Her ring sparkled brightly in the moonlight as they stood on the bridge and gazed at the river rushing beneath them.

McKenzie shook away the thoughts. Jackson was gone. Her memories were all she had left, but they hurt like a slowly healing scab. Her back and legs felt stiff as she straightened up. She changed into her pajamas and dragged herself to bed. After pulling the covers up to her neck, she drifted back to their honeymoon night—how wonderful it had been, being with him, alone. She imagined Jackson lying beside her at that very moment. The familiar ache sliced through her heart. Why had God allowed their life together to be cut short? Now that her husband was gone, what did God want to do with her life?

❧

The following morning, Monica returned to the McGregor Modeling Agency building and approached the receptionist. "May I see Mrs. Cavanaugh?"

"Do you have an appointment?"

"I do not."

"Your name?"

"Monica Baker."

The receptionist called. "Miss Monica Baker to see you."

The receptionist hung up the phone, then turned and pointed to the oak double doors behind her on the right. "Just go through there. It's the third office on the left."

"Thanks."

Monica glanced at the celebrity photographs on the walls as she walked down the hallway. Was that what she was working toward? Could she make it?

Mrs. Cavanaugh greeted Monica at her office door and shook her hand. "It's good to see you, Monica. I heard about your accident yesterday. I'm glad you're okay. Please, have a seat."

If you were so concerned, why didn't you call to find out how I was? "It was a severe accident. I was pronounced dead by the ER doctor at the hospital, but my sister prayed for me, and I was miraculously revived."

Mrs. Cavanaugh's jaw dropped. "Wow! That's amazing! It's a miracle, then, that you're sitting here today."

"Yes. I'm not sure what you were told, but I wanted to let you know I never want to work with that photographer again. I have no hard feelings toward you or this agency and would love to work with you again if another opportunity arises."

With a curt nod, Mrs. Cavanaugh said, "That's very kind of you to say. We'll keep you in mind."

Monica stood up and reached out her hand. "Thanks for your time, Mrs. Cavanaugh. Have a good day."

It was clear. Mrs. Cavanaugh couldn't care less about her and was just patronizing her so she wouldn't sue. She'd never work with that agency again. Time to try something new.

Monica returned to West Hartford and entered the condo. McKenzie wasn't there. She sat at the computer to do a little modeling research on her own. She queried the Backstage site and applied for a Swimwear Fit Model job in New York City.

It took a week to hear back from them. Monica was working out at the New York Athletic Club, located next door to the condo, when her mobile phone rang.

"Monica? Hi! This is Becky from Legends Modeling in New York City."

Her heart raced. "Oh. Hi, Becky! How are you today?"

"Just fine. Thanks for asking. The reason I'm calling is that we loved your photos and would like to bring you in for a test shoot on Thursday at one o'clock in the afternoon. Are you interested?"

"Absolutely! I'll be there."

Thursday morning arrived. Monica could barely contain her excitement. McKenzie drove her to the Union Station bus terminal in Hartford. Monica zipped up the fuzzy brown Sherpa jacket she'd borrowed from McKenzie as they approached the drop-off zone. Small snowbanks abutted the sidewalks. It was chilly with a slight breeze.

McKenzie spoke first. "Remember, when you get to the Port Authority, follow the signs to the subway, then take the Blue A train down to the 23rd Street stop in Manhattan. It's the second stop. Just look at the map on the subway car ceiling if you get confused or lost. They'll announce it over the intercom too."

"Don't worry, McKenzie. I'm a big girl. I'll figure it out."

"I know you will, but since I worked in New York City for several years, I thought I'd help you out."

Monica leaned over and hugged McKenzie. "I know, big sister. I'm just giving you a hard time. Thanks for the advice."

"You're welcome. Call me when you get there, so I know you're okay."

"Will do."

"Oh, and don't talk to any strangers. Got it?"

Monica just waved her off.

Two hours later, Monica exited the bus under the Port Authority building and traveled up the escalators to the shopping area. She passed a gray-haired black man moving slowly with a walker, a terminal worker with a broom and dust bin cleaning up litter, and various harried travelers noisily dragging luggage on rollers over the tile through the hallways. Broadway show advertisements dotted the walls. She followed the signs to the subway, then to the Blue A train sign, and made sure she was headed in the right direction.

Monica shoved through the 23rd Street turnstiles, muddled up the grungy stairwell to the street level, then looked around, trying to get her bearings. She glanced at her phone. She had an hour but wanted to confirm where the agency was before relaxing.

The wind was much stronger here than in Hartford. Perhaps the skyscrapers functioned as wind funnels.

She passed a homeless man sleeping on several cardboard strips, covered with a tarp beside a brick wall. Should she do something? She sighed. Everyone else just walked by. Maybe he'd be awake after her appointment.

Monica walked about four blocks and found the agency. She wanted to be twenty minutes early for her appointment, so she had twenty minutes to kill.

She stopped at a café across the street, was escorted to a table, ordered a cappuccino, and took out her phone. "Hey, McKenzie."

"Hey, sister. How was your ride?"

"Fine. I'm in a café across from the agency on 21st Street. You know, I don't know what it is, but it's exciting being in New York City. There's an energy that permeates this place."

"I know what you mean. I felt it when I worked and lived there too."

"The only downside is all the homeless people. You'd think they would have solved that problem by now."

"Oh, I know, it's terrible, but try not to think about it. Just enjoy your day. There are so many wonderful people and things to do in the city."

"Okay. Please pray my shoot goes well."

"Will do. Call me when you're on the bus heading home. Have fun!"

"Later."

Monica finished her cappuccino and left. She entered the agency's building, with a gray stone façade, then took the elevator up to the third floor. The lobby was much fancier than the McGregor Modeling Agency's waiting room back in Hartford. The oak reception desk, embossed with the Legends Modeling Agency logo in the center, was huge.

The receptionist looked up. "May I help you?"

"Yes. I'm Monica Baker. I have an appointment to meet with Becky."

"I'll let her know you're here. Please have a seat over there."

A few moments later, a woman appeared. She was fiftyish with black hair and fair skin and spoke in a booming voice as she reached out her hand. "Welcome to Legends, Monica. How was your trip?"

"Fine, thank you."

They walked back to Becky's office. Monica sat opposite her. There were provocative shots of models all over the walls of the office.

"As I said over the phone, we loved the pictures you sent us. You're gorgeous in person too. Do you have your portfolio and a comp card with you?"

The compliment lifted Monica's spirit. "I do."

Monica reached into her bag and retrieved a glossy 6 × 9 in. sheet of paper with three of her best shots on one side and her vital statistics on the other—height, weight, bust/waist/hip measurements—along with her contact information. Then she handed Becky a folder containing some other photographs. Monica tensed as she surveyed Becky's face. What did she think?

"Is this all you have?"

"Yes."

"Okay. We'll need to build your portfolio. I've got two test shoots scheduled for you this afternoon. The first is at two o'clock, and the second is at three thirty. Here are the addresses." Becky handed her a piece of paper. "We'll see how these go, then I'll let you know if we'll be moving forward. Any questions?"

"Do you have any suggestions for the photoshoots, or otherwise?"

"Be yourself and be energetic. Own the camera, work with the photographer to get the best possible shots, and have fun. You're lovely, but to be really successful in this business, you'll need to be thinner."

"How much thinner?"

"Please stand up and turn around."

Monica complied.

Then Becky took another look at her comp card. "You'll need to shave two inches off everywhere, which probably means you'd need to lose ten to fifteen pounds."

"Oh, okay. I'll work on that. Anything else?"

"No. That's it for now."

She reached out and shook Becky's hand. "Thank you very much for this opportunity."

Becky nodded, and Monica left. She approached the receptionist's desk on her way out and retrieved a subway map.

❧

The first photoshoot was with a guy who worked out of his apartment. Monica entered a drab-looking building, about fifteen blocks north of the agency, and pressed the number thirty-one button. She was buzzed in within seconds.

A man who was about thirty years old, well-built and tall with blond hair, opened the door. He looked her over, up and down, like she was a piece of meat. Creepy. She glanced around. The place was messy, and the walls were covered with nude photographs. *Better watch out.*

He reached out his hand. "Hi, I'm Frank Chambers. You must be Monica."

She shook his hand. "Yes. Nice to meet you, Frank."

"Becky tells me you're new to New York, trying to break into the business. I'm trying to break into the business too. Maybe we can help each other. Have you been to a photoshoot before?"

"Yes. Several." *He didn't need to know the details.*

"Okay, good. Just relax and have fun. Would you like anything to drink before we get started?"

McKenzie's admonition never to take an open drink from a stranger immediately came to mind. *Who knows what he might put in it?* "No thanks, I'm good."

Frank pointed. "Okay, please put your coat and bag on the kitchen chair over there and stand in front of the white screen."

Monica removed her Sherpa coat, placed it on the chair's back, and then sat down on it. She took off her black flats and placed them in the bag, then took out her black heels and put them on. She stood up, adjusted her snug white tank top and black jeans, then walked over to the front of the white screen. Frank had been watching her every move.

After taking a bunch of different shots from his tripod-mounted camera and complimenting Monica along the way, Frank stepped aside and said, "That's enough. Let's get a few swimsuit shots. You can change in the bathroom over there."

Monica's gut told her to be careful, but she brushed it aside. She really wanted to make it in the modeling business. Becky's decision to move forward with her would be based, at least partially, on this shoot and Frank's evaluation of her. She needed to make it work. Besides, the agency recommended this guy. He couldn't be that bad.

Monica picked up her bag and walked into the bathroom. She noticed there was no lock on the door, so she dressed quickly.

Back in front of the white screen, Frank had her pose at all kinds of angles. He brought over one of the kitchen chairs and had her pose with it in different positions.

Red flags began going off in her head as he gave direction. She walked over to her bag and looked at her phone. "Are we almost done? I need to get to my next shoot."

"Just one more shot." Frank coughed. "Becky said you didn't have a topless shot. Most models have that right on their comp card."

Monica froze. She was genuinely shocked. She didn't even know this guy and had never heard of such a thing. No way would she be another photograph on this pervert's wall. Who knew where else it might end up? On the other hand, this job could be on the line if she appeared uncooperative on her first shoot with this agency. Would Becky not "move forward" with her if she refused? She'd somehow have to get out of it gracefully. "I'm sorry, but I don't have time. I need to get to my next appointment."

Monica picked up her bag and went into the bathroom to change. Her gaze locked on something she'd missed before—a tiny black box in the upper left corner of the ceiling. *He must be filming me. Sick!* She placed the toilet seat down, stood on top of it, reached over, and yanked the box off the wall. She flipped it over and examined it from side to side. It appeared to be a wireless camera of some sort. She instinctively lifted the seat and flushed it down the toilet. She quickly put her street clothes on over her bathing suit, grabbed her coat, and rushed to get out of there.

Frank grabbed her by the elbow just short of the front door. "Must you go?"

She shook him loose. *He's a disgusting pig.* Once in the hallway, she turned and said, "Thanks for your time, Frank. Have a good day."

She took the stairs down, not waiting for the elevator, and got out of the building as fast as she could. Back on the street, she took several deep breaths. How could the agency have recommended someone like that? *Maybe this modeling thing isn't all it's cracked up to be.*

She had only twenty minutes to get to her next shoot.

⤚

The second photoshoot was located five blocks to the west. The quickest way to get there was to walk.

The building had a brownstone facade with teal-tinted windows. A young man leaning against the building smiled as she passed. Monica nodded, then walked up a set of stone stairs to the front door. She pressed a button and was let in. The building was much nicer inside than the last one she'd been to.

She took the elevator up to the second floor. She approached a door with a Locklear Photography sign on the wall beside it and knocked.

"Monica?"

"Yes."

"Hi. I'm Reggie Locklear. Please come in." He turned toward the young woman standing next to him. "This is my assistant. Lawanda James." Monica shook hands with both of them.

Reggie looked to be in his early thirties. He was black, of medium height and build, with a shaved head. Lawanda was also black, about twenty-five, tall and trim, and had beaded hair.

The studio walls were beige, and the room was neat and organized. The camera, lighting, and backdrops were all in place, along with a wooden stool for her to sit on.

This was more like it. Her shoulders relaxed as she smiled for the camera.

About forty minutes later, Reggie stepped from behind the tripod-mounted camera. "That's a wrap, Monica. Nice job today. I think we got some great pictures. I'll plan to send the best ones to Becky this afternoon. Have a great trip back to Connecticut."

"Thanks, Reggie. I'll get changed and be on my way."

Monica looked around in the changing room. No cameras were detected—what a difference from the last guy. Reggie was a total professional and a perfect gentleman at all times. She would love to work with him again someday. She got dressed, picked up her bag, draped her coat over her arm, and walked toward the door. Before leaving, she turned and said, "It was a pleasure working with both of you. I appreciate your professionalism, more than you know."

The elevator was taking forever. Although she was tired, she took the stairs since it was only one flight down. As she approached the midway landing, three men walked into the stairwell from below. She recognized one of them. It was the young man who'd been leaning against the building outside. The other two were older and much bigger.

The young man blocked her path while the others crept behind her. Her stomach clenched in fear as they closed in on her. She screamed. One of the larger men put a thick dish towel over her mouth, muzzling her. A second later, she felt a sharp prick in her rear end.

Everything went dark like someone had flipped a light switch.

CHAPTER 20
PRISONER

IT WAS 11:00 p.m. McKenzie rechecked her phone as she sat on the couch in the condo. No text from Monica regarding which bus she'd taken or when she'd be arriving back in Hartford. Monica could take care of herself, but this wasn't like her. Something was wrong.

She got up and paced back and forth while staring out the window. Was Monica on her way home? Or was she out there lost somewhere? Or hurt?

McKenzie turned her desperate eyes upward. *Father in heaven, please watch over Monica and keep her safe. If she's in any trouble, please get her out of it. In Jesus's name, I pray, amen.*

"Jackson!"

Jackson was sitting on a magenta wingback chair in his library with his feet on an ottoman, reading a book. He looked up. "Yes, Lord."

"Come to me."

He immediately willed himself to God's throne room. Mekoddishkem was standing nearby. "I'm here, Lord."

"Look before you."

Jackson turned his attention toward the sea of glass and saw a woman lying on a bed, handcuffed to a brass headboard. He looked closer. It was Monica. Demons were hovering beside her. "What happened?"

Mekoddishkem walked toward Jackson and placed his hand on his shoulder. "Monica has been kidnapped by sex traffickers."

"What? Oh, no. That's terrible. What should we do?"

"This is part of God's plan for Monica and McKenzie."

"What? God's plan? How can that be? How can any good come from this?"

"God is allowing this terrible event, initiated by Agliarept, to shock Monica out of her complacency. This is exactly what it will be like for her in hell if she doesn't turn from her sinful way of life and accept God's free offer of forgiveness. She is convinced that she'll find happiness and fulfillment through having men stare at her, but that is idolatry, the end of which is death, eternal separation from God."

She'd better repent before it's too late.

McKenzie woke up at 8:00 a.m. on the couch in her living room. She'd been up most of the night waiting, praying, and checking her phone, hoping for a message. It was time to call the Manhattan police to report Monica as a missing person, but she wanted to gather more information first.

She turned on the computer and logged into Monica's email. Fortunately, Monica had given her the password. She found the email from the modeling agency and printed it out. All the details were there.

She called the Legends agency. "May I speak to Becky, please."

"May I ask who's calling?"

"McKenzie Trotman. I'm Monica Baker's sister. She was there yesterday for an interview. It's an emergency."

The receptionist responded, "One moment, please."

A minute later, there was a new voice on the phone. "Hi, this is Becky."

"Hi Becky, this is McKenzie Trotman. You don't know me, but my sister is Monica Baker. She had an interview scheduled with you yesterday. She didn't come home last night, and I'm very concerned."

"Oh, I'm so sorry to hear that. Hopefully, it's nothing, and she'll be appearing at your doorstep before you know it."

"It's not like her not to communicate a change of plans. She would have told me."

"Have you called the police?"

"Not yet. I want to gather some information first. Can you tell me more details about her visit?"

"We only talked for ten minutes or so, then I sent her off to two test shoots."

"Can you tell me who they were with?"

"How do I know you are who you say you are?"

"Understood. I don't blame you. Let me think for a minute… How about if you send the street addresses and phone numbers to Monica's email address. Would that be okay?"

"Yes."

"Could you send it right now?"

"Sure."

A moment passed, and McKenzie saw Becky's email pop up on the screen. "Got it. Do you have any way of knowing whether she made it to those places?"

"Let me check."

Becky responded about a minute later, "I received links to pictures of her from the photographers. So, she made it to both appointments."

"Thank you so much. Did she mention she'd be catching a show, or dinner, or anything else when you spoke with her?"

"No."

"Okay. I'm not sure what else I can do at this point. I'll call the Manhattan police."

"Happy to help. I'm very sorry about this. I hope she turns up soon. Please let me know if there is anything else I can do."

"Will do. I appreciate your help."

McKenzie called the Manhattan Police Department and gave them all the information she had. They opened a case.

An hour later, her phone rang. She picked it up and recognized the 212 area code as being from Manhattan. "Mrs. Trotman?"

"Yes."

"This is Detective McMurray from the New York City Police Department."

"Hello, Detective."

"Any word from your sister?"

"Not yet."

"We've followed up on the leads you provided. We don't have any further news at this time."

"Oh. What else can be done?"

"We'll do our best to find her, Mrs. Trotman. For your information, most missing persons turn up in one to two days."

McKenzie sighed. "That's encouraging, but let's say she doesn't turn up in a couple of days. What might have happened?"

"I don't know for sure. I'd hate to speculate and worry you."

"Enlighten me as to the possibilities."

"One possibility is kidnapping."

"For what purpose?"

"They might want a ransom. Is anyone in your family particularly wealthy?"

"No."

"It says here that she's a model. Is she particularly beautiful or famous?"

"Beautiful, but not famous."

"Well, I hate to say this, but it could be sex trafficking. There's a ring in the New York City area we're trying to crack."

"Sex trafficking?" McKenzie burst into tears. "That's horrible."

"Look, we don't know. We're moving as fast as we can to find her."

"Yeah, but you probably have a hundred other cases you're working on."

"Two hundred."

"If it is sex trafficking, where do you think they'd keep her?"

"In the city for a while, until things settle down, then they'd probably ship her off to another country where she doesn't know the language and can't escape."

"So, we need to move quickly."

"Yes."

"Thank you very much, Detective. You've been very helpful. I pray you'll find her soon."

"Amen."

Chapter 21
Call in the Marines

MCKENZIE TOLD HER parents about Monica's disappearance a day later. They freaked out, as was to be expected. She left out the kidnapping and sex trafficking possibilities shared by the detective.

Her next call was to her brother, a marine stationed in Twentynine Palms, California.

"Duncan?"

"Hey, McKenzie. How-ah-yah?"

"Not good. I'm afraid I have some bad news."

"What happened?"

"Monica's missing."

"What?"

"She was in New York City, doing some modeling."

"Modeling?"

"Yeah, she went to some photoshoots. She was supposed to be back two nights ago but hasn't shown up yet and hasn't texted or called."

"Did you call the police?"

"Yes, they started an investigation and said they'd do their best to find her."

"I'll fly home tonight."

"Why? The police are on it."

"They're overworked, underpaid, and underappreciated, especially in a big city like New York. I'll do my own investigation. Send me the details. I'll get emergency leave and be there in the morning."

"Wow! Great, Duncan. Thanks. See you then."

❧

McKenzie woke up at 7:00 a.m. the next day and checked her phone. There was a text from her brother. He said to meet him at the airport at 7:50 a.m. She needed to hurry.

It took her about twenty-five minutes to get there, but McKenzie arrived on time at the Bradley International Airport in Windsor, Connecticut.

She hugged her brother and started to cry.

"Don't worry, McKenzie. We'll find her."

A man approached and stood next to Duncan. He was tall, very tan with brown hair, and chiseled like a Mack truck.

"This is my buddy, Jarek. He volunteered to help."

She shook his hand. "That's so nice of you, Jarek. Good to meet you."

Duncan and Jarek stowed their marine backpacks in the trunk of her car. Duncan sat in the front passenger's seat, while Jarek sat in the back.

She studied Duncan's face. "You must be exhausted."

"We are. We'll catch a few winks at your place, then head over to New York in a few hours. Do you have the details I asked for?"

"Yes." She handed all the paperwork and notes she had over to her brother.

After they arrived at the condo, Duncan slept in McKenzie's bed, while Jarek rested in Monica's. McKenzie ran out to the store and bought eggs, bacon, pancake mix, and syrup—everything her brother loved for breakfast. She staged the frying pan, mixing bowl, and utensils and waited for them to wake up.

Two hours later, she started the breakfast after she heard them rustling in their rooms.

Jarek said, "Yum! This is great. I haven't had a home-cooked meal in months. Thanks for doing this, McKenzie."

"It's the least I can do for you guys since you traveled across the country on such short notice."

Jarek hitched his thumb toward the hallway. "I noticed some weapons in the hallway cabinet. Are they yours?"

"They were my husband's. He was a marine, just like you guys. He was killed recently, protecting Monica."

Jarek frowned. "I heard. It must have been devastating. I'm so sorry for your loss."

She broke down and cried—the wound was still fresh. Duncan walked over and put his arms around her.

Jarek said, "I'm so sorry, McKenzie. I didn't mean to upset you."

"It's okay. Thanks."

Jarek leaned back. "Duncan told me your husband was a war hero: served two tours in Afghanistan, Silver Star, Bronze Star, and Purple Heart. Very impressive."

Duncan went toward the hallway and said over his shoulder, "We'll be taking the weapons with us."

McKenzie gasped. "What? Take the guns with us? Why?"

"We may have to deal with some pretty bad characters. We might need them."

"Oh. Let me get the key to the gun case."

She opened the door, and both men crowded around the case.

Jarek said, "An M1014 Benelli twelve-gauge combat shotgun, an M4 carbine, and an M1911 forty-five-caliber pistol. Sweet. Do you happen to have another pistol?"

She rummaged through the bottom of the case, retrieved a pistol in a leather holster, and handed it to Jarek.

"A Smith & Wesson Bodyguard .380 pistol in a wallet holster. It'll fit right in my front pocket. Perfect. Do you have any ammunition?"

McKenzie retrieved all the boxes she could find from the case drawer.

Duncan sighed. "It would be nice if we had some body armor."

"Sorry, I don't think we have any of that. Jackson's former best friend is a police officer. I could ask him, but I'd rather not get him involved."

"Agreed. I'll look on the internet and see if we can find a store around here that sells it. We'll also need some burner phones and money."

She raised her hand. "I can run to the bank right now. How much do you need?"

"Two thousand."

"No problem. I'll get another thousand to pay for your plane tickets while I'm there."

Duncan touched her shoulder. "You don't have to do that, McKenzie."

"Yes, I do, Duncan. Jackson left me pretty well-off, so it's not a problem."

"In that case, thank you, Jackson. Can I look through his closet? We'll need some long winter coats."

"Go for it."

Once they were ready, Duncan drove into the city with McKenzie and Jarek and made a stop at the modeling agency. By four o'clock that afternoon, the three of them were sitting in the car outside the Manhattan brownstone where Monica had last been seen.

Duncan glanced at his burner phone. "Okay, McKenzie. Your

appointment with the photographer starts in ten minutes. Send me a text with your new phone as a test."

McKenzie complied.

His burner phone vibrated. "Okay, good. Now, review the plan with me one more time."

"I'll go to the front door, ring the buzzer, and go inside. I'll text you once I'm ready to sit for the pictures. I'll text you again when I change into my swimsuit for more pictures. After that, I'll text you when I'm ready to leave. Then I'll walk toward the subway and take it to the Port Authority. Jarek will follow me on foot, while you follow in the car. I'll then get on the bus to Hartford, and you'll follow behind me, and meet me at the bus station in Hartford."

Duncan nodded. "Perfect. Be sure you stick to the plan precisely. If you don't, we're going to come after you with guns blazing. We don't know when something might happen."

"Got it. Okay, I'm off."

Duncan looked back at Jarek. "See that young guy leaning against the wall?"

"Yeah?"

"Why would he be doing that in the winter. It's cold out there. He took a good look at McKenzie while she was walking by, then he called someone."

"Who wouldn't take a good look at your sister? Oh, sorry. Been out in the desert for too long."

Duncan chuckled. "No problem." His cell phone buzzed. A text from McKenzie had come through. *I'm in. They seem nice.*

About a half hour later, another text came through. *Changing into my swimsuit.*

Jarek tapped Duncan on the shoulder and pointed. "Look."

Two men drove up in a black SUV. The young man who'd been leaning against the wall went over and talked to them. Duncan wrote down the license plate number.

Jarek shoved the front passenger's seat forward. "Maybe that guy's a lookout."

"Maybe."

The young man got into the car with them. They drove around the block and turned into the parking lot behind the building.

Duncan pounded the top of the dashboard with his right hand. "I don't like it, Jarek. It looks like something's about to go down. Grab your thirty-eight. You cover the front door. I'm going to cover the back."

"Got it."

Jarek got out of the car and jogged to the front of the building, while Duncan drove to the parking lot at the back of the building.

A minute later, Duncan called Jarek. "They're sitting in the parking lot, waiting."

"Something is definitely going down."

"Agreed."

Duncan watched as the three men got out of their car and walked toward the building's back door. He got out of his car and followed at a distance, then went inside.

A few minutes later, McKenzie sent a text. *Changing into street clothes.*

Duncan texted her right back and copied Jarek. *Heads up! Three men going in back door, heading up stairwell. Two are huge.*

McKenzie texted back. *Got it. On my way out.*

Duncan hung back until Jarek burst through the front door just as someone was walking out. Jarek ran down the hallway toward Duncan. Jarek withdrew his pistol, then glanced at Duncan as he opened the stairwell door. Three men were standing on the stairwell landing above them. Two of them were holding McKenzie by the arms.

Jarek shot the big guy who wasn't holding McKenzie in the head, killing him instantly. The second big guy took his hands off McKenzie to shoot back, forcing them both against the stairwell wall. Jarek groaned and held his chest. He'd been hit.

Duncan pushed past Jarek and fired two shots. The second big guy fell down the stairs hard… and dead.

The young man tried to run up the stairs, but McKenzie tackled him. Duncan sprinted up, grabbed him, and knocked him on the head with his pistol.

Duncan called out to Jarek. "Are you okay?"

"I'll be fine. Good thing I had the body armor. It hurts like hell, though."

"Let's go out the back into the car with junior here before the police arrive."

McKenzie, Duncan, and Jarek traveled to a desolate spot along the water beside the Con Edison facility in Brooklyn and waited for the young man in the back seat to wake up.

It was dark out when the man started moaning. Duncan leaned over the seat. "What's your name?"

The man glared at him before answering. "Ilya."

"See, no harm in a name. We're just going to talk about a few things." Duncan put his hand on McKenzie's. "I don't want you involved in this. Wait outside while we get some information from him, and let us know if anyone is coming."

"Will do." McKenzie took up a position about forty yards away.

Jarek had the man sit up straight with his hands handcuffed behind him. He was trembling.

Duncan looked him in the eye. This guy knew something, and he would confess… or else. "Here's how this is going to work. I'm going to ask you a question, and you're going to answer truthfully. If you don't, I'm going to put a bullet in your head and dump your body in Long Island Sound. Do you understand?"

The man nodded.

"My sister was taken three days ago from the building where

we shot your friends today." He showed him a picture. "Do you recognize her?"

The man's eyes lit up, but he said, "No."

"You're lying." Duncan clicked the .45 and placed it against the man's head. "Where did they take her?"

"I don't know, I swear."

Jarek got in the back seat with the man and choked him until he passed out.

A few minutes later, the man woke up with the back door open and his head hanging over the asphalt. Duncan had the gun pointed at his face. "Last chance."

Jarek jabbed the guy in his right thigh with a huge hunting knife he'd picked up while getting the body armor.

"Ilya screamed. Okay, okay. 145 Munster. They're in the basement."

Duncan typed the address into McKenzie's Garmin. "There is no 145 Munster. You're lying again."

Duncan fired the gun at Ilya's head, grazing his ear.

Ilya shouted something in Russian.

Jarek said, "This is useless. Let's just kill him."

"No, wait. I'll take you to them."

By this time, it was pitch-black outside. They followed the man's directions and soon approached a run-down building in Queens. The man pointed at it. "That's it, over there."

Duncan stopped the car and turned around. "Where are the entrances."

"There is one in the front and one in the back."

"Where are the girls."

"Go down the stairs, and they're in a large room separated by dividers."

"How many men are in there?"

"This time of night, probably five."

"Are they armed?"

"Yes."

"Is there anything else you'd like to tell me?"

"No."

"Are you sure?" Duncan handed his .45 to McKenzie, then spoke to Ilya. "If we don't come out of there with my sister in ten minutes, I'm going to have her blow your head clean off with this forty-five. Do you understand me?"

"Yeah."

Duncan nodded to Jarek.

Jarek knocked the man out with his elbow.

They went to the back of the vehicle, opened the trunk, and put on long winter coats. Jarek took the shotgun; Duncan took the M4 Carbine. They stuffed extra ammo into their pockets and headed toward the back of the building.

Duncan and Jarek reconnoitered the rear area of the building from a distance. There was one guard outside with an AK-47.

Sleet began falling. Perhaps the weather would conceal their approach.

Jarek handed his shotgun to Duncan and crabbed forward, holding his knife. He hid behind a nearby dumpster, waiting for the guard to turn his back to him. Duncan aimed at the guard with his M4, just in case.

Jarek pounced and quickly dispatched the guard and dragged him behind some nearby bushes.

Duncan jogged to Jarek and handed the shotgun back to him. They moved through the door together, then edged down the stairs quietly into the basement. Hopefully, they could avoid a fight.

They entered a large open room with about ten dividers on each side, set perpendicular to the door. There were curtains between each divider, running parallel to the center walkway.

Duncan walked down the middle of the room, with Jarek guarding his rear, and slowly pulled back each curtain to see if Monica was inside. He went down one end and found two women handcuffed to beds, but no Monica.

He worked his way back—still no Monica.

They continued up the opposite stairs, their guns still pointing forward, and peered into a room on the right. There was a single bed in there with a curtain drawn. He pulled the curtain to the side and looked in.

Monica! She lay on her side with her eyes closed, either sleeping or passed out from drugs. Rage flooded through him. If they'd hurt her, he'd kill every last one of them.

They heard men approaching. Duncan and Jarek both jumped behind the curtain with her. Duncan put his hand over her mouth. She woke up and tried to scream before her eyes focused on him. She quieted.

Duncan got his handcuff key out of his pocket and released her. He pulled her up off the bed and embraced her, then leaned back and put his index finger over his lips. She nodded.

Two men entered the room talking in another language, perhaps Russian. As they pulled back the curtain, Jarek blasted each of them across the room with his shotgun.

Duncan took Monica by the hand. "Let's get out of here."

She could barely walk. She looked drugged out and had big circles under her eyes.

Duncan heard the front door open and pointed for Jarek to position himself with line of sight to the front stairs. A man came bounding down with an AK-47, right into the kill zone. The force of Jarek's shotgun blast walloped the man off his feet and onto his back, dead.

Duncan listened for any additional movement, then whispered to Jarek. "We got four of them. There might be one more."

"Right."

Jarek reloaded and looked up the stairs.

Duncan had to make a decision. Should they go out the way they came, passing through the hallway with all the curtains, or should they go right up the stairs and out the front door? What if that guy out in the car woke up? Would McKenzie have the guts to shoot him? At least he was handcuffed. They'd go out the back—less lighting, better exit.

They went down the center of the hallway again, guns at the ready, with Monica in tow. They made it through the basement, then up the stairs. Jarek went outside first and looked around. Duncan followed him out with Monica.

They heard a click from behind the dumpster. Duncan sprayed it with his M4. There was a moan and crash behind it. "Number five."

Duncan, Jarek, and Monica made it back to the car where McKenzie still held her .45 pointing at the man in the back seat, who was still unconscious.

McKenzie set her gun on the front passenger's seat and threw her arms around Monica. "You're alive."

Monica burst into tears. "Barely."

Jarek pulled the man out of the back seat. There was a lot of blood on his leg. Jarek dragged him over to a vacant lot and dumped him at the far end.

Jarek returned, and Duncan asked him. "Did you kill him?"

"No. He'll probably die of that leg wound anyway."

Duncan nodded. "You should have killed him. Okay, let's get out of here."

McKenzie helped Monica into the back seat. Jarek got in the front passenger's seat, and Duncan began to drive away.

Monica shouted. "Wait! What about the other girls in there?"

Duncan turned to Jarek. "I could call the police on this burner phone, but they might trace it back to Connecticut. Any ideas?"

McKenzie chimed in. "What about pulling the fire alarm."

Jarek spoke up. "I think I saw one near the front door. I'll run in and pull it."

"Jarek! Do you want me to go with you?"

"No, I'll take the thirty-eight, just in case."

"Be careful."

A minute later, Jarek was back in the car. The fire alarm blared in the background. Duncan quickly pulled away from the curb. Every time he looked in the mirror at the back seat, McKenzie was holding Monica in her arms.

Early in the morning, Matvey drove toward the vacant building to check on his business. He quickly turned around when he saw all the police cars and bright yellow police tape surrounding it.

Somebody had discovered his holding area. All the girls would be gone. This would cost him thousands. Not to mention cause him shame with his bosses. Fortunately, each building was isolated, so nothing would lead back to him.

He would find out who did this… and make them pay.

He received a text. *Boss—Ilya is in the hospital.*

Matvey responded. *Send me the address and room number.*

Chapter 22

INVASION

THE FOLLOWING MORNING, Jarek cleaned the shotgun in the living room, while McKenzie was making another hearty breakfast. Monica was still sleeping in her room. They had all taken showers the night before and had put their clothes in the washing machine so McKenzie could wash them right away.

Jarek called out. "McKenzie, do you have the key to the gun case? I'm done cleaning the weapons, and I'd like to lock it."

She responded from the kitchen. "It's in one of the drawers in my bedroom. I'll look for it later."

Duncan came in through the front door.

"Where were you?" McKenzie asked.

"I tossed the M4 in the Connecticut River so no one could trace it back to us. Then I went to the auto parts store and got some upholstery cleaner. After that I went to the car wash and made sure your car was spotless inside and out."

She walked toward her brother. "I feel like a criminal. Maybe we should have called the police as soon as we got to that vacant building, rather than going in there ourselves."

Duncan raised his voice. "There wasn't time. She might have been moved or even out of the country by the time they arrived. Also, the men there might have resisted. Some of the women or police officers might have been injured or killed before SWAT arrived. Why don't you ask Monica how she feels about it? I bet she's glad to be alive and out of that hellhole. Look, McKenzie, this is war. Those were some evil people we got rid of. The world is better off without them."

Monica shuffled into the living room, still in her pajamas and wearing fluffy purple slippers. "I couldn't agree more." She walked over to Duncan and hugged him, then turned and looked at them all. "Thank you so much for what you did for me last night. I can never repay you."

Duncan nodded. "You're welcome, Monica." Then he glared at McKenzie.

McKenzie shook her head and sighed. "What's done is done. What should I do about the police investigation that's still open?"

Duncan quipped, "Tell them Monica decided to go to Las Vegas for the weekend with a rich guy, and she never thought to call you."

"That would be lying."

"Don't get Holy Roller with me, McKenzie. We did what we had to do. Think up something else to tell them."

But what could she say that wasn't lying? Duncan and Jarek didn't deserve to get into trouble for helping. She rehearsed various stories in her mind, but none of them seemed credible. There didn't seem to be a way out. *Please help, Lord.*

A half hour later, her mobile phone rang. It was a Manhattan number. *It must be the detective. Should I take the call? I don't have a story ready. If I don't pick up, the detective may suspect something.* Her head spun. *What should I say?… I can't think straight.*

She let the phone ring a few more times. Finally, she picked up.

"Mrs. Trotman, this is Detective McMurray from the New York Police Department."

Her chest tightened. "Hello, Detective. I meant to call you." *Tell the truth, carefully.*

"We had a major development in breaking up a local sex-trafficking ring and got a lead on your sister. We found a sheet of paper with pictures of her on one side and her contact information on the other. We recovered several girls and young women, but I'm sorry to say, your sister wasn't one of them."

"She's home now."

"What? Oh, that's great! How did you find her?"

"I picked her up in New York last night."

"Wow! Can I talk with her?"

"Sure." McKenzie put her phone on mute. "Monica! It's the detective." She lowered her voice as Monica came out of the bedroom. "He wants to talk to you. They have your comp card. They must have found it at the warehouse. I didn't tell him anything else, except that I picked you up in New York last night."

She took her phone off mute, put it on speaker, and handed it to Monica.

"This is Monica."

"Hello, this is Detective McMurray. How are you doing? Can you tell me what happened?"

"I'm doing okay, under the circumstances. Some men abducted me after a photoshoot and drugged me. I woke up handcuffed to a bed in some dingy warehouse. It was terrifying. Sometime later, as they were taking me to the bathroom, I heard shots. The guard left me, and I ran out the back door. I borrowed someone's phone and called McKenzie. She picked me up last night in New York."

"Do you know who they were?"

"No. They had an accent, though. I think they were Russian."

"Is there anything else you can tell me about them?"

"No. That's all I know."

"Well, thank you for your time, Monica. I'm glad you're okay. Please let your sister know I'll be closing the missing person case."

"Will do. Thank you for following up."

Monica hung up the phone and handed it back to McKenzie. "All set. Case closed."

"Thanks." It still didn't sit well with her, but at least it was over. She went back to cleaning the kitchen. Hopefully, the knot in her stomach would start to unravel now.

Duncan motioned to Jarek. "Let's go out and pick up some beer. We need to celebrate the safe return of my sister and the closing of the case."

Fifteen minutes later, McKenzie's phone rang again. It was her mother.

"Hi, Mom."

"Hi, sweetheart. Your father and I are downstairs. Can you let us in?"

"Really? Wow! What a surprise. I have a surprise for you too."

"What?"

"You'll find out when you come up. Be right there."

She walked over to Monica's room. "Mom and Dad are downstairs. I'm going to get them."

"Did you call them?"

"I called them first thing this morning to tell them you were okay."

"Okay. Let's not share any of the details."

"Right."

❧

Matvey sat in his car with Ilya and another man, Alexei. Matvey had Monica's address written in his notebook, which he'd gotten a few days earlier from her comp card. His notebook was vital to his business success. Even when taking girls from crowded New York, it paid to make sure they didn't all come from the same area. Too much police attention in that case. But it turned out this girl was from Connecticut.

The men watched the entrance to Monica's condo from the first floor of the parking garage next door. An attractive young woman, who bore a resemblance to Monica, opened the door for an older couple. They hugged as if they might be related and then disappeared inside.

Ilya pointed, then spoke in Russian. "That's her. That's Monica's sister. She's the one who set me up."

Matvey smiled. "Good."

He'd make her and the others pay for destroying his business. He'd dispose of Ilya after they were done here. Couldn't have a traitor working for him.

A moment later, a car drove up the ramp behind them toward the second floor and parked. Ilya watched the men as they got out. "Those are the two men who helped her."

Matvey watched in his rearview mirror as they walked by. "Let's go."

The three Russians followed the two men to the condo entrance, then Alexi pulled out his gun and pushed it into one man's back. "Open the door."

Matvey said, "Take us to Monica's place. We want to have a conversation with all of you."

❧

McKenzie walked into the condo with her mother and father. "Look who's here."

Monica stood up from the couch.

Mom screamed. "Monica! How are you?"

Monica ran to their mother, crying. "I've been through a lot, Mom, but I'll be okay."

Monica then hugged their father.

Dad asked, "What happened?"

Monica gave their parents the same story she gave the police.

Dad held her close. "I'm so sorry for what you went through. Do you know who did this to you?"

"A Russian sex trafficking ring."

Anger burned on her father's face. "If I ever get my hands on them, I'll kill them."

Mom put a calming hand on Dad's shoulder, then asked, "Can we use your bathroom, McKenzie? It was a long trip from Marblehead."

"Of course." She gestured to the bathroom off the living room. "Dad, you can use the bathroom in the master bedroom if you don't want to wait."

As Dad disappeared down the hallway, the front door swung open. Duncan and Jarek walked in with their hands up, followed by three men. Two of the men pointed their pistols at McKenzie. A cold chill shot up her spine.

"Who are you? What's this about?" Then, she recognized Ilya. If only Jarek had killed him.

Monica pointed at the last man in line, gritting her teeth. "You! I remember you. They called you Matvey. You're a monster."

The other man waved at the group with his gun and spoke in English with a thick Russian accent. "Everyone! Sit on couches!"

Matvey stared at Monica. "Is anyone else here?"

"No."

They heard a toilet flush. A moment later, Mom opened the bathroom door and walked toward the living room. Her jaw dropped when she saw them, then she screamed.

The unidentified man pointed the gun at her. "Get over here and sit down!"

Mom hesitated.

"Now!"

She moved quickly over to the couch and sat down.

Matvey glared at Mom as he spoke in accented English. "Where is your husband?"

"He went to put a box in the storage cage downstairs."

"Alexei, watch the front door." Matvey turned to the group. "You destroy my business and kill my men. We only ones left. I work very hard for many years to build business. Now I start all over. I will take Monica back with me. She my property." He glanced at McKenzie. "I take her too." Duncan shifted on the couch, causing Matvey to point the gun directly at him. "I want to know why you did this and who you work for."

McKenzie needed to let her father know what was happening, so she spoke in a loud voice. "You Russians have no business coming to our country and enslaving women in your perverted sex trafficking ring. If I had a gun, I'd blow your head off right now."

Matvey chuckled. "Brave words for woman with no weapon."

She huffed. "How would you like it if your sister was captured and taken to work in a brothel?" *Lord, we really need your help right now.* "We didn't set out to destroy your business. We set out to get our sister back."

Matvey grabbed Mom and drilled Duncan with a glare. "Who are you working for?"

McKenzie answered, "We're not working for anyone."

"Shut up! My men very skilled. How you able to subdue them?"

Duncan said, "We are very skilled too."

"Where did you get these skills."

Silence.

Matvey pointed his gun at Mom's head. "Where?"

Duncan said, "The United States Marine Corps."

"Oh, so you're a marine. I think you will be the first to die."

Dad came out of the hallway with the shotgun pointed at Matvey. "No, you die first."

He pulled the trigger and the blasts caught Matvey square in the chest, sending him flying across the room.

Alexei fired back, striking Dad in the shoulder, causing him to fall backward onto the hallway floor. Duncan and Jarek pounced on Alexei and tried to wrestle the gun from him, but he was a big man.

McKenzie and Ilya dove toward Matvey's lifeless body to get his gun. They both got their hands on it simultaneously, but Ilya was stronger. He moved the gun toward her head. McKenzie remembered his stab wound and kneed him in the right thigh. Ilya buckled. McKenzie turned the gun toward him, and it went off, striking him in the head, killing him instantly.

Alexei was winning the battle with Duncan and Jarek and was about to wrestle the gun from them. McKenzie got right up behind Alexei and put her gun to the back of his head. "Don't move."

He started to spin around. She pulled the trigger. Blood and brains flew back at her. She jumped back as Alexei fell to the floor.

McKenzie examined the three assailants. None of them were moving. "Duncan, check to see if they're all dead."

She ran to her dad in the hallway. He was lying on his back. Blood covered the floor beneath him.

McKenzie cradled her dad's head on her lap, just as she had with Jackson when he lay dying a month earlier. Weeping uncontrollably, she cried, "Dad, Dad, are you okay?"

"Yes, McKenzie. I'll be fine."

Behind her, she heard Duncan on the phone, speaking to the 911 operator. "I was so scared. I thought for sure we were going to die. God was with us, but you were amazing. How'd you do it?"

Dad grimaced. "I heard your speech. Good thing the gun case was unlocked. To keep silent, I loaded the gun in the bathroom. Apparently, I got back just in time."

"Yes, you did, Dad. Thank you so much for protecting us."

"You're welcome. Why was the gun case unlocked?"

Because she hadn't had a chance to look for the key yet. "You can thank God for that."

CHAPTER 23
MIRACLE NEEDED

AFTER THE SHOOTOUT in the apartment and a thorough professional cleaning, McKenzie's life returned to its normal routine. In a blink, five months had passed, and she was definitely showing now. It was such a miracle that a human being was growing inside of her. Jackson must be so proud, looking down from heaven on the two of them.

She was extremely meticulous about her health: taking long walks in the summer sun, getting regular checkups, eating only organic foods, and taking her prenatal vitamins daily. She couldn't wait until her baby was born. Still, something was gnawing at her, a feeling that perhaps there was something else she should be doing besides being a mother. Maybe God was speaking to her.

She'd taken care of Monica for a while, but now Monica was back working at a local Starbucks, trying to figure out what to do next. Apparently, the trauma of the whole modeling and sex trafficking tragedy was still plaguing her. From time to time, in the early morning hours, her sister would cry out from her nightmares. Perhaps she should get some help.

McKenzie received an email notification that a FedEx package had been delivered. She went downstairs and picked it up.

The return address indicated it was sent from Aetna. She retrieved a knife from the kitchen and opened the box. Inside was the plaque that had been in Jackson's cubicle. It was a quote from *The Princess Diaries* movie: "The brave do not live forever, but the cautious do not live at all." She smiled as she remembered seeing it for the first time. It was the day she'd brought Jackson's oatmeal to his cubicle while he was still on crutches.

What took them so long to send this?

She spent the rest of the day surrounding herself with his work things. Despite the wait, having these little pieces of Jackson was a treasure.

McKenzie was awakened the next morning by abdominal pain. She tried to ignore it; perhaps it was just part of the gestation process. She went into the bathroom to shower and noticed spotting on her underwear.

She called her gynecologist's office right away. They made an appointment for her later that morning. She texted Sally and asked Sally to go with her. She didn't want to bother Monica at work.

McKenzie's phone beeped. It was a text from Sally. *I'll call my mother to come over to watch the twins. Be there soon.*

Thirty minutes later, McKenzie received another text from Sally. *Here.*

She gathered her things, took the elevator to the first floor, then tearfully wrapped her arms around her good friend. "I'm so scared. I don't know what I'd do if I lost the baby."

"I've been praying ever since I got your text."

"Thank you so much, Sally. That really means a lot. Prayer is so powerful."

Sally stepped back and held McKenzie's hands in hers. "Just remember, you are God's masterpiece. He loves you, and he loves your baby. He will work out everything for your good. He has great plans for you, plans he made before the creation of the world."

McKenzie wiped away her tears with the sleeve of her blouse. "Okay, let's go."

McKenzie and Sally sat together in the doctor's waiting room. Sally squeezed McKenzie's hand when her name was called.

A nurse's aide escorted McKenzie into the gynecologist's examination room. The aide asked her to change into a lavender gown, then took her vital signs. The doctor arrived a few moments later.

McKenzie reached out her hand. "Hello, Dr. Gillespie."

The doctor wore a white coat over her emerald scrubs. "Hello, Mrs. Trotman. What seems to be the problem?"

"I've been having abdominal pain, and I found spots in my underwear this morning. I called your office as soon as I noticed it. Thanks for squeezing me in today."

"I'm glad you called. Let's take a look. I'm going to perform a pelvic exam, followed by an ultrasound."

"Okay."

After the physical exam, the doctor applied the gel and maneuvered the transducer. Halfway up her belly, the doctor reflexively gasped.

Not good. McKenzie leaned forward. "What is it?"

The doctor maneuvered the transducer again several times. "This is very strange, highly unusual." She shook her head and sighed. "I'm afraid I have bad news."

"What?"

Dr. Gillespie sat upright on her stool and looked McKenzie in the eye. "You appear to have an abdominal ectopic pregnancy."

"What does that mean?"

"It's extremely rare. It means the fetus is developing in your abdomen instead of in your uterus."

"What? How can that be?"

"The embryo descended from the fallopian tube and attached to the omentum instead of the uterus."

"What's the omentum?"

"Fatty tissue that covers the stomach and other organs."

"What can be done about it?"

"Your best option is to terminate your pregnancy."

McKenzie cried out, "What? Never!"

The doctor removed her blue examination gloves and looked sternly at McKenzie. "Then there's a good chance you'll die."

McKenzie sat up and glared right back at her. "So be it. Just so you understand, I got pregnant on my wedding night. My husband was killed the following morning. This is my only chance to have his baby. It's all I have left of him. Do you understand me? I must have this baby. Aren't there any other options?"

The doctor sighed. "Termination of the pregnancy is your best option, but it's not your only option. First, I want you to know I understand how important this is to you, but you need to understand just how risky the other option is."

"Okay. Tell me."

"Your baby is right at eighteen weeks. It's not viable outside the womb yet, or in your case, the abdomen. There have been a few cases where surgery was performed, after which the mother and baby survived, but as I said, it's rarely performed and very risky. A large team of specialists would have to be assembled to assist in the procedure. The longer we can keep the baby inside of you, even if it's in your abdomen, the better the baby's chances are of surviving. Another complication is that since the fetus is developing in your abdomen, the placenta will not be delivered during birth. We'd either need to let the placenta be absorbed naturally by your body or remove it surgically. You'll likely lose a lot of blood during surgery and require multiple pints to replenish your body."

McKenzie gulped. "Why wasn't this identified sooner?"

The doctor crossed her arms over her chest. "It wasn't apparent until the baby was more fully grown."

Translation: she missed it. McKenzie frowned and shook her head. "How much time do I have to make a decision?"

"It's hard to say. Ectopic pregnancies normally occur in the fallopian tubes. Only one in sixty pregnancies is ectopic, and of those, only one percent is abdominal. I recommend you get this taken care of right away. How do you feel right now?"

"Better. I'm not having as much stomach pain as I did earlier today. It must be because my friend Sally has been praying for me out in the waiting room."

The doctor snickered. "Let's try monitoring this for a while. Call me right away if you have any more abdominal pain."

McKenzie got off the examination table. "No offense, Doctor, but I'd like to get a second opinion. This is way too important for me to make a snap decision right now. I'd like the OB/GYN staff at St. Francis Hospital to weigh in if you don't mind." *I doubt their first reaction would be to perform an abortion.*

"No offense taken. Let's get you scheduled for an appointment at the hospital right away."

This situation was dire. She couldn't go it alone. She needed God to help her through this. She had to get away to somewhere peaceful so she could pray. "Can I run home to get a few things?"

"I wouldn't recommend it. I'd rather have you checked out at the hospital right away."

"Please have your office call me as soon as the appointment is made. I promise I'll go once they call."

The doctor shook her head. "It's your life."

"Yes. It's my baby's life too!"

McKenzie burst into tears as soon as she locked eyes with Sally, then collapsed into her arms. The other people in the waiting room were probably staring but so what.

She explained everything to Sally in the car a few minutes later.

"Don't you worry, McKenzie. We're going to get the whole church praying for you."

"Thanks. I think we're going to need a miracle."

After being dropped off at the condo, McKenzie packed a bag, then got Monica, who had arrived home from work, to drive her to the cemetery. McKenzie shared the difficult news with her on the way.

As McKenzie stepped out of the car, her phone pinged with a voicemail from the doctor's office. She ignored it… for now.

McKenzie walked toward Jackson's grave with Monica following behind. It was a cloudy June afternoon of about seventy degrees Fahrenheit. Twigs on the ground scrunched as she knelt before Jackson's headstone and raised both hands. "Father in heaven, you answered my prayers to spare Monica's life. Please answer them again. I need your help right now. Nothing is too hard for you, Father. Please save my baby. Don't let my baby die."

Tears dribbled down her face.

Monica moved toward McKenzie, then placed a hand on her shoulder.

McKenzie continued, "This is all I have left of Jackson, Father. Please have mercy on my baby and me. Don't let my baby die! Please! Save my baby. In Jesus's name, I pray, amen."

Jackson stood by, invisibly, weeping with McKenzie as she prayed. After she got up to leave, he returned to the throne room of God and threw himself prostrate on the floor. As he was about to pray, he heard Jesus speaking to the Father on behalf of McKenzie and their baby. Jesus, the Holy One of God, our only Savior, was interceding for them. How wonderful is our God! How magnificent He is! He loves us so much. "Thank you, Lord Jesus. Thank you, Father. Thank you, Holy Spirit. Thanks for all you've done and all you continue to do on our behalf each day."

⤪

McKenzie listened to the voicemail from Dr. Gillespie's office as they walked back to the car. They'd made an appointment for her at the hospital, but it was in thirty minutes. Monica had to drive fast to get them there on time.

McKenzie arrived at the St. Francis OB/GYN department. She was escorted into an examination room, then instructed to put on a gown and sit on the examination table.

A team of obstetricians entered the room. "Mrs. Trotman, I'm Dr. Sanford, Chair of the Department of Obstetrics and Gynecology at St. Francis Hospital. Per your request for a second opinion, provided to us through Dr. Gillespie, my team and I plan to thoroughly examine you to determine if there is anything unusual about your pregnancy."

About ten minutes later, Dr. Sanford spoke directly to McKenzie with the other doctors standing by. "Mrs. Trotman, we agree with Dr. Gillespie's diagnosis—you have an abdominal ectopic pregnancy. Since you're not in any immediate pain and the bleeding has stopped, we're going to send you home. I strongly caution you to refrain from any heavy lifting or anything strenuous. We'd like to wait until your baby is at least at thirty weeks before performing the surgery. This will ensure the baby's lungs are fully developed before delivery.

"This operation will be very complex and require involvement from various teams of health professionals. We'll start planning the operation tomorrow in case the situation changes and we need to retrieve your baby sooner."

"Then there's a chance you can save my baby?"

"Absolutely."

McKenzie choked up. "Praise, God. Thank you so much, Doctor."

Thank you, Father.

The doctor handed her a business card. "You're welcome, Mrs. Trotman. Call us right away if you experience any more abdominal pain."

"Will do. Thanks again."

Chapter 24
Unexpected Journey

THREE MONTHS LATER, McKenzie lay on a hospital bed, having her stomach shaved in preparation for the abdominal ectopic surgery. The anesthesiologist arrived with a resident and informed her of what they'd be doing. First, they'd give her a sedative, followed by a general anesthetic once she was in the operating room. Then, they left, saying they'd be back in a few minutes.

Monica stood by her side. Her mother, father, Jackson's father, and Sally were in the waiting room.

McKenzie bit her lower lip. "The doctor said there's a chance I won't make it through the surgery."

Monica teared up.

McKenzie reached for her hand. "I want you to know that I love you very much. Please tell Mom, Dad, Duncan, and Sally that I love them too."

"I will."

"Everyone's been so wonderful to me after Jackson's death. I want you to know that I'm not worried if I don't make it because I'll go straight to heaven and be with Jesus forever. Promise me you'll think about giving your life to Jesus one day too."

Monica paused for a moment. "I promise."

"I know we haven't talked about this, but I want you to take care of the baby if something happens to me."

Monica's tears broke free, and she gripped McKenzie's hand tightly. "It would be my honor."

"Mom and Dad can help too."

"Of course. Let's not talk anymore about dying. You're going to be fine, and you're going to have a beautiful, healthy baby."

A nurse helped McKenzie onto the gurney. The anesthesiology resident arrived and explained she'd be injecting the sedative now. She watched as the resident injected the sedative in her catheter.

An instant later, McKenzie rubbed her eyes, disoriented. Where was she? White pockmarked tiles were right in front of her face. She peered closer. Those were ceiling tiles. How could she be on the ceiling? She shifted and flipped over. She gasped… she was hovering in the air above the operating room. A pregnant woman lay on the table with her stomach slit open, but something was wrong. The doctors and nurses were scurrying around, working frantically.

The voice of her surgeon, Dr. Sanford, drew her attention. Wait… the pregnant woman was her. What was happening? How could she be hovering in the air like this? *Jackson said the same thing happened to him when he was injured. Maybe I'm having an out-of-body experience… or maybe I'm dead.*

She cried out, "Jesus, what's happening? Oh, God, please save me and save my baby. Help me, Lord Jesus. Please help me! Save me!"

A huge personage suddenly appeared right beside her in the air. She screamed. The being was about seven feet tall and wore an impossibly bright white robe with a golden sash. It must be an angel. Jackson had said an angel appeared to him after he'd been struck by the hit-and-run driver.

The being reached out and touched her shoulder. "Do not be

afraid, McKenzie Trotman. I am Mekoddishkem, the angel who appeared to your husband last year."

"An angel. Wow!" She looked into his eyes. They were glowing. "Why am I here? Why is this happening to me? What's going to happen to my baby?"

"Do you remember your husband mentioning The Wall?"

"Yes."

"I'm going to take you there and show you important things."

Her emotions exploded in a kaleidoscope of terror and excitement. But no fear could keep her from learning and experiencing all that the angel had in mind.

Mekoddishkem motioned to her. "Touch my robe."

She did, and they were transported up through the ceiling, then through various rooms in the floors above them, and finally up into the sky. They kept going up through the atmosphere and into outer space, whizzing at incredible speed past planets, asteroids, and stars.

A bright light appeared, and they entered through a fold in space. Mekoddishkem opened a white door with a golden handle. They walked through it onto a gray landing. McKenzie looked about fifty yards to her left at a massive white translucent structure with circles on it, like portholes on the side of a ship. As they walked closer, she noticed each circle had a golden rim around it.

"Is this The Wall, Mekoddishkem?"

"Yes."

"Each portal provides access into the past, present, or future of anyone who was ever conceived?"

"That is correct."

They were now standing right next to The Wall. "What do we do now?"

"First, I must show you how things stand now. Ask to be taken into your portal in the present."

"Okay." She faced The Wall. "Take me into my portal in the present."

Portals zipped by from left to right at incredible speed. Then The Wall shifted rapidly upward. Finally, it stopped with a particular portal directly facing her. McKenzie and Mekoddishkem were whisked inside.

They were back at the hospital room, hovering over her body again. Machine alarms blared as the doctors worked on her and shouted instructions.

Suddenly, hundreds of beings appeared. They were sword fighting. Half wore bright, shining robes like Mekoddishkem, while the other half wore dark, tattered clothing. The latter group had long greasy hair, oversized yellow teeth, and disfigured faces that were reptilian in texture.

"Who are they, and why are they fighting?" she asked.

"They are fighting over your baby, McKenzie. The angels want him to live, while the demons want him to die."

"It's a boy?"

"Yes."

Jackson would be so happy. "That's wonderful, Mekoddishkem, but why would demons want to kill my baby?"

"They believe God has a very important purpose for your child."

"What is that purpose?"

"That is not for you to know at this time, McKenzie. It is enough for you to know that he has an important role to play in God's plan for humanity."

"What should I do?"

"Teach him God's ways. Read the Bible with him. Disciple him. Pray for him continually, as he will be prone to wander."

"I am the Lord's servant."

Mekoddishkem smiled.

"McKenzie!" The voice came from behind her, striking a familiar chord, but it was out of context. Could it be? She turned around. "Jackson? Is it really you? I can't believe it. It is you."

Jackson was wearing a bright, shiny robe, just like Mekoddishkem. He ran to her and hugged her. She fit into his arms perfectly, just like always. They both wept loudly.

"It's so good to see you."

"It's wonderful to see you too, Jackson."

Mekoddishkem interrupted, "We must go. The time is short."

She protested, "Why? Haven't I died? I don't want to go back. I want to stay here with my husband."

Jackson held her hand. "I know you want to stay, but you must go. God has important plans for our son. You must raise him well and teach him to follow Jesus. Don't worry. God's angels will be watching over you and our son. I'll be looking in on you from time to time too. We'll see each other again soon. Until then, I will miss you very much. I love you, McKenzie." His earnest face took a downturn. "Oh, and Monica is in great danger. Pray for her. Reach out to Pam too."

Mekoddishkem and McKenzie exited her portal and returned to The Wall. She fell to her knees, weeping. "I don't want to go back. Please let me stay. I want to be here with Jackson."

"I understand, but it can't be done." Mekoddishkem said nothing more and waited for her.

She finally calmed down but couldn't stop thinking about Jackson.

"I understand this is very difficult for you, but we need to move quickly. I have more to show you. Ask The Wall to take you into your future."

"Wait a minute. I'm sorry, but I can't just compartmentalize like that. I'm not like Jackson. I need time to process all this and talk it out."

Mekoddishkem stood before her, silently.

Either he wasn't willing to give her the chance to spew her emotions, or he would stand their impassively while she did. Neither option satisfied her. She sighed. *Well, I can't stay here forever.* "Fine. God only knows what you're going to show me next. Take me into the future in my portal."

They were instantly transported to a dirt road that traversed the middle of a cornfield. The stalks were about eight feet high. Twenty feet down the road, a man stood beside a boy, who was sitting in a wheelchair. The man had his hand on the boy's shoulder. They were looking away, so she couldn't see their faces.

Meanwhile, about forty demons stepped out from either side of the cornfield onto the road. They drew their swords menacingly as they invisibly approached the man and the boy. Angels instantly appeared and stood between the pair and the demons.

"Mekoddishkem, I've seen this scene before in a dream. What does it mean?"

"It will be revealed to you at the proper time. Keep praying for your son. As I said, he will be prone to wander."

"Will do. Mekoddishkem, I had another dream. This one was about Monica. I saw her in hell while I was standing beside Jesus."

"Ask to be taken to your sister's portal in the future."

McKenzie and Mekoddishkem returned to The Wall. She faced it and said, "Take me to Monica Baker's portal in the future."

They were taken to a cave. A light emanated from the end of a dark, narrow passageway that was carved into the rock. They walked down it and turned into the lit room. A woman lay on a bed inside. She was crying. One of her hands was chained to the iron headboard. McKenzie looked at the woman more closely. It was Monica.

"This is horrible. Poor Monica."

An enormous demon entered the room. Mekoddishkem pointed at him. "This is Lord Agliarept. He's the demon king who oversees the New England portion of the United States."

"Really. I didn't realize there was such an office, but it makes sense because the Bible talks about rulers and principalities in the heavenly realms."

"Agliarept plans to have Monica killed soon so he can make her his queen. She'll be on a chain at first, but she will eventually become so evil that a chain will no longer be needed. Then, at the end of her days, she will be cast into the lake of fire to suffer forever with the demons and any other person whose name is not written in the Book of Life."

Her poor sister. What a horrible fate. McKenzie placed both hands on Mekoddishkem's arm. "What can be done to stop this?"

"You must lead her to Christ. You have two months."

McKenzie woke to find herself lying in a hospital bed.

Dr. Sanford spoke to her, even though she hadn't opened her eyes yet. "The anesthesia should have worn off by now. How are you feeling, Mrs. Trotman?"

McKenzie opened her eyes. "A little groggy, Doctor. How are you?"

The surgeon smiled. "Fine, but you're the one who just had surgery, not me. I'm happy to report you have a healthy baby."

She shrieked. "Oh, praise God! Thank you so much, Doctor."

"You're welcome."

"How did the operation go? It looked like you lost me a few times."

Dr. Sanford's jaw dropped. "What do you mean?"

"I saw you and the rest of the team scurrying around trying to save me."

"That is true, but I don't know how you could have known that."

"I had an out-of-body experience. I was hovering above the operating room and saw the whole... Oh, I guess this must sound pretty weird."

"It certainly does. Are you're okay? It sounds like you were hallucinating."

"Did you lose me a few times or not?"

"Yes."

"How could I possibly have known about that if I didn't actually see it for myself?"

"You couldn't have."

"Correct. You don't have to believe me, Doctor. It's your choice. I just want you to know there's a spirit world beyond our own. Everyone will one day die and become a part of it. When you die, you go to one of two places—heaven or hell. I urge you, in the strongest possible terms, to be reconciled to God through his Son, Jesus Christ."

Dr. Sanford folded his arms. "Thank you for sharing that, Mrs. Trotman. Getting back to your question, you required eight pints of blood during the surgery, so you'll need to stay in the hospital until you're fully recovered. We decided to leave the placenta in your abdomen to avoid further blood loss. Your body will absorb it on its own over time. We'll need to monitor you regularly to ensure there are no complications."

"Understood. Can I see my son now?"

"I thought you didn't want to know the gender?"

"An angel told me I would have a boy and that he would be an important part of God's plan for humanity."

Dr. Sanford huffed. "I'll have your son brought in to you right away."

McKenzie breathed a sigh of relief. *Thank God everything worked out.*

A nurse appeared about five minutes later. "Mrs. Trotman, here is your son." She placed the newborn in McKenzie's arms. The baby was sleeping. She kissed him on the forehead, savoring this first moment.

Her parents and Jackson's father strolled into the room a short time later, followed by Monica and Sally. They were all smiling. But Mr. Trotman had tears in his eyes.

As they circled her bed, McKenzie glanced over at the door and paused for a moment, hoping against all hope that Jackson would suddenly appear and bound through the door to join them.

McKenzie said to her father-in-law, "I wish Jackson were here." She tried to fight back the tears, but couldn't, unleashing a torrent of emotion.

Mr. Trotman raced to her side. "I wish he were here too." His chest heaved. "And Elaine would have loved being a grandmother."

Mr. Trotman stepped back from her bed, wiped away his tears with his shirtsleeve, and straightened up. "Let's not think about that right now, McKenzie. This is a happy occasion. You have a wonderful, healthy baby boy, and I have a wonderful, healthy grandson."

Sally sauntered over to the hospital bed and clasped McKenzie's hands in her own. "I'm sure he's watching from heaven right now."

"I know that's true," McKenzie said.

"Congratulations. What's his name?"

"Jack." She gestured to her mother. "Mom, would you like to hold your grandson?"

Her mother grinned. "Of course." She reached out and took Jack in her arms.

"Would you mind taking him to the couch over there? I want to talk to Monica for a moment."

"Sure." Mom, Dad, and Mr. Trotman walked over with Jack to the sitting area.

McKenzie took Monica's hand in hers and spoke softly. "Monica, I didn't tell you this earlier, but I've been having dreams about you. I dreamed I was standing beside Jesus and saw you across a canyon. You were in hell, suffering in terrible agony. You were pleading with me to save you."

Monica teared up and placed her other hand over her mouth.

"While I was on the operating table, I died for a short time and had an out-of-body experience. I met an angel, the same angel Jackson told me about. He took me to The Wall, and I saw Jackson. He was fighting for you and said you were in great danger. I then traveled into your future and saw you crying and chained to a bed. You were serving as the new queen to a demonic lord. The angel said you'd one day be thrown into the lake of fire if you didn't change your ways and turn to Jesus for forgiveness. You're running out of time, Monica. You need to make a decision soon."

Monica frowned. She released McKenzie's hand and walked over to the couch. At McKenzie's questioning glance, she put up a hand as if saying she couldn't talk about it right now. Monica gave a small smile as she sat beside Mom and her new nephew.

Jackson stood nearby with Mekoddishkem. "I'm so happy for McKenzie. What a thrill it must be for her to hold our new baby. I wish I could hold him."

"You will, one day."

"What's going to happen to Monica?"

"That is up to her."

911

MONICA LEFT MCKENZIE at the hospital and returned to the condo. The kitchen was a mess. They'd been in such a hurry to get to the hospital after McKenzie's water had broken that there'd been no time to clean up. Monica loaded the dishwasher and cleaned off the counters with a damp cloth. Everything had to be neat and tidy when McKenzie arrived home with the baby the next day. What an exciting time this was. *Maybe it will be my turn someday.*

Monica traipsed through the living room. It was a mess too. Then she glanced into her bedroom. The whole condo needed to be cleaned up. Housekeeping wasn't her thing, but she'd do it anyway; if not for herself, then for McKenzie and her new nephew.

She entered McKenzie's room, looking for the vacuum. A FedEx box sat on the floor beside her nightstand. It had already been opened. The return address indicated it had been sent from Aetna. Something prompted her to peek inside. She probably shouldn't—after all, it was McKenzie's, not hers—but she did it anyway. There was a plaque and some other small items inside. A pamphlet fell to the floor. The title was "Steps to Peace with God." She read it. Now she understood, for the first time, that Jesus had given his life to pay for her sins. Jackson had given his life for her too. The "dream" about Jackson and the angels came to mind.

She dropped the pamphlet back in the box. She'd have time to ponder all this religious stuff later. Right now, she needed to get the condo ready for McKenzie and Jack.

The demon assigned to watch Monica smiled as he watched her guardian angel depart. "Master Botis will be very pleased."

He called for his master, who arrived within seconds.

Botis asked, "Why did her angel leave?"

"I don't know, master."

"Very well."

Botis approached Monica and touched her heart.

Monica organized the books and magazines on the oak coffee table in the living room. Then she folded the multicolored Afghan blanket, which had been knit by Jackson's grandmother, and laid it over the back of the burgundy leather couch. Afterward, she vacuumed the living room and the hallway to the bedrooms.

The next room to attack was her bathroom. She placed her hair straightener and hairdryer in the cupboard under the sink, then neatly stored her makeup accouterments in a plastic box in the medicine cabinet. There was hair all over the sink, bathtub, and floor, plus mildew in a few spots on the shower wall and curtain. She wiped everything down with a sponge, then got on her hands and knees with Clorox wipes to make sure all the germs and mildew were gone before the baby got home.

Monica suddenly felt light-headed. She sighed and settled onto her bed. She shouldn't be this tired, but McKenzie and little Jack would be coming home tomorrow, so she had to get the cleaning done today. It had to be done right; McKenzie would notice.

Monica got up and stripped the sheets off her bed, picked the dirty clothes off the floor and threw them into the hamper, then stuffed the rest of her things in the closet and drawers where they belonged. After making her bed and vacuuming her room, she dragged the upright over to the master bedroom.

McKenzie's room was already pretty neat, so there wasn't much left to straighten out. Monica stripped the sheets off the bed, started a laundry load, then returned, made the bed, and vacuumed.

The oak crib Mr. Trotman had purchased was already fully assembled and positioned by the window in McKenzie's room. The sheets and cushions around the crib's inside edges were embroidered with a Noah's ark theme. A white pajama onesie hung over the front railing.

A white wicker bassinet was set beside the bed, with a matching changing table against the wall near the walk-in closet.

After all this, Monica plopped down into the cranberry overstuffed sitting chair by McKenzie's bed. Why was she so tired? Cleaning was hard work, but she shouldn't be *this* tired.

Suddenly, A crushing pain squeezed her chest, like a vise tightening all around her. Pain pulsated in her left arm, and she began to sweat. Then she started getting even more tired. Her limbs dragged on her like heavy weights. She grabbed her phone, called 911, and gave her location. She fell to her knees, feeling delirious, then crawled to the front door and opened it. Everything went black.

Monica awoke on her back. Two demons were hovering over her. She cried out, "Oh, God! Help me, Jesus. Save me!"

One of the demons had his gnarly fingers on her forehead. Her spirit was being extracted from her body as if the hose from the vacuum cleaner was attached to her head. "Oh, God, not again."

The extraction was soon complete. She looked down at her lifeless body. The two demons edged over, and each clasped one of her arms tightly.

"Help me! Jesus, save me. Jackson, where are you?" *I should have listened to him. Oh, God, why didn't I listen to him… I didn't listen to Sally or McKenzie either. What am I going to do?*

The two demons abruptly released their grip and retreated down the hallway to her left. A sparkling white light appeared on her right. An angel stood before her with a drawn sword in his hand.

Monica fell to her knees and breathed a sigh of relief.

Suddenly, what must have been a hundred demons appeared. The angel thrashed back and forth at them with his blade, but the sheer numbers were too much. He couldn't have seen the first two demons sneaking behind him and grabbing her. She screamed as they pulled her upward and out of the condo complex. She thrashed back and forth, trying to extricate herself, but their grip on her arms was too tight.

Downtown Hartford appeared directly beneath them. They continued heading east. They cruised over Cape Cod in what seemed like seconds. It was like looking out the window of an airplane, watching the ground whiz by at incredible speed. Soon, they were out over the open Atlantic Ocean. The wind was so forceful her lips flapped.

A landmass appeared, albeit briefly; it must have been Spain or Portugal. They were over a sea again soon afterward, most likely the Mediterranean.

They hovered over a mountaintop somewhere in the desert, then descended into a cave opening. They glided to the back of the cave and proceeded through solid rock into a massive cavern with thousands of people standing in a line below. They were all naked. Beside them was a large hole in the cavern floor. Blistering heat and glowing red light emanated from it.

Another demon appeared, glared at her intently, then eyed her up and down. "Whoa! I can see why the master wants you."

She looked down, and her stomach clenched in embarrassment. She was naked too. Her two transporters released her. The new demon grabbed her by the arm. "I am Botis, sent by my master to retrieve you."

"Who is your master?"

The demon struck her in the face, sending her flying to the ground. "You will only speak when commanded to! Agliarept will teach you your place. Get up, slave."

She burst into tears. Botis grabbed her by the arm and dragged her into what must be Agliarept's chamber. He threw her to the floor before the throne.

Agliarept stood. "Botis, is that any way to treat my new queen?"

Monica froze. *Queen.* Exactly what McKenzie had told her. This demonic lord wanted her to be his queen.

Botis withdrew from her, bowed to his master, and edged backward away from them.

She trembled uncontrollably before Agliarept. He approached her. There was the look of desire in his eyes. He must be seven feet tall. His chest, thighs, and arms were all abnormally massive and muscular. Horns appeared from under each ear, curved upward, and met about six inches above his head.

Agliarept's jaw dropped as he gaped at her. "You're finally here and more beautiful than I imagined." He turned toward one of his attendants. "Quick! Give my new queen a robe."

A demon approached from the side and gave Monica a sparkling silver robe covered with jewels.

Agliarept motioned with his hand. "Come to me."

Her body trembled as she approached him and peered into his cold, dead eyes.

∾

Botis grumbled under his breath. Why should he do Agliarept's dirty work without reaping any of the benefits? Why couldn't he have a beautiful slave girl like Monica for his own? Would he remain under Agliarept's thumb forever?

Agliarept would be occupied for a while. This was his chance.

Botis rocketed to Satan's throne room.

Satan looked down from his throne. "Botis, where is your master?"

Botis knelt. "He is occupied, my lord."

"Occupied? Doing what?"

"He is with his new queen, Monica Baker... Jackson Trotman's sister-in-law. I killed her per your orders. I know how important it is that you be informed of any developments regarding the traitor Jackson, so I thought I would bring this to your attention immediately."

"Excellent, Botis. You shall be rewarded. It appears Agliarept's lust has overshadowed his duty to ensure the longevity of my kingdom."

Botis stood, then walked backward away from the throne with his head bowed.

Chapter 26

Rescue

Jackson was in Renoir's painting studio, busily drawing a vase of flowers. The voice of Jesus interrupted his reverie. *Is he calling me?* Jackson immediately put down his charcoal pencil and traveled to God's throne room, unsure of what to expect. Mekoddishkem was already there. Together, they stood before their King.

Jesus leaned forward. "Jackson, the demon Botis just killed Monica before her appointed time. This was done without my prior direction or approval. Mekoddishkem, take a legion of angels to hell and retrieve her. Then take his master, Agliarept, and put him in a cell in the Abyss where he will be held for judgment."

Mekoddishkem responded, "Yes, Lord."

Jackson and his guardian angel bowed, then stepped backward from God's throne.

He walked alongside Mekoddishkem as they left the throne room. "How many angels are in a legion?"

"About six thousand."

"Whoa!"

Jackson and his guardian angel approached a golden gate, about twenty feet high, embedded within a limestone wall. They walked

214

on golden cobblestones through the entranceway. Mekoddishkem nodded his head to the two guards. "I need to speak to the commander immediately. I have orders from the King."

One of the guards escorted them past various buildings, each expertly constructed with limestone façades and gold-framed windows. They entered a stadium-sized courtyard surrounded by more buildings. A flagpole stood in the middle. The flag was white with a red cross embossed on it. They proceeded over limestone cobblestones to the rear of the courtyard and entered the main building. They turned right and found at the end of the hallway a doorway with a red rectangular sign over it. The word *Aluf* was emblazoned in gold on it.

"Mekoddishkem, what does *Aluf* mean?"

"First leader of a group, like your commandant of the Marine Corps."

"Thank you."

Mekoddishkem guided Jackson to the legion commander's office. The commander stood as they entered. "Mekoddishkem!" His voice boomed. It reminded him of a marine colonel he served under in Afghanistan, a man Jackson would have followed anywhere. Of course, this angel had to be the commander.

Mekoddishkem relayed the orders they'd received from King Jesus. The commander had a subordinate blow a shofar. Thousands of angels immediately assembled in the courtyard and fell into formation. Jackson could only stare at them. The marines were a pretty tough lot, but they were nothing compared to this outfit.

The commander explained the mission to his unit. The legion of angels departed, flying in formation through the air like a flock of geese. Mekoddishkem and Jackson followed behind.

Demons guarding the entrance to hell were quickly dispatched by the onslaught of angels. An alarm was sounded. Huge numbers of demons appeared. A fierce battle erupted between the ancient forces of good and evil.

The commander peeled off from the fighting with about fifty angels. Jackson and Mekoddishkem followed them to Agliarept's chamber. They overpowered the demons guarding it, walked inside, and found Monica with one hand chained to an iron bed, wearing a robe. Agliarept's jaw dropped as he stood beside the bed. His countenance turned to anger once he recognized Mekoddishkem. Agliarept picked his sword up off the floor and lunged at the angel, swatting at him with fierce blows.

Jackson went over to the bed, took Monica's hand to stretch out the links, and shattered the chain with his sword. She threw her arms around him. "Oh, thank you, Jackson. Thank you for coming to rescue me from this monster. Let's get out of this hellhole now."

"Jesus orchestrated the whole thing, Monica. Thank him."

Monica glanced upward, raised her arms, and shouted, "Thank you, Lord Jesus!"

Jackson eyed the commander. "Let's get out of here!"

Suddenly, a powerful-looking creature came through the cavern wall. Jackson grunted. "Satan."

Jackson glanced back at Mekoddishkem for help, but he was still occupied with Agliarept.

Botis snuck up behind Agliarept and cut his master's Achilles tendon with his sword, causing him to buckle. Seizing the opportunity, Mekoddishkem struck Agliarept down, then eyed Botis.

Botis fled.

Jackson struck at Satan's neck with his sword, but the Evil One flicked it away effortlessly.

Mekoddishkem cried out, "Jackson!"

Jackson looked over. His guardian angel tossed a sword to him. He recognized it instantly. It was the sword that had been mounted in the training center.

Satan lifted his hand and transported Jackson into another

underground chamber. Jackson raised the sword, but for just a moment, he stood staring at Satan's strikingly handsome features.

He shook his head to clear it, then assumed a fighting position. "What do you want with me, Satan?"

Satan waved his hand, and an ancient iron door creaked open. As the seal was broken, air rushed out, filling the chamber with a putrid stench, giving Jackson the dry heaves. "Come with me."

Jackson hesitated, but then curiosity got the better of him. Satan escorted him through the doorway. The brilliance of Jackson's God-given countenance lit up the entire hallway, which seemed to extend forever. Dozens of wormlike creatures scurried away to avoid the light. Cries of agony emanated from between the iron bars of each cell as they passed. So sad. Jackson had trouble breathing; there was so little air. After walking about fifty yards, Satan pointed at one of the cells on the left. "Open that one."

Jackson studied the cell door. It was made up of six or seven vertical iron bars that were about four feet high and six inches apart, all braced by four horizontal bars. The edges of the door were crusted over with rust. It appeared not to have been opened for many years. The caked-on rust splintered off as he lifted the latch and opened the door.

Satan spoke. "Come out, slave!"

A naked man slowly crabbed his way out of the cell before them. He tried to stand but could not. He was severely bent over, like someone with osteoporosis. His whole body was covered with bite marks, welts, and filth. He slowly, and with great effort, managed to straighten up. The man's eyes practically popped out of their sockets when he recognized Satan. The man bowed deeply to the evil overlord.

He turned toward Jackson, then quickly shielded his eyes with one hand. Jackson's shimmering white robe and skin were blinding the man. But the man studied Jackson as his eyes continued to adjust.

A few seconds later, the man put his hand down by his side. "Jackson. Is that you?"

Jackson raised his brows. "Yes. Who are you?"

"Don't you recognize me?"

Jackson shook his head. "No."

"I'm your grandfather."

Jackson caught his breath. "Pappi?"

"Yes."

He fell to his knees. Tears streamed down his face. "Oh, Pappi. Pappi. What are you doing here? You should be in heaven with Grandmother."

"You're right, Jackson. I chose a different path."

He stared into his grandfather's eyes, searching for any ray of hope. Finding none, he pitied him. "I'm so sorry for the terrible suffering you're going through, Pappi."

"I'm paying for my owns sins, Jackson. I should have let Jesus pay for them."

Satan slapped Jackson's grandfather across the face, sending him crashing against his cell door.

Jackson scowled at Satan as he helped his grandfather to his feet.

His grandfather's present suffering was nothing compared to what awaited him in the lake of fire. He'd be thrown in there right after the great white throne judgment. Just thinking about it was too much to bear.

His pity turned to anger. He glared at Satan and pointed a finger at him. "You put my grandfather here, Satan. You deceived him, the same way you deceived our ancestors, beginning with Adam and Eve."

Satan smiled. "It gives me great joy to see your grandfather suffer, Jackson, and to see you suffer because he's suffering."

A thought popped into his head. Could he break his grandfather out of hell? Would Jesus allow it? He placed his hand on his grandfather's shoulder, thinking.

Satan broke the silence. "Would you like to trade places with him?"

Jackson was stunned. Did Satan know his thoughts? Probably not, but he was new to all this. Even though Satan pretended to be God, he wasn't. That aside, maybe there was a way to get his grandfather out of this awful place. Was there anything in the Bible to indicate this was possible? He remembered the apostle Paul had been willing to change places with the Jewish people and go to hell instead of them, but that was all Jackson could muster. Jesus had already made the great exchange, our sin for his righteousness. People had to choose whether to accept his offer of forgiveness or turn it down. This could only be done while they were living. The truth settled over him. There was nothing he could do to help his grandfather, no matter how badly he wanted to get him out of hell. His grandfather's fate was sealed, forever.

Jackson looked back at his grandfather. "I'm so sorry, Pappi. I wish I could help you, but there's nothing I can do."

Pappi's eyes squinted as he drew closer. He reached out and held Jackson's hand. "I know, Jackson. I'm so proud of you. You made the right choice. Please tell your grandmother she was right. I should have listened to her. And please tell her I miss her."

Jackson sobbed for a moment. Eventually, he turned to Satan. He remembered Mekoddishkem's admonition not to believe anything Satan said, and if forced, to only respond to him with Scripture, as exemplified by Jesus when Satan tempted him. "The Lord rebuke you, Satan. There's nothing in the Bible that says a person's destiny can change after they die."

"I got your grandfather out of his prison cell, didn't I?"

"Yes."

Satan led Jackson out of the prison hallway with his grandfather trudging behind them. Satan closed the iron door and addressed Jackson's grandfather. "Sit over there against the wall until I call for you."

His grandfather sat on the stone floor and breathed deeply. Relief shone on his grandfather's face.

"You see, Jackson. I'm more powerful than you think. I can ease your grandfather's suffering if you obey me."

Satan might be telling him the truth… or not. He couldn't take a chance. And yet, what if he could help his grandfather? Perhaps his grandfather didn't have to go back into that awful cell. What should he do? He narrowed his eyes at Satan. "I'm listening."

❦

Satan led Jackson to a city in the clouds. It was within the earth's atmosphere but must be only visible and accessible to those dwelling in the heavenly realms. The buildings were either gray or dark brown and misshapen. Garbage was strewn all about the ground, and ruins from unfinished construction projects were prevalent. The contrast to heaven—where completed buildings shone brilliantly of pure gold and fine jewels—was striking.

Above them, demons floated everywhere. They eyed Jackson with disdain but fell prostrate, trembling with fear, once they realized Satan himself was escorting him.

Satan took Jackson into a dark cavernous chamber. "Does this room remind you of anything?"

Jackson looked around. Six marble steps were leading up to an ornate throne. Burning torches hung on the wall behind it. A pair of golden lion statues sat on either side of each step and one beside each armrest. The number six must be significant. It was in the Bible somewhere, maybe Kings or Chronicles. The room was ornate, so it must have been someone rich… "King Solomon's throne room?"

"Outstanding, Jackson. You know your Bible."

"You know it too; only you distort it to suit your purposes."

"There, there, Jackson. No need to be rude." The devil opened his arms. The walls surrounding the throne room seemed to dissolve, revealing bird's-eye views of various cities. The Statue of Liberty in New York City was on one panel, the Washington Monument on another, the House of Parliament in London on a third, and other panels displayed Mecca in Saudi Arabia and the Temple Mount in Jerusalem. "This is where I rule the world from, Jackson."

"Wow!" He was genuinely impressed but had to catch himself. He had to remain alert and on guard, lest Satan deceive him, as he had countless others before him.

"I know you control the world, Satan. The Bible says so in 1 John, chapter five. However, you can't harm God's people unless God allows it, as it says in Job, chapters one and two."

Satan didn't say anything.

Jackson placed his hands on his hips. "What do you want with me, Satan?"

"Getting right to the point. I like that about you, Jackson. Let me show you around first, then I'll answer your question."

Where's he going with this? Beware! The Bible said Satan's greatest downfall was his pride. How could Jackson take advantage of that to help his grandfather and protect his family back on earth, especially Monica, from Satan's minions? But wait. Could Satan read his mind? Not likely. Satan could tempt him by planting thoughts into his head, but only God could know his thoughts. He began to plot a strategy.

The phrase *know your enemy* popped into his mind. *Where did that come from?* Oh yeah. It was a saying from Sun Tzu's *The Art of War*. He needed to know what he was up against when dealing with the most powerful evil force in the universe. The best way to understand him and learn his objectives was to go along and pander to his vanity. "How, exactly, do you control the world, Satan?"

"A fascinating question, Jackson. I'm so glad you asked. The first step is to make sure the world doesn't believe I exist."

"What?" Jackson huffed. "That's odd. I thought you wanted

people to worship you. That's what you asked Jesus to do when you were tempting him."

Satan chuckled. "That will come later, at the appointed time. You must first understand that I've been around for a very long time. Thousands of people die every hour. It's enough, for now, for me to see the horror on their faces when they realize they'll be suffering in hell, then spending the rest of eternity in the lake of fire, largely because of me. It's a pleasure I never tire of."

Jackson couldn't help but gag. *What a sick being.* He dared not verbalize his thoughts, however. Not if he could get Satan to reveal more of his strategy first. "What's the next step?"

"To get humanity to believe they're inherently good—that by working a little harder and doing good deeds, they can reform them-selves, atone for their past mistakes, and in the process, make the world a better place."

"That seems reasonable and even admirable on the surface, but Jesus said no one is good, except God."

"Look how successful I've been in changing many people's minds about that."

"How did you do it?"

Satan's eyes lit up. "Change begins in the mind. I've single-handedly transformed many cultures over the centuries. I'm very proud of that. I've done it by working through key individuals to invent philosophies and religions that have nothing to do with Jesus, that man that I killed on the cross."

"You mean Jesus Christ, the Son of God, who is seated at the right hand of the Father and willingly gave up his life to save humanity? I recall seeing you in his throne room not too long ago asking for permission to kill my family."

Satan bristled.

Better be careful. Tone it down, or he won't talk anymore. "Who are some of the people you've used over the centuries?"

"I already have the eastern cultures firmly in my grasp. They are buried in Hinduism, Buddhism, Confucianism, and other religions contrary to the teachings of the God of Abraham, Isaac, and Jacob. Your feeble missionaries go to these places to share their flimsy religion, but my slaves kill them whenever prompted to do so by me."

"Only after God allows you to. God finds a way to get his message to those he has chosen."

Satan screamed, "Stop interrupting me with your lies!"

Jackson felt cool and calm inside, not intimidated as he had been in the marines whenever a senior officer yelled at him. It must have been the Holy Spirit dwelling within, strengthening him. Perhaps those in God's throne room were watching him right now, and God was helping him through this confrontation. "I speak the truth but will not interrupt you any longer."

Satan guffawed. "Ha! What is truth?"

Those were the words Pilate used before ordering Jesus to be crucified. Satan must have given those words to Pilate. Fascinating! Jackson opened his mouth to accuse Satan of being the 'Father of Lies,' as Jesus had done, but bit his tongue. He needed to know more about Satan's grand strategy for the world, so he could figure out how to help his family. "Please continue without interruption."

"That's better. My focus now is on the West, particularly that last bastion standing in the way of me establishing my one-world government on earth."

Satan paused, apparently testing him to see if he could keep his mouth shut.

"I'm talking about the country of your origin, Jackson. Your precious little United States of America. It has been challenging to conquer, but I'm getting closer. It shouldn't take much longer to work out my plan fully. It's inevitable, you know. I will succeed."

It's inevitable you'll be cast into the lake of fire one day. No reaction, confirming Satan couldn't read his mind.

"My plan has been underway from before your country even came into existence. In its early years, most of the people serving in your country's government followed your God. The seeds I planted, starting in the eighteenth century, took many years to germinate, but we are now very close to seeing them blossom.

"Who did I use, you asked? Philosophers Jean-Jacques Rousseau and Georg Wilhelm Friedrich Hegel. They were beneficial in persuading these dumb sheep that humanity was fundamentally good and would ultimately find fulfillment in their brief pathetic lives by living communally, governed by absolute reason and living in perfect harmony.

"The next phase was a continuation of those ideals, but with God removed from the equation. Enter my underling Karl Marx, who argued the fruits of capitalist industrial expansion should be shared by all workers, not just the robber barons who exploited them. These ideas took hold in other less sophisticated, less educated, and less developed nations, but not in your beloved United States. The checks and balances embedded in your government's Constitution, along with your people's independence and religiosity, make adoption of these revolutionary ideals much more difficult to achieve. Rest assured, however, that these obstacles will soon be obliterated. How, you might ask? By dismembering the core foundations of your society.

"It begins by confusing what a family is. The traditional family with a male husband who works outside the home and a female wife who stays home to raise the children is an anachronism that must be crushed. Enter male husbands and male wives, female husbands and female wives, and transgender husbands and wives. Implant the idea that women can only find meaning and fulfillment in life by working outside the home. Challenge the headship of the man as paternalistic victimization of women. Foment permanent opposition between whites and minorities, portraying whites as privileged and non-whites as victims. Argue for the tolerance of all different cultures, languages, and people groups, even if they vehemently oppose the Judeo-Christian heritage of your country. Blame the problems of the world on the imperialistic policies of the United States. Attack the flag and the Pledge of Allegiance as symbols of that imperialism. Tear down borders, so the people lose their identity as Americans. Attack the churches and synagogues as antiquated and judgmental, defusing their influence by making them irrelevant. Take prayer out of the schools and remove it from public events. Attack the Bible as unscientific and subjective, as full of myths and old wives' tales. If anyone opposes us, call them homophobic, racist, or judgmental. Change the focus away from what the Bible says about the family and other institutions to what each individual feels is right or wrong, as guided, unbeknownst to them, by me.

"The battle I just described was fought with prior generations and continues being fought with the current generation. Some will never join us. Such opponents will one day be killed, but my followers have not yet matured enough in the United States to implement that form of discipline. It worked quite nicely in Nazi Germany under Hitler, in Russia under Stalin, in China under Mao Tse-tung, and in Cambodia under Pol Pot. I look forward to the day when another servant of mine will accomplish these same objectives in the United States. Then our victory will be complete—a one-world government controlled by me for the good of all.

"Part of my long-term strategy is to cultivate sympathy in the next generation to our way of thinking. This is best accomplished through indoctrination within the public schools. Why fight the parents directly when we can easily go around them? For example, teach kindergarteners to question their gender. Maybe they were born a boy but were really meant to be a girl. More importantly, if we can convince them they got here by accident, through evolution, then there's no need for them to believe in or follow God.

"Lying, disinformation, character assassination, and subversion of the letter and spirit of established laws and policies are all acceptable in this war against the putrid offspring of the God of Abraham, Isaac, and Jacob. Dehumanize your adversaries to the point that everyone thinks they are evil. Show no mercy. Encourage addiction to drugs and alcohol as a way of eliminating a whole swath of the population and creating the social problems that go along with that lifestyle.

"We can't afford to adhere to principle, honesty, or integrity. Such things have no place in this war. The stakes are too high, and the time too short. Accuse them of the very thing we are doing. Knock them back on their heels. Never let up. Attack, attack, attack! Remember at each step along the way in this global struggle to use whatever means necessary to achieve our larger objectives. The end always justifies the means.

"You know how messed up this world is, Jackson. There's so much poverty, so much death, so much hatred, and there's no end in sight. I want to bring order and stability into the world. As I said earlier, I've been around for a very long time and know what's best for everyone. I can only achieve this if I gain control of your country's major institutions—the government, media, businesses, schools, and all the other aspects of American culture. I need this power to purge those who oppose us and implement a utopia for the benefit of all."

Satan studied Jackson, then paused for an uncomfortably long period of time. It may have only been a minute, but perhaps it was two or three. Was Satan testing him again?

Finally, Satan spoke. "You have obeyed by not interrupting me. That's good."

Jackson raised his hand.

Satan responded, "You're still waiting for an answer to your question, correct?"

"Yes."

"I want to offer you a job, Jackson. I want you to serve on

my United States team. You would report directly to the lord of New England."

Jackson scoffed. "Agliarept? The demon lord who hates my guardian angel and who ordered the killing of my boss, my daughter's mother, and my sister-in-law?"

"Yes. One and the same. Don't worry. We'll let bygones be bygones. Okay?"

Interesting. Satan is not aware Agliarept will be put in a prison cell. That confirms he's not omniscient.

"Why should I believe you?"

"You don't have a choice."

"I always have a choice. What if I say no to your job offer?"

"I'll personally murder your entire family."

He couldn't lose McKenzie and the baby. But he also couldn't work to destroy his own country. But was any of this true? Pappi was lost—nothing he could do about that. McKenzie and the baby would have guardian angels, so Satan was lying; he couldn't kill them. If Agliarept was to be put in a prison cell, that meant his boss would have to be someone else—perhaps that monster, Botis.

Wait a minute. What am I thinking? How could I even consider a deal with Satan? Mekoddishkem said not to believe a word Satan said.

Jackson had all the information he needed. There was no longer any reason to keep up appearances. "Jesus said you are a liar and the 'Father of Lies.' You deceived Adam and Eve and countless people since. You even had me in your grasp at one time, but no longer. I am a child of the Most High God." He took a deep breath and firmed his jaw. "I will never work for you."

Satan seethed at him like a wolf ready to devour its prey. Nearby demonic servants scurried away, as if something terrible was about to happen. The devil paused, then laughed, and with a booming voice declared, "You mean the three gods, don't you, Jackson—Father,

Son, and Holy Spirit? The last time I checked, one plus one plus one equals three."

That statement rolled around in Jackson's head for a moment. How should he respond? Then a thought came to mind. "The last time *I* checked, one times one times one equals one."

The devil clapped as he looked around. "Oh, good one, Jackson. You really got me there. Do you think I've never heard that one before?"

Jackson stopped himself. It was a great comeback, but it wasn't Scripture. He had to be fully alert. What would Satan try next?

"That's some loving God you have, Jackson, allowing your own grandfather to suffer in hell like that."

Jackson teared up. "Liar! You heard my grandfather. He chose to go there by consciously rejecting God's offer of forgiveness. The Bible says God is not willing that any should perish, but that all should come to repentance. Yet, he does not leave the guilty unpunished. My grandmother said my grandfather didn't want to be with God in heaven."

Satan chuckled. "I'm sure he's thrilled with his decision now."

Jackson pointed. "You blinded him, you fiend. Look at the misery you've caused him, as well as the billions who came before him and the billions who will come after. How can you be so hateful?"

Satan smiled. "I *can't* hurt God, but I *can* hurt his children. Would you like me to show you other members of your family whom I've killed over the millennia and have imprisoned in the earth beneath us? Would you like to see more of them?

"Perhaps you'd like to see other people you knew in life, who are now dead and in hell. Would you like to see your old boss, Fred? Too bad your flimsy witnessing didn't work. Or maybe you'd like to see Dexter, the man who beat you to a pulp after raping your wife at college. Have you ever imagined what that was like, someone else ravishing your wife? Ha, ha! No love lost there, I bet.

"What about Ronaldo, Monica's ex-boyfriend, the man who killed you. He's *way* down in the Abyss. I bet that makes you feel good, doesn't it? Deep down, you're glad he's there being punished, aren't you?"

Jackson shouted, "The Lord rebuke you, Satan!"

Satan replied in a mocking voice, "The Lord rebuke you. The Lord rebuke you. Aren't you tired of saying that, Jackson?"

"I'm saying it because it's biblical, it's true, and it works. That's exactly what the angel Michael told you when you were fighting with him over Moses's body."

Satan shook his head. "You're not supposed to be here, Jackson. It's written in the parable of the rich man and Lazarus that no one can cross over from heaven to hell and no one can cross over from hell to heaven. You're violating God's rules."

"You're twisting the Scripture, taking it out of context. I was sent here to retrieve Monica. I didn't come on my own."

"You're in my realm now. I don't have to follow God's rules here. I'm going to enjoy destroying you."

Raphael's admonition came to him: *You must be so confident in your skills that you know your opponent will lose.* "You can't destroy me. I'm a child of the living God."

Jackson removed his sword from its scabbard and assumed a fighting position. *He had bested Botis. He would defeat Satan too.*

The devil turned to one of his guards. "Give me a sword."

The guard threw a leather scabbard at Satan. Satan removed the sword and discarded the scabbard.

Jackson attacked first, but Satan easily deflected his blows. Jackson continued fighting with all the skill he could muster, but Satan seemed barely flustered.

Then Satan took the offensive. Jackson successfully deflected the blows for a time, but Satan was relentless. Satan continued pressing. Jackson winced when he was nicked on one arm, then the other.

Satan then nicked him on the face. This was a game to him. Jackson's confidence ebbed. He was getting beaten—badly—but he would not give up. He would *never* give up. *Think!* What else could he do? Should he cry out to Mekoddishkem for help like he'd done before? Should he cry out to Jesus? His Lord could easily defeat Satan.

Why did he always have to call out for help? Why couldn't he defeat Satan on his own? He was hopelessly outmatched.

Satan laughed as he nicked Jackson again and again, without mercy. Finally, Jackson fell to the ground, weak and breathing hard. Satan stood over him, gloating.

What else could he do? Wait! What was it that Mekoddishkem said? *Don't believe a word Satan says.* What did he say after that? *Fight Satan with the Word of God.* That was it. He was fighting Satan on Satan's terms—with a sword. He should be fighting Satan on God's terms, with a different type of sword—the Word of God. How foolish he'd been. Now he knew he couldn't lose.

Jackson stood.

Satan tilted his head.

"Satan! You are a defeated foe." Jackson lowered his sword and began citing Scripture:

"It is written, *The one who is in you is greater than the one who is in the world.* Satan, by the authority of the Word of God, Jesus in me is greater than you.

"It is written, *The seventy-two returned with joy and said, 'Lord, even the demons submit to us in your name.'* Satan, by the authority of the Word of God, you must submit to me.

"It is written, *And these signs will accompany those who believe: In my name they will drive out demons.* Satan, by the authority of the Word of God, I drive you out.

"It is written, *Resist the devil, and he will flee from you.* Satan, I resist you. By the authority of the Word of God, you must flee... Be gone!"

Jackson leered at Satan. The devil's face quickly became beet-red; he turned and fled his own throne room. Jackson looked around. The demons darted away from him as well.

Jackson cheered, then stopped himself. Jesus commanded his followers not to rejoice that the spirits would submit to them.

Jackson returned to Agliarept's bedchamber. Then he took Monica by the hand.

He brought Monica's spirit to the hospital room where her physical body lay. McKenzie sat in a wheelchair, her arms stretched out over Monica's body, even though she had just delivered their baby. Her hair was a mess, and she was dressed in a polka-dot johnny with flip-flops. Someone from the hospital must have called to tell her Monica was in the emergency room. Since McKenzie was already at the hospital, she would have just come downstairs. She was bent over, grimacing in pain from the surgery. Her eyes were closed, but her lips were moving as she prayed silently.

Jackson released Monica's hand. "Tell McKenzie I love her, and I can't wait to see her again soon. Tell her I look forward to meeting our wonderful son in heaven one day." Monica smiled as she looked back at him. Her spirit faded and became enmeshed in her physical body.

Monica gasped for air. McKenzie screamed.

Monica struggled to sit up as she gawked at McKenzie. "Where am I?"

McKenzie wrapped her arms around Monica. "The hospital."

Monica groaned. "The hospital? Again? What happened?"

"The ambulance workers found you sprawled on the floor beside the front door of our condo. They applied CPR until you arrived at the hospital. The emergency room crew took over and continued CPR but were unable to revive you. They pronounced you dead shortly afterward."

Mekoddishkem appeared and stood invisibly beside McKenzie

and Monica. Jackson looked toward him and asked, "Does McKenzie have any idea how powerful her prayers are?"

"No. Most people do not."

A beam of light descended from heaven and aligned in the form of a cross on Monica's forehead.

Sally ran over from the other side of the room and gaped at Monica. "You're alive. It's a miracle."

Monica folded her hands. "Sally, what must I do to be saved from hell?"

Sally shouted for joy, then looked over at McKenzie. "Ask your sister."

McKenzie straightened up. "Me?"

"Yes."

McKenzie grasped Monica's hands. "Pray with me, word for word." Monica bowed her head. McKenzie paused, then looked up. "Actually, what's most important is not the exact words you use, but what's in your heart. Tell God what's in your heart."

Monica sighed. "Dear Lord Jesus, you are the Son of God. I'm so sorry for all the terrible things I've done. I don't want to live like that anymore. Thank you for dying on the cross to pay for my sins. Please forgive me and save me from hell. I'm yours. I promise to serve you all the days of my life. Amen."

McKenzie hugged Monica. "You've just made the most important decision of your life. The Bible says there is much rejoicing in heaven over one sinner who repents."

Monica pointed toward heaven. "I bet Jackson is rejoicing too." She then reached over and hugged Sally.

McKenzie nodded. "I bet you're right."

Sally asked, "Why now?"

Monica ran a hand through her tangled hair. "At first, I was terrified of going to hell. But escaping hell is not enough. I needed a real rescue from the things I've done and the dark parts of my heart.

Now, I have a peace I've never known before, like everything is going to be okay. This peace must come from Jesus. He's done so much for me. I want to follow him forever."

Jackson jumped up and down as he hugged Mekoddishkem. "Praise God! Monica is finally saved. Now I don't have to worry about her anymore... What was that light?"

Mekoddishkem said, "The veil was removed from Monica's heart."

Monica, McKenzie, and Sally all embraced, putting smiles on the faces of Jackson and Mekoddishkem.

Mekoddishkem grasped his hand. "Your first mission has been accomplished, Jackson. What are you going to do now?"

Jackson grinned. "Whatever the Lord wills."

Chapter 27
RAGE

SATAN CONVENED HIS senior staff in his throne room. He sat upright on his throne with both forearms on the armrests.

"I can't believe you allowed Monica to defect to the enemy." Satan looked to his left and his right. "Arise."

The lions all came to life but remained at their stations, growling at the demonic spirits trembling before them. Moans erupted from Satan's lieutenants. Apparently, the memory of Agliarept's recent mauling was still fresh in their minds.

Satan leaned forward. "Don't you understand how important this is? If we don't stop the prophecy, we'll all end up in the lake of fire. Every one of you has failed me, especially Agliarept." Satan swept a hand around the room. "Where is he? Agliarept's lust may have doomed us all."

Several responded, "We don't know where he is, master."

"I'll deal with him later. Go throughout the land and determine if the resurrection of the enemy army has occurred."

"Yes, master."

"And bring Agliarept's underling, Botis, to me."

"Yes, master."

❦

An hour or so later, Botis arrived in Satan's throne room, holding his nearly severed arm by his side. He was surrounded by all Satan's lieutenants.

One of the demons spoke up. "Master, there is no evidence the enemy army has been resurrected. Many followers of the Nazarene still walk the earth."

Satan sighed. "That's good news for us all. We've been given a reprieve. This must not be allowed to happen again—ever. We must ensure all the relatives of this Jackson Trotman are killed immediately. Do you understand me?"

"Yes, master."

"Botis!"

Botis came trembling before Satan and fell to his knees. "Yes, master."

"Where is Agliarept?"

"He was defeated in battle by the angel Mekoddishkem. One of my warriors told me he was then imprisoned in the Abyss by order of the Nazarene."

"Botis! You are now the commander of the New England principality."

Botis hid his smile. He dared not show any emotion. The slightest misstep might incur Satan's wrath.

Satan walked down from his throne, grabbed Botis by the front of his robe, and restored his severed arm. Botis erupted with glee. "Thank you, master."

Satan pulled him close and glared into his eyes. "The only living offspring of Jackson is his son, Jack, correct?"

"Yes, master. I know of none other."

"Kill him."

Should he ask Satan if he'd gotten God's permission to kill Jackson's son? No. Agliarept had been mauled by the lions after asking that exact question. Botis glanced over at one of them. What must it have been like to be sliced by the teeth of not just one but all of them?

He was at a crossroads: If he complied with Satan's request, he'd avoid immediate punishment but would surely incur future punishment from God. If he declined Satan's request, he'd be immediately mauled by a pride of lions, then punished by God at a later date anyway for all the other bad things he'd done.

Avoidance of immediate pain seemed the best course of action. "Yes, master."

Botis bowed as he left Satan's throne room.

Back in Agliarept's… or rather, *his* throne room, Botis gave orders to his warriors to wait for an opportunity to kill the baby. It wouldn't be easy since at least one guardian angel would be watching over both of them.

CHAPTER 28

NEW BEGINNINGS

MCKENZIE, ACCOMPANIED BY her mother and father, walked into the hospital parking garage. Her father was carrying her son in a brand-new car seat. It was gray and cushioned, but Jack was so tiny the straps barely kept him in place. She stowed him in the center of the back seat, securely fastening the seat belt, so the car seat faced backward in her Volvo. Her mother drove while McKenzie sat in the back and listened carefully for any chirp out of him, hoping to get home as soon as possible so she could hold him again. Her father followed behind in their car. The stitches from the surgery gnawed at her a bit, stinging whenever she moved, but it was just temporary.

Twenty minutes later, McKenzie trudged into the condo. Her dad lugged the car seat with Jack, while her mom brought in her overnight bag. Both were placed on the oak living room floor. She locked the door behind her, then glanced around. The living room and kitchen were spotless. She took sleeping Jack out of his car seat and walked down the hallway toward her bedroom. Her parents were right behind her. She glanced in Monica's room on her right and the common bathroom on the left. Monica had done a great job cleaning up the place. Too bad she had to spend a few more days in the hospital.

The bassinet, changing table, and crib were just as McKenzie had left them. She changed Jack's diaper, carefully sanitizing the area where the umbilical cord had been, then changed him into his new pajama onesie. The breastfeeding was difficult, but Jack conked out soon afterward.

Her parents stayed in Monica's room that night rather than travel back to Massachusetts, so they could enjoy their first grandchild and visit Monica in the hospital.

About ten o'clock that evening, McKenzie collapsed into her bed, first checking Jack in the bassinet to make sure he was okay. What a miracle—this little human being had come out of her body!

"Oh, Lord, please protect my precious son and I from the evil one. In Jesus's name, I pray, amen."

Two days later, Monica returned from the hospital and opened the condo door. It was good to be home.

McKenzie was sitting on the couch in the living room nursing Jack. "Monica! How are you?"

"Doing a lot better, thanks. The doctors said I had… Wait a minute, I wrote it down." She pulled a piece of paper out of her plastic hospital bag. "Hypertrophic cardiomyopathy."

"Sounds serious."

Monica closed the door and locked it. "Very. They said my heart muscle is too thick. It's inherited. They had to install an ICD."

"What's an ICD?"

Monica looked down at the piece of paper. "Implantable cardio-verter-defibrillator. It'll shock me if something goes wrong with my heart again."

"You poor thing. You've been electrocuted, kidnapped, and now you've had a heart attack." McKenzie uttered a strangled snicker.

"I'm sorry. I shouldn't be laughing. What did you ever do to deserve all this?"

Monica laughed. "I'm a slow learner, I guess. God used these trials to draw me to him. I trust the rest of my life will be much less eventful."

McKenzie shook her head. "He will protect you, but I wouldn't count on your life becoming uneventful. I've noticed the closer I draw to Christ, the more I get attacked spiritually. I guess you'll have to experience that yourself to know what I'm talking about."

Monica sat on the love seat, perpendicular to McKenzie. "So, how's Jack, and how do you like being a mom?"

"Jack's doing great! It's exhausting, but I wouldn't change a minute of it. I just love this little guy so much. Isn't he precious?"

"Absolutely. He's so cute! He has Jackson's eyes." Monica reached over and tugged on his little foot. "You know, McKenzie, I don't think I should go back to modeling."

McKenzie tilted her head to the side. "Really. Why?"

"None of it's real. Most of the pictures are photoshopped to make the models look more enticing. They're selling an image that men will long for. In turn, women want to be just like that image, so men will long for them. It's all extremely shallow, concerned with outer beauty rather than inner beauty."

"Very profound. I've been praying about this. I know it must be a tough decision. I mean, it was your dream to be a model."

"Yes, but I don't mind. I'll find another dream. Perhaps God has something else for me to do."

"I'm sure he does. What do you think it might be?"

"I don't know. Maybe warning girls and young women about the potential dangers of modeling and sex trafficking."

McKenzie nodded. "That's a great idea. Do you remember the human trafficking chapter that I started in Marblehead? Maybe we could get involved in something like that. We should find an existing human or sex trafficking prevention organization in Connecticut and figure out if we'd fit in. If not, we could start our own. We could start a blog or even write a book about your experiences. The sky's the limit."

"Why not."

"Okay. You take the lead in researching this. I need to focus on little Jack right now, but I'll help in any way I can."

"Sounds like a plan."

⌁

McKenzie awoke the following morning with a compelling need to pray for Pam. After all, Jackson had specifically mentioned her by name. "Oh, Father, thank you so much that you love me and gave me an opportunity to see Jackson. What an incredible, out-of-this-world blessing it was. It will sustain me for the rest of my life. Lord, I'm sorry I haven't been praying for Pam. I've been so busy taking care of Jack that I've forgotten to do much of anything else. Jackson planted the seed, the Alpha class watered it, but only you can make it grow in Pam's heart. Please let me know if there's anything else I can do to help her. In Jesus's name, I pray, amen."

Later that morning, a thought came to her. She should invite Pam to dinner. Excuses came to mind: *I hardly know her*; *If she's sick, she might get the baby sick*; *I'm too busy*. McKenzie pushed those aside and called Pam at work, inviting her to dinner at the condo on Friday.

When Friday evening came and McKenzie answered the door, Pam immediately reached out her hand and shook Jack's foot. "Hi Jack! It's so nice to meet you. Oh, McKenzie, he's so cute."

"Thanks. Please come in. You can put your coat in the closet over there. I'm so glad you could make it."

"Thanks for inviting me. Your timing is perfect. I've been meaning to speak to you but have been so busy at work that I haven't gotten around to it."

"Great. Can you hold Jack while I get dinner ready?"

"Sure. I'd love to."

Monica walked out of her bedroom. "Hi, Pam. I see you've already met Jack. Isn't he adorable?"

"He sure is."

After dinner, Pam complimented McKenzie on the haddock, then McKenzie excused herself to get Jack ready for bed.

❧

While McKenzie was occupied in the bedroom, Monica sat at the kitchen table with Pam. Might as well tell Pam her good news. "I prayed to receive Jesus as my Lord and Savior last week."

Pam blinked at her. "You did? Why?"

"I was terrified of going to hell. You may not know this, but I suffered a heart attack last week and had an out-of-body experience. I was floating in the air above my body. I cried out to Jesus to save me. Two demons came and were taking me to hell when an angel arrived and stopped them. Seconds later, maybe a hundred demons showed up. It was too many for the angel to fight, so the two demons took me to hell. Then, Jackson and a bunch of angels later came and rescued me."

"Jackson?"

"Yes. He sparkled like an angel in his white robe. Hell is a horrible place, Pam. Trust me. You don't want to go there."

Pam sat up straight. "Jackson told me I'd been there."

"Really? When?"

"I had a heart attack at the office about a year and a half ago. Jackson gave me CPR and saved my life. He told me I cried out while he was reviving me. He said I was pleading with him to get me out of the fire. I don't remember any of that actually happening, but I believe him."

"You were definitely in hell, Pam, and that's where you're going to end up permanently unless you change the direction of your life right now."

"What should I do?"

"Do what I did a week ago. Pray to Jesus and ask him to be your Lord and Savior."

"How do I do that. I don't know how to pray."

"Just use your own words. Act like you're talking to a real person, which you are. Talk to him honestly from your heart."

Pam looked upward. "Jesus, I don't want to go to hell. I've done a lot of bad things, and I'm sorry. I don't want to be like that anymore. Please forgive me and make me clean. Please be my Lord and Savior. Amen."

Monica reached over and hugged her friend. "I'm so proud of you, Pam. Perhaps McKenzie can help us figure out what to do next."

"Of course, I will." McKenzie was standing in the doorway to the bedroom with a grin on her face. Obviously, she had heard Pam's confession of faith.

Monica returned her grin. The journey forward might not be clear, but at least they had each other.

❧

Thanksgiving was at the Bakers' house in Marblehead, Massachusetts, that year, as it had been for decades. Jack was nine months old, and he crawled all over the house. He was particularly interested in his grandparents' stairs. Grandma had a gate set up, blocking the stairs, so he'd have to explore elsewhere. Anything not nailed down went into his mouth. He was a very active boy with tons of energy. Jack was able to grab the coffee table and lift himself to a standing position. He'd be walking in no time.

The Bakers lived in a hundred-year-old two-story redbrick

colonial. The house had oak hardwood floors, stylish crown molding, and beautiful furniture they'd inherited from their grandparents. Mrs. Baker had a knack for decorating, and Mr. Baker was pretty handy around the house.

There was a knock at the door. Mrs. Baker opened it and cheered when she saw her son standing on the concrete doorstep. He'd made it! They hadn't been together since the bloody incident with the sex traffickers at McKenzie's condo. Duncan had Jarek with him.

Mrs. Baker put her arms around her son. "What a surprise! I thought you couldn't make it home for Thanksgiving this year. So glad you're here. And I see you brought Jarek with you."

Duncan smiled. "Yes, we managed to get leave just in time for Thanksgiving."

Mrs. Baker hugged her son's friend. "Welcome to our home, Jarek."

Jarek scanned her eyes. "I hope it's okay for me to be here."

"Of course. We're glad to have you."

Her husband approached. He hugged Duncan and shook Jarek's hand. "Hey, Jarek, how are you? Would you like a drink?"

"I'm fine, sir. How's your shoulder doing? I know it's no fun getting shot."

"Not too bad. I've lost some range of motion. I'm an electrician, you know, and I work with my hands, so I've had to make some adjustments, but I'm thankful to be alive and still able to work."

"Glad to hear it. That was awesome how you charged into McKenzie's living room with the shotgun and took out that guy. You saved us all."

"You're welcome. When were you shot?"

"Rescuing Monica from the sex traffickers. Fortunately, I had body armor on, but it still hurt a lot."

"Oh, I didn't know that. McKenzie just said you went to New York City to pick up Monica after she'd escaped from the sex traffickers."

"Oh. I guess they didn't want to worry you. I think I'll take that drink now."

❧

Monica waltzed into the room wearing a knee-length crimson red dress with gold heels. Her natural blond hair was back, without the highlights, and pulled to one side over her right collarbone. She pulled up short at seeing the guys.

Jarek was staring at her with his mouth hanging open. She shied away at first but then glanced back at him, checking to see if he was still looking, which he was. She walked right up to Jarek and shook his hand, then hugged Duncan.

Jack crawled into the room.

Duncan commented, "Wow, McKenzie. He's so big. Can I hold him?"

"Of course." McKenzie picked up Jack and handed him to Duncan.

Duncan grinned from ear to ear. "Hi, Jack. I'm your Uncle Duncan."

Jack squirmed in his uncle's arms, clearly indicating he wanted to get back on the floor.

Jarek turned to Monica. "The last time I saw you, you'd just gone through hell with the kidnapping and home invasion. Now you look beautiful!"

Monica smiled at Jarek's compliment.

"Something's different about you, though. You look… well, much more at peace."

She guided him into the living room. "Jarek, I never got to thank you for all you did for me that night in New York City. I was really out of it, drugged up, so I didn't know what was going on. I really appreciate you and Duncan rescuing me." She let out a long sigh. "I just can't let that happen to anyone else. I'm working to prevent child sex trafficking with an organization called Love146 that is based in Connecticut."

"Good for you. I'm glad you're helping others and doing something meaningful with your life." Jarek flashed her a radiant smile that made her stomach squirm.

"You're doing something meaningful with your life too—defending our country. I know that only one percent of the population is on active duty in the military at any one time, so you and my brother are pretty special people. I know is sounds cliché, but thank you for your service."

"That's very nice of you to say, but what else is going on with you? You've changed somehow. I can't put my finger on it."

"I became a Jesus follower like McKenzie. That must be why I seem more at peace."

Monica and Jarek were inseparable the rest of the evening.

Nine months later, a year and a half after he'd given the kill order, Botis arrived to check on the demon who was monitoring Jack.

The demon spoke. "Nothing to report, sir."

As McKenzie was washing off the tray from Jack's high chair, she accidentally knocked an open bag of cough drops from the kitchen counter onto the floor. The cough drops were strewn everywhere. She got on her hands and knees to pick them up, then popped one of them into her mouth. Jack stood nearby, observing.

The kitchen timer went off, and she moved to the oven, putting her back to the boy.

Botis stood beside the demon with his arms folded, eyeing the nearby guardian angel. Cough drops still littered the floor. This was too good an opportunity to pass up. He edged as close as he could to little Jack. "Go get one of those candies and put it in your mouth. It will taste yummy."

Jack found one under the kitchen table and complied.

Jackson burst onto the scene and slashed at Botis with his sword. "How dare you try to kill my son!"

Botis bolted, not wanting to be dismembered again by the prince who defeated Satan. The other demon fled right behind him.

❧

McKenzie retrieved two gray quilted oven mitts out of a kitchen drawer and pulled the salmon out of the oven. She checked the middle with a knife. It was done. Then she stuck the knife into the sweet potato and determined it was done too.

A wheezing noise came from the other side of the kitchen, but she dismissed it and started cutting up the food for Jack.

The noise sounded again. It was coming from under the kitchen table. She bent down. Jack's face was blue. He was pawing at his throat. She pulled him out from under the kitchen table and smacked him several times on the back, but it didn't do any good. Then she tried pressing hard on his stomach, but that didn't work either.

She scanned the floor. A few cough drops that she hadn't picked up yet rested in the corner. *He swallowed one!* Instinctively, she grabbed Jack by the ankles, turned him upside down, and then patted him firmly on the back several times. The cough drop pinged against his teeth as it toppled out of his mouth onto the floor.

She flipped him right side up, then held him directly in front of her, eyeball to eyeball. "Don't ever put those things in your mouth again! Do you understand me?"

Jack nodded his head up and down, then began to cry.

She sighed. "Oh, I'm sorry, Jack. I didn't mean to yell at you. Are you okay?"

He sniffled. "Yes, Mommy."

She held him tight. "Mommy was very scared because you were choking. Mommy should not have left those cough drops on the floor. She should have picked them up right away. Don't ever take things off the floor and put them in your mouth again. Okay? Do you understand me?"

"Yes, Mommy."

"Good boy."

She hugged Jack again, then put him back on the floor.

She got on her hands and knees to make sure there were no cough drops left on the kitchen floor. Jack had done exactly what she had done—picked a cough drop off the floor and put it in her mouth. She needed to be more careful next time.

That evening, McKenzie knelt beside her bed and prayed. *Oh, Lord, thank you for sparing Jack's life today. I'm so sorry I wasn't paying attention to what he was doing and that I was harsh with him. He just did what he saw me doing. Please help me to be more careful next time and set a better example. He's a good boy. Please protect him from any harm. In Jesus's name, I pray, amen.*

McKenzie took a deep breath and remained kneeling, clearing her mind, and waiting for the Lord to speak to her. A few minutes later, a question came. *I'm focusing all my time and energy on Jack, which is appropriate at this stage of his life, but is there something else you want me to do?*

Monica had found purpose in her life. He was now using her to help others recover from the horrors of sex trafficking. God had truly taken the ashes of her life and made them beautiful.

Lord, are there ashes in my life that you want to make beautiful?

She waited patiently for several minutes. Thoughts of her own abortion came to mind: waking up at the Brown infirmary after being raped, discovering a month later she was pregnant, agonizing over what to do next, never discussing it with her parents, going to the Planned

Parenthood clinic in Providence, Rhode Island, the procedure, the pain, and the shame and regret that persisted long afterward.

Having Jack brought into focus what had been lost. Another human being could have been walking the earth right now if she hadn't had that abortion. In retrospect, she should have taken time off from school, had the baby, and given him or her up for adoption. That's what she should have done, but that's not what she did. She couldn't change the past. God had completely forgiven her, so she needed to forgive herself and move on with her life. There was no point dwelling on the past.

Was it really that simple? Were the next steps in dealing with this tragedy that concrete? Had she ever truly grieved for her baby?

Oh, Lord, you know my heart. You know how sorry I am for what I've done. Thank you for forgiving me. Please take good care of my baby. I look forward to meeting him or her in heaven one day. Please take the ashes of my life and make them beautiful. In Jesus's name, I pray, amen.

Another thought came to mind as she got up to leave. *Whoever loses his life for me will find it.*

❧

The following Sunday, McKenzie greeted Sally in the church lobby while on her way to drop Jack off at the Sunday school class for two-year-olds.

Sally knelt to his level. "Hi, Jack! How are you today? Can I get a hug?"

Jack lifted his arms and complied. He'd been to Sally's house many times, usually asleep in his car seat, while his mom met with her for discipleship.

Sally then hugged McKenzie. "Listen. There's a pro-life rally at the State Capitol on Wednesday. The Family Institute of Connecticut is organizing it. Would you like to come?"

McKenzie couldn't believe it. "Wow! I was just praying about how I could get more involved. Sure, I'd love to come. What time?"

"Noon."

"Okay, let's talk Wednesday morning to confirm."

"Great! See you then."

✎

A scene came into view in the sea of glass that captured Jackson's attention.

About five people were standing on a sidewalk beside a wrought iron fence outside of a building. "Wow! McKenzie is one of them." They held signs that read Choose Life and Don't Stop a Beating Heart. *They must be protesting at an abortion clinic.*

Two black teenage girls walked past the assembly on the sidewalk, then stood at the locked gate, waiting to be escorted in. McKenzie walked calmly toward the girls. "Excuse me, miss. Can I talk to you for a second?"

The taller girl glared at her. "We're here for an appointment. You're not going to stop us."

McKenzie put Jack down and held his hand. "Do you see this child?"

The girls looked away and didn't say anything.

"This is Jack, my two-year-old son."

The shorter of the girls looked at the toddler, while the taller one continued looking away.

"Would it be okay for me to kill my two-year-old son?"

The shorter girl guffawed. "Of course not."

"Why not?"

"Well… It wouldn't be right."

"Why?"

"It would be murder."

"Oh. I see. It would be murder. Well, what if my child was one year old. Would it be okay for me to kill him then?"

"No."

"What if he was one month old, just an infant? Should I be allowed to kill him?"

The shorter girl paused. "No, it would still be wrong because he'd be just a baby."

"Agreed. What if he was just one day old?"

"The same. It would be wrong because he had already been born."

"Okay. We agree so far, then. That's good. What if my son were minus one day old?"

"Minus one? What do you mean?"

"What's your name, miss."

The shorter girl hesitated. "Summer."

"Nice to meet you, Summer. Are you the one who is pregnant?"

"I think so."

"I'm McKenzie. What I'm asking, Summer, is if it would be okay for me to kill Jack if he was still in my belly and going to be born the very next day. Would that be wrong?"

The abortion attender arrived at the gate, opened the door, and looked sternly at the girls. "Don't listen to these kooks, girls. They're crazy. Everything we're doing here is perfectly legal."

McKenzie yelled out as the girls walked toward the abortion facility, "Think about it, Summer! It's not too late to leave. You don't have to go through with this. We can make sure your baby gets a good home if you can't give her one. I'll be praying for you."

The two girls and the attendant disappeared into the building.

McKenzie prayed. "Oh, Lord, please be with Summer and help her to do the right thing. Please save her baby, in Jesus's name, I pray, amen."

A few minutes later, a car drove up to the gate and honked. There was a teenage white girl in the passenger's seat. She had wavy blond hair and blue eyes. It looked as though she'd been crying. The driver was a man of about twenty. He had tanned white skin, black hair, and a trimmed three-day beard. His eyes were stern and focused, much like the stone-cold eyes of the shark Jackson had seen off the beach at Block Island. An attendant came to the gate and opened it. The couple drove in without being spoken to by the abortion protesters.

The scene switched to inside a beige waiting room, and Jackson had to reorient himself. The white couple sat beside an oak magazine rack on brown-cushioned chairs. The two black girls sat opposite them. A brass ceiling fan spun above them. They had no idea that Jackson was watching from heaven, along with God and the great cloud of witnesses.

The glass office window slid to one side. A woman from inside spoke. "Amanda?"

The blond girl glanced over at the young man, bit her lip, then stood up and walked over to the window. "Right this way, please, miss."

Amanda followed the woman into an office.

The woman sat at a desk and reviewed Amanda's information on a portable electronic device. "How old are you?"

Amanda sat opposite her. "Sixteen."

"Do you have your driver's license?"

"Yes." Amanda retrieved a brown wallet from her pink backpack.

The woman looked over the license and returned it to her. "Thank you, Amanda. What can I do for you today?"

"I'm pregnant."

"What do you want to do about it?"

Amanda sniffled. "I'm not sure. My boyfriend wants me to get an abortion."

"Is that what *you* want?"

Amanda shifted in her chair. "I don't know."

The woman leaned forward on her desk. "Well, it's your body, Amanda; you can do whatever you want."

"What about the baby?"

"It's not a baby yet. It's just a fetus."

"Will an abortion hurt the baby… I mean, fetus?"

"Not at all. It's just a glob of cells. It won't feel anything."

"What about me. Will it hurt?"

"You'll experience some discomfort, but we'll give you something for it, and you'll be back to normal in just a few days. We have some wonderful doctors and nurses here who will take good care of you."

"I haven't told my parents about this yet. Should I?"

"You're sixteen, so you don't have to. That's the law in Connecticut. This really should be a personal decision between you and your healthcare professional."

"Good. My mother is very religious, so she'd probably freak and try to talk me out of it."

"Look, Amanda, hundreds of women have abortions here every month. It's nothing to worry about."

"Do the women ever feel bad afterward?"

"Most don't, but you have your whole life ahead of you. Do you really want to wreck all your dreams to stay home and take care of a child for the next eighteen years? Are you ready for that kind of responsibility?"

"Well, no."

"You can have another child when you're married and are better able to take care of it. Besides, having babies costs a lot of money. You need to have a job and a place to stay before having one." The woman shrugged. "Remember, you can do whatever you want. It's your body."

"What about adoption?"

"That certainly is an option, but do you really want to go through the trouble of getting extremely fat, then undergoing the pain of childbirth, only to have the baby ripped away from you and given to someone else at the end? All your friends at school and family members will be talking about you. Everyone will know you're pregnant once that stomach of yours starts bulging out. I've had three children, and I can tell you from experience that being pregnant isn't easy. You're pretty uncomfortable for most of the nine months."

The clinic employee leaned back in her chair. "At sixteen, you should be out partying with your friends, not stuck at home for the next decade or two taking care of a kid."

Amanda sighed. "That's true. I don't want to quit school and get a job or stay home twenty-four seven with a kid. I want to have a good time."

"The decision is yours, Amanda. Once again, you can do whatever you want; it's your body."

"What will my friends and family think?"

"No one has to know."

"Okay."

Amanda reached into her backpack and handed the woman a wad of bills. The woman smiled as she counted the money. Then she had Amanda sign a series of forms electronically. Afterward, Amanda was taken to another room and given a johnny to change into. Sometime later, she was given drugs through an IV and escorted on a gurney into an operating room.

Jackson peered at her stomach and was able to see the four-month-old preborn baby boy resting comfortably in his mother's womb, sucking his thumb, oblivious to what was about to happen.

The doctor inserted a suction tube into Amanda's body. The baby instinctively pulled back as best he could, trying to snuggle farther up into the protection of his mother's womb. Guided by the doctor, the tube latched onto the boy's right leg and began pulling. The boy's face scrunched in pain as the suction pulled harder and harder. Jackson looked away in horror as the boy's leg was finally ripped whole from his torso.

Jackson cried out in anguish, "Oh, no! How can this be happening?"

Jackson continued watching, even though he didn't want to. Step by step, the doctor methodically continued dismembering the child. The left leg was stripped off next—more horror, more agonizing pain. The torso was then cut in two and sucked out, followed by the head.

Two angels arrived, visibly shaken. It didn't matter that they must have seen this drama many times over the years. They didn't seem numb, only sad. The angels retrieved the baby's soul from what was left of his body in the nearby waste canister and took the tiny boy with them. There was no cheering in heaven over the addition of another soul to God's family, just stunned silence.

Mekoddishkem turned to Jackson and whispered, "It's America's Holocaust."

The picture switched again, and they were standing in the waiting room as before. Summer began talking to her friend. "What do you think about what the woman with the baby outside said?"

"Who, McKenzie? The clinic lady was right. She's a religious kook. Don't pay any attention to her. You need to do what's right for you."

"Dawn's son was so cute, though. I mean, my baby isn't minus one day old, as in her example, but she or he probably is minus six months old or so."

"That's crazy. It's not minus anything. It's just a fetus. It's not a baby."

Summer shook her head. "It may not be fully formed yet, but it's going to be a baby someday."

There was a call from the attendant behind the glass window. "Summer?"

Summer stood up and approached the window. "I'm sorry, I've changed my mind."

The woman opened her mouth, likely to ask why, but Summer

was already halfway to the door. Without looking at her friend, she flung open the door.

On the way out, she muttered under her breath. "I hope that protester outside really can help me find a good home for my baby."

The heavenly assembly cheered.

Jackson raised his arms in triumph, "Yay! Well done, McKenzie."

He moved away from the sea of glass and retreated to his throne, far in the distance from God's throne. Although it was fascinating to witness all these different events, it was emotionally draining. He'd had enough for one day. And yet, these types of scenes must play out thousands of times per day before God. He sees them all. He's grieved by the tragedies and delighted by the victories. It's all part of his master plan to rescue those who want to be saved from a terribly corrupt and fallen world. The stakes are incredibly high. The eternal destiny of billions of precious human beings hangs in the balance every hour of every day.

At least he hadn't asked Mekoddishkem or Jesus why the abortion of Amanda's child wasn't stopped. Better not to be rebuked again, even though Jesus had been extremely gracious toward him following his comment about the Catholic priest.

The bad things that happen in this world were often the terrible price paid for having free will, the power to choose to do good or evil.

Everything the clinic worker told Amanda during her abortion appointment was a lie. Perhaps hers was the greater sin. The preborn baby had experienced excruciating physical pain, and Amanda would likely endure terrible physical pain many days after the abortion. But her mental pain, anguish, and guilt would be far greater. That pain would last a lifetime. *Oh, Lord, please use this tragedy to draw Amanda and the abortion clinic worker to yourself. Your forgiveness is their only hope for a new life on earth and later in heaven. I pray these things in Jesus's name, amen.*

CHAPTER 29

FULFILLING WORK

JACKSON AND HIS angelic companion stood outside the construction site. "Mekoddishkem, is there anything I can do to help prepare places for people?"

"What would you like to do?"

"Well, I was a pretty good project manager. I could do that."

The angel looked at him, stone-faced. "What would you *like* to do?"

Jackson responded instantly, "Whatever the Lord wants me to do."

Mekoddishkem sighed. "What would *you* like to do?"

Jackson thought for a moment. "*I* would like to paint pictures."

"Did you learn a lot during your class with Brother Caravaggio?"

"Yes, I did. The drawing felt so natural; it came so easily to me. I was a stick-figure guy on earth, but now I'm able to capture the real essence of the things I'm drawing."

"Great! Why don't you continue with your painting classes?"

"I'd like to, but it will take time away from my sister and daughter. I barely know them."

The angel shrugged his shoulders. "Perhaps you should bring them with you."

Jackson exclaimed, "Wow! I never thought of that. I bet they'd love it. Can we go to Brother Renoir this time instead of Brother Caravaggio?"

Mekoddishkem nodded. "Of course, Jackson, but you understand that is a totally different style of painting."

"I understand, but I think they would like that style better. I would like it better too."

The angel smiled. "Very well. I will make the necessary arrangements and will let you know when your appointment with Brother Renoir will be."

"Thank you, my good friend."

"You are welcome, Jackson."

Sometime later, Mekoddishkem escorted Jackson, Susan, and Joy into the painting studio of the renowned French Impressionist artist, Pierre-Auguste Renoir.

The canvas virtuoso glanced over and smiled as the youthful entourage entered. He beckoned them to sit on three nearby stools surrounding a vase of flowers. Each stool had a sketch pad and charcoal pencil already on it. Jackson glanced back at Mekoddishkem, who was standing in the doorway, smiling. *It is so unselfish of him to take me around heaven and wait for me while I take painting lessons.* "I never expected to be doing this in a million years."

Jackson sat on his stool and studied his favorite artist of all time. He'd seen photographs of Renoir as a young man in the late 1800s—pale white skin, medium-length brown hair with a mustache and beard, wearing a charcoal-gray double-breasted coat, and sporting a serious and somber disposition. Like everyone else in heaven, he was now wearing a white linen robe. His facial features were the same, but the serious and somber look was gone, replaced by a countenance of exuberant joy.

Renoir's presence in heaven was a surprise. Although he was raised Catholic, Renoir seldom, if ever, set foot in a church. During his life on earth, he had a wife, along with a mistress he never told his wife about, and multiple children by both. He was a chain-smoker with a nervous tic where he rubbed his index finger under his nose incessantly. He was a man of great anxiety and great contradictions—sometimes passive, other times aggressive; sometimes indecisive, other times clear-minded; sometimes shy, other times forceful. He didn't like being separated from his contemporary painting friends, who included Cezanne, Monet, Pissarro, and Sisley. He spent money freely and was often out of it, relying on wealthy patrons to support him during the early years of his career.

Renoir completed over four thousand works of art during his lifetime on earth. He never portrayed French society's problems and evils in his paintings, nor did he paint conventional, lifelike portraits. Instead, he captured idealized versions of people, perhaps trying to reflect what they could be rather than who they were. Renoir once told a friend his primary goal in painting was to spread joy.

Jackson surveyed the four walls around the studio. All were covered with paintings, each of which, at first glance, was a masterpiece. He could have stared at just one of them for hours, but that shouldn't have surprised him. After all, Renoir had been in heaven for the last hundred years, perfecting his technique.

A painting of a woman hung on the wall directly in front of him. It reminded him of the *Two Sisters (On the Terrace)*, a painting he loved and had a framed print of in his condo. He'd seen the original and literally spent hours studying and admiring it during two separate visits to the Art Institute of Chicago. The woman jumped off the canvas in a way he'd never seen before. Her face was so precise in detail and exuded an inner joy. The background was composed of various brightly colored hues applied with alternately heavy and light brush strokes, all permeated by soft, translucent light. Renoir once wrote he could paint a portrait in six two-hour sessions. Did it take him a shorter time to paint a portrait in heaven?

Jackson turned to his right and was met by a huge painting that reminded him of *Luncheon of the Boating Party*. Jackson had seen the original on a visit to The Phillips Collection, a museum in the Washington, DC, area while recovering from wounds sustained as a marine in Afghanistan. The painting he was now viewing also contained a large number of distinct personalities and subplots. He took a few moments to view it from different distances and angles, admiring how it seemed to change with each new step.

"Magnificent, Brother Renoir. It is a great honor to meet you and to view your work, especially with you standing right here beside me."

"Thank you, Jackson, the honor is mine. God gifted me to paint in this way, so I give him all the glory. What can I do for you today?"

Jackson stood between the two girls. He put his left arm around Susan's shoulder. "This is my sister, Susan." Susan reached out her hand, and Renoir shook it. Jackson then put his right hand on Joy's head. "This is my daughter, Joy."

"Such a beautiful family you have, Jackson. You must become models for me. May I paint all of you right now?"

Jackson's jaw dropped. "You want to paint us? Now?"

"Of course. It will only take me an hour or two."

Jackson was incredulous. "An hour or two?"

Renoir nonchalantly answered, "Of course. Do you have the time now?"

Jackson responded emphatically, "We absolutely have the time now. It would be a great honor to be painted by you, Brother Renoir."

Renoir nodded. He had Jackson stand directly behind the two girls, who were then seated on wooden stools. The great French Impressionist master was painting him and his family. How amazing!

"Wait! What about the scene behind us. Could you paint us at another location?"

"Of course. Where would you like to go?"

"The tree of life."

The group was transported with Mekoddishkem to the river which flowed from the throne of God. Fruit trees of all kinds grew on both banks of the river.

They came upon a massive tree that straddled either side of the river, bearing a fruit he'd never seen before. "What is that tree?"

"That is the tree of life."

Jackson walked along a golden sidewalk, reached up, and took a piece of the fruit. It was pear-shaped and copper-colored. As soon as he did that, another instantly appeared in its place. He took a bite. It was the best fruit he'd ever tasted. Energy from it instantly penetrated every muscle of his body.

Renoir was extremely focused while he worked. He'd periodically ask Jackson to alter his stance or have the girls change the position of their hands and feet. Surprisingly, Renoir didn't produce a drawing first, but he probably didn't need one. Renoir vigorously applied brush strokes to the canvas resting on a wooded easel with its back facing them. Thankfully, the rheumatoid arthritis that had plagued him in his later years was now gone.

Time passed. He didn't know how much, exactly, but it seemed to go by quickly. Renoir looked up from his easel. "It's finished, Jackson. Would you like to see it?"

Susan and Joy hopped off their stools and ran straight to the opposite side of the easel. The first thing that struck Jackson about the painting was Renoir's portrayal of the girls' hair. It was so exquisite, so detailed and lifelike; amazingly well done. Similar to his painting *Madame Charpentier and Her Children*. The daughters' hair in that family portrait was incredibly lifelike as well. He'd seen the original during a visit to the Metropolitan Museum of Art in New York City.

The group returned to the studio. Renoir had the girls pick up their sketch pads and charcoal pencils, and he drifted off with them to a nearby room. Jackson stayed behind, studying the freshly painted masterpiece in detail. How could something so beautiful be created so quickly? He could stand there for hours, staring at it.

He caught himself and sighed. He needed to go sit with Susan and Joy. He'd have plenty of time to look at the picture later.

After a short time of drawing, Susan, Joy, and Jackson handed their sketches to Renoir. He paused and thoughtfully considered each one. After praising Susan's and Joy's work, he turned toward Jackson and said, "You will become a great painter one day if you work hard."

Jackson teared up. "Thank you, Brother Renoir. That means a great deal coming from you. May I ask a favor?"

"Of course."

Jackson placed his hand on Renoir's shoulder. "Would it be possible to borrow your painting of us for a while? I want to spend time studying and admiring it, and I'd also like to show it to the rest of my family."

"Borrow it? Of course not."

Jackson blinked at Renoir's reaction. Had he overstepped?

Before he could apologize, Renoir responded, "You must take it. It's yours."

"What? Take it? Are you sure? Really? Oh, thank you, Brother Renoir. I never imagined I'd have an original Renoir painting in my home and never dreamed I'd be included as one of the subjects in it. What a great blessing."

"You are most welcome, Jackson."

He pulled in a deep, satisfied breath. He had a clear purpose for his life here in heaven. His mind was focused. He couldn't believe it was possible to be this happy.

CHAPTER 30
RIPTIDE

THE MEETING HALL was filled with folding chairs and parents shifting in their seats.

McKenzie sat up straight when her son's name was called.

"Jack Trotman."

Jack, now twelve years old, stood. He was wearing an olive-green Boy Scout uniform as he walked to the front of the hall.

The scoutmaster handed Jack a badge enclosed in a small wax paper wrapper. "Jack is being promoted to First Class tonight." He shook Jack's hand. "Congratulations."

Jack smiled and returned to his seat as McKenzie and the other parents clapped.

Her gaze wandered around the room as she waited for all the other boys to receive their awards. She read through several banners hanging on the walls:

Scout Law:	Scout Oath:	Scout Motto:	Scout Slogan:
A scout is Trustworthy Loyal Helpful Friendly Courteous Kind Obedient Cheerful Thrifty Brave Clean Reverent	On my honor, I will do my best to do my duty to God and my country and to obey the Scout Law; to help other people at all times; to keep myself physically strong, mentally awake, and morally straight.	Be prepared	Do a good turn daily

Thankfully, Jack was being steeped in traditional values each week, as they would surely make him a better citizen and a better person, but impressing the Word of God on his mind and heart was even more important.

The following morning, McKenzie sat with Jack at the breakfast table for their daily devotional. She was reading from Ephesians 6:10–17:

Finally, be strong in the Lord and in his mighty power. Put on the full armor of God, so that you can take your stand against the devil's schemes. For our struggle is not against flesh and blood, but against the rulers, against the authorities, against the powers of this dark world and against the spiritual forces of evil in the heavenly realms. Therefore put on the full armor of God, so that when the day of evil comes, you may be able to stand your ground, and after you have done everything, to stand. Stand firm then, with the belt of truth buckled around your waist, with the breastplate of righteousness in place, and with your feet fitted with the readiness that comes from the gospel of peace. In addition to all this, take up the shield of faith, with which you can extinguish all the flaming arrows of the evil one. Take the helmet of salvation and the sword of the Spirit, which is the word of God.

"Mom, what does all that mean?" He put a piece of toast into his mouth and chewed it.

McKenzie put down her glass of orange juice and cleared her throat. "It means that just as there are God the Father, God the Son, God the Holy Spirit, and the holy angels living in the heavenly realms who are good, there are also Satan and demons living in the heavenly realms who are bad. The Bible says the forces of evil rule over our world. That's why it's so messed up.

"There are battles between good and evil going on all the time in the heavenly realms that we know nothing about because they operate in a dimension invisible to us. These evil forces especially hate Christians and often attack them, hoping to turn them away from God because they're a threat to their plans and because Christians will one day rule the world with God instead of them."

"Are demons like monsters?"

"Yes, only demons are real and monsters are make-believe."

"That sounds scary."

"It is."

"How do demons attack people?"

"Primarily through the mind. Just look at each piece of the armor in Ephesians, chapter six, and that will tell you how they attack us."

"What do you mean?"

"Well, take the *Belt of Truth*, for example. Why is that mentioned?"

"I don't know."

"Satan and his demons will attack you with lies. The only way to avoid being fooled by them is to know the truth."

"What are some of the lies they tell?"

"They say that the theory of evolution is fact and that we got here on earth by accident, but the truth, as noted in the Bible, is that God created us."

"So, evolution is a lie?"

"In terms of an explanation of our origins, yes. There is scientific evidence for cells in our body changing, like when you have a cold, but there is no scientific evidence that a frog somehow evolved into an ostrich over millions of years."

"What else?" Jack lifted his spoon and began eating his oatmeal.

"The *Breastplate of Righteousness* means we should always strive to do the right thing. Satan, or one of his demons, will tempt us to do the wrong thing and then condemn us afterward if we actually do it. It's pretty twisted.

"The *Gospel of Peace* means we should rest in the fact that Jesus paid the penalty for our sins by dying on the cross, resulting in peace between us and God. Satan tries to get us to work our way into heaven by performing good deeds.

"The *Shield of Faith* means we should believe God's promises as written in the Bible. Satan tries to get us not to believe them.

"The *Helmet of Salvation* means we should trust that Jesus has saved us from hell and will welcome us into heaven. Satan tries to convince us we're not saved.

"The *Sword of the Spirit* means we can use Bible verses as an offensive weapon against Satan's attacks. Reciting Bible verses puts

Satan on the defensive. The Bible says to resist the devil, and he will flee from you."

Jack picked up his plate, bowl, and silverware, and placed them in the kitchen sink. "Wow, Mom, that's an awful lot to understand. Is it okay if I didn't get it all?"

"Sure. You can study it later. It takes a lifetime to grow into a mature Christian, but what I taught you this morning is very important. It's time to brush your teeth and finish getting your backpack ready. We'd better get going soon. I don't want you to be late for the last day of school."

⸎

The next day was Saturday and the start of summer vacation. McKenzie and Jack hopped into the car and began the hour-and-a-half journey to Watch Hill Beach in Westerly, Rhode Island. It had been McKenzie and Jackson's favorite beach while Jackson was still alive. Jack had grown to love this place too. In past years, he'd particularly looked forward to riding on the Flying Horse Carousel, but he was too old for that now. Her baby was growing up. These days he simply enjoyed the ice cream at the St. Clair Annex more than anything else.

The parking was expensive, at least double what they were charging at nearby Misquamicut State Beach. They walked on the concrete sidewalk up the hill from the parking lot, past Taylor Swift's summer mansion that was perched on the highest point overlooking the ocean, then down a pebble and dirt path to the beach below.

McKenzie smiled at the expanse of soft sand. It was the most beautiful beach in the world.

The waves were great for bodysurfing that day. There were no lifeguards at the beach, so as a precaution, McKenzie set up her beach chair and umbrella beside the border to the Ocean House Hotel beach, which did staff a lifeguard.

Jack spent hours riding his boogie board on the waves. She made it a point to never take her eyes off him.

Her phone rang, and she dug for it in her bag. "Hi, Mom. What's up?"

Her mother's voice had become gravelly since she'd retired from teaching, but the Boston accent was as pronounced as ever. "Hi, honey. Where are yah?"

"I'm at the beach with Jack."

"Oh, that sounds like fun. Is he done with school for the year?"

"Yes."

"I was just calling to see if you and Jack would like to come up to the North Shore for a weekend, or perhaps a week, sometime this summer."

"Sure. Let me check my calendar." She fetched the calendar book out of her beach bag and looked at July. She glanced up. Jack was pretty far out, apparently waiting for just the right wave. "Hold on."

She got up and walked down to the surf. She waved at Jack to come in closer, which he did.

Then she returned to her beach chair and picked up the phone. "Mom?"

"Yes, honey."

"July Fourth weekend looks good."

"Okay. That's good for us too. Sounds like a plan. I'm looking forward to it."

"Me too. Take care. Love you."

"I love you too, honey. Oh, before you hang up, there's a nice young man from our church whom I'd like you to meet. Maybe I could invite him over for dinner one evening so you could say hello."

"Mom, please. I'm really not interested, but thanks for offering."

"Sweetheart, Jackson has been gone twelve years now. He was the love of your life, but you deserve to be happy again."

"I am happy, Mom. I don't need a man to make me happy."

"Okay, sweetheart. I understand. But just think about it. Okay?"

"Love you. Bye, Mom."

McKenzie huffed, then scanned the shoreline for Jack. He wasn't there. She shifted her gaze farther out but still didn't see him. Suddenly, the hotel lifeguard appeared in her peripheral vision, running into the ocean with a small, bright red flotation device clasped to her right arm.

Jack's boogie board was flipping in the surf, but no Jack. She got up and ran down to the water to investigate. *Don't panic. He's got to be around here somewhere.*

She surveyed the beach and water again but couldn't find him. She screamed, "Jack! Jack! Where are you? Jack!"

⁛

A strange voice spoke to Jack in a whisper. "Glad I brought my goggles. I wonder if there's any money or jewelry on the seafloor that someone might have lost."

A gleaming object rested about five feet down. He took a deep breath and dove to the bottom. As he got closer, it appeared to be a piece of metal. Once he reached the bottom, he picked it out of the sand and held it in front of his face. A small tin food container someone had discarded or lost. Nothing special. He started to surface because he was getting short on air but was suddenly caught in a strong current that pulled him out to sea.

Jack looked up. The water was getting deeper. Ten feet of water over his head, then fifteen. He had to get air as soon as possible. He struggled toward the surface with all his might, but he couldn't get there. *Only a few seconds left. I can't take any more.*

Then, out of oxygen, he did what he had to do. He let out all his air and breathed in the saltwater. It offered relief for a second, but this was short-lived. As he gasped for more air, everything suddenly turned black, like someone had turned out the light.

When he awoke, he looked down. A horrid-looking creature with yellow teeth was holding him by the ankle. He tried with all his might to escape, but it was useless. Out of desperation, he prayed. *Jesus, come quick. Save me from this demon.*

As bright as the sun, the image of a man suddenly appeared directly opposite him, suspended in the water about ten feet away. The man pulled out a sword and began slashing at the creature.

The creature fled, then the man returned and looked directly into Jack's eyes. It was the man from the picture on his mother's vanity. It was his father, and he was smiling. Jack smiled back.

Suddenly, his body lurched as something or someone abruptly pulled him to the surface.

❧

A crowd had formed on the shoreline, watching as the lifeguard dove underwater again and again. The buoy attached to her arm gave a clear indication of where she was frantically searching.

McKenzie paced back and forth on the sand. This was just like what had happened years ago on the beach at Block Island, only this time it was her child who was missing.

She screamed again. "Jack! Jack, where are you?" *How could I have been so stupid and irresponsible?*

The lifeguard surfaced and began dragging a person toward the beach. It was Jack! She shrieked and ran into the water to help pull his limp body onto the beach.

The lifeguard laid him on his back and began CPR. She performed several rounds but without success.

McKenzie raised her hands upward and cried out, "Oh, God in heaven, please save my little boy. In Jesus's name, I pray, amen."

Another round without success.

Please, God. Please help. Jesus! We need your help right now.

The lifeguard tried again, this time giving a sharp thrust to Jack's stomach. Water erupted from his mouth, and after a coughing fit, he began breathing normally.

She hugged her boy. "Oh, Jacky, Jacky, I'm so glad you're safe. Thank God."

She released her son, stood, then knelt beside the lifeguard and hugged her too. "Thank you so much for saving my son. How can I ever repay you? I'm so sorry I wasn't watching him. I got distracted by a phone call."

"You're very welcome, ma'am. I'm just paying it forward."

"What do you mean?"

"Someone saved me from drowning a long time ago, and I lifeguard every summer, hoping to return the favor."

"That's very honorable. I was just thinking about a rescue I saw years ago on Block Island."

"How long ago?"

"Let me think. Jack here is twelve, and I had married his dad about a year before that, and then we were both working on Block Island seven years before that, so it was twenty years ago."

"I was rescued on Block Island twenty years ago. Which beach?"

"Let me think. It was the one with the cliffs."

"Mohegan Bluffs?"

"Yes, Mohegan Bluffs."

"You're kidding? That's the beach where I was saved."

McKenzie placed her hand on her chin. "I remember it was a little girl in a purple bathing suit who was saved. She was probably eight years old."

"I'm twenty-eight. I don't remember what I was wearing, but purple is still my favorite color. That's an amazing coincidence."

"I don't believe in coincidences. God orchestrates things for a reason. Let me tell you something more amazing. This boy's father is the one who saved you."

"Really? That's incredible. Where is he now?"

"In heaven. He passed away before Jack was born. It was the day after our wedding night, as a matter of fact."

The lifeguard placed a hand on McKenzie's forearm. "I'm so sorry. I wish he were here so I could thank him."

"You already did."

Jack sat up. "I saw Daddy underwater. He was as white as lightning, and he smiled at me."

McKenzie's jaw dropped. "What do you mean?"

"He saved me from a demon who was holding me underwater."

"What? Have you been reading Ephesians, chapter six? Are you sure this isn't your imagination running wild, Jack?"

"Yes, Mom. I'm sure. He was attacking the demon with his sword."

The lifeguard chuckled. "That's quite a dream you had, Jack."

Jack stood. "It wasn't a dream. I saw it with my own eyes. Angels and demons are real. The Bible says so."

McKenzie smiled at the lifeguard. "We just read about angels and demons in the Bible yesterday." She studied Jack. "Are you sure?"

"Yes, Mom."

"Okay." McKenzie turned to the lifeguard. "Once again, how can I ever repay you?"

"You already have."

"What's your name?"

"Ashley."

McKenzie shook her hand. "Nice to meet you, Ashley. I know my husband saved you physically twenty years ago and that you saved our son physically today, but are you saved spiritually?"

"What do you mean?"

"I mean, are you trusting in Jesus to wipe away all your sins so that you can spend eternity with him in heaven one day?"

"Honestly, I don't know what you're talking about. I don't know anything about Jesus or sin."

"Come with me." McKenzie, Ashley, and Jack all went up to the place where McKenzie had been sitting on the beach. She reached into her beach bag and pulled out a New Testament. McKenzie wrote her name, phone number, and email address on the inside cover, then handed it to Ashley. "Read this book cover to cover, then call or email me. This book will change your life forever. Promise?"

"Promise."

CHAPTER 31
SAVED

BOTIS APPEARED BEFORE Satan in his throne room, shaking like a leaf.

"What do you have to say for yourself, Botis?"

"I tried my best, master. I drowned the boy, and he was unconscious, but his father, the traitor Jackson, appeared and attacked me while I was holding the boy underwater. Then a human lifeguard appeared and saved the boy. It wasn't my fault, master."

"Wasn't your fault? Of course, it was your fault. You failed me." Satan looked to his right and his left and issued a command. "Arise, attack."

The entire pride of golden lions was on Botis within seconds.

The following Sunday, Jesus summoned Jackson to the throne room. They observed his son, Jack, walking down the hallway at church. Jack approached his youth leader and asked to speak with him privately. They went into his office.

"Pastor, what must I do to be saved?"

Jackson wept from joy.

After Jack prayed to receive Jesus as his Savior, a golden cross appeared on his forehead. "Praise God. Lord Jesus, will my family be safe now?"

"I know the plans I have for your family, Jackson. Everything will be accomplished soon."

With a big smile, Jackson observed his son's baptism from God's throne room. Jack stood in the pool at the front of the church, dressed in a white robe. A pastor stood beside him, holding his hand. "Jack, why do you want to be baptized today?"

"Because it's a commandment."

"That's true. Anything else?"

"Because I want to show the whole world, and everyone in the heavenly realms, that I'm a Christian."

The pastor smiled and raised one arm upward. "Jack Trotman, by your profession of faith, I now baptize you in the name of the Father, the Son, and the Holy Spirit." He guided Jack down into the water, fully immersing him.

Peace and contentment washed over Jackson. He would see his son in heaven one day.

A moment later, a light from heaven shone on the pastor as he began his sermon. "Lots of people plan for retirement, but few plan for postretirement."

Word got back to Satan that Jack Trotman had become a follower of the Nazarene. Satan assembled his senior lieutenants and told them to survey the whole earth to determine if the enemy army had been resurrected.

They returned about an hour later. "There are still followers of the Nazarene walking the earth, master, and as best as we can determine, no resurrection of the enemy army has occurred."

Botis lay in pieces before Satan's throne. *Pathetic.* Satan walked over and touched his remains. Botis was reassembled into his former self. "I may still have use for you, Botis."

Botis nodded, then moved away, trembling, and stood beside Satan's other lieutenants.

Satan returned to his throne and addressed his underlings. "Once again, we are fortunate that the resurrection of the traitors did not occur. This is puzzling to me. Jackson Trotman must have another child out there somewhere. Search everywhere."

All of them answered at once, "Yes, master."

Satan leaned back on his throne. "I was certain Jackson's son was the one. Keep trying to kill him, just to be sure."

Botis replied, "Yes, master."

"Who could it be if it's not him?" Satan mumbled under his breath.

CHAPTER 32
THE PROM

JACKSON HADN'T LOOKED in on McKenzie for quite a while. It wasn't that he didn't love her; it was just that his mind was now so fully occupied by all that was available to him in heaven—painting, concerts, piano lessons, museums, and even visiting other planets. His greatest treasure, however, was basking in the love of God, face-to-face. Besides, God would have called him if there was a problem.

It was a beautiful day in late spring, sunny and about seventy degrees Fahrenheit, when he checked on her. McKenzie stood before his grave. He gasped the second he saw her. She'd aged. Not in a bad way. She was still beautiful, but crow's-feet had emerged around her eyes, and the rest of her face seemed weathered. A streak of gray ran through her hair on the right side. It didn't matter, somehow. Life had gone by quickly, like a vapor, but her inner beauty hadn't faded. In fact, she was stronger and more powerful in spirit than ever before, a force to be reckoned with in the heavenly realms.

"It's hard to believe, Jackson, but our son is seventeen years old. Jack loves baseball. Hall High School won the conference championship this year, and Jack was selected first-team, all-conference. He's an outfielder, just like you were, and he had a three forty batting average.

You'd be very proud of him. He didn't make the all-state team, and he's probably not good enough to play Division I baseball in college like you did at UConn, but he might be able to make a Division II or III team. Regardless, he's really enjoyed the sport over the years, from Little League up through high school.

"We've started looking at colleges. He likes UConn. His grades and SAT scores are good, so he should be able to get in. We're planning to visit Brown next week; not sure he'll get in there, though. It's even more competitive than when I applied. There are some Christian colleges on his list too—Gordon, Liberty, and Taylor. He likes Gordon. We haven't seen Liberty or Taylor yet. I don't want to push him in either direction. He needs to make up his own mind since he'll have to live with whatever decision he makes. It's his life to live.

"I never got to tell you this while you were alive, but I want to thank you for purchasing life insurance before we got married. What a blessing it's been. It would have been tough to work and raise a child as a single parent. I invested the money, and we have enough to pay for his college. Most importantly, having this money enabled me to pour my life into him without having to worry.

"It's been more than seventeen years since you were taken from me. I miss you so much." She paused to gather herself. "I hope you're having a good time with Jesus and God the Father in heaven, and with your mother, your sister, and your many other relatives dwelling there. But down here, it's lonely. The only thing that's keeping me sane is reading the Bible every morning with Jack, attending the ladies' Bible study at church, and volunteering in the pro-life movement.

"Oh, I forgot to tell you. Jack has a date for the junior prom tomorrow. Her name is Katarina, and she's very nice. She's a cute redhead with blue eyes. They've known each other since middle school. She lives in Avon and is in the high school youth group with Jack at church."

McKenzie sighed. "Well, I guess that's it. Take care, sweetheart. I love you."

Jackson waved out of habit as she got up to leave. "I love you too, sweetheart. I'll see you again very soon."

If only he'd been there to play catch with his son as he grew up. It would have been one of the greatest joys of his life. He'd have to ask Jesus for two gloves and a ball, so they could make up for lost time when they were reunited in heaven one day.

If McKenzie only knew the joys awaiting her on the other side, she wouldn't be so downcast in spirit. Although she couldn't see it, the Spirit of Jesus was right there inside of her, guiding and comforting her. But for now, for a short time, she'd have to suffer. This was designed to make her faith grow stronger and her dependence on God grow deeper. For when the precious things of this life were taken away from her, she had nothing left to hold onto except Christ. *Just keep God in the forefront of your mind, McKenzie, and everything will work out for the best.*

He prayed that God would fill the void in McKenzie's life left by his passing. She could get married again. After all, the Scriptures allowed her to remarry if she wanted to. But McKenzie hadn't faltered. So far, she hadn't wanted anyone else. Her love for him was unbending.

Jackson looked in on McKenzie the next day. It was mid-May, cloudy, and a comfortable sixty-five degrees Fahrenheit. Jack stood in the Rose Garden on the West Hartford side of Elizabeth Park. Like his father, he was six-foot-two and muscular with jet-black hair and fair skin. He looked dapper in a black tuxedo, while his date wore a full-length black chiffon dress. Katarina was about six inches shorter. Her curly red hair bounced as she stepped toward Jack and handed him a small white box. Katarina didn't have a cross on her head, but it was just a date.

"Thanks, Katarina." Jack opened it and took out a white boutonniere with a pin stuck through the supporting green neck. Katarina reached up to pin the boutonniere on the left lapel of his jacket.

Then Jack handed Katarina a pink box containing a wrist corsage. She smiled and put it on.

The couple stood arm in arm directly behind a series of horseshoe-shaped trellises covered with pink roses. McKenzie and Katarina's parents smiled as they busily took pictures of the couple with their mobile devices.

Other prom-bound couples were playing out the same ritual nearby.

Jack drove Katarina from Elizabeth Park to the Farmington Marriott. They entered the ballroom and stood by the wall as they waited in line to find their seating assignments.

They were just friends and had been for a long time. So, it wasn't really a date. But Katarina wasn't playing fair. The makeup and lipstick were new on her. She was captivating, which tangled his insides up. She looked like a magazine model, as if he didn't even know her. The other guys were staring at her too, wondering who she was. Jack became so enamored he got tongue-tied, and he leaned against the wall, reminiscent of his days at middle school dances.

Katarina shoved him hard on his pecs.

Jack chuckled. "What was that for?"

"Snap out of it, boy. The night is young."

That was all it took. He relaxed, and after dinner, they went out on the dance floor and had a great time.

After the DJ played the final song, Jack returned to the table with Katarina and collected their belongings. As they walked out of the ballroom, he smiled and offered his arm to her. She smiled back and took it.

They went outside and began the long walk to the United Technologies parking lot. He had parked his car there because they weren't able to find a spot at the hotel.

A thin, disheveled, balding man, about five-nine and in his midthirties, approached them from behind a bush just outside the hotel property. He displayed a knife in his right hand. "Give me all your money. Now!"

Katarina squealed. Jack took her hand. "I'll handle this."

Jack glanced into his eyes. The guy looked possessed. He must be high. Jack felt for his mom's Smith & Wesson Bodyguard .380 pistol. It was concealed in his right pants pocket in a wallet holster. After learning about his father's shooting death, the kidnapping of his aunt, and the invasion of his mother's home by sex traffickers, he'd never go to a public event without it. He had the upper hand, but the other guy didn't know it.

He would be justified in shooting him but decided on a peaceful approach. It wasn't worth killing someone over a few dollars. He reached into his left rear pants pocket, pulled out his wallet, and handed the man all the money he had.

The man's eyes widened as he looked Katarina up and down. "Now give her to me."

Jack pulled Katarina behind him, gave her the car keys, and said, "Go to the car and call nine-one-one."

Suddenly, an idea popped into his head. He slipped off his jacket and wrapped it around his left forearm. If it came to a fight, he could take this guy. "Back off. I don't want to fight, but I will if I have to."

The guy lunged. Jack blocked the jab with his covered left forearm, then kicked his assailant in the groin. As the man stood there, moaning and hunched over, Jack turned and broke the man's left kneecap with his right heel, a move he'd learned from a friend who'd taken karate.

The man made a quick swipe at him. Searing pain shot through

Jack's thigh. The guy had stabbed him. Jack fell to the ground. His leg really hurt, but he could deal with it.

He tried to get up… but couldn't.

Enraged, the assailant cried out, then limped toward Jack, knife in hand.

No choice. Jack pulled the .380 out of his pocket, turned off the safety, and shot the guy in the chest.

The man slumped over sideways beside him, dead. Blood flowed onto the pavement between them.

❧

Jackson had been standing nearby, praying for his son. Unfortunately, Jack would carry the burden of having killed someone for the rest of his life, but there had been no choice. Even so, he'd have some answering to do with the police about that pistol since he wasn't old enough to carry a permit. At least he and Katarina were still alive.

The next events occurred like clockwork. It sickened Jackson every time he saw it. Two demons arrived and retrieved the dead man's soul.

Suddenly, a demon came out of the man's body—it was Botis!

Jackson inflicted a gaping wound in Botis's torso with all his might.

Botis cried out in agony.

"How dare you try to kill my son again. In the mighty name of Jesus Christ, be gone, you monster."

Botis scampered away as fast as he could.

A police car arrived. The officer quickly affixed a tourniquet to Jack's leg and applied pressure on the wound with a large gauze bandage. Katarina rushed over as he lay on the ground. She propped up his head on her lap and held his hand. "Jack. Are you okay? Are you hurt?"

"Yeah, he got me with his knife. I'll be okay." He looked down at his leg. "It looks like I've lost some blood."

"I'm here for you, Jack. Hang in there. Okay?" Tears filled her eyes.

Jack's eyes drifted closed. He was losing consciousness.

The wound must be worse than Jackson had thought. When he'd been shot in Afghanistan, he'd passed out as well. "Father in Heaven, please get my boy some help. He needs it right now. Please heal him. In Jesus's name, I pray, amen."

In heaven, Jesus would also be interceding for Jack.

CHAPTER 33
PREPARING

THE IMAGE OF Jack's late father on his mother's nightstand, smiling and handsome, wearing his marine officer dress blue uniform, had hung in Jack's mind ever since he was old enough to understand what it meant. Even though Jack had never met Jackson, he wanted to be like him. Hopefully, his dad would be proud of him when they met in heaven one day.

During the incident on prom night, Jack had gotten a taste of how it felt to protect someone. He'd recovered and gone off to college, but academics never fulfilled him. He needed that sense of purpose again, so he'd joined the marines right after college.

In early September, Jack drove down Interstate 95 from Connecticut to Quantico, Virginia, orders in hand. He stayed in a motel just off base the night before he was due to report. He was pretty tired from the trip and tried to get as much sleep as possible but ended up watching TV until about two in the morning.

Jack walked out to his car the following morning after a crummy breakfast at the motel. It was unusually hot and humid for this time of year. Was he doing the right thing? His stomach burned like acid had been poured into it.

He drove to the base entrance, showed the marine guard his orders and ID, and was allowed to pass through. He followed the signs to the Officer Candidate School reception area and parked his car. His backpack was crammed with everything listed on his OCS packing list: money, collared shirts, pressed slacks, running gear, flip-flops, towels, and toiletries. He left many of his personal belongings in the car.

Inside, he was directed to a warehouse where he was issued standard marine equipment, including a web belt, two canteens, a shovel, camouflage covers and utilities, pant belts, socks, and boots. Everything issued was then stuffed into an olive-green marine duffle bag.

The next stop was the barbershop. Jack couldn't watch as his wavy, jet-black hair was lopped off. He refused to look in the mirror afterward.

He was then directed to a classroom and told to sit in one of the available chairs, along with all the other candidates. The senior officer in charge gave a quick orientation, then ordered the staff to come forward. As the drill instructors entered the hall, they began yelling and screaming at the candidates, flipping over tables, throwing chairs, and demanding they get outside immediately. Every subsequent command had to be properly and speedily obeyed without question or hesitation.

When they were finally ordered back to the squad bay, which contained perhaps thirty bunk beds with storage trunks for each candidate, they were told to bring all their stuff outside and dump it on the blacktop so it could be inspected. Absolute perfection would later be demanded regarding how each rack was to be made, how shoes were to be shined and aligned beneath it, and how the gear was to be stowed in the trunk.

Much of the first three weeks were focused on the basics—physical fitness training, running the obstacle course, classroom instruction, and drilling on the parade deck. Their instructors demanded absolute obedience. Jack was evaluated after each event. The staff would decide if they wanted to make him a leader of other marines. One of the most interesting challenges was the Quigley, a trench filled with muddy swamp water that had to be navigated while fully immersed in combat gear and while the candidate attempted to keep his M16 rifle dry.

One member of his platoon was dropped from OCS due to an injury, and another dropped on request after deciding the Marine Corps wasn't for him.

Liberty was granted after the third week. Jack had a nice steak dinner with some of his buddies at a local restaurant. It was a relief not to have someone screaming at him to finish his food right away. After eating, he went back to the motel, relaxed in the hot tub for about fifteen minutes, then went to his room and crashed for twelve hours.

Jack returned to base Sunday evening. His instructors woke him up at the crack of dawn the next day. After physical training and breakfast, he struggled to stay awake in Marine Corps history class.

The next big test was SULE, or Small Unit Leadership Evaluations. During this phase of OCS, Jack had to work with his team to overcome logistical challenges, including a simulation in which they had to transport a wounded marine up a steep, muddy embankment.

Ten weeks passed in the blink of an eye. In mid-November, it was time for graduation. What had once been a ragtag mob of civilians was now a well-oiled, lean-green machine. Jack marched with pride on the parade deck to his platoon sergeant's staccato commands. His mother and girlfriend would be in the stands, watching. Hopefully, his dad was also watching from heaven.

Jackson had been basking in the presence of God for a long time. Perhaps he'd been lying before the throne for a few days; maybe it had even been weeks or months. Time was a funny thing in heaven.

The focus was more on experiencing God's joy in the present, than in dwelling on the past or the future.

Praise just kept pouring out of him. He couldn't help it. God filled him to overflowing with immeasurable joy. Even his pores oozed praise. He couldn't explain it, but that was how it was. He couldn't get enough of God's goodness.

Out of nowhere, it occurred to him that he should visit the women in his life—his mother, sister, and daughter. So, just like that, he got up and left.

Jackson knocked on the door to Rachel's house.

"Hello, Jackson. It's been a while. How are you?"

"Fine, Rachel. I'm looking for my sister and daughter. Do you know where they are?"

"They're not here," Rachel replied. "Susan and Joy moved out quite a while ago. They're living at your mother's house now."

Jackson thanked her, then left. He hadn't been to his mother's new heavenly home yet. This should be quite a treat.

Jackson willed himself to the entrance of his mother's home. It was a massive eighteenth-century French chateau fit for a queen. He counted ten white-trimmed floor-to-ceiling windows on the first floor, the same on the second, then smaller windows on the third. The perfectly symmetrical redbrick façade, accompanied by a gray slate roof, was truly magnificent.

He knocked on the front door and was quickly greeted by his mother. "Jackson! What a surprise. It's so good to see you. Where have you been?"

Jackson looked around the lobby. Eighteenth-century furniture was everywhere—a writing desk with a chair, a grandfather clock, and period paintings he'd have to study later.

"I got caught up in worshipping God, Mom. I don't know how long I was there. I suddenly realized I should spend time with you, Susan, and Joy."

"Oh, trust me, Jackson. It's not been a problem. I've thoroughly enjoyed getting to know your daughter. Joy is such a delight. I want to be with her all the time now. It makes up for not having any grandchildren of my own while I was on earth."

"I'm so glad, Mom. It seems you've found meaning and purpose here." Jackson fidgeted. "I guess you know Joy better than I do."

"God comes first. I get that. You'll have all eternity to get to know your daughter better. But so that you know, spending time with your daughter has been the most wonderful part of my life. I couldn't be happier."

Joy burst into the room and dove into her grandmother's embrace. She looked up at Jackson and calmly said, "Hi, Daddy."

He descended to his knees and opened his arms. Joy strolled over to him and allowed him to hug her.

"Where have you been, Daddy?"

"With God."

"Oh."

Jackson scanned his daughter's eyes. "Would you like to go with me to Brother Renoir's studio for a painting lesson?"

"Sure, Daddy. Can we bring Melody?"

Jackson stood up. "Who's Melody?"

Mom responded, "McKenzie's daughter."

A sprightly toddler with brown pigtails entered the room. She was the spitting image of McKenzie.

Jackson gulped.

Mom pointed at Jackson. "This is my son, Melody. He's also Susan's brother and Joy's daddy. Most importantly, he married your mommy after you came to heaven."

Melody lit up, then ran over and hugged Jackson around his thighs. "What's my mommy like?"

"I'm so glad you asked, Melody. She's nice, kind, smart, beautiful, and lots of fun to be with. She's also a powerful follower of Jesus. We love each other very much. I'm sure she's looking forward to meeting you one day."

Melody scrunched up her brow. "Are you my daddy?"

Jackson chuckled, then quickly caught himself. "No, I'm not."

Melody took his hand. "Did you know my daddy?"

Jackson sighed. Memories of Dexter immediately came to mind—their fights, his rape and murder attempts, and him being tortured in hell. "Yes, I did, Melody."

"What is he like?"

How could he answer in a way that wouldn't hurt her feelings? After all, she was only a toddler. She didn't need to know everything. On the other hand, he had to tell her the truth. "He did not believe in Jesus or follow him."

"Will he be coming to live with Mommy and me in heaven?"

"No, he will not, sweetheart."

Melody paused, then put her hand on her chin. "Will you be my daddy?"

Jackson gasped, then chuckled nervously. "God is your real daddy, Melody."

"I know, but will you be my other daddy?"

"We'll have to ask your mommy when she gets here, but… well… I'm sure she'd say yes. So, yes, Melody. I will be your other daddy."

Melody lifted her arms, wanting to be picked up. Jackson complied. She hugged him around the neck. Such strength for a little toddler.

Soon, they left for Renoir's studio where Jackson continued preparing beautiful Impressionist paintings for McKenzie's and Monica's future homes in heaven, as well as Jack's. Hopefully, they'd like them when they got here.

A while later, Jackson visited Jack's graduation. Katarina and McKenzie smiled as Jack received his gold second lieutenant bars.

Katarina still didn't have a cross on her forehead. Hopefully, that would come in time.

He prayed God would watch over his son as he embarked on the next chapter of his life. With Jack as a marine, his guardian angel would certainly have his work cut out for him.

CHAPTER 34

NEW BIRTH

THREE YEARS LATER, Jackson hovered invisibly beside McKenzie in the hospital waiting room as their first grandchild was about to be born. Her hair was fully white now. She'd changed a lot from the young woman who'd given birth to their son. Jack's newborn eyes had been a blue hue he'd never seen before or since, except perhaps in heaven. The day of his son's birth didn't seem that long ago. Twenty-five years went by pretty fast in heaven.

Jackson breathed a sigh of relief as he surveyed the squad of angels assigned to protect his earthly family. It was so gracious of God to have granted his request for additional protection. He didn't want his heaven-dwelling mom, sister, or daughter to be there, just in case there was trouble. They watched in heaven from a distance instead.

Jackson's dad was in the waiting room with his new wife. It would be a proud moment for his dad—his first great-grandchild. *The new wife looks young. Quite a huge ring on her finger. That didn't take long. Wonder what Mom thinks? It's his right to remarry, according to the Bible, so she must be okay with it.*

Jack suddenly appeared at the sliding glass door entrance to the waiting room. He ignored everyone else and zeroed in on McKenzie. "Mom, I need you to come with me. Right now!"

Jack rarely, if ever, addressed her like that. Something must be wrong. McKenzie got off her chair and rushed toward her son. He looked grave. Of course, this would be a less joyful occasion than normal anyway, due to the baby's in utero spina bifida diagnosis, but something else must be going on.

Jack spoke as they walked briskly down the hallway. "The baby was born, but he hasn't started breathing yet. We need you in the room right away to pray."

They burst through the doors into the delivery room. The baby was lying on a cushioned table on his back. One nurse was applying chest compressions, three at a time, while the other controlled the oxygen flow through a mask placed over the baby's mouth and nose. They exchanged commands out loud to keep in sync with each other.

"One, two, three."

"Breathe."

"One, two, three."

"Breathe."

"One, two, three."

"Breathe."

McKenzie walked over to the table and grasped one of the baby's feet, trying to stay out of the nurses' way. She tuned out the noise and began to pray aloud. "Oh, Father in heaven. Nothing is too hard for you. Please rescue this precious little boy and let him live. We need your help right now, Jesus. Please help us. Don't let my little grandson die. Please, Jesus. Please don't let him leave us. You saved Monica and Jack when they desperately needed you. This baby desperately needs you right now. Please save this little boy. In Jesus's name, I pray, amen."

The doctor injected something into the baby through his umbilical cord.

"One, two, three."

"Breathe."

"One, two, three."

"Breathe."

"One, two, three."

"Breathe."

❦

Jackson prayed alongside McKenzie. They were in complete agreement.

Thousands of demons suddenly appeared, like spaceships in a *Star Wars* movie abruptly descending out of hyperspace. They were led by Satan and were there to fight. Surely this small contingent of angels would be no match for them. Jackson pulled out his sword. The demons quickly overwhelmed the small angelic contingent, and one of them placed his hand on the baby's chest.

The nurses' efforts weren't effective.

McKenzie lost her composure, tears streamed down her face. "Oh, Father, please don't let this little boy die. Send a legion of angels if you have to, but please don't let my grandson die."

Instantly, a legion of angels suddenly appeared about forty yards away. The archangel Michael was leading them. Jackson and the angels beside him ran to Michael's side.

Jackson raised his sword. "Yeah! Way to go, McKenzie!"

Everyone looked to Satan to see what would happen next.

Jackson glanced back at the delivery room. The demon no longer had his hand on the baby's chest, but the baby was still not breathing.

He glanced up and down the line of assembled angels. All had long swords drawn that were lifted high. He stared at Michael, waiting for a signal. Michael charged directly at Satan. Jackson followed right after him, along with the rest of the angels. Thousands of spirit beings quickly came to blows in hand-to-hand combat. Jackson had never seen anything like it, even in a 1930s swashbuckler movie.

The demons soon retreated. Jackson looked over and saw that his grandson was breathing on his own now. "Praise, God! Thank you, Jesus."

Once again, no one in the earthly realms would have had any clue what had been happening in the heavenly realms… with the possible exception of McKenzie.

CHAPTER 35
LOSING YOUR LIFE

JACK AND KATARINA named their baby Samuel.

A week had passed since they'd brought her grandson home from the hospital. McKenzie had given them space to begin their new journey, but it was odd that they hadn't reached out yet. She picked up her phone to call Jack. There was no answer, so she left a voicemail. "Hey, Jack, it's Mom. I hope you, Katarina, and the baby are doing well. I'd love to see you guys. Please give me a call when you get a chance and let me know how things are going."

A day passed, then another. Soon a full week had passed. McKenzie called Jack a second time. Once again, he didn't pick up. *Odd.* "Jack, this is Mom again. I miss you guys. I hope everything is okay. Please call me. I'm worried about you."

After two more days of no returned phone calls, McKenzie had to act. She drove from Connecticut to Virginia the following day to find out what was going on.

She knocked on the door of their apartment. Katarina answered it. Her red, rumpled hair crept over her shoulders. Brown circles hung beneath her eyes. They narrowed as she spoke. "What do *you* want?"

Stunned by her tone, McKenzie paused to gather her thoughts.

Don't let her use your words against you later. "You had a baby three weeks ago, and I haven't heard from you or Jack. What do I want? I want to see you, my son, and my new grandson. Jack hasn't returned my calls. I got worried. I didn't know if he was alive or dead. May I see them now?"

"Jack hasn't come home from work yet, and the baby's sleeping."

"Oh, that's okay. I'd love to see Samuel, even if he's sleeping. Is there anything I can do to help?"

Katarina gritted her teeth. "I don't want your help."

"Honey, what's wrong."

Katarina raised her voice. "I'm not your 'honey.' What's wrong? You're what's wrong. You and everyone like you. How could a loving God allow my precious little boy to be born with a horrible condition like spina bifida? What did he ever do to deserve that?"

"He didn't deserve it, but we live in a fallen world, Katarina. God originally made everything perfect, but sin corrupted the creation. We don't know all God's ways or why he allows terrible things to happen to some people, but we know he's for us. We know that no matter what happens to us, it's ultimately for our good. Don't you remember Romans 8:28? 'In all things God works for the good of those who love him, who have been called according to his purpose.'"

Katarina huffed. "Well, I don't see how this can work together for anyone's good. I don't want anything to do with your God, and I don't want to have anything to do with you. Go away, and don't ever come back here." Katarina pointed her finger at McKenzie. "Don't call, don't text, don't write, and don't send any presents. Just go away and leave us alone."

Katarina stepped back into the apartment, slammed the door, and locked it.

McKenzie stood there, bewildered and confused, for a moment. Sure, Katarina was dealing with a lot. But what could have possibly led to such a vitriolic outburst of anger? Finally, she walked to her car, closed the door, and bawled her eyes out.

❧

That night, at the hotel, McKenzie was driven to her knees to pray. *Lord, why is this happening? How can it be that I'm not allowed to see my son or grandson?* Jack had been her life. Now he'd been taken away too. She'd never get to know Samuel, and her grandson would never get to know her.

McKenzie prayed continually for weeks, asking God to intervene, to help Jack and Katarina come to their senses and bring about a reconciliation. The weeks turned into months—still no contact.

Daily routines became tedious and dreadfully dull. Every morning was the same thing: get up, put on the oatmeal, floss and brush her teeth, take a shower, get dressed, do dishes, take out the trash. How many thousands of times had she done these things, and how many thousands of times would she have to do them again.

Her family couldn't believe what was happening. Jack had been such a great son. Her mom and sister tried reaching out, but Jack rebuffed them too.

Monica and Jarek had two children now—a little girl and a little boy. Their video calls were the highlight of her week, but that job was overshadowed by the sadness of how Katarina had robbed her of the chance to know her grandson.

The silence continued for years. There was nothing to look forward to, nothing to live for. Just as King Solomon had declared everything meaningless, "a chasing after the wind," in the book of Ecclesiastes, there was no enjoyment, no pleasure in anything she did.

That evening, she knelt and prayed, "Lord, you've taken away my husband, my son, and now my grandson. I have nothing left. There's nothing here for me, nothing on this earth I desire. I don't want to live anymore. Take whatever years I have left and do whatever you want with them. Please speed your return. I can't wait to be with you and Jackson in heaven one day."

Over the years, she'd never stopped praying for Jack and little Samuel. She prayed that God would keep them safe and help Jack repent and honor his mother so that he would have a long life. She prayed for Katarina too. After all, Jesus had instructed his disciples to pray for their enemies.

McKenzie had read through the Bible many times over the years, studying it carefully and memorizing key portions of it. But while she knew the Bible well, she wasn't sure if she knew the author of the Bible well and if he even knew her. Jesus's words from Matthew, chapter seven were particularly troubling:

Not everyone who says to me, "Lord, Lord," will enter the kingdom of heaven, but only the one who does the will of my Father who is in heaven. Many will say to me on that day, "Lord, Lord, did we not prophesy in your name and in your name drive out demons and in your name perform many miracles?" Then I will tell them plainly, "I never knew you. Away from me, you evildoers!"

Was Jesus going to tell her one day that he didn't know her? Was that even possible? After all, she'd been following him for years. What was the will of the Father, anyway? She looked it up in the Matthew Henry commentary: First, believe in Christ; second, repent of sin; third, live a holy life; fourth, love one another; and finally, hear and do the sayings of Christ.

She believed in Christ and had repented of her sin. But had she believed and repented enough? Was the life she'd lived holy enough? Did she love her neighbor thoroughly enough? Did she teach about Christ frequently enough?

Foul, horrible thoughts that she couldn't repeat to anyone filled her mind. She immediately put on the armor of God and attacked her harasser with Scripture, but the assaults continued. Day after day, she fought them, but she could not conquer them on her own.

A deep, overwhelming dread permeated her mind and emotions. She'd never been so depressed before. What could she do? A thought of ending it all came to mind. The gun case was just down the hallway. It could be over so quickly. Her pain would be gone, and she'd be with Jackson right away. No more waiting, no more loneliness.

She buried her head in her hands until the feeling passed. A few moments later, she regrouped. If she had killed herself, she'd have to explain to God why the last act of her life was murder—the murder of herself. One of the Ten Commandments was not to commit murder. The thoughts continued plaguing her, so she called her friend. "Hi, Sally. It's been a long time. How are you?"

Sally's cheerful disposition jumped through the phone. "Hey, McKenzie. Good to hear from you. I'm doing just fine. How are you?"

"Not good. Do you remember the problems I was having with my thoughts years ago?"

"Yes. As I recall, I gave you several Scriptures to quote in the name of Jesus."

"That's correct. It worked back then, but it's not working now. I've doubted my salvation too. I've been praying, putting on the armor, and calling out Scripture, but the thoughts keep coming, and they are much more powerful this time."

"Perhaps it's a more powerful demon attacking you. Or perhaps it's Satan himself."

"What do I do?"

"Do you recall the passage where the disciples could not cast out some demons themselves, and Jesus cast those out for them?"

"Yes."

"You don't have to fight all your battles yourself, McKenzie. Instead, you can ask Jesus to fight them for you."

That evening, she did just that.

The following afternoon, her mind was clear. The bad thoughts were gone. First, she was relieved, then her relief turned to joy. "Wow! Jesus healed me. This is amazing! I've never experienced anything like this before."

Suddenly, an evil thought crept in, then another. She went to her bedroom, closed the door, knelt beside her bed and prayed, "Lord Jesus, please keep me out of the mud. I don't want to go back in the mud. Save me, Jesus! Please save me!"

Her mind cleared again. She vowed from that day forward to always stay near to God in prayer. She never wanted to go back to that dark place again.

The next day, McKenzie came across a verse in Zechariah, chapter thirteen that spoke to her. She'd had a spirit of impurity. There was no doubt Jesus had delivered her from it.

Now, reading the Bible wasn't just an intellectual exercise. God was real. He'd heard her prayer and healed her, personally. No doubt God knew her. All her determination, discipline, and self-sufficiency were not enough. She needed Jesus to help her overcome the world.

Weeks passed. She prayed formally on her knees, every morning and evening, and informally throughout the day, sharing her thoughts with God all the time. Amazingly, her mind had remained clear.

Other things changed too. She was watching less television, going to bed earlier, and sleeping better. The to-do list of the things she'd been putting off for months got done in a day. She was bolder when sharing Christ with others.

She asked Jesus to fix any other areas of her life that needed fixing, even those she wasn't aware of. She wanted to please God in every way and make him proud of her.

McKenzie finally understood Galatians 2:20: *I have been crucified with Christ and I no longer live, but Christ lives in me. The life I now live in the body, I live by faith in the Son of God, who loved me and gave himself for me.*

She'd been missing Jesus's joy and the abundant life he'd promised. She'd known Jesus in her head but not in her heart. How could she have followed Jesus all these years but not known him or been known by him? And what about the other people in her church? They needed to experience this close relationship with Jesus too.

God had worked out everything for her good. He'd used the fractured relationship with her son and daughter-in-law to help her die to herself and live for Christ. She needed God all the time now. She needed God every hour, just like the song said.

CHAPTER 36

RECONCILIATION

ON A RANDOM Saturday while she was arranging flowers, McKenzie's doorbell rang. She went to the front door and opened it. It was Jack. "Jack! Is that really you?"

He'd filled out and his hairline had receded, but it was still her boy. McKenzie hugged her son as he opened the storm door, weeping as he embraced her.

Jack looked into his mother's eyes. "I'd like you to meet someone."

She followed Jack outside as he went to his car and opened the trunk. He took out a wheelchair and then pushed it to the front passenger's side door. He opened it and lifted a boy, about ten years old, into the wheelchair. "This is Samuel, your grandson."

McKenzie fell to her knees in front of the wheelchair and grasped Samuel's hands. The boy's eyes studied her. Tears streamed down her face as she spoke. "Oh, Samuel, it's so good to finally meet you."

Samuel smiled. "It's nice to meet you too."

Jack placed his hand on McKenzie's shoulder and gently pulled her to her feet, then he ushered her aside. "I'm so sorry about everything, Mom. Katarina cracked when Samuel was born. She couldn't handle the pressure of raising him. We got divorced two months ago, and I have full custody."

"I'm so sorry, Jack."

"So am I. I had no idea things would end up like this. It was so unfair how we treated you all these years. Please forgive me."

McKenzie paused for a second. Though she'd been hurt by their actions, the joy of seeing them canceled out all those old feelings. God had finally answered her prayers. "Of course, I forgive you."

Samuel looked at the bouquet in McKenzie's hands. "What are those flowers for, Grandma?"

Being called Grandma was music to her ears. "These are for your grandpa's grave. He died before your father was born. I was just on my way over to the cemetery where he is buried."

Jack touched her elbow. "We can go with you. It's been a long time since I visited."

"Sure, but first, your visit calls for a celebration. Let's scrounge up your favorite meal—New York Strip steak and fresh corn on the cob."

"Whoo-hoo! Sounds like a plan."

McKenzie got in the back seat of the car. Jack placed Samuel in the front seat, then put his wheelchair in the trunk.

They traveled to a specialty meat store in Bloomfield. McKenzie gave Jack some money and stayed in the car with Samuel.

"So, Samuel, how do you like school?"

"It's fine."

"Do you have many friends there?"

"Not really. Some of the kids make fun of me because I'm in a wheelchair."

"That's very wrong. They shouldn't do that. It's not your fault you're in a wheelchair."

"I know. You're right, Grandma."

"What's your favorite subject?"

"I like English because we get to read stories."

"Oh, what kind of stories do you like?"

"*Star Wars.*"

"Do you like Luke Skywalker?"

"Yes."

"That's cool."

Jack got in the car, turned around, and placed the paper bag containing the meat in the back seat beside McKenzie. She leaned forward and pointed. "Take a right out of the parking lot and then a left at the traffic light. That will take us to a local farm where we can get the corn on the cob."

The group arrived at the farm stand. Samuel gawked at the corn. It was about eight feet high, ready to be picked. "Can I touch the cornstalks?"

"Of course." McKenzie went to buy the corn at the farm stand while Jack got out the wheelchair and pushed Samuel toward the cornfield.

She returned to the car. Since Jack and Samuel weren't back, she wandered over to the cornfield. She walked toward an opening in the corn. As she turned the corner, she looked down a dirt path and saw Samuel sitting in his wheelchair with Jack standing beside him. They were looking away from her and Jack had his hand on Samuel's shoulder.

McKenzie gasped. It was the exact image she'd seen in her dream and the exact image Mekoddishkem had shown her through The Wall. "Oh, Father, please protect my son and grandson from Satan and his minions. Please send a legion of angels to protect them right now. In Jesus's name, I pray, amen."

Not sure what all this meant, she kept it to herself.

⁕

They returned to McKenzie's house in West Hartford, Connecticut—the house Jack had grown up in after McKenzie sold the condo.

Jack wheeled Samuel backward up the front porch steps, then into the house. They went into the kitchen, and Jack positioned Samuel beside the table.

Jack then sat down at the table. "It's good to be back."

McKenzie put the teapot on the stove. "It's wonderful having you back. How have you been, other than the divorce?"

Jack shifted in his chair. "It's been awful. She got the house and half of our savings. To make things worse, I lost my job last month. These crises have forced me to reassess my priorities and figure out what's truly important. I realized I was missing God in my life, so I started going to church again with Samuel."

She placed her hand on Jack's. "I'm so sorry for all the trials you've been through, but I'm glad it's brought you closer to God."

Jack looked at Samuel. "You love your youth group, don't you, Samuel?"

"Yes, we have a great time, and everyone is very nice to me. I'm learning a lot about God too."

McKenzie perked up. "That's wonderful, Samuel. What are you learning about God?"

"That he loves me just the way I am, and he has great plans for me."

"That's true, Samuel. Do you know what his most important plan is for you?"

"No."

"To be in heaven with him someday."

Samuel had a puzzled look on his face. "What is it like in heaven?"

He has so much to learn. "It's a wonderful place where God the Father and Jesus live with the angels and all the people who loved him while they were alive."

"Like Grandpa?"

"Yes, like Grandpa."

"Does everyone go to heaven?"

"No. Only people who believe Jesus is God's Son and that he paid for their sins by dying on the cross."

"I believe that."

"You do? That's wonderful. Have you ever told Jesus that you're sorry for the bad things you've done and that you don't want to do them anymore?"

"No."

"Have you ever asked Jesus to forgive you?"

"No."

"Have you ever told Jesus that you want to obey his commands as laid out in the Bible and that you want to follow him for the rest of your life?"

"No."

"Would you like to do that now?"

"Of course. I love Jesus."

"Fantastic! Let me lead you in a prayer, the same way your grandpa led me in a prayer, and the same way your daddy's youth pastor led him in a prayer when he was a boy."

CHAPTER 37

IN THE TWINKLING OF AN EYE

JACKSON KNEW IN his spirit that McKenzie was coming to visit his grave. He left his painting and rushed to be with her. Her face had become wrinkled with age, yet her eyes were as bright and vibrant as the day he'd met her. Their conversations were a treasure, even though she couldn't hear his responses. He'd given up trying to communicate directly with her years earlier, choosing instead to wait for her to speak. It was unusual for her to come this late in the day.

She approached his grave with flowers in hand and placed them beside his gravestone. How thoughtful of her. There was a man and a boy in a wheelchair beside her.

"Jackson, I brought your son, Jack, and your grandson, Samuel, to visit with me today."

She knelt beside Samuel and said, "I speak out loud to Grandpa because I believe he can hear me from heaven. Can you tell Grandpa what you did a few minutes ago, Samuel?"

"I accepted Jesus as my Savior!"

Jackson jumped for joy. He looked for confirmation on their foreheads. His wife, son, and grandson, all had crosses glowing on them. Praise God for his blessing.

At just that moment, he heard Jesus calling for him. Jackson hesitated. Couldn't he spend a little more time with his family? Then again, he couldn't wait to rejoice with Jesus that his grandson was now a Christian.

Jackson appeared in the throne room. God's heavenly household stood before their thrones. Legions of angels hovered above. He'd never seen everyone assembled all at once like this.

Jesus turned to the great assembly. "This is a momentous day. The Father has declared that today is the day I go to gather my church."

Jackson switched his gaze to Mekoddishkem. "Is this the rapture?"

"Yes."

"Fantastic! I've been waiting so long. Why today?"

Jesus called aloud, "Jackson."

When the Holy One of God mentioned his name in the great assembly, Jackson startled. "Yes, Lord."

"Today is the day I will gather my church. The last person the Father has chosen before the start of the great tribulation has been saved."

Why is Jesus telling me this? "Who was the last person, Lord?"

"Your grandson."

Jackson teared up. "Does this mean..."

With a radiant smile, Jesus said, "Yes, Jackson, today you will be able to see McKenzie and hold her in your arms again."

He jumped high in the air, overcome with emotion. "Thank you, Lord."

Jesus said, "Mekoddishkem."

Mekoddishkem straightened up. "Yes, Lord."

"Go to McKenzie and show her what we discussed."

Jackson raised his hand. "Can I go with him?"

"No, you will need to wait a little longer, Jackson. You will see the rest of your family very soon."

Jesus nodded, and then a mighty angel raised a massive, ancient trumpet to his lips and blew into it. The sound was deafening and would surely get the attention of everyone in heaven.

A deep, powerful voice then exclaimed, "Qum," a command to arise.

৵

A nearby internment was about to begin at the cemetery. People were milling around, talking softly. The coffin rested beside a rectangular hole in the ground. Chairs were neatly arranged opposite it.

Samuel looked at them. "What are they doing, Grandma?"

"That's a funeral, Samuel." McKenzie pointed. "Someone just died, and they are burying their body in that hole in the ground. If that person was a Christian, their spirit will go up to heaven to be with Jesus."

Suddenly, no one in the funeral party moved a muscle. Everyone appeared to be frozen in time. Everyone except McKenzie, her son, and her grandson. She rushed to one of the men standing in the funeral party and nudged his shoulder. He didn't budge. She looked up and saw a blue jay suspended in midair, but its wings weren't flapping.

Samuel was crying. "Grandma, what's happening?"

She grasped her grandson's hand. "I don't know, Samuel."

She gazed upward and saw what appeared to be a fiery comet dropping out of the sky. The object seemed to be headed directly toward the cemetery. As it continued its descent, she picked Samuel up and held him tightly against her chest.

The ground trembled as the massive object crashed into the earth about twenty feet in front of them, causing her to lose her balance. The being landed in a crouched position with his back to them as if to brace the impact. He rose up slowly, turned, and stared directly at McKenzie. His face, hair, and clothing were as white as lightning, and he had a golden sash across his chest.

McKenzie screamed and fell prostrate to the ground with Samuel, trembling with fear. Jack dropped to his knees beside her, shaking like a leaf.

The angel walked over to them and placed a hand on each of their shoulders. The fear left her immediately. She looked up. "Mekoddishkem?"

"Yes, McKenzie. It is I." The angel dipped his head. "I am here to grant you an extraordinary gift—the privilege of seeing the dead in Christ rise to meet their Lord."

McKenzie stood and looked out into the cemetery.

Suddenly, the top burst off the coffin at the internment.

Samuel clung to her.

"What was that?" she asked.

Mekoddishkem crossed his arms. "You will see."

The man in the coffin sat upright, looked around, raised his arms in victory, and shot up into the sky.

A few seconds later, a skeleton rose from the ground directly in front of an old Civil War era gravestone. The dirt had not been disturbed. An invisible force began skillfully weaving tendons and flesh over the dry bones. Finally, the body was covered with a shimmering white linen robe.

The person gasped his first breath and stared at McKenzie, incredulous. He appeared to be about thirty years old, and a look of extreme elation came over his face. Then he was whisked away, straight up into the clouds.

Numerous skeletons passed up through the ground without disturbing the dirt. New bodies were weaved for a woman, a boy, and a man who had been buried nearby. More people could be seen blasting up into the clouds from the old Memento Mori cemetery about three-quarters of a mile away. Colonial-era Native Americans and other departed souls emerged from unmarked graves near the river and meadows below, then rose into the clouds.

Nearby, ashes appeared in the air and settled into two piles on the ground. The piles began swirling and, eventually, formed into a man and a woman who were quickly swooped upward.

"Why is everyone around me frozen in time?" McKenzie asked.

"So that you could be shown the dead in Christ arising," Mekoddishkem said. "These events happen very quickly, in the twinkling of an eye."

Suddenly, a skeleton appeared above Jackson's headstone. After the body was reconstituted, Jackson smiled and looked directly at McKenzie and then at Jack and Samuel. He opened his mouth but apparently didn't have time to say anything before he was whisked straight up into the air. McKenzie jumped up as high as she could, screaming wildly and crying with joy.

The bodies soon stopped traveling into the sky. Then, Mekoddishkem rocketed back into the clouds, and time resumed where it had left off.

The members of the funeral party looked around at each other in confusion. Several women screamed when they saw the burst open coffin with no body in it. "What just happened? Where's my father?" one of the men asked.

"It's the rapture, Reverend!" McKenzie yelled to the minister of the funeral party. "An angel just showed me the dead in Christ rising from their graves. The man in the coffin was taken up to heaven too."

The minister looked around. "Listen to me! The dead in Christ are raised first and then those living in Christ. Those of us who are Christians will be taken up into the sky very soon. If you are not a Christian, you will be left here on earth. If you are left, please go and find a Bible. Read it and believe every single word it says. Admit you're a sinner, then accept Jesus as your Savior, and follow him the rest of your life. He died on the cross to pay the penalty for your sins. You're going to go through a terrible time of God's judgment called the tribulation. Whatever you do, don't accept the mark of the Beast. Your eternal destiny depends on it."

As soon as the minister had finished speaking, McKenzie was pulled up into the air from the ground as if she were connected to a long, taut bungee cord. The familiar landmarks on earth gradually faded from view as she flew higher and higher into the sky. After reaching a certain altitude, she met other saints in the air, including her son and grandson, all seemed a little scared and confused but also as deliriously happy as she.

They looked around and waited there momentarily as other souls soared up from below to be with them. Then, as a group, they were all mysteriously guided east across Connecticut, Rhode Island, Massachusetts, and the Atlantic Ocean, finally stopping in the air above the Mount of Olives in Jerusalem. McKenzie had seen a picture of this place online.

There before them was a vast multitude of people suspended in the air, surrounding a single source of light emanating from what looked like a man. The great cloud of witnesses was crying, "Holy, holy, holy is the Lord God Almighty, who was, and is, and is to come!"

Samuel pointed to the light. "Grandma. Is that Jesus?"

Tremendous energy and joy surged through her. "Yes, Samuel."

Samuel gasped. "Look at me, Grandma! My body is fixed. It's straight now."

McKenzie exclaimed, "Praise God! No more spina bifida for you, Samuel. It's a miracle. Thank you, Jesus."

"Grandma, you look so young now! You're beautiful."

The arthritic joint pain was gone. She had more energy than she could ever remember. There were no wrinkles on her hands; her skin was like that of a baby. "It looks like Jesus gave me a brand-new body too. Thank you, Jesus."

McKenzie joined in the chorus with her son and grandson by her side. In the distance, a group of people traveled toward her—the angel, a man, a young girl, and two toddlers. Mekoddishkem broke off from the group as they drew closer, and Jackson came into view.

She rushed toward him and embraced him with all her might. Joy flooded through her in a tidal wave. Finally, they were reunited. His kiss on her lips was the most wonderful she'd ever known.

Their grandson raced after her, shouting, "Grandpa! Grandpa!"

Jackson scooped Samuel up into his arms and held him close, then he put the boy down and lost his composure as he embraced his son for the first time.

One of the toddlers rushed toward McKenzie and cried, "Mommy! Mommy!"

Who could this be? She gasped. Of course. She knelt and embraced her daughter, mixing tears with kisses. "I'm so sorry for not keeping you, baby. I'm so sorry."

"It's okay, Mommy. I love you!"

McKenzie couldn't stop kissing her.

Finally, she pulled back and stood. McKenzie then grasped Jackson by the hand, and as tears of joy flowed down their faces, they both turned to worship their King.

Notes on Speculation

As stated in the Author's Note section, I tried to adhere to the Scriptures and key extrabiblical sources when writing this book but relied on my educated imagination in cases where these sources were silent. I detail these speculations below, so there is no confusion about which components of the novel are found in the Bible and which are not.

- Age of redeemed bodies in heaven—see endnotes 19 and 158

- Ability of residents in heaven to visit the earth—see endnote 92

- Involvement of residents of heaven in spiritual warfare—see endnote 93

- Golden cross invisibly emblazoned on the foreheads of believers on earth—see endnotes 97, 160, 166, 236, and 289

- Glowing faces of the redeemed in heaven—see endnote 112

- Welcome feast on the first day of arriving in heaven—see endnote 120

- The idea that the Holy Spirit does not restrain evil in hell—see endnote 151

- Treatment of people in hell—see endnote 153

- The idea that our prayers may be accessible to others in heaven—see endnote 161

- The idea that residents of heaven can see events on earth

through the glassy sea in God's throne room—see endnotes 193 and 238

- The idea that there will be artisans in heaven helping prepare places for future arrivals—see endnote 224

- The description of the angel's barracks—see endnote 251

- The Christian flag description—see endnote 252

- The description of Satan's throne and throne room—see endnote 2 and 262

- A dove invisibly descending on believers when baptized—see endnote 317

- The idea that the rapture will not occur until all people God has chosen have been saved—see endnote 345

- The idea that an angel will speak the word Qum when announcing the rapture—see endnote 347

- The idea that everyone raptured will assemble in the air above Jerusalem—see endnote 353

- The notion that the redeemed will sing a particular song when worshipping Jesus in the air above Jerusalem following the rapture—see endnote 354.

AUTHOR'S REQUEST

Thanks for reading *The Battle*. If you enjoyed this novel, please write a review on Amazon using this link: *https://www.amazon.com/stores/ author/B07HQ8G3MJ/*. Just a few words are extremely helpful to me and readers searching for a book like this.

Other installments in the *Heavenly Realms* series are planned. You can follow me on Amazon to be immediately notified of any upcoming releases.

If you'd like to receive my weekly Christian devotional blog, schedule a Zoom call with your book club, or reach out to me directly with a personal message, please contact me on my website at *https:// rickstockwell.com*.

Thank you very much for your support.

Rick

ACKNOWLEDGMENTS

First, I would like to thank God the Father, God the Son, and God the Holy Spirit for giving me the vision, insight, energy, knowledge, and tenacity to write this book. I could not have done this without their help and guidance. God's Word does not return void (Isaiah 55:11)!

I would also like to acknowledge fellow authors who have gone before me.

1. Those who sought to understand what goes on in the heavenly realms: Randy Alcorn, Paul Enns, Erwin Lutzer, John Burke, Donald Barnhouse, Todd Burpo, Don Piper, Warren Wiersbe, and Bill Wiese.

2. Those who provided valuable apologetics: Ken Ham, regarding creation vs. evolution; Dean Halverson, regarding the world religions; and Sebastian Gorka, regarding the war against the soul of America.

3. James Scott Bell for his book about plot and structure, and Nancy Kress for her books about character development.

4. Jerry Jenkins for his course entitled Your Novel Blueprint.

Several friends and family members also provided valuable feedback and insights: Donna Stockwell, Chris Stockwell, Phil Stockwell, Lois Hales, Jim Silk, Anne Silk, Denise Przystawski, Bob Sullivan, Pastor Rob O'Neal, Dave Wittmer, Bob Kagels, and Marilyn Kagels.

A huge shout-out to my editor, Janice Boekhoff, who did a fantastic job restructuring the original manuscript and making numerous recommendations to improve it.

Any errors or omissions are my own.

Book Club Questions

1. What was your first impression of the book?

2. What did you like most about *The Battle*?

3. What did you like least about *The Battle*?

4. What were the major themes of the book?

5. What were the main characters' primary motivations (e.g., Jackson, McKenzie, and Monica)? Did they achieve their goals?

6. How did the characters change throughout the story?

7. Did you connect with any of the characters? If so, how?

8. What new things did you learn? How did the book impact you?

9. What unanswered questions do you still have?

10. Were you satisfied with the ending?

11. Do you believe in spiritual warfare? How do you imagine conflict in the heavenly realms occurs?

You may contact the author at www.rickstockwell.com if you have any questions or would like to invite him to your book club.

Appendix A—Prophecy Primer

Note: Genuine Christians hold various points of view regarding the end times. Plenty of books are available on this topic. The following summarizes the point of view from which I wrote this book.

A Christian is someone believes Jesus is the Son of God (John 3:16; Romans 10:9), repents of their sinful way of living (Luke 13:3), and gives up their life to follow Jesus (Mark 8:34–38). There is much, much more to the Christian life, but that is where it starts.

When a Christian dies, they go directly to what is known as the "intermediate heaven" (Luke 23:43). They will reside there with God—the Father, Son, and Holy Spirit—plus the holy angels, and all the Christians who died before them and after them until the "rapture."

The rapture occurs when Jesus leaves the intermediate heaven, accompanied by the Christians residing there, and reunites them with perfect/incorruptible versions of their former physical bodies. After that, he causes the Christians who are currently alive on earth to join him in the sky with their new bodies (John 14:1–3; 1 Corinthians 15:51–57; 1 Thessalonians 4:13–18). The rapture could occur at any time, and no one knows when it will happen except God (Matthew 24:36; Mark 13:32). Following the rapture, Christians will stand before the judgment seat of Christ (bema judgment) to receive rewards for what they did in life (1 Corinthians 3:11–15; 2 Corinthians 5:10; Romans 14:10–12). In parallel, a seven-year tribulation period will begin, during which an agreement will be made between the antichrist and Israel. Halfway through the tribulation, the antichrist will break the agreement and the wrath of God will be poured out on the earth (Daniel 9:24–27; Revelation 6–19). The purpose of these events is to bring about the conversion of Israel and to judge living unbelievers. Raptured Christians will not be on earth at the tribulation's beginning (1 Thessalonians 1:10).

At the tribulation's conclusion, Jesus will physically return to the earth (i.e., the second coming—Revelation 19:11–16) to destroy his enemies at Armageddon, which is Greek for Megiddo, located in Israel (Revelation 16:16; 19:21). Those who became Christians during the tribulation will appear before Christ at the sheep and goats judgment and be rewarded according to what they did in life. Those who did not become Christians during the tribulation, along with the Beast and False Prophet, will be thrown into the lake of fire (Matthew 25:31–46; Revelation 19:20). God will resurrect Old Testament saints during this period (Daniel 12:1–2).

Following these events, the millennium will begin, during which Christ, assisted by select Christians (Luke 19:11–27), will rule over the earth for a thousand years (Revelation 20:4, 6). Satan will be bound and thrown into the Abyss during this period and will be unable to interfere with events on earth (Revelation 20:2). People born during this period will become both believers and nonbelievers. At the end of the millennium, Satan will be released from the Abyss (Revelation 20:7), gather the non-Christians (of Gog and Magog) from the four corners of the earth, and they will surround the city of Jerusalem, seeking to destroy God's people there (Revelation 20:8–9). God will destroy Satan and his followers with fire from heaven (Revelation 20:9–10).

The great white throne judgment will then occur. At that time, everyone whose names are not written in the Book of Life—Satan, fallen angels, demons, and unredeemed people—will be judged and thrown into the lake of fire for all eternity (Revelation 20:10–15).

Following the great white throne judgment, God will create a permanent new heaven and a new earth (Isaiah 65:17; 2 Peter 3:13; Revelation 21:1). Jesus Christ will rule with Christians appointed to assist him. Once he establishes his kingdom, he will turn it over to God the Father (1 Corinthians 15:24). The new Jerusalem, the city of God, will descend from heaven to the new earth, and God will dwell there with redeemed humanity for all eternity (Revelation 21).

The unredeemed go immediately to hell when they die (John 3:18). Their punishment will vary according to what they did or did not do during their life on earth (Mark 12:40; Luke 12:47–48; 20:47; Revelation 20:12). Hell is located within the earth (Numbers 16:30, 33; 1 Samuel 28:11–13; Job 7:9; 11:8; 17:16; Psalm 55:15; Proverbs 1:12; 7:27; 9:18; 15:24; Isaiah 7:11; 14:9, 15; Ezekiel 31:15–17; 32:21, 27; Amos 9:2; Matthew 12:40) and is where the unredeemed will suffer in a world characterized by darkness (Matthew 8:12) and fire (Matthew 13:42; Mark 9:43, 48). They will suffer physically and spiritually as they await the great white throne judgment (Luke 16:23). Then they will be cast alive into the lake of fire for all eternity (Matthew 25:31–46; Revelation 20:10–15).

THE MAJOR RELIGIONS of the world share at least one thing in common: the Golden Rule. Stated in various ways, it boils down to this principle: *Treat others the way you'd like to be treated.* Due to the nature of this content, I was unable to include it in the body of the novel but think it's important to include here. By showing how different each religion is, I hope to dispel the notion that "all paths lead to God."

The following information is taken from Dean Halverson, *The Illustrated Guide to World Religions* (Bloomington, Minnesota: Bethany House Publishers, 2003).

Buddhism. Founded by Siddhartha Gautama in the sixth century BC. The first part of his life was lived in luxury in Nepal, sheltered from the world. When he ventured outside his father's palace, he encountered great suffering. He decided to leave his family—including his wife and children and vowed to discover how to eliminate suffering. After practicing extreme asceticism and nearly dying from lack of food, he vowed to meditate until he reached enlightenment. It's said he attained enlightenment and became known as Buddha. He concluded that the path to enlightenment is through the Middle Way, the Eightfold Path of moderation that avoids the extremes of asceticism and luxury. Over the centuries, many variations of Buddhism developed. Heaven, known as Nirvana, is believed to be an abstract void. The follower must adhere to the Middle Way and accumulate enough karmic merit for entry. In contrast, the way to heaven according to Christianity is to recognize that we've done wrong, repent of our sins, ask God to forgive us, and believe Jesus paid the penalty for our sins on the cross.

Confucianism. Confucius was the prime minister of the State of Lu in China during the fifth century BC. At the age of fifty-six, he traveled throughout China hoping to restore peace and security by reestablishing the old Ritual-Music Culture. Twelve years later, he returned home, having failed in his mission. Confucius concluded that change could not occur through top-down cultural/political imposition but could only be achieved through individual moral responsibility. God seemed too far away, so the concept of *T'ien*, or "heaven," was developed, which encompasses all things, including people. He argued that each person had the potential to actualize their humanity through *jen*—a return to, and living out of, their original goodness—and become one with heaven. Confucianism is more of a value system than a formal religion, with its adherents focused on living good lives today rather than the afterlife. In contrast, Christianity teaches that people are not good but are sinners who are dead spiritually. The dead cannot actualize themselves to become one with God. They are wholly dependent on Jesus to make them alive spiritually by transferring his righteousness to their account so that they can live with God forever in heaven.

Judaism. Judaism is the religion practiced by the Jews. It's generally based on the Tanakh, or Hebrew Bible, completed about 165 BC, and the Talmud commentaries. There are two versions of the commentaries: one completed in the fifth century AD and the other in the sixth century AD. There are three primary branches of Judaism—Orthodox, Conservative, and Reform. The Orthodox Jews believe the Torah—the first five books of the Hebrew Bible—is God's inspired word given through Moses, who led the Jews on an exodus out of Egypt to the promised land, known today as Israel. The Torah is regarded more highly by Orthodox Jews than the other books of the Hebrew Bible, which in its entirety is known to Christians as the Old Testament. Conservatives believe the Hebrew Bible is the word of God and man, while the Reform Jews believe the Hebrew Bible is a human document that can serve as a guide for moral living. Many Orthodox Jews believe in life after death (e.g., Daniel 12), but many Conservative and Reform Jews do not, thinking people live on in their accomplishments and the minds of others. In contrast to many Conservative and Reform Jews, evangelical Christians, like Orthodox Jews, believe the Old Testament is the inspired Word of God. They also believe this about the Christian New Testament. Jews who believe in the afterlife strive to *earn* their way to heaven by observing the law, while Christians *believe* their way to heaven by trusting that the sacrifice of Christ on the cross was sufficient to pay for their sins and make them perfect before God.

Hinduism. Hinduism originated in what is now India in about 1,500 BC. It holds that behind many gods stands an all-inclusive impersonal *force* called Brahman, which manifests itself in three forms: Brahma (Creator); Vishnu (Preserver); Siva (Destroyer). Each manifestation has at least one spouse. Vishnu is further divided into ten incarnations called *avatars*. It's estimated there are 330 million other gods in Hinduism. Many Hindus also believe the world is an illusion. Another major tenet of Hinduism is the law of karma (i.e., you reap in this lifetime what you sowed in previous lifetimes) and reincarnation (i.e., how someone lives this life determines the type of body they'll receive in the next life—insect, animal, or human). Christianity, like Hinduism, adheres to the concept of reaping what you sow but states there is one God in three persons—Father, Son, and Holy Spirit. Jesus, the Son, came to a real earth and died a real, agonizing death on the cross to pay for our sins. Christianity also teaches we have only one life to live, and at the end of that life, we will be judged.

Islam. In 610 AD, at the age of forty, the prophet Muhammad stated he began receiving revelations from the angel Gabriel. At first, Muhammad thought these revelations were demonic, but his wife convinced him they were divine. These revelations were later recorded in a book called the Qur'an, which states that 124,000 prophets were sent into the world, each for a different time. The highest-ranking prophets were given divine revelation: Moses (Torah), David (Psalms), Jesus (Gospels), and Muhammad (Qur'an). Each person has two angels assigned to him or her for their entire life; one to record the good deeds and one to record the bad. Each person will one day stand before God and be judged. Those whose good deeds outweigh their bad deeds will be sent to Paradise, while those whose bad deeds outweigh their good deeds will be sent to hell. Christianity agrees with Islam that the Torah, Psalms, and Gospels are divinely inspired and that every person will one day be judged by God. Christianity is not in agreement with Islam regarding how to get into heaven. Rather than hoping their good deeds outweigh their bad, the Christian believes Jesus's death on the cross was sufficient to pay for all their sins, and thereby qualifies them for entry into heaven.

Selected Bibliography

Alcorn, Randy. *Heaven.* Carol Stream, Illinois: Tyndale House Publishers, Inc., 2004.

Barnhouse, Donald Grey. *The Invisible War.* Grand Rapids, Michigan: Zondervan, 1965.

Bisutti, Kylie. *I'm No Angel: From Victoria's Secret Model to Role Model.* Carol Stream, Illinois: Tyndale House Publishers, Inc., 2013.

Burpo, Todd. *Heaven is for Real.* Nashville, Tennessee: Thomas Nelson, 2010.

Bell, James Scott. *Write Great Fiction: Plot & Structure.* Cincinnati, Ohio: Writer's Digest Books, 2004.

Boom, Corrie ten. *Each New Day.* Old Tappan, New Jersey: Fleming H. Revell Company, 1977.

Burke, John. *Imagine Heaven.* Grand Rapids, Michigan: Baker Books, 2015.

Enns, Paul. *Heaven Revealed.* Chicago, Illinois: Moody Publishers, 1989, 2008.

Enns, Paul. The *Moody Handbook of Theology.* Chicago, Illinois: Moody Publishers, 1989, 2008.

Gorka, Sebastian. *The War for America's Soul.* Washington, DC: Regnery Publishing, 2019.

Halverson, Dean. *The Illustrated Guide to World Religions.* Bloomington, Minnesota: Bethany House Publishers, 2003.

Ham, Ken. *The New Answers Book 1.* Green Forest, Arkansas: Master Books, 2006.

Ham, Ken. *The New Answers Book 2*. Green Forest, Arkansas: Master Books, 2008.

Ham, Ken. *The New Answers Book 3*. Green Forest, Arkansas: Master Books, 2009.

Ham, Ken. *The New Answers Book 4*. Green Forest, Arkansas: Master Books, 2013.

Kress, Nancy. *Write Great Fiction: Characters, Emotion & Viewpoint*. Cincinnati, Ohio: Writer's Digest Books, 2005.

Lutzer, Erwin W. *One Minute After You Die*. Chicago, Illinois: Moody Publishers, 1997.

Mac, Toby, and Tait, Michael. "Bulletproof"—George Washington (1755). *Under God*. Bloomington, Minnesota: Bethany House Publishers, 2004. http://www.undergodthebook.com/story01.cfm.

Wiersbe, Warren. *The Strategy of Satan*. Carol Stream, Illinois: Tyndale House Publishers, Inc., 1979.

Wiese, Bill. *23 Minutes in Hell*. Lake Mary, Florida: Charisma House, 2006.

Note: *Having formal endnote references in the body of this novel would do irreparable damage to its readability. The citations below will (a) ensure credit is appropriately attributed, and (b) guide those wishing to pursue a particular topic further.*

Author's Note

1. Randy Alcorn argues for the importance of using our imagination when contemplating heaven in his book, *Heaven* (Carol Stream, IL: Tyndale House Publishers, Inc., 2004), pages 15–22. Note: This monumental book contains thousands of Scripture references, but the opinions and speculations expressed should not be considered to be as authoritative as Scripture itself.

Chapter 1 Critical Mission

2. There is no description of Satan's throne in the Bible. The depiction of his throne in this book comes directly from 1 Kings 10:18–20, a description of King Solomon's throne.

3. The leaders of a failed attempt to assassinate Adolf Hitler were hung from the ceiling using piano wire and meat hooks as recorded on this website: https://www.jewishvirtuallibrary. org/operation-valkyrie-the-quot-july-plot-quot-to-assassinate-hitler. Satan may have inspired Hitler to do this.

4.   The idea that Satan may be able to heal fatal wounds comes from Revelation 13:3.

Chapter 2 *Nothing Impure*

5.   The inference from Revelation 20:4–6 is that the unredeemed will reside in hell for at least a thousand years before being cast into the lake of fire.

6.   The reference to the lake of fire comes from Matthew 25:31–46 and Revelation 20:10–15.

7.   The angel description comes from Daniel 10:5–6.

8.   Biblical references to guardian angels include Psalm 34:7; 91:11; Matthew 18:10; Acts 12:15; and Hebrews 1:14.

9.   Jehovah Mekoddishkem means "The Lord who sanctifies."

10.   The statement "All the days ordained for me were written in your book before one of them came to be" comes from Psalm 139:16.

11.   The reference to God wiping away every tear comes from Isaiah 25:8 and Revelation 7:17; 21:4.

12.   The reference to angels escorting us to heaven comes from Luke 16:22 and is also mentioned in Paul Enns, *Heaven Revealed* (Chicago, IL: Moody Publishers, 2011) page 39, and Lutzer, pages 56–57, 78.

13.   Revelation 21:21 states each gate in heaven is made of a single pearl.

14.   Revelation 21:12 states there is an angel guarding each gate.

15.   Revelation 21:19–20 states the base of the wall surrounding heaven consists of twelve different minerals.

16.   The reference to light emanating from the wall surrounding the city of heaven comes from John Burke, *Imagine Heaven* (Grand Rapids, MI: Baker Books, 2015), page 104. Note: This book contains numerous accounts of near-death experiences in which the people involved argued they went to heaven or

were on the way to hell. The author provides hundreds of Scripture references to reinforce the authenticity of their stories. They appear credible but should not be considered to be as authoritative as the Bible itself.

17. The reference to people in heaven wearing white linen robes comes from Revelation 19:8.

18. The reference to loved ones waiting for us in heaven comes from Jonathan Edwards, *Heaven: A World of Love* (Amityville, NY: Calvary Press, 1999), page 18, quoted in Alcorn, page 329.

19. We do not know at what age people will appear in the intermediate heaven since this information does not appear in the Bible. The speculation is that those over thirty will revert to the age of thirty—their peak, while those under thirty will remain at the age at which they died on earth and be reunited with their physical bodies at that same age during the rapture. Their bodies will then mature to the age of thirty during the millennium.

20. The reference to Sunday school teachers possibly waiting for us in heaven comes from Burke, page 86.

21. The reference to a deceased sister waiting for us in heaven comes from Todd Burpo, *Heaven is for Real*, (Nashville, TN: Thomas Nelson, 2010), pages 93–97.

22. The reference to an angel guarding each gate to heaven and making sure the name of the person who wants to enter is written in the Book of Life comes from Lutzer, page 108 and Burke, page 252. The biblical reference is Revelation 21:27.

23. The reference to the believer's eyesight becoming enhanced in heaven comes from Burke, pages 62–63, 113.

24. The reference to the dimensions of the wall surrounding heaven comes from Revelation 21:17. It is also mentioned in Enns, page 26, and Lutzer, page 108. There are various opinions on whether the 144 cubits (216 feet) refers to the height or the thickness of

the wall. The NIV Study Bible translates it as "thick" (but states in a note it could also mean "high"). Dr. Lutzer understands it to mean "height." Dr. Enns states that it is unclear whether it means "high or wide."

25. The reference to a river in heaven flowing from under God's throne comes from Revelation 22:1 and Burke, pages 104–105. The idea that people may enter the river to receive a final cleansing comes from Burke, page 305.

26. The mention of an incredibly bright light emanating from God's throne comes from Burke, page 22. The primary biblical references for this are Revelation 21:23 and 1 John 1:5. Other biblical references include Psalm 118:27; Isaiah 60:19; and 1 Peter 2:9.

27. The verse 2 Kings 5:14 states the prophet Elijah told Naaman to cleanse himself seven times in the Jordan River to remove his leprosy.

28. The reference to nothing impure being allowed into heaven comes from Revelation 21:27.

29. The reference to the redeemed receiving a warm welcome into heaven comes from 2 Peter 1:11 and is mentioned in Enns, page 41.

30. The reference to Jackson walking along a golden pathway in heaven comes from Revelation 21:21.

31. The reference to people in heaven having different colored sashes comes from Burpo, page 87.

32. That the redeemed will be filled with joy comes from Psalm 16:11.

33. The reference to everything in heaven exuding light comes from Burke, page 181.

34. The reference to buildings in heaven made from gold and jewels comes from Revelation 21:18, 21 and is cited in Enns, pages 25–26.

35. The sound of rhythmic chimes heard in heaven comes from Burke, page 117. The reference to rocks crying out comes from Luke 19:40.

36. The ability of believers to feel the light emanating from the throne room comes from Burke, page 33.

37. The reference to Jackson being called by God to "come up here" is extrapolated from Revelation 4:1b.

38. The image of Jackson trembling in fear is extrapolated from Daniel 10:17–18.

39. The reference to anyone who looks at the face of God will die comes from Exodus 33:20.

40. The reference to Jesus helping us stand comes from Lutzer, page 79.

41. The reference to Jesus's pierced hands is from Burpo, page 67 and John 20:24–31, along with Psalm 22:16.

42. The description of Jesus comes from Revelation 1:13–15. (Any attempted description by the author would fall short.)

43. The life review comes from Burke, pages 23; 140–141; 149–150; 241; 243–244; and 249.

44. The reference to everything being in "full view of the LORD" comes from Proverbs 5:21.

45. The reference to "love covering a multitude of sins" comes from James 5:20 and 1 Peter 4:8.

46. The reference for Jesus telling Jackson, "Well done, good and faithful servant," comes from Matthew 25:21.

47. The reference to Jesus radiating out of a person comes from Burke, page 65.

48. The judgment seat of Christ (bema judgment) for believers comes from 1 Corinthians 3:11–15; 2 Corinthians 5:10; Romans 14:10–12. See Appendix A for the context regarding when this occurs.

49.   The reference to God wiping away every tear comes from Isaiah
      25:8 and Revelation 7:17; 21:4.

50.   The description of God the Father and the four creatures around
      the throne comes from Revelation 4:3–8. (Any attempted
      description by the author would fall short.) See also Burke,
      pages 312–314.

51.   God the Father stated he was "well pleased" with Jesus in Mark
      1:11 and Luke 3:22. Jesus's righteousness transfers to all true
      believers. Therefore, God the Father would be "well pleased"
      with Jackson.

52.   The reference to there being perfect peace in God's presence
      comes from Isaiah 26:3 and Burke, pages 195, 276.

53.   The idea that communication will primarily be telepathic in
      heaven comes from Burke, page 34 and elsewhere in that book.

54.   The idea that the brightness of an individual's countenance may
      vary by person in heaven comes from Burke, page 65.

55.   The idea that there is no rush or timetable in heaven comes
      from Burke, page 132.

56.   The reference to there being a throne in heaven reserved for
      Jackson (and all true believers) comes from Ephesians 2:6.

57.   The reference to cherubs, seraphs, archangels, and angels comes
      from Donald Grey Barnhouse, *The Invisible War*, (Grand Rapids,
      MI: Zondervan, 1965), page 69.

Chapter 3 Payback

58.   Angels carried the body of Lazarus to Father Abraham's side
      in Luke 16:22. The assumption is that demons will carry the
      unredeemed to hell, as mentioned in Erwin Lutzer, *One Minute
      After You Die* (Chicago, IL: Moody Press, 1997) page 25, quoted
      in Wiese, page 124.

59.   The idea that a person can be indwelt by a demon is found
      in Matthew 8:16; 10:1; 12:27; 12:43–45; 17:14–20; Mark

3:15; 5:12; 9:29; 16:17; Luke 4:33–36; 8:2; 8:26–39; and Acts 16:16–18.

60. We do not know the location of the entrance to hell or if there are multiple entrances. According to Revelation 9:13–15, four angels were bound at the river Euphrates and will be released one day to kill a third of humanity, so perhaps the entrance is somewhere in that vicinity.

61. The logic for having approximately 10,000 people standing in line at the Abyss opening is that 5,000—10,000 people die per hour throughout the world, and most of them will not be going to heaven, according to Matthew 7:14.

62. The idea that everyone will be naked in hell (aka the Abyss) comes from Bill Wiese, *23 Minutes in Hell* (Lake Mary, FL: Charisma House, 2006), pages xv and 37. Biblical references include Job 26:6; Revelation 3:18; 16:15.

63. The reference to there being a horrible stench in hell comes from Wiese, page 7.

64. A mark on the forehead indicates allegiance to God (Revelation 7:3; 9:4; 14:1; 20:4; 22:4) or the devil (Revelation 13:16; 14:9–10).

65. The leaders of a failed attempt to assassinate Adolf Hitler were hung from the ceiling using piano wire and meat hooks, as recorded on this website: https://www.jewishvirtuallibrary. org/operation-valkyrie-the-quot-july-plot-quot-to-assassinate- hitler. Satan may have inspired Hitler to do this.

66. It's not known if demons would sexually assault people in hell, but the Holy Spirit will not be restraining evil there. Biblical references to fallen angels having sexual relations with women include Genesis 6:1–4; Jude 1:6–7.

67. The *Radical Abiding* discipleship program, developed by Bob and Allie Stevens, utilizes the STAR method.

68. Oswald Chambers advocated the idea that discipleship helps people get closer to God. See *Oswald Chambers His Life and Work* (London: Marshall, Morgan & Scott, Ltd., 1959).

69. The notion from the theory of evolution that fishes evolved into amphibians, which evolved into reptiles, which evolved into birds and mammals is mentioned in Ken Ham, *The New Answers Book 1* (Green Forest, AR: Master Books, 2006), page 9.

70. The explanation of the process of DNA passing from parent to child, in which the child inherits 23 chromosomes from each parent, came from Ken Ham, *The New Answers Book 1*, (Green Forest, AR: Master Books, 2006), page 228.

71. The reference to one square inch of DNA containing the equivalent amount of information to 7 billion Bibles comes from Ken Ham, *The New Answers Book 2* (Green Forest, AR: Master Books, 2008), page 113.

72. The reference to mutations causing a loss of genetic information comes from Ken Ham, *The New Answers Book 1*, (Green Forest, AR: Master Books, 2006), page 168. A "loss or reshuffling" of genetic information is mentioned in Ken Ham, *The New Answers Book 3* (Green Forest, AR: Master Books, 2010), footnote 8, page 274.

73. There is no scientific observation of lifeless chemicals organizing themselves into living things, according to Ken Ham, *The New Answers Book 2* (Green Forest, AR: Master Books, 2008), page 211.

74. Statistics about the human body came from Ken Ham, *The New Answers Book 3* (Green Forest, AR: Master Books, 2010), page 159.

Chapter 5 Spiritual Attack

75.   Ephesians 6:10–17 contains a description of the armor of God.

76.   Jesus commanded Satan to leave him, as recorded in Matthew 4:10. Children of God can do the same to any demonic spirit attacking them.

77.   The believer can recite 1 John 1:8–9 to claim God's forgiveness for their sins following their confession.

78.   God does not want us to dwell on our past sins, as noted in Philippians 3:13–14.

79.   The idea that feelings can lie to a person comes from Pastor Rick Warren's *Daily Hope* radio program, date unknown.

Chapter 6 Unwelcome Visitor

80.   The reference to Satan being perfect in beauty and proud in bearing—looking much like the other angels, but bearing a haughty expression comes from Ezekiel 28:12b.

81.   The reference to Satan "roaming through the earth and going back and forth in it" comes from Job 1:6–7.

82.   The reference to the Lord speaking to Satan and saying, "Have you considered my servant Jackson?" is adapted from Job 1:8.

83.   The reference to Satan accusing the saints (i.e., Jackson) comes from Revelation 12:10.

84.   The reference to Jesus calling Satan a murderer and a liar comes from John 8:44.

85.   The concept that Jackson is a new creation comes from 2 Corinthians 5:17.

86.   The reference to Jackson being a member of God's household is adapted from Ephesians 2:19.

87.   The reference to Jackson's sins becoming "white as snow" is adapted from Isaiah 1:18.

88.   The reference to a hedge of protection surrounding Jackson comes from Job 1:10.

89. The phrase, "The Lord rebuke you," comes from Zechariah 3:2 and Jude 1:9.

90. The idea that Satan knows his time is short comes from Revelation 12:12.

91. The idea that a Christian residing in the intermediate heaven would be given permission to visit the earth is speculation. The idea that Jackson would even desire to do this seems contrary to Isaiah 65:17, "The former things will not be remembered, nor will they come to mind." The context for this verse is the eternal kingdom (after the millennium), not the intermediate heaven.

92. The idea that redeemed Christians will be warriors in God's army is inferred from Revelation 19:13–14 but explicitly stated in Revelation 17:14. The context for these passages is Armageddon (Megiddo in Hebrew), the location of the final battle between God and Satan. Another reference is Burpo, page 138. That the redeemed might be involved in heavenly realms warfare before then is speculation.

93. The angelic use of swords as weapons in the heavenly realms comes from Numbers 22:23, 31; 1 Chronicles 21:12, 16, 27, 30; and 2 Chronicles 32:21.

94. The idea that redeemed people in heaven will need to know how to fight with a sword comes from Burpo, pages 136–138. Biblical references to the army of heaven fighting alongside Jesus, including both angels and believers, comes from Revelation 19:14. A definitive reference to believers fighting alongside Jesus comes from Revelation 17:14.

95. The following website provided historical broadsword fencing techniques: https://www.youtube.com/watch?v=dvu-XUu2ytY.

96. The idea that a golden cross is emblazoned on a believer's forehead, invisible to us in this world, is speculation based on the fact that angels will be able to distinguish the redeemed from the unredeemed, as noted in Matthew 24:31 and Mark

13:27. A mark on the forehead indicates allegiance to God (Revelation 7:3; 9:4; 14:1; 20:4; 22:4) or the devil (Revelation 13:16; 14:9–10). Burpo mentions on pages 73–74 that the redeemed in heaven, and possibly those on earth, have a "light" or halo over their head.

97. Biblical references to guardian angels include Psalm 34:7; 91:11; Matthew 18:10; Acts 12:15; and Hebrews 1:14.

98. The reference to the battle being against the spiritual forces in the heavenly realms, not flesh and blood in the earthly realms, comes from Ephesians 6:12.

99. The reference to only approaching the king's throne when called upon comes from Esther 4:11.

100. The reference to approaching the throne of grace with "freedom and confidence" comes from Ephesians 3:12.

101. References to Jesus being seated at the right hand of God the Father include Matthew 22:44; 26:64; Mark 12:36; 14:62; 16:19; Luke 20:42; 22:69. Another reference is Burpo, page 100.

102. The reference to the throne room shaking when God the Father spoke comes from Isaiah 6:4.

103. The reference to God knowing what we need before we ask comes from Matthew 6:8.

104. The idea that God knows our thoughts is noted in 1 Chronicles 28:9; Psalm 44:21; 94:11; Proverbs 15:11–12; 16:2; Jeremiah 17:10; 23:24; Matthew 9:4; and Hebrews 4:13.

105. The idea that God the Father is not distant or unapproachable but filled with love, just like Jesus, comes from John 10:30; 14:7.

106. The concept of God giving people time to repent comes from Revelation 2:21.

107. The idea of no one coming to Jesus unless the Father draws him comes from John 6:44.

108. The idea that people must respond to God's call comes from James 4:8.

109. The idea that no one can come into God's presence unless Jesus paid for their sins comes from Revelation 21:27.

110. The concept that God withholds judgment to allow the believer time to repent comes from Romans 2:4, as cited in Paul Enns, *The Moody Handbook of Theology* (Chicago, IL: Moody Publishers, 2008), pages 344–345.

Chapter 8 *The Mansion*

111. The speculation that people in heaven will have glowing faces comes from Exodus 34:29–30, which notes the radiance of Moses's face after spending forty days on Mount Sinai with God.

112. The reference to the height of heaven being 1,200 stadia (1,400 miles) comes from Revelation 21:16b.

113. The reference to a building in heaven containing 396,000 stories, each 20 feet high, comes from Enns, pages 25–26.

114. The idea of the redeemed in heaven being able to will themselves to other locations comes from Alcorn, page 430, and Burke, page 135.

115. The reference that King David would rather be a doorkeeper in the house of the Lord than dwell elsewhere comes from Psalm 84:10.

116. The possibility of there being multiple homes for us in heaven comes from Burke, page 270.

117. The idea that the home Jesus prepares for us is more spectacular than we ever imagined comes from 1 Corinthians 2:9 and is cited in Burke, page 27.

118. The reference to the architect and builder being God comes from Hebrews 11:10.

119. The idea that there will be a welcome feast on the first day of arriving in heaven is speculation. The Wedding Feast of the

Lamb, described in Revelation 19:9, will not occur until all the
redeemed have arrived in heaven after the rapture (see Appendix
A for context).

120. Jackson's reference to taking the lowest seat at the banquet is
based on Luke 14:8–12, and cited in Barnhouse, page 221.

121. The reference to the architect and builder is God comes from
Hebrews 11:10.

122. The idea that communication will primarily be telepathic in
heaven comes from Burke, page 34, and elsewhere in that book.

123. The reference to the Great Commission comes from Matthew
28:18–20.

124. The idea of eating in heaven comes from Luke 22:29–30 and is
noted in Alcorn, pages 291–298. Other references include Luke
24:41–43, in which Jesus eats a piece of fish in his resurrected
body, and Matthew 26:29, in which Jesus says he will not drink
wine again until he drinks it with his disciples in heaven.

125. The idea that the redeemed may sleep in heaven comes from
Hebrews 4:1–11 and Revelation 14:13 and is referenced in
Alcorn, pages 317–318.

126. The idea that there will be work to do in heaven comes from
Genesis 2:15 and is referenced in Alcorn, page 319.

127. The idea of having a tutor assigned to us in heaven comes from
Alcorn, page 309.

128. The idea of there being a common language in heaven, or
the innate ability to understand other languages, comes from
Alcorn, pages 363–365.

129. The reference to nothing being "too hard" for God comes from
Genesis 18:14 and Jeremiah 32:17, 27.

130. The reference to God gifting us with unique talents and abilities
on earth, and by derivation, in heaven, comes from Exodus
31:2–3.

131. The idea of having fellowship with other believers in heaven comes from Alcorn, pages 117, 323–324, and Enns, page 16.

132. The concept of there being no marriage in heaven comes from Matthew 22:30, Mark 12:25, and Luke 20:35.

133. The reference to how people in heaven will feel about loved ones in hell is discussed in Lutzer, pages 118–119.

134. The idea of people in heaven being able to see activities on earth comes from Alcorn, pages 69–71.

Chapter 10 The Museum

135. The idea that God will give those who love him more than they can ask or imagine comes from 1 Corinthians 2:9.

136. The idea that communication will primarily be telepathic in heaven comes from Burke, page 34, and elsewhere in that book.

137. References to the omnipresence of God (i.e., being in multiple places at the same time) include 1 Kings 8:27; Psalm 139:7–10; Proverbs 15:3; Isaiah 57:15; Jeremiah 23:24; Matthew 18:20; and Acts 17:27.

138. The reference to being indwelt by the Holy Spirit comes from Luke 11:13; John 14:17; 1 Corinthians 6:19–20; and Revelation 3:20.

139. The idea that there may be museums in heaven came from Alcorn, page 243.

140. The idea of there being children in heaven who have not yet reached the age of accountability (i.e., are not yet old enough to understand sin and the gospel remedy for it) is discussed in Lutzer, pages 93–102.

141. The reference to Jesus wiping away every tear comes from Isaiah 25:8; Revelation 7:17; 21:4.

142. The reference to laying down one's life for their friends comes from John 15:13.

143. Pilot had Jesus flogged before his crucifixion, according to Mark

15:15. Other references include Isaiah 50:6; 52:14; 53:1–12; and Psalm 22:1–21.

144. The reference to many people attending the crucifixion comes from Luke 23:27a.

145. The actual crucifixion of Jesus is described in all four gospels: Matthew 27:32–50; Mark 15:21–37; Luke 23:26–46; and John 19:17–37.

146. The reference to Jesus's pierced hands and feet is from Burpo, page 67; Psalm 22:16; and Luke 24:39–40.

147. The reference to a gut-wrenching stench in hell comes from Burke, page 228, and Wiese, page 7.

148. The idea that our past sins are fixed in concrete comes from a radio sermon delivered by Pastor Chuck Swindoll on his *Insight for Living* broadcast, date unknown.

149. The idea that we can let Jesus pay for our sins on the cross or pay for them ourselves in hell comes from a message by John Piper, source/date unknown.

150. It is speculation that the Holy Spirit does not restrain evil in hell because the people there desire separation from him and his attributes (e.g., mercy).

151. The Ten Commandments appear in Exodus 20 and Deuteronomy 5.

152. Angels in hell reside in dungeons, according to 2 Peter 2:4, and are bound in chains according to Jude 1:6. That some of the unredeemed in hell will receive similar treatment is speculation.

153. The concept of there being different levels of punishment in hell comes from Mark 12:40 and Luke 20:47.

154. The reference to God not being willing that any should perish but that everyone would come to repentance comes from 2 Peter 3:9.

155. The Sermon on the Mount appears in Matthew 5–7. The

first section of this passage, called the Beatitudes, is found in
Matthew 5:3–12.

156. Jesus healing the leper immediately after delivering the Sermon
on the Mount is found in Matthew 8:1–3.

157. The reference to children taking physical form at various ages
in heaven, depending on when they departed this earth, comes
from Alcorn, pages 288–290. That preborn children who died
on earth will also take physical form in heaven is speculation.
However, Burpo, pages 120–123, addresses this. The Bible does
not record at what age people will appear in the intermediate
heaven. This book speculates that people who arrive at heaven
over thirty will revert to age thirty upon arrival, as that is their
physical peak. Those who arrive younger than thirty will remain
at that age in heaven and receive new bodies of that age at the
rapture, then grow to maturity during the millennium. See
Appendix A for a definition of these terms. Another reference
is Burke, page 94.

158. The reference to Jackson's daughter, Joy, not having a name
because he and the mother, Cassandra Alvarez, never named
her is extrapolated from Burpo, page 94.

159. The idea that a golden cross is emblazoned on the forehead of
believers, invisible to us in this world, is speculation based on
the fact that angels will be able to distinguish the redeemed
from the unredeemed, as noted in Matthew 24:31 and Mark
13:27. A mark on the forehead indicates allegiance to God
(Revelation 7:3; 9:4; 14:1; 20:4; 22:4) or the devil (Revelation
13:16; 14:9–10). Burpo mentions on pages 73–74 that the
redeemed in heaven, and possibly those on earth, have a "light"
or halo over their head.

160. The reference to a person's public or private thoughts being
accessible to other people in heaven is not in the Bible, so it
should be considered speculation. However, all our thoughts are

accessible to God, as noted in 1 Chronicles 28:9; Psalm 44:21; 94:11; Proverbs 15:11; 16:2; Jeremiah 17:10; 23:24; Matthew 9:4; and Hebrews 4:13.

161. Satan had to obtain permission from God to inflict woe on Job and his family, as noted in Job 1 and 2.

162. The Roman emperor Nero dipped Christians in tar, impaled them on poles around his palace, lit them on fire, then declared, "Now you truly are the light of the world." More information on this topic is available at https://www.conservapedia.com/Nero. Satan likely inspired the concept of impaling people on poles.

163. The idea that Satan may be able to heal fatal wounds comes from Revelation 13:3.

164. The leaders of a failed attempt to assassinate Adolf Hitler were hung from the ceiling using piano wire and meat hooks, as recorded on this website: https://www.jewishvirtuallibrary.org/operation-valkyrie-the-quot-july-plot-quot-to-assassinate-hitler. Satan may have inspired Hitler to do this.

Chapter 12 Torn Between Two Worlds

165. The idea that a golden cross is emblazoned on the forehead of believers, invisible to us in this world, is speculation based on the fact that angels will be able to distinguish the redeemed from the unredeemed, as noted in Matthew 24:31 and Mark 13:27. A mark on the forehead indicates allegiance to God (Revelation 7:3; 9:4; 14:1; 20:4; 22:4) or the devil (Revelation 13:16; 14:9–10). Burpo mentions on pages 73–74 that the redeemed in heaven, and possibly those on earth, have a "light" or halo over their head.

166. The idea that a church staff member might not be a true Christian comes from Warren Wiersbe, *The Strategy of Satan*

(Carol Stream, IL: Tyndale House Publishers, Inc., 1979), pages 115–116.

167. The reference to "Lord, don't you know me," comes from Matthew 7:22.

168. The reference to a "great cloud of witnesses" comes from Hebrews 12:1.

169. The reference to there being demonic lords and hierarchies of leadership in the heavenly realms comes from Barnhouse, pages 128–129, 132.

Chapter 13 Reunion

170. References to lifting hands during worship include Nehemiah 8:6; Psalm 63:4; 134:2.

171. The story about George Washington's battle at Fort Duquesne during the French and Indian War comes from an extract called "Bulletproof" from Toby Mac and Michael Tait, *Under God* (Bloomington, MN: Bethany House Publishers, 2004).

172. The idea that people in heaven will know when a loved one will be arriving comes from Alcorn, page 446.

173. The reference to the redeemed receiving a warm welcome in heaven comes from 2 Peter 1:11 and is mentioned in Enns, page 41.

Chapter 14 High Stakes

174. The reference for McKenzie telling Satan to get "behind her" is derived from Matthew 16:23; Mark 8:33; and Luke 4:8 (NKJV).

175. The idea that believers in heaven may explore the universe comes from Alcorn, pages 430–432.

176. The idea of being transported rapidly from one location to another comes from Alcorn, pages 257 and 284; and Lutzer, page 92.

177. The concept of Satan, and therefore demons, being able to make suggestions to people comes from Matthew 16:21–23.

178. The idea of the Holy Spirit convicting people of sin comes from John 16:8.

179. The Billy Graham Evangelistic Association publishes the "Steps to Peace with God" tract.

180. The idea that the devil can blind the minds of unbelievers comes from 2 Corinthians 4:4.

181. The concept of Satan sifting people like wheat comes from Luke 22:31.

182. Insights into the world of modeling came from Kylie Bisutti, *I'm No Angel: From Victoria's Secret Model to Role Model* (Carol Stream, IL: Tyndale House, 2013), pages 5, 11, 21, 54, 66, 69–72, 76, 107, 154, 172, 214, 234–235, 242–243, and 245.

183. The idea that nothing is "too hard" for God comes from Genesis 18:14; and Jeremiah 32:17, 27.

184. The reference to "faith coming by hearing, and hearing by the Word of God" comes from Romans 10:17 (NKJV).

185. The reference to being seated with Christ in the heavenly realms comes from Ephesians 2:6.

186. The reference to God using suffering to make us worthy of his kingdom comes from Corrie ten Boom's *Each New Day* (Old Tappan, NJ: Fleming H. Revell Company, 1977), pages 108–109. The Scripture reference is 2 Thessalonians 1:4–5.

187. McKenzie's request to have God fill her with the Holy Spirit comes from Luke 11:13: *If you then, though you are evil, know how to give good gifts to your children, how much more will your Father in heaven give the Holy Spirit to those who ask him!*

188. The judgment seat of Christ (bema judgment) for believers comes from 1 Corinthians 3:11–15; 2 Corinthians 5:10; Romans 14:10–12. See Appendix A for the context regarding when this occurs.

189. The reference to ruling with Christ during the millennium period comes from Revelation 5:10.

190. The idea that what appears to be an accident from our perspective may be ordained or allowed by God comes from Exodus 21:13. It's also discussed in Lutzer, pages 158–159.

191. The idea that God provides each person with an opportunity to respond to his call to salvation comes from Alcorn, pages 347–348.

Chapter 16 Neither Are Your Ways My Ways

192. The reference to there being a glassy sea before the throne of God comes from Revelation 4:6. The idea that residents of heaven can view events on earth through it is speculation.

193. The idea that people in heaven are dressed in white robes comes from Revelation 4:4b.

194. The idea that there are thrones for the redeemed residing in heaven comes from Ephesians 2:6.

195. The reference to everything being in "full view of the Lord" comes from Proverbs 5:21.

196. The reference to their being a "great cloud of witnesses" in heaven comes from Hebrews 12:1.

197. The reference to Jesus being the only way to heaven comes from John 14:6.

198. The reference to the death of the saints being precious in God's sight comes from Psalm 116:15.

199. The reference to our thoughts not being the same as God's comes from Isaiah 55:8.

200. The reference to there being no greater expression of love than to lay down one's life for a friend comes from John 15:13.

201. The idea that God provides each person with an opportunity to respond to his call to salvation comes from Alcorn, pages 347–348.

202. The reference to God not being willing that any should perish, but that everyone should come to repentance comes from 2 Peter 3:9b.

203. The reference to Jackson being called by God to "come up here" is extrapolated from Revelation 4:1b.

204. The reference to the redeemed being able to sit on God's throne comes from Revelation 3:21.

205. The idea that God transferred Jesus's righteousness to the true believer's account comes from Romans 4:22–25.

206. Bible verses pertaining to abortion include Job 31:15; Psalm 139:13–16; Isaiah 49:1; Jeremiah 1:5; Luke 2:21; Galatians 1:15; and Ephesians 1:4.

Chapter 17 Alpha

207. The *Alpha* film series is available via this link: https://alpha.org/preview/alpha-film-series/

208. The reference to homosexuality being an "abomination" to God comes from Leviticus 18:22, 20:13 (NKJV).

209. The Sermon on the Mount quotation regarding not judging others comes from Matthew 7:1–5.

210. The principle of not judging others outside the church comes from 1 Corinthians 5:12–13.

211. Jesus spoke of confronting those involved in sin in Matthew 18:15–17.

212. God's plan for marriage comes from Genesis 1:27–28; 2:24; and Mark 10:6–12.

213. Biblical references to sexual immorality include Leviticus 18:1–30; 20:10–21; Romans 1:24–27; 1 Corinthians 6:9–20; Ephesians 5:3–5; and Revelation 21:8.

214. The story of the woman caught in adultery comes from John 8:1–11.

215. The reference to God's existence is "obvious from the creation,"

and that we are "without excuse" if we disagree with that, comes from Romans 1:18–20.

216. The Scripture, "The fool says in his heart, there is no God," comes from Psalm 14:1; 53:1.

217. A reference to God being "holy" and "righteous" is in Revelation 15:4.

218. A reference to God being "perfect" is Matthew 5:48.

219. The idea that all human beings, regardless of religious affiliation or lack thereof, have a conscience, and are therefore accountable to God comes from Romans 2:14–16.

220. The reference to "From everyone who has been given much, much will be demanded" comes from Luke 12:48.

221. The reference to no one having the ability to adhere to the tenets of the major religions, no matter how hard they try, was derived from Burke, page 163.

222. The reference to the architect and builder is God comes from Hebrews 11:10.

223. The idea that specially gifted artisans may work on projects in heaven is speculation based on Exodus 31:2–5.

224. The reference to people resting from their labors in heaven comes from Hebrews 4:3–11 and Revelation 14:13.

225. The reference to people having meaningful work in heaven comes from Alcorn, pages 155 and 321.

226. The reference to God preparing a place for us comes from John 14:2–3.

227. The reference to God knowing who will become Christians before creating the world comes from Ephesians 1:4.

228. The reference to there being much rejoicing in heaven over one person who repents comes from Luke 15:7.

Chapter 18 The Battle for One Soul

229. The reference to nothing being "too hard" for God comes from Genesis 18:14 and Jeremiah 32:17, 27.
230. The reference to Jesus bringing the widow's son back to life comes from Luke 7:11–17.
231. The reference to Jesus bringing his friend Lazarus back to life comes from John 11:38–44.
232. The reference to legions of angels comes from Matthew 26:53.
233. A reference for a person's spirit returning to their body after death is Luke 8:55.
234. References to people waking up in the morgue include https://www.ranker.com/list/real-people-who-woke-up-in-morgue/amy-robleski.
235. The idea that a golden cross is emblazoned on a believer's forehead, invisible to us in this world, is speculation based on the fact that angels will be able to distinguish the redeemed from the unredeemed, as noted in Matthew 24:31 and Mark 13:27. A mark on the forehead indicates allegiance to God (Revelation 7:3; 9:4; 14:1; 20:4; 22:4) or the devil (Revelation 13:16; 14:9–10). Burpo mentions on pages 73–74 that the redeemed in heaven, and possibly those on earth, have a "light" or halo over their head.
236. "The prayer of a righteous person is powerful and effective" passage comes from James 5:16.

Chapter 20 Prisoner

237. The reference to the sea of glass comes from Revelation 4:6. It's speculation that beings in heaven can see events on earth through it.
238. The description of the makeshift brothel in the abandoned warehouse was inspired by the movie *Taken* (France: EuropaCorp, 2008; United States: 20th Century Studios, 2009).

Chapter 21 Call in the Marines

239. The description of the makeshift brothel in the abandoned warehouse was inspired by the movie *Taken* (France: EuropaCorp, 2008; United States: 20th Century Studios, 2009).

Chapter 23 Miracle Needed

240. The reference to a person being God's masterpiece comes from Burke, page 75.
241. The reference to God working everything out for our good comes from Romans 8:28.
242. The reference to God having great plans for us comes from Jeremiah 29:11; Psalm 138:8; and Ephesians 2:10.
243. The reference to God knowing his plans for us from before creating the world comes from Ephesians 1:4.
244.
245. The real-life survival story of a mother and baby in England following an abdominal ectopic pregnancy is available via this link: https://www.dailymail.co.uk/health/article-2008476/Themother-risked-ectopic-baby.html.
246. The reference to nothing being "too hard" for God comes from Genesis 18:14; and Jeremiah 32:17, 27.
247. The reference to Jesus interceding for us with God the Father comes from Romans 8:34. The Holy Spirit also intercedes for us, as noted in Romans 8:26–27.

Chapter 25 911

248. The Billy Graham Evangelistic Association publishes the "Steps to Peace with God" tract.
249. Monica's decision to put off a decision for Christ had tragic consequences. A reference to making a decision now is found in 2 Corinthians 6:2.
250. There are many New Testament passages portraying demons

harming people. For example, Matthew 15:22 states "My daughter is demon-possessed and suffering terribly."

Chapter 26 Rescue

251. Builders used limestone (aka Jerusalem stone) in the construction of many Old Jerusalem dwellings. That the angel's military quarters would be of similar construction is speculation.

252. The flag mentioned had a white background representing purity and a red cross representing the blood shed by Jesus for all humanity. That such a flag exists in heaven is speculation.

253. *Aluf* is a senior military rank in the Israeli Defense Forces. It is a Hebrew word that means "champion" in English.

254. Legions of angels are referred to by Jesus Christ in Matthew 26:53.

255. The notion that there are entrances to hell comes from Matthew 16:18; Job 17:16; 38:17.

256. The reference to the presence of putrid smells and reptilian wormlike creatures comes from Burke, page 232.

257. The idea that we can let Jesus pay for our sins on the cross or pay for them ourselves in hell comes from a message by John Piper, source/date unknown.

258. Refer to Appendix A for a discussion of the great white throne judgment and lake of fire.

259. The apostle Paul's willingness to go to hell for the Jews comes from Romans 9:3.

260. The reference to "The Lord rebuke you, Satan" comes from Zechariah 3:2 and Jude 1:9.

261. The idea that a person's eternal destiny cannot be changed after they die comes from Daniel 12:2; Ecclesiastes 9:6; and Hebrews 9:27.

262. Having Satan's throne room located in a "city in the clouds" is

speculation based on Ephesians 2:2, which states Satan is "the ruler of the kingdom of the air."

263. 1 Kings 10:18–20 contains a description of King Solomon's throne.

264. The reference to Satan controlling the world comes from 1 John 5:19.

265. The reference to Satan not being allowed to harm believers without God's permission comes from Job 1:12; 2:6. See also Psalm 105:15; 1 John 5:18.

266. The reference to the pride of Satan comes from Isaiah 14:12–15.

267. The pretext for Satan tempting Jackson comes from Matthew 4:1–11. There will be no temptation in heaven, as noted in Alcorn, pages 299–304.

268. The reference to "know your enemy" comes from Sun Tzu's *The Art of War*.

269. The reference to no one being good except God comes from Mark 10:18 and Luke 18:19.

270. The reference to Jesus being seated at the right hand of God comes from Luke 22:69; Ephesians 1:20; and Colossians 3:1.

271. The reference to being indwelt by the Holy Spirit comes from Luke 11:13; John 14:17; 1 Corinthians 6:19–20; and Revelation 3:20.

272. The question "What is truth?" spoken by Pilate before the crucifixion of Jesus comes from John 18:38.

273. The references to Jean-Jacques Rousseau, Georg Friedrich Hegel, Karl Marx, and other facets of Satan's plan to build a one-world government came from Sebastian Gorka's *The War for America's Soul* (Washington, DC: Regnery Publishing, 2019), pages 55–65.

274. The reference to Satan being the "father of lies" comes from John 8:44.

275. The reference to God "not wanting anyone to perish but everyone to come to repentance" comes from 2 Peter 3:9b.

276. The reference to God not allowing the guilty to go unpunished comes from Exodus 34:7.

277. The idea that the devil can blind the eyes of unbelievers comes from 2 Corinthians 4:4.

278. The reference to the archangel Michael disputing with the devil about Moses's body comes from Jude 1:9.

279. The reference to no one being able to cross from heaven to hell or from hell to heaven comes from Luke 16:26.

280. The reference to "the one who is in you is greater than the one who is in the world" comes from 1 John 4:4b.

281. The reference to demons submitting to Christians comes from Luke 10:17.

282. The reference to Christians driving out demons comes from Mark 16:17.

283. The reference to "resist the devil, and he will flee from you" comes from James 4:7.

284. The reference to not rejoice that the spirits submit to him comes from Luke 10:20.

285. The reference to Jesus being the "Holy One of God" comes from Mark 1:24; Luke 4:34; and John 6:69.

286. The reference to fallen angels kept in dungeons held for judgment comes from 2 Peter 2:4.

287. A reference for a person's spirit returning to their body after death is Luke 8:55.

288. "The prayer of a righteous person is powerful and effective" passage comes from James 5:16.

289. The idea that a golden cross is emblazoned on a believer's forehead, invisible to us in this world, is speculation based on the fact that angels will be able to distinguish the redeemed from the unredeemed, as noted in Matthew 24:31 and Mark

13:27. A mark on the forehead indicates allegiance to God (Revelation 7:3; 9:4; 14:1; 20:4; 22:4) or the devil (Revelation 13:16; 14:9–10). Burpo mentions on pages 73–74 that the redeemed in heaven, and possibly those on earth, have a "light" or halo over their head.

290. The reference to there being much rejoicing in heaven over one sinner who repents comes from Luke 15:7.

291. The reference to the Holy Spirit removing the veil from a person's heart comes from 2 Corinthians 3:14–16.

Chapter 28 New Beginnings

292. Insights into the world of modeling came from Kylie Bisutti, *I'm No Angel: From Victoria's Secret Model to Role Model* (Carol Stream, IL: Tyndale House, 2013), pages 5, 11, 21, 54, 66, 69–72, 76, 107, 154, 172, 214, 234–235, 242–243, 245.

293. Taking the ashes of someone's life and making them beautiful again is gleaned from Isaiah 61:3.

294. "Whoever loses his life for me will find it" comes from Matthew 16:24–25.

Chapter 29 Fulfilling Work

295. The idea that we will continue serving God in heaven comes from Alcorn, pages 319–321 and 396–397; Enns, page 142; Lutzer, pages 113–114.

296. The Impressionist master, Pierre-Auguste Renoir, was raised Catholic and seldom, if ever, set foot in a church, according to Barbara Ehrlich White, *Renoir: An Intimate Biography* (London: Thames & Hudson Ltd., 2017), page 23.

297. The reference to Renoir having a wife and a mistress with children from both comes from White, page 132.

298. The reference to Renoir being a chain-smoker with a nervous tic

who rubbed his index finger under his nose constantly comes from White, page 12.

299. The reference to Renoir being a man of great anxiety comes from White, page 21–22.

300. The reference to Renoir being a man of contradictions who could be passive/aggressive, indecisive/clear-minded, or shy/forceful comes from White, page 135.

301. The reference to Renoir not wishing to be away from his painting friends comes from White, page 140.

302. The reference to Renoir's paintings never reflecting society's problems comes from White, page 49.

303. Renoir painted idealized versions of his subjects rather than portraits, as noted in White, page 52.

304. The reference that Renoir, later in life, claimed to be a Christian believer who wanted to "spread joy through his painting" comes from Lawrence Hanson, *Renoir: The Man, the Painter and His World* (New York, NY: Dudd, Mead & Company, 1968), page 280, cited in https://www.movieguide.org/reviews/Renoir.html.

305. References to the characteristics of the art of Impressionist painting come from White, page 33.

306. Various authors discussed Renoir's rheumatoid arthritis in Licia Maria Henrique da Mota, Fernando Neubarth, Leonardo Rios Diniz, Jozélio Freire de Carvalho, Leopoldo Luiz dos Santos Neto, "Pierre-Auguste Renoir (1841–1919) and Rheumatoid Arthritis," National Library of Medicine, May 20, 2012.

307. The reference to people in heaven having a clear purpose comes from Alcorn, page 226.

Chapter 30 Riptide

308. The passage cited from the book of Ephesians, which describes the armor of God, comes from Ephesians 6:10–20.

309. The idea that the forces of evil rule over our world comes from
     1 John 5:19.

310. The idea that Christians will one day rule with Christ comes
     from Revelation 3:21, 20:4.

311. The reference to Satan being the "father of lies" comes from
     John 8:44.

312. The reference to "Resist the devil, and he will flee from you,"
     comes from James 4:7.

Chapter 31 Saved

313. Jack's question to his pastor, "What must I do to be saved?"
     comes from Acts 16:29–31.

314. The reference to God having great plans for us comes from
     Jeremiah 29:11; Psalm 138:8; and Ephesians 2:10.

315. The reference to baptism being a commandment and that it be
     done in the name of the Father, Son, and Holy Spirit comes
     from Matthew 28:19.

316. Baptism by immersion represents the death and burial of
     Jesus Christ and the death of the old nature of the person
     being baptized.

317. The reference to the power from heaven coming upon the pastor
     while he delivered his sermon comes from Burpo, page 125.

Chapter 32 The Prom

318. The reference to life going by quickly, like a vapor, comes from
     Job 7:7; Psalm 39:5; 102:3; 144:4; James 4:14.

319. The reference to inner beauty comes from 1 Peter 3:4.

320. There are many references to Christians being indwelt by the
     Holy Spirit (aka the Spirit of Jesus). One is 1 Corinthians 3:16.

321. The reference to a Christian (McKenzie) being allowed to
     remarry after their spouse has died comes from Romans 7:2–3
     and 1 Corinthians 7:39.

322. Angels carried the body of Lazarus to Father Abraham's side in Luke 16:22. The assumption is that demons will carry the unredeemed to hell, as mentioned in Erwin Lutzer, *One Minute After You Die* (Chicago, IL: Moody Press, 1997), page 25, quoted in Wiese, page 124.

323. The idea that a person can be indwelt by a demon is found in Matthew 8:16; 10:1; 12:27; 12:43–45; 17:14–20; Mark 3:15; 5:12; 9:29; 16:17; Luke 4:33–36; 8:2; 8:26–39; and Acts 16:16–18.

Chapter 34 New Birth

324. The reference to women and children not being involved in battles in the heavenly realms comes from Burpo, page 138.

325. The reference to a Christian (Jackson's father) remarrying after their spouse has died comes from Romans 7:2–3 and 1 Corinthians 7:39.

326. The reference to nothing being "too hard" for God comes from Genesis 18:14 and Jeremiah 32:17, 27.

327. The reference to praying in Jesus's name comes from John 14:14; 16:23–24.

Chapter 35 Losing Your Life

328. The reference to God initially making the world perfect comes from Genesis 1:31.

329. The reference to sin corrupting the world comes from Genesis 3:17.

330. The reference to everything being meaningless comes from Ecclesiastes 2:11.

331. The reference to honoring your father and mother resulting in a long life comes from Ephesians 6:1–3.

332. The reference to praying for our enemies comes from Matthew

5:44. That our enemies may be in our household comes from Matthew 10:36.

333. The Matthew 7 passage quoted is from Matthew 7:21–23. An excellent sermon by Pastor Joe Funderburk of Valley Community Baptist Church, delivered on 09/06/22, is available via this link: https://www.youtube.com/watch?v=v_ZMUHSCg_Q&list=P LqJz0vlEXgjWvAC0Z7vosXpodPfrNxC_K&index=19

334. The information regarding the Father's will comes from the *Matthew Henry Commentary on the Whole Bible,* public domain, Matthew 7:21–29.

335. The reference to the armor of God comes from Ephesians 6:10–17.

336. The concept of Jesus giving someone a clear mind comes from Mark 5:15 and Luke 8:35.

337. The idea of God keeping us out of the mud comes from Psalm 40:2.

338. The reference to a spirit of impurity comes from Zechariah 13:2.

339. The reference to McKenzie overcoming the world comes from 1 John 5:4–5.

340. The reference to Jesus's joy comes from John 15:11.

341. The idea of dying to self comes from Galatians 2:20.

342. The hymn "I Need Thee Every Hour" was written by Annie S. Hawks and Robert Lowry in 1872.

Chapter 37 *In the Twinkling of an Eye*

343. The reference to God presiding over the great assembly in heaven comes from Psalm 82:1.

344. The reference to no one knowing the rapture's date (i.e., when Jesus will return to earth for his church) except the God the Father comes from Matthew 24:36 and Mark 13:32. See Appendix A for additional information about the rapture. It's

speculation that the rapture will only occur after everyone God has chosen, up to that point in history, is saved by him.

345. The trumpet blast at the rapture comes from Matthew 24:31; 1 Corinthians 15:52; and 1 Thessalonians 4:16.

346. The reference to the voice of the archangel at the rapture comes from 1 Thessalonians 4:16. That the archangel would utter the Hebrew word *Qum* at this time, which means "to arise" in English, is speculation.

347. An angel placing hands on someone to remove their fear comes from Daniel 8:17–18 and Revelation 1:17.

348. The reference to departed saints physically coming out of the grave comes from Matthew 27:52 (after Jesus was crucified and buried in the tomb). The Civil War veteran's resuscitation illustrates this concept. The remains of the other departed saints passing through the dirt illustrates they were given resurrection bodies (like Jesus had in John 20:19). While the former illustration may be what happens at the rapture, it's more likely the latter will occur.

349. The ability of God to reinfuse dry bones with flesh and blood comes from Ezekiel 37:1–14.

350. Biblical references to the rapture are 1 Thessalonians 4:13–18; John 14:1–3; and 1 Corinthians 15:51–57.

351. The reference to the rapture occurring quickly, in the twinkling of an eye, comes from 1 Corinthians 15:51–52.

352. The reference to the sky bursting with light when Christ returns comes from Luke 17:24. That the redeemed would be assembled in the air directly above Jerusalem is speculation.

353. The statement "Holy, holy, holy is the Lord God Almighty, who was, and is, and is to come" comes from Revelation 4:8. The four living creatures around the throne never stop saying this. That the redeemed would do the same at the rapture is speculation.

354. The Golden Rule principle—*treat others the way you'd like to be treated*—is inherent to all major religions. Norman Rockwell's notes used to create his Golden Rule painting are accessible via this website: https://www.nrm.org/2018/03/golden-rule-common-religions/.

355. Information about Buddhism comes from Dean Halverson, *The Illustrated Guide to World Religions* (Bloomington, MN: Bethany House Publishers, 2003), pages 49–65.

356. Information about Confucianism comes from Halverson, pages 66–83.

357. Information about Hebraism (Judaism) comes from Halverson, pages 125–153.

358. Information about Hinduism comes from Halverson, pages 85–102.

359. Information about Islam comes from Halverson, pages 103–124.

www.ingramcontent.com/pod-product-compliance
Lightning Source LLC
Chambersburg PA
CBHW051318190726
48290CB00001B/206